I0600238

All We Have to Remember

Volume One of
the Seventh Layer Saga

C.R. Ware

Book Cover by Reece-Alexander Norris-Paterson

First edition, 2025

For the Architect of Dreams, who is a father
to all in the dark of night.
and
To my Dad, who wanted to be the cool sports dad,
but was willing to be the cool nerd dad for his kids.

CONTENTS

The red blades began with a promise.

In the seventh-layer world, amongst the poorest of men, lived a woodcutter and his wife.

They were cruel people who hated their life and their lack of children.

The spouses blamed each other for their shame and in doing so only deepened their pain.

Until the day he arrived. A workman, appearing weak and in rags, offered to share with the couple out of the little he had.

Despite their cruelty, the couple was moved by his generosity.

"Keep what you have," they told him, "and let us instead share with you the shelter of our land."

The instant they said this, the stranger was changed from a wretch to a wonder.

They saw now that this was no mere man, but that a true power had come in disguise to their land.

"Great One leave us," the couple then pleaded, "For, great as you are, we are hollow and shameful people."

"And yet," said the Great One "in your shame you chose to give when you could have taken. So, I will show, that you have not been forsaken. I will ask for something from you, but not more than you can give."

"Ask Great One, and it will be yours." The couple agreed.

"You have been wicked, but this day you showed kindness and care. Continue this way, and this I will give." Declared the Great One. "I will give you three children. Each will be beautiful and with lives greater than you could provide. Of them, the third will be given the most. They will start a family all of their own and receive, for all their descendants, a gift that none can take away. From that line, your family will rise, generation to generation, but heed me. This promise comes with a warning. If you or your descendants forget yourselves and this promise, then you will rise only to fall."

The couple promised dearly that they would hold to his words. When they had, he vanished, leaving no sign behind.

With no name left, the couple began to call this the Great One, Azaz.

The end and the beginning.

PROLOGUE

WITHIN HER SMALL CASTLE, Dread Rose shook her head, disappointed. The ancient kyate-siv tribe peered down a hallway of her small castle at wounded and dead soldiers. Each had served Dread Rose to the end, but failed, as evidenced by the fact that their bodies cluttered the doorway where the lone beastman still stood barring her and her last soldier's path.

The remaining man took a desperate stab at the guardian with his spear. The beastman, an usarumai warrior, seized the haft with hands layered in thick bestial hide and pulled the spear past his body, dragging the soldier with it. With his free hand, the warrior latched onto the soldier's scalp.

The elderly spellcaster had heard the stories of the iron grip of an usarumai but this was the first time Rose saw a beastman actually live up to them. With his left, the usarumai shattered the wooden haft of the spear with his grip alone. With his right hand, he tightened his hold on the soldier's head.

Her soldier screamed, but only for a moment, before the beastman's left dropped the remains of the spear and silenced him.

The usarumai looked down the hallway at her, panting and letting out an untamed snarl.

Rose clicked her tongue. "I sent six men against you, and all they've managed is to barely scratch you. To think we'd have so much trouble in our own house." She looked down at the animal at her side. "Valathien, kill him."

She'd designed Valathien to be an enhanced guard dog. With a body as large as a great mountain hound's, his skin rippled with scales and tufts of hair. He prowled on claws made to produce rancid wounds. His elongated maw was cultivated with rows of gleaming teeth. The muscles of the creature's strange face had also been altered, so as Valathien worked his jaw in preparation for the kill, the bizarre movements only added to his intimidating appearance.

As Rose watched her pet stalk the usarumai she lamented that she was too old now to participate in the battle herself. She would have to live vicariously through her creation.

The beastman's eyes became more nervous with each step Valathien took. For a moment Rose wondered why, then she remembered that he'd seen her pet go to work once already.

"Are you wishing you'd stayed in your cell yet?" she asked.

The usarumai looked over his shoulder, through the prison door he guarded.

"Ah, are you going to beg for mercy after..." Then she followed his gaze to see something new.

Around the door, someone was watching. She might not have seen him if he hadn't flinched in pain. He hid mostly behind the doorframe, but as he twitched, she saw him and the crimson light that flickered across his skin. She recognized him as another of her prisoners, the human boy, but what was that light?

She stood confused, having never seen the like before. Even more strangely, she could not feel any magic. Was she so old now that even that sense was abandoning her, or was this some unintended effect of what she'd done to the boy before his imprisonment? She should be able to sense it if it was, but she could feel nothing.

"How odd," she mused.

Hearing Rose's words and seeing where she watched the beastman's growl deepened and he began to work his hand expectantly.

"Now why are you protecting him?" questioned the dread.

The usarumai warrior made no reply, keeping his eyes trained on the monstrosity prowling towards him.

"Have it your way. Valathien."

Her pet lunged at the command and the warrior threw one of the downed soldiers in Valathien's path, but the creature tore through the remains easily.

Jaws wide, he lunged again for the beastman's throat. The usarumai's hands snapped out, each catching one part of the maw, keeping it from closing on him. Valathien's sharp teeth sank into the beastman's hands as his hind legs planted themselves on the ground and pushed forward using the powerful muscles Dread Rose had developed in him. Raised on his rear legs, the creature was nearly as tall as the usarumai.

The usarumai was locked with his hands holding back Valathien's jaws, so Rose's pet used his claws to rake the sides of his prey.

Roaring his defiance, the usarumai warrior continued to fight back as Valathien's jaws closed slowly in. Rose found it impressive that he was able to hold them back at all. The beastman looked over his shoulder one last time and then straight into the jaws of Valathien.

To Rose's surprise, he smiled.

Through laboring breaths and growling words, the beastman spoke in their tongue. "Yona sarumai... tai tahano."

She spoke very little of their language but enough to understand this.

"I can still be loyal."

The beastman became serious once again and cried out in words she could not fully understand, which morphed into a roar so loud she was sure it shook the masonry.

Rose's eyes widened, and she took an involuntary step back. She couldn't even hear herself over the roar as she gasped, "Impossible."

As the roar faded, a new sound reached her. Valathien yelped and squealed, his previous efforts with his powerful legs to fight forward now reversed. Valathien whimpered as he fought with all his strength to get away, but he couldn't.

The iron grip of the usarumai held him fast and fought back Valathien's jaws. The creature tried to fight back, to stop its jaws from being forced open further, but the beastman fought with reckless strength.

Rose cursed as she realized that another one of her few remaining creations was going to be destroyed. She didn't fear the beastman but she knew she was too old now to fight against him if the warrior came for her next. Glaring, she retreated further into her fortress as she looked for the reinforcements which were doubtless already on the way.

Rose couldn't understand how this had happened. How did the beastman get out of his cell? What was that red light on the boy? And, even if he was an usarumai, how had any tribesman overpowered Valathien? None of it made any sense.

"I don't know what in all of the layers of the world is going on, but he will pay for Valathien. There is only one way out of this passage. He will not escape, both he and that boy will be back in chains by dawn."

However, that was not to be. When, soon after, Rose returned with a company of guards, she found more of the impossible awaiting her. The dungeon of stone walls, without windows and only one door, was empty. The boy, the beastman, and the possessions she'd taken from them were all gone, with no sign of how they vanished.

Beyond those stone walls, the usarumai was finally able to slow his run. It was dusk, and the long shadows of the trees he hid within would give him cover for now. Dropping the supplies he carried in one hand he carefully laid down the form slumped over his other shoulder.

Having caught his breath, the warrior checked his side where Rose's strange abomination had clawed at him. The wound burned with infection. With every step, it felt as if the claws tore at him anew. He needed to stop and rest, to treat the wound, but the witch and more of her pets would be after him soon, possibly even her marauders. If he lightened his load, maybe he could make it.

He looked down at what he carried. All he had was a small sack of provisions and the boy. For an instant, he thought about leaving him behind, but no.

Just after they'd made their impossible escape, the boy fainted. The red light of the Akai had faded from his skin soon after, but the warrior knew what he'd seen. The boy was a red blade, a real red blade.

In his rest, the boy's face was slick with sweat and his body jerked through his heavy breathing. The usarumai looked at him with tears beginning to burn in his eyes.

"Why me?" he asked in his native tongue. "I am not... I am one of the *ja*. Why me?"

There was no reply, and the usarumai shook his head.

"There is no time for this." He was one of the *ja* but was promised a new name and a new life free of that shame. To abandon was the path of the old life, the path of the dead.

The warrior looked down at his wound again and knew the path he was on now.

"One last chance for one good act." The usarumai turned his eyes to the rising moon. "I can still be loyal."

An owl peering down at them hooted loudly and Baruoka-*ja* of the usarumai knew it was time. With a groan, he lifted the boy and the bag onto his shoulders and fled into the night.

CHAPTER 1

"OVERALL, NOT A BAD morning," Ghen mused, watching the sun's slow rise.

The ball of light shone nicely for early spring, and Ghen had gotten an early start on the road. Sure, breakfast might not have been his best work, but even Ghen's old mule was behaving, and Bo almost always took issue with something. Yet not today.

"Yep, not a bad morning."

The cart drummed a rhythmic rumble as it plodded down the dusty country road. The old road was out of the way for most of the world, but it was still worn with ruts from many trips and long service to country folk and ranchers like Ghen.

"You know, girl," he said to the mule, "I'm happy we got us a break from tilling, but I'm ready to be home."

Bo shook her mane and snorted.

"Oh, don't be ornery. It's not my fault the blade broke. If anything, I would think you're as guilty as I am. The one time I get you moving quick, and you hit a stone the size of Mr. Noren's ego."

Bo ignored him and continued to trudge towards home and her stall.

Ghen grinned. It was a shame that he'd needed to buy a new plow blade, but the old one was too far gone. The trip to Marden Hallows would be worth it, though, if the next crop turned out a good yield.

"Of course, there is plenty more than plowing that's gonna need doing after three days off the land. Hopefully Jirus... Well now, what's this?"

Ghen found himself distracted by a little fella walking ahead on the road. Bo was gaining on him quickly. At first, Ghen thought it was a local kid, but as he got closer, he recognized him.

"Remember him, Bo?" he asked the mule. "We saw him heading out just when we pulled into Marden."

The odd boy had asked him for directions to Henaden, the big trade city a few days north. Around these parts strangers tended to stick out as most everyone knew one another, that was unless they were a merchant of some sort.

"You're no merchant, though," Ghen muttered to himself.

He looked sort of like a beggar, but Ghen had never seen a beggar with a sword. His clothes weren't quite rags, they were tough cloth of a subtle brown. It reminded Ghen of his uncle's old military coat from his time in the Watchmen Brigade. What made him look so much like a beggar was that the coat, and everything else he had, was dusty, torn, and wrinkled from long travel.

He wasn't tall, but the more Ghen looked at him, the more Ghen began to think he was older than his height suggested. Especially when Ghen had seen his eyes in Marden, he'd seen an edge that'd made him want to steer clear.

Add to that the sword the stranger carried, and Ghen was sure he would do just that. He'd noticed the hilt the first time the little stranger asked for directions, but now he wasn't wearing the thick coat he had before. Ghen now spied a second shorter sword next to the first.

Ghen had never learned the sword, but these looked different from the ones he was used to seeing, they were thinner and slightly curved. Not that he knew swords well. His uncle had let Ghen hold his short sword a couple of times when he was a youth, but that was the beginning and end of his experience with such things. What good would a rancher have for a sword?

No, this kid was definitely out of place. Ghen had been ambushed by thieves once already and there were more stories of attacks all the time. Ghen swallowed hard and tried to keep an eye out as his cart rolled past the stranger.

As Ghen steered around the kid, the small fella threw up a hand. "Eh, hold, please."

His words were said oddly. The stranger spoke with intentionality and focused on each word like he was trying to make sure he said it correctly.

Despite his care, the boy's accent still dominated his speech. It made Ghen think about the words a second before their meaning struck home. The rancher pulled on the reins and Bo slowed to a halt.

He wanted to go on, but the kid had asked for help. Ghen was nervous, but just ignoring him wasn't what good folk do.

As the kid took a step closer, Ghen got another good look at him, especially now that he no longer wore his coat. It wasn't just his accent that was clearly foreign.

Like Ghen, he was human, but that was where the similarities ended. His features and voice made him somewhere in his late teens, but he was half a head shorter than he should have been. His hair was dark and straight, its ends raggedly cut short, likely by one of the blades the boy carried. His skin held an almost darker marigold color, and the shape of his eyes was more drawn than Ghen's. It wasn't the shape of his eyes that held Ghen's attention, though. It was the look *in* them.

He looked worn. Like his clothes, his eyes bore a dusty bearing of long miles and longer struggles. Sleepy, suspicious, wary, and exhausted looks flew across his face with every flick of movement.

Ghen was not sure what to make of him, but that gaze just felt wrong. The rancher held the reins tight, ready to kick Bo into a hurried start, but said nothing.

Despite the worn eyes, the stranger was grateful that Ghen stopped and bowed slightly. "I seek Henaden, a city. I think I travel the right way, but I am not sure. Do you know Henaden? Is this the way?"

Ghen sat for a moment, not sure exactly what was going on. The stranger's face was stern, but he wasn't exactly unfriendly. There was no doubt that this was the same kid from a few days before. Still, that made him more odd, not less. He didn't seem like he was making a joke, but then why was he asking about this?

"You're headed the right way," Ghen explained. "Stick to this road and don't make any turns and you ought to be there in about a little less than a week since you're on foot." Then adding, "Just like I told you the other day."

His features might have been different from Ghen's, but his expressions were still clear. Surprise, worry, and a little confusion ran quickly over the boy's face.

"Eh... yes. Forgive me." He bowed again. "I did not recognize you." He added cautiously, "I trust your earlier directions. I sought only assurance." Regaining the rest of his composure, he asked another question. "Between Henaden and where we are now, are there any towns or cities?"

"There's a couple of farms and ranches between here and there." Adding again, "Just like I told you the other day."

The stranger winced slightly before nervously bowing. "Thank you."

Clearly unsure of what else to say, he spun on his heel and quickly started stomping away. Ghen had the inclination to let the peculiar little fella go but...

"Hold your horses, kid."

The short stranger halted but didn't turn.

Ghen let Bo walk a little further until he caught up.

The kid's jaw was clenched, and he looked down at the tops of his ragged boots. At first, Ghen wondered if he was angry, then almost laughed at himself when he realized he was, just not at Ghen. He was embarrassed and angry at himself.

He was odd alright and maybe even a little dangerous, but he was a kid after all. Ghen came to a decision, "You can hop on if you want," he said, patting the seat. "I can take you a couple of miles before I turn off the main road. Just... when I tell you to get off, you go." Ghen's eyes drifted to the sword hilts.

The boy blinked in surprise. "Eh... Thank you." Then he bowed again.

What was with that bowing? It just made Ghen feel off. All the nobles of the country were off in places like Roldea or Cobaden to the east. Ghen had never bowed to anyone and had definitely never been bowed to before.

The boy leaped from the ground onto the seat with effortless and surprising agility.

It was Ghen's turn to blink. "Goodness kid, you're a spry one. Uh, why don't you put your gear in the back?" He thumbed toward the open back of the cart.

The young man hesitated, but with a slow sigh, he pulled off his pack, setting it behind them, along with his weapons. However, it didn't escape Ghen's notice that when he put them in the back, the kid placed everything of his as close to himself as he could.

Once the boy was settled, Ghen held out his hand, as good folk should, but the young man looked at it, confused. Before Ghen could say anything, he became even stranger.

He tilted his head as if listening to someone Ghen couldn't see, nodded, and then finally reached out and shook Ghen's hand in the most awkward way imaginable.

"I'm Ghen Jarden. I... uh hope you don't get offended or nothing, but kid, you're an odd one."

The kid withdrew his hand and avoided Ghen's eyes. "I am Em Dèr, and yes, I know."

Ghen. Em rolled the name in his mind. It was a strange name, but his own name was strange to him now. While Em was not thrilled that this man asked him to set aside his weapons, he was in no position to refuse.

Still, he'd made sure to keep them close. 'Ghen' seemed kind, but that did not make him trustworthy.

Many people act kind to begin with, when they really aren't, a little voice agreed. It was the older voice this time, the one Em called Instinct. It came through clearly in Em's ear, but no one else heard so much as a whisper. *That doesn't mean he might not be genuinely kind though, Little Em. Make sure you're not being rude.*

Em knew the voice of Instinct well. It was one of two he'd heard since waking. Instinct came through in lofty tones and somehow always sounded as if it were on the edge of grinning. The other voice was deeper, bigger, and more stoic. A calm base that when roused sounded like it was speaking through a bestial growl. That was Nature.

Even to Em, the voices speaking from out of his shadow were strange, but these two were his only guides. The message said to trust Nature and Instinct, and he would.

Em decided he would accept Ghen's kindness but would not be caught off guard by another betrayal. Or, at least, he guessed it would be another betrayal.

Em gave Ghen another inspection. He was taller than Em and probably stronger. His face was covered with a curly beard that was a rusted dark brown with flecks of silver. Bumping down the road, the man wore an easy smile, one that was comfortable on his face. All his clothes had dust from the road, save for a straw hat he wore with a wide brim. Patches on his clothing spoke of its long service to its owner.

Despite his smile, the driver's eyes darted from the road to Em and back.

Well would you look at that Little Em, he's afraid, Instinct said, amused. *Probably as scared of you as you are of him.*

Em spoke back in his mind. *I, at the least, have reason to be. He does not, if he keeps his word, I have no reason to trouble him.* Em's only real plan was to get to Henaden.

How's he going to know that? Instinct questioned with an unseen grin. *As strange as he seems to you, have you considered how even more strange you are to him? This is his home, after all.*

And not mine? Em asked.

Em knew the answer before Instinct said a thing. *Sorry, Little Em, but no.*

"So, are you one of the watchmen?" Ghen initiated, jolting Em from his internal conversation.

When Em deciphered the question, he still did not understand it. What was a watchman? He knew the word, the name brought to mind an idea of a group of militia protectors. Ghen, however, was clearly talking about something more official. He considered trying to lie and saying yes, but if that brought further questions, what would he do then? If he refused to answer, his ride might be shorter than Em would like.

"No, what is a watchman?"

Ghen spluttered. "What?!" It apparently had not been the best response if Em wished to be ignored. "You're joking. How did you get through Marden or half the places this side of the Manaford River without hearing of the Watchmen Brigade?"

"I am... an odd one?" Em said, hoping Ghen would leave him alone.

"No kidding. So, what are you doing out here then? Unless you climbed over the mountains, you didn't come straight north to get to Henaden. As we've covered, you don't exactly fit our local crowd."

"Ghen-*sa*, I..."

"It's just Ghen, you can drop the sir."

Sir? Em hadn't said, 'sir.'

Instinct laughed. *But he thinks you did. Sir is their word of honor, and sa is yours.*

Then I will not correct him. Em said to the know-it-all second voice. Out loud he said, "Yes... Ghen." It felt off putting not adding the *sa* honorific to a senior.

Ghen let the reins go slack and, no longer being driven, the lazy mule slowed bit by bit until it became distracted enough to stop.

They sat in an awkward silence for a long time.

"Kid," Ghen said slowly, "I hope you don't take offense at me. I'm not trying to be rude, but I am going to be honest. You worry me."

Em averted his eyes.

"Kid, if you want Bo to go on, I'm going to need some kind of answer. You're hiking around with two swords and I'm not even sure you are from Ifeldia. Since we've got that war with Yongarad on our borders, I'm a little nervous."

Yongarad, Ifeldia, Em wasn't even sure what those were. Nations, he guessed, but that wasn't a real help. He kept silent.

Ghen began to breathe in shorter breaths, obviously unnerved by Em's stillness. "I... I need you to be straight with me. You look like military, and not ours. Are you one of them Marauders?"

Like a twig snapping beneath a heavy boot, something shattered inside Em.

NO! the other voice, Nature, shouted. This voice wasn't old, it was strong and powerful. It howled the word so loudly that Em yelled it out himself in sudden anger and glared venomously at the startled man.

Then it was gone, everything receding into its natural place and Em felt ashamed.

"I beg your forgiveness," Em said, lowering his head. "I am not one of these marauders, and I should not have spoken so. I will take my leave."

He tried to stand but only got halfway when a hand gripped the hem of his shirt.

Ghen watched him with, was that pity?

"Sit down," he said.

Em stayed as he was.

Ghen sighed. "Please, kid."

Slowly, Em settled back.

"You don't need to apologize, kid. If anything, maybe I do. You're a stern one, but that doesn't mean you ain't good folk. I'm sorry if I offended you, but with all that's going on these days, I have to worry for my family."

Em said nothing.

"I guess it isn't quite fair for me to ask a bunch about you without telling a bit about myself." Ghen flicked the reins, and the mule began to tramp forward again. "Ifeldia may be at war, but I'm a rancher. Raising cattle mostly, don't really raise pigs anymore, but got a few goats despite how much the little snots run me ragged. I also grow as much grain for my stock as I can. Oh, and of course I've got old Bo here to take care of." He nodded at the mule.

Bo snorted as if she understood and was even annoyed that she'd been left for last.

"Don't be rude," Ghen chided the animal. "As I said before, I've got my little family as my helpers. They're good folk. Jirus, he's a relative of mine, can be a little interesting, but he's good too once you know him. That's about it, I'm a simple fella as far as it goes."

Finishing, Ghen turned his gaze toward Em. It was his turn now.

This was going to take some explaining, and Em did not want to do that. Yet, from the expression on Ghen's face, there was no choice. If he didn't say something, Ghen might not feel safe, and then what would happen? Em could imagine being tracked by a hunting party as he searched for Henaden, and then falling asleep and... it would get worse. He had more than enough difficulties without all of that.

Taking a long, deep breath, Em resigned himself. He was not sure he could lie well enough to get out of this, which left him with the truth.

"Speaking truth, Ghen-*sa*," he said, accidentally adding the honorific, "I do not know."

Ghen tensed when Em reached into the back of the cart, but relaxed when he realized the young man was reaching into his bag instead of towards one of his scabbards. From there, he drew out his notebook. Most of the pages were blank, but throughout the book, a light and precise hand had left many letters. His own hand, but he had no memory of writing it. Opening the first page, Em became suddenly reluctant to hold it out to Ghen.

Are you afraid? Nature asked in its deep growling base. As if it wasn't obvious.

With a huff, Em held out the book.

Ghen looked at the open book and then pushed it back towards Em. "I'm driving. Read it to me, would you?"

Em wasn't sure if that was the real reason or if the rancher either couldn't read or just noticed Em's conflict about handing the book out. Either way, he looked at the page. He already knew what it said by heart. He'd read it this morning until he'd memorized every word. At least, memorized for now.

He read aloud, as clearly as he could in his accented voice:

> You go by the name Em Dér.
> I know you are confused, and I know why. You have forgotten
> again. I am writing this message to warn you. If you sleep, you
> will forget. I know this because I am you, a you that has been
> forgotten. That is what our life has become, living for a day
> to die in our sleep. Then, a new Em rises tomorrow with no
> memory of who we were.
>
> Em, even as I write this to you, I wonder how long we have
> been this way. I do not know who we once were or who we
> are supposed to be now. All I know is what I have been told,

which I will pass on to you. We forget everything each day, but there is a chance to be whole again. This curse or sickness we have can be cured, Em.

In the city of Henaden is a master of magic known as Master D'gui. Our guides told me Master D'gui will help us. I do not know why, but this may be our only chance. Trust Instinct and Nature, they will see us to our goal.

Also, you should know that whatever has been done to our mind has not affected everything about us. You will find that our body remembers much of what our mind cannot.

Seek Henaden, find Master D'gui, and find who we are supposed to be.

That is all we have to remember.

From the Em of yesterday.

Finishing, Em closed his notebook and waited. Ghen kept his eyes on the road, his casual smile now an intense glare at the dusty way ahead.

He will call me a liar, Em told Instinct.

I disagree, the older, cheerful voice of Instinct said lazily as it took its place back from the more bestial voice of Nature.

Ghen sat hushed for a long time, the thump of the cart cresting small stones the only interruption to the quiet morning. Finally, Ghen pulled off to the side of the road.

Em was not going to wait to be told to 'get off' and 'get out,' he knew. The moment the cart stopped, he started to get out.

"Where are you going?" Ghen asked.

Em paused, before settling back.

Ghen gave his mule enough slack for her to graze at the side of the road, then tied the rest of the reins off. Reaching into one of his pockets, he brought out a scuffed wooden pipe. After taking a moment to stuff it and light it, he soon began to puff a small cloud of smoke.

The rancher watched his mule dig at the grass, slowly breathing in and out and deep in a veil of thought that Em had no window into.

"Can I see that book?" he asked after a long time, turning and holding out a hand.

Instead of holding it out, Em gripped it tighter. He needed this book.

"It's alright," Ghen said softly. "I promise I'll be careful with it."

With an effort, Em slowly lifted the book out. He hated this, but he still saw no other choice. Ghen reached out cautiously to take it and was careful as he opened the cover.

"It's written in Ifeldian," Ghen said with some disbelief.

"You are surprised?"

"I guess, are you from around here then?"

"I do not know," Em said bitterly.

Ghen winced. "Oh right, sorry kid. Hey, do you know what you wrote this with? This first page is ink, but," he looked at a few of the following pages, "these aren't all the same."

Em chose not to answer. He'd seen the differences, too. Throughout his travels, he'd obviously made his record with whatever was available.

Ghen realized Em wasn't going to comment and took a long pull on his pipe. With that, he leaned back and read. His eyes scanned slowly down the page, digesting each word. Then, when his eyes reached the bottom, he went back to the top and read it again. Then a third time.

When he completed this, he delicately turned the pages. The notebook wasn't fragile, but Em appreciated the care Ghen took. Even though Ghen was being careful, Em felt like a taut string. His spirit was rigid, stretched to its limits, and ready to jump at the man to protect his leather-bound treasure.

A few pages in, Ghen's mouth curled in confusion. "What's this?"

He held the book where Em could see the page. It was a mix of names and symbols. He knew what it was.

"They are places and directions."

Ghen nodded. "I get it now. You've got Marden Hallows here at the end, and this symbol, you said it's a direction?"

Em nodded.

He pointed to the symbol, and a drawing shaped like a twisted arrow with lines jutting in each direction from the bent stem. "North?"

"Yes."

He read over the other ones for a long time and then sighed. "You know you're lost, right?"

Em averted his eyes. "I know where I need to go now."

"And you did before," Ghen said, indicating a different name. "This one says Tiberonen. Now I've never been there, but I know where it is. It's a small town east of Henaden. The entry you have a few lines down is Peldia, that one is far west of Henaden. In other words, you passed it."

Em didn't say anything, he'd already guessed that from the directions afterward. It was why, despite having directions, he had stopped Ghen on the road. He needed to be sure he was on the right path.

Ghen eyes softened. "It's hard to get around, isn't it?"

Em didn't answer.

Ghen tapped his chin with his pipe. "I don't recognize half of these names. Wherever you came from, it wasn't close, I don't think. That's if you are telling the truth, of course."

"Of course," Em muttered irritably.

Ghen held up his hands in something like a surrender. "Sorry, didn't mean to make it sound like that. It's just a lot to take in, kid. Here, I think I've read enough."

Ghen held out the notebook and Em accepted it greedily.

Unable to resist, Em retrieved it and skimmed through it again. Whether he was checking for damage or simply reminding himself of its contents, he wasn't sure, perhaps both.

Despite giving back the journal, Ghen did not immediately begin to drive Bo forward. Instead, he leaned back, to stare into the distance, sending up wisps of smoke to blur his view.

Em finished his review and placed it back in his bag, wrapping the book in the cloth he kept it in to make sure it was protected.

"You forget everything... Well, that story is either dumb, bold, or true," he muttered. "It would make a sorta sense though from what I've seen of you. Not that I've ever heard of Master D'gui, but that doesn't mean much. I've never met a magician, not sure I've ever wanted to."

He chewed the end of his pipe for a minute, then suddenly brought his hand down on the cart with a loud slap.

The mule's head jerked up and turned towards the rancher with annoyance.

"Oh, you're fine, go back to your grazing. You, on the other hand," Ghen said, turning his body so that he more or less sat facing Em, "I need you to do something for me. Look me in the eye and tell me that everything I read in there is the truth."

Em opened his mouth, but Ghen held up a finger.

"Kid, before you answer, think hard. I'm serious about this."

Did he really have to justify himself to Ghen? He had his notes, his two swords, and the direction to go on. He could leave now, and Ghen would more than likely leave him alone. Even if he did not, Em was beginning to wonder if he should even care.

Yet something stayed him.

It was Instinct, who, in a mischievous voice, said dramatically, *Oh Little Em, don't be that way. Try trusting a little more.*

The tone threw Em off. Could Instinct be trying to trick him? No, he couldn't. If he couldn't trust the journal, then he had nothing to trust at all.

He met Ghen's eyes. "Yes, it is true. I... I do not know who I am." A chill ran up and down Em's spine when he finished speaking. He felt bare, exposed.

Ghen, however, smiled. "Come on Bo, let's get going." Reclaiming the reins, he led the cart back on the road.

Em sighed internally with relief. He still wasn't sure if Ghen believed him, but it sounded like there was less of a chance that anyone would try to chase him down later. Getting a ride was also something of a boon, the cart's progress would be better than his own. Nevertheless, he found he was still a little unhappy.

Why? he asked Instinct. *Why did you make me do that?*

Instinct said nothing, but there was a feeling. A grin, and what Em might have sworn was a wink. It wasn't malicious, but it still made Em grit his teeth.

"Em? Are you alright?" Ghen asked.

"Eh? Ah yes, I am well."

"Okay, you looked a bit rough there for a second."

"It was nothing," Em said a little too quickly.

Ghen scrutinized Em out of the corner of his eye for a moment before blowing out a long stream of smoke. "You know, Em, look in the back of my wagon. What do you see in there?"

Confused but happy about the change of topic, he complied. "I see my things and a large blade."

"For a plow," Ghen explained. "See Bo broke the old one I had and..."

Bo snorted irritably.

"Fine, *we* broke the old one too badly to be repaired."

Em was beginning to wonder if the animal could actually understand Ghen.

The rancher continued, "Had to go buy a new one unexpectedly. I've lost three days of work due to the back and forth between Marden and home. That's a good bit to lose without planning. Thing is, I've got an idea. Do you know what nightroot is, Em?"

"A plant, I have no memory, but I still know things. I simply do not know how I learned any of it." Em replied defensively.

Ghen nodded. "I guess that's what your notes meant by trusting Instinct and so on. I was meaning to ask about that. 'Instinct' was written oddly in your notes. Like it's a person, is there something to that?"

Em hesitated, but there was no point in hiding it. "It is a voice that is not a voice. A feeling of words, images, and people. To me, Instinct and Nature are a person or maybe people... It is hard to explain, they have no face I can see but they are there. They... are my guides."

"And these voices are what tell you all you know and where to go?"

"Not everything, they are not how I know the meaning of words. Even when Instinct and Nature are silent, I know things. I believe that is what my message meant when it said my body remembers what my mind does not."

"Hmm," Ghen said thoughtfully. "I can't say I really get your meaning, but it's clear you do. So, I'll leave it there. Anyways, we were talking about nightroot. I grow a little bit of it. It sells nicely in season and brings in some extra halaks. The time to sell the root is actually soon, somewhere in the next two weeks is about when the season to sell starts. The problem is I can't sell it in Marden, which is closer to me. Instead, I have to make the longer trip to Henaden.

"These three days to get the plow have cost me time, though. It will make that trip hard, especially 'cause I haven't done all the prep for it. With that in mind," Ghen grinned slightly, "how about we make a little trade? If you walk to Henaden, it will take you five days to a week to get there. If you ride on my cart, we can do it in two or three."

Em looked up from the road and met the man's eyes.

"Here's my deal," the rancher finally said. "You work with me for three days. I'll feed you, give you a safe place to sleep, and then make sure you get to Henaden. No getting lost, and you really won't lose any time. Myself, I get to sell my little patch of nightroot and make up the lost work with your extra labor."

Em was suspicious. This was not as simple as it seemed. Once he slept, his memory would fade away. Tomorrow, he would be vulnerable to whatever Ghen said if he didn't have his journal.

His sickness and how susceptible it left him nearly made Em refuse, but his greater fear won out. He'd already passed Henaden without realizing it.

Could he risk making that mistake again? Would he be lost forever? No, he needed to find Master D'gui, and soon. He could not tolerate this forever, and would not.

One way or the other, he would see the end of these cursed days.

So, slowly, Em nodded. "Why would you do this? We just met."

The rancher bellowed with cheery laughter. "Why? This is just what good folk do."

Em wasn't sure what Ghen meant by that. He might have asked, but the man spoke first.

"There's a lot wrong in this world, Em," the rancher said, turning to the rising sun and the breaking blue above. "But bad as things may be, it's not a bad morning."

CHAPTER 2

GHEN STEERED THE CART off the main road and onto a narrow byway that ran parallel to a long fence. The moment the fence came alongside, Ghen said, "And just about here is where my little homestead begins. It's a Jarden legacy, according to Pop. The land's been ours since before this was even part of Ifeldia."

At this point, it was drawing near to midday, and cicadas hummed to praise the light high in the sky. Em blinked away the glare as he let his gaze drift over the land, which rose and fell like the dip and crest of gentle waves. In the pasture they rode past, many of Ghen's cows marched east in a lumbering mass, shadowing the cart.

"Forgive me Ghen-*sa* I—"

"Ghen," the rancher reminded him.

"Ghen," he corrected. "I do not follow your meaning."

Ghen scratched his head. "So, your friend Instinct doesn't know everything then. Well, I can tell you a few things as we go on, but Ifeldia is where you are. It's our country, nice and proud we are of it too."

"I understand." Em wasn't sure he did, but perhaps he should learn to. If Ifeldia was the name of the country in which Master D'gui lived, he should avoid being ignorant. Then he noticed again the herd of cattle that trailed the cart. "Why do your animals follow us?"

Ghen smiled at the crowd sauntering after them, occasionally flicking their thin tails in expectation. "They're hoping I brought them a little something from out of town, but they can graze right where they are."

Em leaned back and forth to match the curves and dips of the unwieldy dirt road as they continued so he wouldn't tip out of his seat. Ghen adjusted himself easily to the familiar contours of his home as he listed off his family to his new guest. He had a wife, May, and two daughters. The youngest, Amiria, carried the name of May's mother, while the elder, Kaddley, had already seen five falls. While these were his only children, there was also a boy among them.

"And the boy isn't your son?" Em inquired when Ghen didn't immediately elaborate.

"He's not," Ghen said.

"Is he more help, like I am to be?"

"Ha! I wish. I really can't afford a full ranch hand. You may think our deal favors you but, compared to some folk, you're cheap labor. Jirus is the son of one of my cousins. Sadly, Ol' Mahden died in an accident with his horse. Jirus's mother didn't take the accident well, she's gone too." Ghen did not give any more details on her death. "It was a rough time for a lot of the family and Jirus got it the worst. After they were gone, I took him in. That's what good folk do after all."

But as he went on about this relative, it became clear that Jirus wasn't exactly held in high regard. Ghen clearly cared for him, but couldn't trust him. The rancher made a clear warning that Em was to keep an eye on his belongings.

"Honestly," Ghen sighed "even when we find him with things that aren't his. I think I pity Jirus more than I'm angry with him."

Em was interested in meeting them all, but he would take Ghen's advice around the younger boy. Em didn't have much to take, but what he did have was precious.

"There it is," Ghen said, pointing. "Home."

In the distance, something broke the natural waves of land, rising from where many fence lines met. Coming closer, Em began to make out that it was two somethings. What looked like a home and what might be a barn.

That is an odd lodge for his beast, Nature commented. *Is it not too small?*

Em agreed with Nature on that point. He looked at the squat building close to the ground and wondered how large Ghen's ranch could be if this was his barn. Neither his barn nor nearby home was very tall, instead both were long and rectangular. That did not make the barn, however, seem much more impressive.

The house was equally puzzling. Built on stone supports at the corners, the house's main walls were wooden logs, large and bound by resin. The roof was thatched, yet through its center, a fifth pillar protruded. It took him a moment to realize this pillar billowed smoke. It was a chimney? Then why did it rest in the center of the house? That looked wrong, despite Em having no memories of seeing a chimney any other way.

Along the side of the home were four wooden shuttered windows, each flung wide to let the cool air flutter through the home. Outside sat two wooden chairs and a small box, likely used as a substitute for an outdoor table on his porch. The simple furnishings, once a stained copper color, were faded to a dull gray with only hints of their former shine. Opposite the porch, the barn stood as a big wooden obstruction to whatever view might lie beyond.

As the cart was rolling toward the barn, Em noticed the front door wasn't wide enough for the cart to go through. "Do you leave your cart out of doors?"

"Not quite," Ghen said with a chuckle. "You'll find barns around here are built differently than other places. What you're looking at is the front door. We'll bring the cart in around the back."

As Bo pulled them around the edge of the barn, Em could see a larger set of doors with a lock. Ghen hopped out of the cart and pulled out a key. Deftly, he swung the doors out. The inside of the barn was in shadow, but Em's vision adjusted enough that he noticed the entrance sloped down from the door.

"It goes underground?" Em said incredulously.

"Like a lazy dwarf's hollow," Ghen joked. "See, here we dig our barns into the ground a little. I'll explain why later, but, as I'm sure you've guessed, the cart here needs to go down. Hop out and give me a hand."

Jumping down from his seat, Em began to investigate the inside, his curiosity stoked. The earthy musk of animals reached him first but wasn't overpowering as he took in the interior.

The sloping ramp wasn't steep, but as it ran down, it became clear why the barn was long instead of tall. The walkway led far down to a landing with an open floor. Around the ramp and this landing were many stalls for livestock, except where a part of one wall was set aside for a workbench and crates. The ambiance, from the tools left on the workbench to the earthen floor where clumps of straw were strewn about carelessly, gave the barn a very settled look.

"What do you think?" the rancher asked.

"I think I was hasty when I thought your barn was too short."

Ghen bounced his brows. "We country folk have a few clever tricks." Ghen nodded towards the mule. "Take a hold of Bo with me. It's easier to get her down with the cart when there's two of us."

Em felt the long-served scuffs and scores on the ramp as they made their way down. Then, Em noticed there was also a slight clopping sound with each step he took.

"It's hollow." Em muttered to himself as he surmised the meaning of the echo.

He wondered why. Storage perhaps?

Now that he was inside, his eyes adjusted, and Em saw that a landing and running boards were built above the ground floor to create even more space above. He caught a glimpse of a door on the landing. No doubt, that was the front door Em had seen before. In one corner next to the landing was a staircase to get up and down. The running boards above upheld a hayloft on one side and many racks of long farming tools on the other. The landing and loft were supported by cross beams going out to the sides of the platforms to the ground with supports below them.

At the base of the ramp was a spacious walkway where the cart was given room to maneuver as Ghen turned Bo aside. Lifting the large blade for his plow out of the cart, he let out a relieved breath.

"It's good to be home. Hey, I know we just got here, but I want to see what that Instinct of yours might know. Do you think you could unhook the cart from Bo and put her and the cart in there and there?" Ghen gestured to an empty stall and another space with wheel marks leading from it where the cart must usually be stored.

Em was being put to work immediately then. "Yes, that will be done Ghen-*sa*," he said snapping into an automatic rhythm.

"No need to be so tight kid, and uh you said the sir thing again."

Em bowed. "Forgive me Ghen..." He caught himself this time.

Ghen's mouth quirked before he suddenly cocked his head. "Goodness, how old are you, anyway? Do you know that?"

Em thought about it, but there was nothing among his notes, and neither Instinct nor Nature made any comment. Finally, he shook his head.

"That's too bad, but you can't have seen more than twenty falls, for sure. My guess is less than seventeen. I'm all for you being polite, but listen, kid, you're going through enough. I promise I'm not trying to make your life any harder, and I won't if I can help it."

"Thank you," Em said, bowing, but more relaxed this time.

"Good. I'm going to go to the house and talk with May about what's going on. She'll want to know, and she'll tan my hide if she thinks I tried to hide it. Oh, and with Bo, don't bother taking all the straps off of her, just unlatch her from the cart. I'm hoping to hook her up to the plow before the end of the day. I doubt she'll care to notice the difference since she's not wearing a bit in her mouth. If you run into a problem, I'll be back quick, and we can work it out then."

Ghen sauntered up the small staircase in the corner and went out the front door. The small stairs were wide and steep as they spiraled up and out of view. Seeing no reason to wait, Em started on his work.

I like him, he is trusting, Nature said stonily. *You could run off with his animal, but he does not fear that.*

Em looked up to where the rancher had disappeared. *If anything,* Em thought in reply *it comforts me to think that he trusts me now.*

Perhaps you can trust him. Instinct's older voice chimed in.

He has genuine kindness, but that does not mean I should trust him. I will be mindful, but, as you said before, I will not be rude. Whether I trust him or not, it would be unwise to anger my host.

Unhitching the mule was a simple process once Em began, but his unpracticed hands still took two to three minutes to detach them all. The mule, though she tossed her head when Em first reached for her, behaved well enough for him to lead her to her stall. After putting Bo away, Em turned to pull the cart into its home.

Only when he turned around, there was someone in his way.

A boy, shorter than Em, with curly hair and mischievous eyes, who could not have seen the autumn leaves fall more than twelve times based on the soft features on his face, even if he bore one bruised cheek. If Ghen was right about Em's age, that made this boy four to five seasons his junior.

From Ghen's description, Em had no doubt this was Jirus. Em's fist clenched as he saw Ghen's warning had proved accurate. The younger boy was rooting through Em's things and already held one of Em's swords in hand.

Neither of Em's swords were long. Even this one, which he considered his longsword, was made to be used with one hand if needed, so it needed to be light. The blade was less than three feet by the local measures, but the sword's hilt was slightly longer than it needed to be so that it could accommodate two hands for versatility. The single edge formed a slight curve from the tip down to the squared guard of the hilt.

His short sword was a mirror image of the longsword, only smaller in all its dimensions. The guards and hilts had no inlays of precious metals, but to Em, they were worth more than gold from the scratched steel tips to the corded handles. They weren't extravagant weapons, but they were *his* weapons.

Once Jirus saw Em watching him, he drew the long blade and, Em thought, began holding it like a fool. He gripped the sword with both hands, but his grip was too tight. He pointed the sword at Em with his arms almost fully outstretched, leaving him with no range of motion.

We both know you can close the distance and take it back, Instinct's old voice said lazily, and carefully added, *So please, don't freak out Little Em.*

Despite Instinct's warning, Em was tempted to crush this upstart. This morning Nature had taken pains to train him, and he could tell this was a common occurrence. Without even realizing, Em constructed how to take the weapon back easily. Despite not remembering all of his practice, his body remembered what his mind could not.

Jirus wouldn't be a challenge, so Em took Instinct's advice and held himself back.

"You must be Jirus-*so*," Em said calmly, deciding, despite being the senior, to treat Jirus with respect.

The boy blinked, Jirus hadn't expected Em to know his name.

"Who are you?!" Jirus demanded, obviously trying to hide the fear in his voice.

"I am Em." He bowed slightly, but Jirus didn't bow in return. Em let that disrespect pass. "Ghen-*sa* has invited me to stay here for three days. I will work in exchange for his guidance to Henaden and the use of his cart. If you do not mind, return my weapon." Em kept his voice calm but firm, extending a hand as he spoke.

Jirus took half a step back and said emphatically, "No! You stay right there."

Em took a deep breath. Ghen at least had been careful with his things, but seeing someone not only steal his sword but use it poorly was irritating. Unlike Ghen, Jirus definitely could not be trusted.

"Would you lower my sword?"

"Quit making demands! I have the sword, and that means you're going to listen," Jirus insisted.

"So, the one without a weapon must listen?" Em asked as his limited patience ran out.

The dash was almost unconscious. Em moved in a cold and quick maneuver. Grabbing the part of the blade pointed at him with his outstretched left hand, he avoided wrapping his hand over the sharp edge. Now, with even a light hold, Em pulled the sword past him. Since Jirus's arms were fully extended, he had no length to give and was pulled forward. Without the right footing, the small tug sent Jirus stumbling forward.

With another quick and practiced sequence, Em was able to disarm the boy and reclaim his weapon with a quick pull. With the sword in his right hand, Em pushed Jirus away with his left. The boy fell back against the cart in a daze after the sudden blur of motion.

With a familiar flick of his hand, the sword spun into a proper grip. Em did not want to appear intimidating though, so he let his arm and weapon fall slack at his side.

"Forgive me, but I am protective of my things. In the future, please leave them to my care."

Jirus didn't reply, but the boy's snarling expression made Em uneasy. This might not be the last time Jirus would go digging through his belongings. Despite the fierce expression, the color in the boy's face drained slowly.

Jirus had been jumpy when he still held the sword, now being the hare under the proverbial fox's paw, the effect was magnified.

Em decided maybe he needed to try to put Jirus more at ease. "I am not your enemy. You do not need to fear me."

With wounded pride, fear quickly turned to anger. "I'm not scared of you. You, you—"

"Jirus!" Ghen came down the stairs like a stampeding animal. "What in the jaws of the horizon is going on here?!"

Realizing how this must look, Em holding his drawn sword in hand and Ghen's relative shouting, Em felt suddenly ashamed.

Jirus quickly answered. "This stranger was here trying to steal Bo. When I came in, he pulled out his sword and attacked me."

Ghen let out a false laugh. "Boy, I haven't known Em very long, but I would bet all the land in my name that if he'd attacked you, you wouldn't be here to talk about it."

Em felt ashamed. "Forgive me, but his tale is not fully false. Jirus-so had my sword and I... reclaimed it."

"Mind if I ask you why?" Ghen queried cautiously. "'Cause Em, I've stuck my neck out for you here."

"Ghen-sa, he had my sword and acted as if he might use it. I admit I am protective of my things, but I still think it was best. Neither he nor I are hurt." Or at least, Em hoped that was the case. Jirus had hit the cart, but he looked fine.

Ghen studied Em's eyes again, and the rancher's features softened. "Alright. Sorry if I came off stiff, but good folk do have to stand up for family. Also, did you go to sleep while I was gone? I told you, drop the sir."

Despite the remaining tension, the small joke relieved Em. "Forgive me. I will remember... for now."

"Good." A smile started to find its way back onto Ghen's face. Then it faltered as he turned to his relative. "Jirus, as you've noticed, this is Em.

He'll be with us for a bit. Since you didn't know him, I won't call you out for this, but I want you to head into the house."

"Why?" he asked, annoyed.

"'Cause May has a job waiting for you. Just like she apparently did most of the time I was gone. The odd thing is," Ghen's tone of voice made it clear he did not find it odd in any way whatsoever, "she said she could barely find you when she needed help."

The younger boy shrugged. "How is that my fault?"

"'Cause we both know you were avoiding work," Ghen said, growing aggravated. "I trusted you to take care of things while I was away, Jirus, and you didn't. Now, Em is going to be doing work for his food, a place to sleep, and a ride. Right now, you get food, a bed, clothes, and the pleasure of my company for next to nothing. Now shape up or you are going to find the old phrase 'you don't work, you don't eat' is more than just an adage we country folk toss around."

Jirus opened his mouth to argue, but Ghen cut him off.

"Don't! I don't want to hear it. I trusted you, Jirus. May has to take care of the girls. She can't be everywhere at once, but instead of helping, you went off to do who knows what. If I can't trust you to act like good folk should, then I will need to get a mite tougher. Now, hurry up and go to the house."

Jirus's eyes narrowed but he wisely said nothing. Instead, he chose to angrily stomp as he went up the stairs toward the house.

Ghen turned to address his guest. "Sorry to do that in front of you. I'm not the kind of person who likes being mad, especially in front of guests, but even good folk got to get tough now and again."

"I do not blame him Ghen-s... eh Ghen." Em said catching himself, "We both acted in haste."

"Don't be offended, but I hope you and he both quit that habit. Running headlong in life sounds like a good idea until you hit a wall." Something in his own words made Ghen's face brighten as he recalled something. "Oh, you were wondering about our barns, right? Do you know why we dig them down like this?"

"No. It would be a lot of labor for no gain that I can see."

The rancher gave a sly smile. "That you see, yet."

Ghen led Em toward the back wall of the barn, walking alongside the ramp towards the back door. At the corner where the wall met the slope, a small door was built into the side of the ramp. Ghen grabbed a lantern by the door and quickly lit it before opening the door and stepping in.

"We all use this part of our barns to grow two things," he called from within, "mushrooms in late summer and early fall, and nightroot in late winter and early spring. You have to do it then, or it might be too cold or hot to get a good crop where we are."

Entering, Em had to bend awkwardly to keep from hitting his head despite his smaller height. When he was finally able to glance around, he didn't see anything at first. All that was obvious was dirt and wooden planks laid out to keep you from treading directly on the earth.

Yet as his eyes adjusted, he began to make out shadows that did not move with the swaying of the lantern. More focus revealed small black shapes, like many veins, crisscrossed over the soft dirt.

Instinct's shadowed voice came in a breathy whisper. *Nightroot.*

CHAPTER 3

EM'S EYES TRACED THE night-black veins that wove across the floor when the lantern light began to shift back towards the exit.

"We shouldn't stay too long, or the light might hurt the plants," Ghen explained.

"Is this all your nightroot?" Em asked before Ghen left. "To make a trip to Henaden, would you not need more? This is not a large square of earth."

Ghen paused. "No, that's all I need. Nightroot can't be grown in patches much bigger than this. If you tried, it would starve the ground and kill the roots. Also, you can't just grow nightroot anywhere. The soil also has to be just right. This stuff used to be almost impossible to find, but we locals figured out how to grow it a few generations back. It's more common now than it's probably ever been, but still rare enough to be valuable."

As Ghen left the little hidden planter, his voice still carried through the opening. "I'll probably only get one full bag because we're going a little early. That's the thing though, it's still worth the trip. Ground up, the little root can be used to make some neat things by herbalists. Normally, I wouldn't take the cart to Henaden, since it's only me and the bags. Instead, I'd just ride Bo to make it faster. Of course, we will this time, I don't think Bo would like both of us on her and I'm too lazy to walk."

"I did not know nightroot was that valuable," Em admitted as he followed Ghen out.

"Valuable enough for everyone in the area to build their barn around the idea. The local farms and ranches all sell it, as well as a few other places to the west and north of Henaden. We're really the only ones who can. Even for us, if we don't treat it just right, we can accidentally ruin the whole crop." Ghen added with genuine pride in what he and his fellow locals could do, but his pride faded to something like embarrassment as he continued.

"So, actually, there was another reason I wanted to show you this. Sorry to put you to work so quickly. You look tired, but if we're going to Henaden in three days, we need this gathered by the end of tomorrow. Before we can take it, we have to let it dry for nearly half a day. Otherwise, the root could spoil while we're on the road. Like I said, we have to treat it right or it won't be worth a thing.

"I know it's not the kind of thing good folk usually do, sticking their guests in dark places like this, but would you mind pulling the root this afternoon? We'll go eat a quick bite at the house first. Then I can come back here with you and show you how to do it. If you run into a problem, I plan to fix the plow here in the barn. That means, for a while at least, I'll be right nearby where I can help."

For a moment, Em was alarmed at the idea of being shut in a dark space. Yet, he suppressed the thought that Ghen was planning some attempt to steal from him. If that was his plan, then he wouldn't suggest they leave first to share his family's meal, it left too many chances for Em to escape.

"One last word of warning," Ghen said as they took the stairs. "My wife May is the greatest thing that's ever happened to me, and my girls are a close second, but they can be a little... talkative. Around these parts, May is known to talk without most folk getting a word in. I'm sorry if she asks you a bunch of questions and doesn't give you a chance to answer. It's just her way, and I promise she's being friendly."

"I have little to say. I do not mind being silent." Personally, Em would be glad to say nothing at all.

The rancher paused, thinking it over, then shrugged. "Fair enough."

Ghen swung the front door of the barn open, and Em found himself back between the house and the barn. Since they'd passed before, a new addition had appeared. A woman, obviously May, waiting for their arrival with hands on hips and a polite smile on her face. However, Em found her somewhat striking. Her hair was a bright red, and her skin's complexion wasn't as naturally dark as her husband's, both of which seemed very strange to Em.

"Hello, you must be Em," she said cheerily. "It's nice to meet you, but before you go in, I wanted to apologize. I didn't know anyone was coming to stay, and the girls left out a bit of a mess. We'll pick it up as we can, but please excuse it in the meantime."

Em lowered his head respectfully. "Thank you May-*se* for allowing me into your home. I will not mind. I am the one intruding."

"Don't be silly," May said good-naturedly. "You're very..." she paused for half a breath, "polite, but we'll get things straightened soon. For now, though, I set out some bread and cheese on the table. It's a small meal, but I promise to make a larger supper. Also, I'm not sure what '*se*' is, but thank you, and just 'May' is fine."

"I see..." This family was difficult. All the same, Em was about to let her know that a simple meal was more than suitable, but she spoke first.

"Now come along, there is no sense in us standing around out here. You've come a long way and the food's out." Briskly, she turned and beckoned them in.

Em noticed Ghen was failing to hide a smile. The rancher was right, she did like to talk.

As they stepped into the house, Em had the sudden urge to remove his shoes and almost did, until he noticed that neither Ghen nor his wife did so. They showed no sign of planning to either, so Em kept his on. The strangeness of keeping them on bothered Em slightly the whole time he was in the home.

Beyond this, however, the home was quite comfortable.

The building was simple, but with no internal walls except around a washroom, the effect was that it easily felt like one spacious room. On the far side of the house, three beds and a smaller crib were bunched together. A few steps from the foot of these rested their strange fireplace in the center of their home.

The round chimney was a stone pillar that bulged like a large, upturned bowl at its base. There was a gap at the bottom of the bowl, where five rods supported it. Looking in as he got close, Em noted there was also a larger support in the center of the fireplace that reached up to the base of the bowl. Between the smaller supports were thin metal sheets that ran on rails to suspend themselves over the flames. It took Em a moment to realize that this was so the fireplace could double as a kind of stove.

At the base of the fixture was a small pan where the ashes were collected, which was cleaned regularly. This fireplace and its design made sense, but for some reason, Em couldn't see it as anything but strange. Wherever he'd come from, things like this were not normal.

Beside the fireplace, two sitting chairs were arranged on one side, and across from them, a table set for their midday meal. Near the front and back doors of the home, the house was divided, with one section holding a small washroom, while the rest was arrayed with cupboards and counter space making up the kitchen.

As Em settled awkwardly at the table and took all of this in, May marched around the house. Her red hair swayed this way and that, and she kept talking all the while as she put all things in order. Not that there was much out of order. Despite being described as a mess, the house was quite orderly.

May comfortably talked on and on about local weather, gossip, and more. She spoke so fast that Em couldn't keep up and missed many details, but it didn't matter. As Ghen had foretold, May was quite capable of speaking enough for both of them. Finally, she paused her lecture to manage her youngest daughter and Em wondered how long the silence would last.

The answer was, not very long.

"Mama says you'll be with us for the night." This was not a question, but a statement. Kaddley, the elder daughter, was her mother's child. She didn't ask questions she wouldn't answer herself if given the time. Though, while she shared her mother's personality, she'd inherited her father's dark curly hair.

Without waiting for Em to reply, Kaddley launched into a perky but repetitive description of who all of her family was before trying to pick up where her mother had left off about the weather.

The other daughter mumbled quietly to her mother as her older sister carried on. Amiria, called Ami by her family, was still learning to talk. Em wondered if she would inherit the talkativeness too or if she would be relegated to silence with her father.

Em noticed that Jirus was nowhere in sight, but there was a missing portion in the food served. He'd either already eaten or taken his food with him to wherever he was now.

"Now aren't you being kinda rude, little lady?" Ghen said. "You haven't let Em here say a word."

The little girl deflated slightly, and Em shook his head.

"She may speak. I do not mind taking time to listen."

"Oh!" Kaddley said. "Your voice sounds funny! Have you heard..." and off she went again.

Throughout the remainder of lunch, Em managed no more than half of a sentence. Instead, he nodded along as he ate. Even though the conversation was one-sided, Em felt strangely relaxed. He began to sit less resolutely in his chair and even lean back in an imitation of Ghen. It felt... good.

It's been a while since you were able to enjoy having company, hasn't it? Instinct asked.

Perhaps. I do not remember.

Ghen had obviously already told May and Kaddley of his condition. Multiple times, they both expressed how sorry they were for him. Almost immediately, this was followed by some diatribe about a neighbor, or about how they had both heard 'the strangest thing' recently.

Em began to wonder if they would go on all day until May peeked out the window and, guessing at the time, decided they'd rested enough.

"I know we're having fun," she said with the clap of her hands bringing the full room to attention, "but we all have things we need to do. Em, you can leave your stuff right here at the table."

At the mention of his things, Em's grip tightened. "Forgive me, but I wish to keep them."

May raised an eyebrow, but nodded. "Well, alright, but just know you have the option to leave them here whenever you want. I'll make sure the girls here don't get into anything. As for Jirus, I may not know where he always is, but this is *my* house. Nothing happens here that I don't know about. I won't let him mess with anything of yours if you do decide to leave it. Now go on both of you, get out there."

May shooed them out with as much haste as she'd beckoned them in, but Em still kept with him all his possessions, determined to keep them in sight at all times.

Once back in the barn, Ghen brought Em back to the patch of nightroot. Em hesitated at the door to the dark room.

"Is there another job I might do?"

Ghen hesitated. "Well, honestly, if we are going to go to Henaden together, this has to be done soon. Either you or I need to do it, at least for a little while. If you think you can work on putting the plow together, I'm willing to stay in here a while."

Em looked at the wooden contraption next to the workbench and the large blade Ghen had purchased for it. He could figure it out, he was sure, but his work would be poor and Ghen had said the last blade had broken under poor management. He didn't want to be responsible for this new blade being ruined.

"No," Em sighed. "I will pull the root for now. However, I will keep my things with me."

"That's fine. Step on in and I'll show you how the work is done."

It took a moment for them both to get settled into the small space, but once they were reasonably comfortable, Ghen explained the process. He even showed Em a few examples of how to begin harvesting the root and then watched Em do it once or twice before leaving him to work on his own.

Em was tempted to try the plow after all when Ghen mentioned that constant light could hurt the roots, meaning the work of pulling them had to be done without any light at all. Being in the dark didn't bother Em, but the idea of being closed in was unpleasant. Yet in the end, he conceded and allowed himself to be left in shadow.

It wasn't long until the cramped space was uncomfortable, and after an even shorter time, the tight space was nearly maddening. Em was short compared to Ghen, but even he had to crawl on his knees when he reached toward the lower end of the ramp. He desperately desired to stretch out, but the slightest movement left him bumping into the ceiling or some support while digging in the dirt for the thin roots.

Luckily, the work itself quickly became simple. It was a job that trusted feeling more than sight. He ran his hand over the top of the rough earth until he touched the smooth, and oddly cool, round body of the root.

As Ghen had told him, pulling the vein of root was easier if he pulled up a part at a time, working his way along the top of the root until he pulled up the whole thing. The roots grew long sprouts that burrowed deep beneath the surface veins, and if he pulled up too hastily, he would lose more than he'd collect.

The more Em pulled, the more he began to see that the nightroot was much larger than he first thought. Each time he pulled up a whole strand of nightroot he stowed the lengths in a pouch Ghen had given him.

Em wondered if the roots shrank when dried because otherwise, he couldn't see how all of it would fit in only one or two bags. They were little more than small grain sacks, and even one root coil created a noticeable bulge in the sack.

The trick to pulling nightroot, Ghen had explained, was not to tear the root. According to him, it had a larger chance of rotting if an end was left open to the air. If a root was ripped, Em would have to tie both of the torn ends into small knots which should save the root from rot.

The process was slow and tedious, but Em realized he had nothing better to do. If Ghen's words and estimations were true, Em would lose almost no time getting to Henaden, all while knowing he wouldn't have to worry about where his next meal would come from.

When he'd awoken this morning, he hadn't had a clue what to do or how to do it. Only after reading his notebook and taking time to gather himself had he found his way, trusting his notes to figure out in which direction Henaden lay.

Before leaving, he'd found some leftover cooked meat. That was the only food he'd had. The fur gave Em the impression it'd once been a kind of rodent. An obvious gift from his past self. Thinking of all he must have forgotten, the Em of yesterday felt like a different person.

While under Ghen's roof, he wouldn't have to worry about what he would leave for the Em of tomorrow. That was enough of a reason to work for the rancher, but it wasn't all. Em had to admit Instinct was right. Sitting at the table with Ghen's family, Em knew he missed having others. He wouldn't tell Ghen, it wasn't his business, but Em guessed he would enjoy the rancher's company.

"Gaki marō," Em growled angrily, as he heard the *thwick* of another root tearing.

Em muttered to himself, irritated by the torn root. He was becoming more certain that he'd never done anything like this before since his body's memory was no help in this task. This was the fourth or fifth end he'd have to tie off. Unlike the previous tears, Em was sure he could have avoided this one if he had been more focused.

As he struggled to tie the root off, he wished again for a little light. The root was so small it was easy to lose track of. Ghen had taught him how to tie it without seeing, but it was still difficult.

"What I need is just a little... light."

A quick flicker of red radiance filled the small space and Em jumped upright as a jolt of pain rocketed up his arm. With a thud, Em's head banged on the low ceiling above. He sat down, or maybe fell, groaning. Sitting there, he rubbed the top of his head soothingly.

Em heard Ghen's voice come through the ramp above him. "I should have warned you. Sometimes if the ground is dry, there can be some little shocks. They're not bad, just surprising. A man a while back called it static, whatever that means, but I'll bet hitting your head hurt worse." It was muffled, but Em heard the rancher laugh. "That ceiling has claimed a few noggins. Welcome to the ranch!"

Em ground his teeth. Hurt, embarrassed, and irritated, he sat for a moment rubbing his arm. He wasn't sure what locals might mean by static, but something about that red light felt wrong. Besides, his shocked arm hurt worse than the... never mind, the headache was getting worse.

CHAPTER 4

AFTER ANOTHER HOUR OR more of pulling, Ghen came to the door of the ramp. "How're you doing in there?"

Em only grunted in reply.

"Finish pulling that root you've got and come out. Otherwise, you won't be able to stand up straight tomorrow."

Happy to comply, Em made quick work of the coil of root and stuffed it into the sack. Before leaving, he collected his bag and swords. On his hands and knees, they'd quickly become more cumbersome, so he'd taken them off and set them by the door.

When he finally came out, he could feel Ghen was right, stiffness had already set in. Ghen held out a skin of water while Em was stretching. His back cracked and popped as he twisted. Finishing, Em took the drink gladly. Looking down at himself, he saw that he was covered head to toe with earth and detritus.

Almost as if Ghen could read Em's thoughts, he said, "Don't worry about your clothes. I've got some spare stuff you can wear while you're here to work, they'll be big on you, but you'll only need them for a day or two. We'll have a wash day before we leave. So, all your stuff will be clean and ready for our trip. Till then there's something else you can do for me. I promise to let you have sunshine this time."

"Yes, that would be nice," Em said with a slight groan.

The rancher led Em up the ramp, out of the barn, and to the other side of his house. There they came upon what Ghen explained was a small smokehouse and an old tree stump. Lying beside the stump, a small pile of large logs on one side and a small number of split ones on the other side. Em guessed his job would be splitting even more wood.

"I figure you may be better at this than pulling roots since you've got that sword," Ghen commented. "Using an axe might not be the same, but what do I know?"

"I can do this," Em said. "This job at least is familiar in a way."

"Hey! That's good. Winter is about through with us, but we still need split wood to heat the stove. Don't worry about splitting the whole pile, just get enough to fill that smaller rack by the back door, and we should be fine." Ghen gestured to a small wood rack with a few small logs and split wood still on it.

"Yes, Ghen-s—" He caught himself again, at least he was getting better at it. Em looked at the three tools resting on the log for a moment and stopped Ghen before he walked off. "Ghen, I have a question."

Ghen turned and glanced at the tools. "Something wrong? I thought you said this one was familiar."

"It is. What I do not understand is what these are for." Em pointed to what he could only describe as a small metal ramp, or oversized nail, that lay next to a large hammer.

Ghen paused a moment before bursting into laughter. Em's confusion mounted, and he stared at the objects again, unable to guess their purpose. It was a hammer and an instrument like a chisel, but thicker at the base.

Ghen wiped his eyes briefly as he explained. "Em, there's a chance you've split wood before with an axe, but around here the trees are hardwood. If you think the axe will be enough to do the job, you're in for a surprise. You start the log with the axe and make a dent. Then stick the wedge," he gestured to the small metal ramp, "in the crack. Once you do that, hit the wedge with the hammer and it'll split."

Studying the objects, Em began to understand the concept, but he still asked Ghen to split one to make sure. The process was just as he explained. He took the axe to the log, pulled it out, placed the 'wedge' in the crevice he'd made, and struck it with the large hammer. The blade of the wedge drove through, and the log toppled apart in pieces.

"It is a chisel of a kind," Em muttered to himself. "Only to split instead of carve."

Finishing his demonstration, Ghen sauntered away with a grin, a chuckle still lingering from Em's question. Despite seeing the example, Em couldn't shake his curiosity as he set a new log on the stump.

Hmm. Instinct pondered in Em's shadow. The young man could hear the voice grinning, but he wasn't sure at what. *You've definitely split logs with an axe before.*

Trusting the voice, and a little curious, Em brought the axe down hard, hoping to fracture it with only the axe. The tool's head hit the log and bit into it, but the log didn't split. Instead, his strength resounded back, running up the axe handle into his arms. Em recoiled as if he'd been bitten and shook off his arms as the force of it burned.

A hearty laugh from behind meant that Ghen had stayed to watch for a moment. Then there was more laughter rolling around in Em's shadow, as a merry Instinct laughed somewhere beyond sight.

Em didn't turn around, his face burning. The way of the sword was familiar, but the way of the rancher was obviously not. It seemed Instinct was trustworthy most of the time but had a mischievous side. Em wondered if Instinct and Nature truly had a will all of their own.

Next time, he tried doing things Ghen's way, and it was annoyingly effective after his own failed attempt. Admitting defeat, Em adopted Ghen's method as his own. The more wood he split, the more natural the new process became.

As time stretched, Em entertained himself by thinking about other things. He found himself looking at the chimney of the house again and thinking of all he'd noticed within. While the building was packed with people, furniture, and possessions, the way the family bustled around within never made the home feel cramped.

As Em's thoughts lingered on Ghen's family, he eventually decided they were good company. Perhaps someone else might have found all their constant talking rude, but Em didn't mind. May and Ghen charged an orderly house, and while May was slightly more stern, she was acting as friendly as her husband had.

It wasn't much, but after considering their actions throughout the day, Em felt more comfortable with the little trust he was placing in them.

While their treatment of him could still be some lie, their blatant affection for each member of their family made his worries seem dramatic.

They care deeply for their own, Em said to his shadow. *Do you know if there are people who care the same for me?*

I do, but you have other concerns, Nature answered with a low growl. *Someone is watching you.*

His senses jumped at the warning. It was true, now that his mind no longer wandered, it tracked. He followed the shuffle and slight blurs of motion in the distance. He kept splitting logs, pretending not to have received the warning. More subtly, he observed.

Little turns with the swing of the axe, pausing to set aside split wood, by these he surveyed all around. Yes, they were watching.

There were three of them, and Em recognized at least one, Jirus. The boy was sly, but Em was wary of him. All three were hard to make out at first, but as they moved, Em caught fleeting glances and slowly formed a mental image of them.

Three boys, he guessed, the other two were taller and likely older than Jirus, but the one was Jirus himself. Every so often, they moved. Em could only guess it was so they could get a better view of him. But why? Was an outsider that entertaining?

He kept working, ignoring them, until a fourth pair of eyes fell on him. Of course, when Kaddley watched him, she wasn't hiding. She simply walked out of the house and strode happily over to him.

"Mama says to come inside and get cleaned up before dinner."

Em looked up, only now noticing that the light of day was past its peak and already the colors of the sky began to lose to the red army that dominated the rise and fall of each day. Time had become a haze in the rhythm of work, and looking at the wood rack, he realized he'd split more than enough.

"Thank you. I will come soon."

"Okay." Kaddley giggled. "You've been in the nightroot, you're all dirty."

"Perhaps I should brush myself off, then."

"Per... perhaps?" the little girl said, trying to puzzle out the word.

"Maybe," Em explained, and the girl nodded.

"Perhaps you should," she said in a childish imitation of his accented voice.

Em could not help smiling. It felt oddly good.

You ought to do that more often, Little Em, old Instinct said.

"Do you know where Jirus is?" Kaddley asked.

Em thought carefully about how to answer, as his last interaction with Jirus hadn't gone well. Would forcing his junior out of hiding go any better?

"Nearby," he said.

"Okay," Kaddley said. The little girl took a few steps past Em, cupped her hands around her mouth, and shouted, "JIRUS! MAMA, WANTS YOU!"

Unable to stop another smile, Em gathered up the wood from his labors and strode to the house so that Jirus could come out of hiding. The moment he stepped in, May met him at the door to inspect him.

"Oh, that dirt gets everywhere. Be sure to wash your hands before you sit at my table," she told him, guiding him toward the washroom.

After cleaning his hands, Em stepped into their living area and the thick rich air that only comes with cooking meat filled his nostrils. Slabs of beef seasoned with herbs from the family's garden sizzled on the fireplace cooking grates next to a tall lid. When May lifted the lid to check on its contents the earthy smell of cooked potatoes joined the aroma of the beef. The symphony of smells was a sudden reminder to Em of just how good a proper meal could be. This was going to be far better than a leftover rodent.

A comment, that he decided to keep to himself.

Ghen walked in a moment later and saw Em. "Good, they already went and got you. I pulled some of the roots myself and then hung it all so that part could start to dry. Tomorrow, I'll show you how it's done."

"Ahem." May cleared her throat, looking pointedly at the pools of earth Ghen was tracking in.

"And I'll be back in a second after I brush some of this dirt off," Ghen added.

The moment Ghen stepped back in, May asked without looking up from her work, "Did you finish with the plow?"

The rancher swelled. "Of course, my dear. It wasn't great that the blade broke, but at least I was almost done when it did. Bo's had a good day, and we finished the field. I even gave her a little treat for not being a twit."

"Then will you and I plant seed?" Em asked, guessing at the next step.

"Actually, we need to let it rest first. When I get back from Henaden, I'll get around to that. Don't worry though, there's another field that's already been plowed. Since the blade broke, it's all rested, too. Tomorrow, when we aren't pulling nightroot, all of us will head out and start seeding that..." Something behind Em caught the rancher's eye. "Jirus, did you get that fence mended that May set you on?"

Jirus's secret entry had not gone as he hoped.

"Yes, the bull wasn't anywhere near the broken part. I don't know why it was such a problem." Jirus's voice was full of contempt.

"Good folk can't tolerate broken equipment. If the bull had found it broken, he would have gone through the gap and a whole lot further. Then you would have wished you'd decided to fix it on your own. Chasing down that old boy is no fun at all, take it from me."

"Azel and Jhoen don't have to do stuff like this," Jirus argued.

Ghen shook his head. "Those boys' parents can afford hired hands for all seasons. The only reason we have Em here is because he's riding with me to Henaden as a kind of trade. Besides, their farm doesn't need a bull, a ranch like ours does. So, we need to keep it where we can get to it. Does that make sense?"

"Yes sir," he replied lazily. To his mind, Jirus was done with this conversation.

Ghen raised an eyebrow, but let it slide. May was beginning to set the table, and the rancher lent a hand. It was not long before they all sat down to eat.

Em ate slowly, focusing on maintaining his discipline. The meal tasted as good as it smelled, and with each bite, his hunger grew. Still, he made sure to stay polite and not overeat, despite the temptation.

The matron of the house saw through that hesitation. "Eat what you want, Em. You're skinny as a pole and probably haven't been able to get a full stomach in a long time. Just don't make yourself sick."

"Thank you, May-*se*." Em said respectfully, reaching forward to refill his plate.

"So, what does that mean?" Jirus asked. "That *se* and *so* stuff."

"Forgive me, it is a habit of mine, I would guess." Em did his best to explain based on his limited knowledge. "They are terms of respect, *sa* and *se* for older men and women *so* and *si* for younger."

The boy toyed with the food on his plate. "That a thing from your home?"

"I assume so. However, I am not sure where my home is."

"Well, you look like a marauder to me."

Except for the young Ami, the rest of the table fell silent.

Em's fist clenched, and he felt the heat rise in his face.

Before Em could reply in haste, Instinct cut in. *Leave it alone, Little Em. He doesn't know any better.*

Marauder, that name. All Em had were impressions, something about them made him sick. They worked for... someone or something. Em's mind wandered through a fog of dark, tangled images and sensations. None of them were clear thoughts, and there were no words to give them form. All he knew was that whoever these marauders were, they were people Em had met before, and he did not want to meet again.

"I am not one of these marauders," Em replied slowly, pacing his breath, letting his anger cool as he spoke. "I do not know who the Marauders are. Something tells me they are a group, but I have no love for them. I have forgotten much, but that much I know."

Jirus sniffed derisively. He either doubted the answer or was disappointed by it. "So much for not using broken equipment."

"Jirus!" May's voice flared, but her eyes were chilling. Em was surprised to see such a change in the friendly woman. "First you ask if he's one of those killers, then you insult him in front of all of us."

Jirus gaped. "Look at his clothes! He's a foreigner and Azel says those people are all trouble. He thinks—"

May's voice ran to a fever pitch. "Jirus! You will not speak to a guest of mine or anyone else's that way or I will show you wrath that would make the monsters of Yongarad cry for their mothers. Do you understand me?"

Jirus shrank under the colossal weight of May's gaze.

Once she was sure Jirus was subdued, May turned slowly, like the spin of a typhoon until she came to her husband. Ghen, at this point, was trying to avoid her gaze with everyone else. Finding he'd caught her ire, he got ready to speak, but she silenced him with one pointing finger.

"This behavior has gone on like this too long, Ghen. You help him straighten up." Her words were careful and clear. "There will be no more of it or I'll have both your hides."

Ghen nodded slowly and rubbed his left temple with one hand, trying to appear apologetic.

Kaddley stood up to say something, but it died on her tongue when May shut her down with a glance.

With order restored, May settled back, and the table resumed the meal.

What surprised Em was that within five minutes, the table drew back to the merry and grateful mood of before, as if nothing had happened. The only exception was Jirus, he noticeably did all he could to avoid eye contact with May for the time being.

Once they were all finished, and the girls were being put to bed, Ghen invited Em outside to talk. Em collected his things from the house and followed the rancher out into the cool early spring air.

The sun was setting behind distant trees, but some of its light still remained. On one side, the sky was painted by an auburn brush, while on the other, streaks of deep blue whispered the comfort of the oncoming night. The daylight chime of cicadas faded as an orchestra of crickets tuned their instruments for the song of the sleeping.

"We're planning to have you camp out in the hay loft. I hope this won't offend you, but I'll be locking the barn up. If you forget everything, I don't want you just wandering around. I... uh, I hope you understand." Ghen kept his tone level, clearly trying not to make Em nervous.

"That is the right thing to do," Em said, and for the hundredth time since waking, hated the strange forgetfulness that plagued him. Once again, he had no choice but to trust the rancher. However, Em also needed to make sure he could keep to his goal even if the rancher did try to betray him.

"Is there a lantern or some light in the barn? If tomorrow morning is anything like today, I will be very confused and will need to read through my notes twice before I know how to act. Ah!" Em realized. "I will also need to make a note about our deal and why I am here. Otherwise, I'm not sure what might happen."

"Good thought, I could have a hard time convincing you I'm good folk after locking you in a barn. Do you have anything you can use to write with in that bag of yours?"

"I have materials, but I do not think they are very good."

"Don't bother with them then. May writes letters to family in Cobaden, so we have ink and the like, that'll work nice. I'll get you some before you set down for the night."

"Thank you."

Em paused, just admiring the sounds of a day's end. This would be his last day, after all.

Tomorrow, some other Em would take his place. One with no memory of this day's bright beginning or beautiful end. This Em wished to remember, to be, just a little longer.

"Em..." Ghen began mournfully.

"Yes?" Em didn't turn away from the coming night, not yet.

"I wanted to make sure I said I'm sorry about what's happening to you. That probably doesn't make you feel any better, but you need to know. I can't even start thinking about what I'd do in your place."

It didn't make him feel better. If anything, Em only mourned himself all the more, but he appreciated the care he was being given.

Em sighed in his heart. *The me of tomorrow will be well cared for.*

If you think that, Nature rumbled in Em's shadow, *why not trust him? It is not easy to trust, but he has done nothing that speaks of ill intent. Remember, child, there is safety in metal but no comfort. The Em of tomorrow, as you call him, will worry for himself. Should you wish for advice, then listen to me. Tonight, at least, trust and be at peace.*

The voice was right, Em had to admit. Even if Ghen betrayed him while he slept, he would never know.

Okay, he told Nature, and to Ghen he said, "I trust you Ghen-*sa,* for today at least, you have my trust. I cannot speak for who I will be tomorrow, but I choose to have peace tonight."

"Thank you," Ghen said kindly. "If there is anything else I can do to help you settle, let me know."

"There is one other question I have," Em said slowly.

"Ask away."

"Marauders, what are they? Not the word, I can feel they are more than a word. A group, a dangerous one."

"They are that. This about what Jirus said?" Ghen asked.

"Yes," Em said. "When you see me, do you see a marauder?"

"Well," Ghen answered slowly, "I don't. I've never seen a marauder and I thank the heavens for that. Thing is, Jirus hasn't either, he's just talking nonsense. The boy he mentioned, Azel, may have put the idea in his head, but he's seen as little as any of us. He's just a neighbor boy who makes trouble.

"You're certainly dressed like a fighter and not one from Ifeldia. That's probably where the idea came from, but who knows if yours is marauder gear? I doubt it. There are always stories about what kind of people they are and I'm not sure you fit the description."

"Stories can be exaggerated."

Ghen nodded. "That's true, but Uncle Grady saw them firsthand. Most of the things I know about the greater world I learned from him. Long ago, he was one of the watchmen." Realizing Em wouldn't know them either, he quickly explained. "They're a militia that's separate from the army. They take people the army won't or can't take. For a season, my uncle went out with them to see the world for himself. The short version is the Marauders are a lot like the Watchmen Brigade, separate from the army, save they work from Yongarad. While the watchmen don't take criminals, marauders aren't supposed to care. Their reputation is... dark."

As the night's shadow settled in, another darkness rose from deep within Em's heart. "You do not know my reputation. Even I do not."

"Okay kid, listen closely." Ghen sounded irritated. "You're a little grumpy and worn to the nub, but even so, you didn't rob me when we first met. I didn't hear of a thief in Marden after you passed through. I didn't hear you ever say a rude word to anyone, even when Jirus toyed with your sword. Now you want to tell yourself you might actually be one of those Yongarad monsters? No, that just sounds crooked. So, don't you put that nonsense in your head."

"Yongarad." Em repeated the name. "That is the nation your Ifeldia is at war with?"

"Well, you know... well I guess you don't." The rancher shook his head. "I have a feeling this won't be the last time I'm going to have to tell you this."

"You're probably right about that. If there is much you need to say, then..."

Ghen waved Em off before he could finish. "No, you're entitled to your answers. It's a country, see, not quite as big as ours— Well, wait, maybe they are... Argh, I need to start at the beginning."

"Please wait." Em insisted. "If your tale is long, telling me will not matter. Save it please, I will write to myself to ask you about it tomorrow. If this place is at war, that is something I need to know about. He, the Em of tomorrow, will write down whatever is important."

"If that's how you want to do it, that's fine with me," Ghen said.

"Thank you, Ghen... Ghen." Em fought to keep off the honorific but still bowed.

Ghen huffed. "I still don't get all the bowing and *sa*, I could have sworn you were saying sir, anyways, I guess it's just you. If it's easier to add it at the end of my name, go ahead, like I said, you've got it hard enough. I won't make it harder. Now, should we get you that quill so you can be ready for bed?"

"Not yet, I would like more time before I rest."

"Got something else you need to do?"

"Yes, in my notes I am told that it is my body that remembers, not my mind. Nature says that comes from his teachings and constant practice.

Would you mind if I practiced before I am locked in the barn?" Em asked, tapping the weapons at his hip.

Em expected Ghen would resist, but instead, he smiled. "Why not? Let's see what you can do."

CHAPTER 5

Would you mind if I practiced before I am locked in the barn?" Em asked, gripping the weapons at his hip.

I'm pleased Gha... would... we... what we... Vernier...

see what you can do...

To the west of where Em primed himself, and Ghen prepared to learn what he could of his guest, two others were thinking they knew quite enough about him.

Em had never mentioned to Ghen the eyes that had followed him while he was splitting wood, but if he had, Ghen would have guessed they belonged to the two brothers Jirus was always trying to imitate, Azel and Jhoen Colrage.

Neither of the brothers liked or disliked their neighbor, Jirus. He was entertaining, and they enjoyed impressing him, but neither could accept him fully because of the other. Azel, the older, thought that accepting a boy so much younger than he was as a friend would make him look childish. His younger brother, Jhoen, feared that his older brother would think less of him if he tried to seriously befriend Jirus. So, neither did.

Despite their neutral disposition, both of them shared a dream with Jirus. Each of them wished to go on adventures and become a hero of legend.

The brothers, however, had an experience that Jirus did not. Their father, Ned Colrage, had been enlisted in the Watchmen Brigade. He'd traveled many places while in that service and come to despise all those who came from beyond Ifeldia's boundaries. This natural dislike was something both of his sons had inherited. So, from the moment Jirus brought word of the 'unfamiliar swordsman,' the sons of Ned Colrage were convinced he was nothing but trouble.

As the sun was setting on the Jarden farm, it was also casting weak orange light on the road the boys traveled home. As they went, the brothers discussed that 'Em' and the trouble he was surely going to cause.

"I bet he's a thief, running from the law," Jhoen guessed. "He probably grew up doing it. It's probably all anyone ever does where he's from."

"Maybe," Azel said slowly. "I still think he could be a marauder. Dad said they always wear those coats that make them blend in with the swamps on the other side of the mountains. His coat looked like it could do that."

"Yeah, but..." Jhoen tried to think of something smart and impressive to say. "But he's too small. The stories all say marauders are scary, he wasn't scary, I could take him."

Azel smiled wickedly. "Mayb— Hey, what's that?"

He'd become distracted by something up the road which he soon made out was a large tent assembled on the side of the byway. Small as the tent was, it was striking and attractive. A red velvet cloth adorned with gold tassels, featuring a matching symbol, a circlet of gold with pointed palisades descending into an inverted crown.

As they drew closer, they saw a man sitting in front of the tent, tending a small fire. A fragrant scent rose from the flames, and as soon as the brothers caught it, they were instantly entranced. Equal parts sweet and savory, the aroma was a sharp reminder that they hadn't intended to stay at the Jarden ranch for so long and had gone without food for hours.

Neither could help drawing nearer. The man looked up at their approach. He was in travel clothes, but lavish ones. Gold filigree was woven into every cuff and collar, and the cavalry sword at his hip was so covered in jewels that it sparkled in the failing light even if the man kept his body mostly in shadow. His face was a mask of wisdom with a strong jaw, experienced wrinkles, and flowing hair of fine silver. Yet, despite his many markers of age, one glance at him was enough to see that he'd once been both strong and handsome. Even while his looks and strength might have been slightly lessened with age, it was clear his wealth had not.

"My good luck continues," the rich man said, with a voice far clearer than his age would suggest.

"Sir?" Azel said. "I don't know what you mean by that, but you know you're on our father's land, don't you?"

"Oh?" queried the man. "I didn't know any of the nobles owned land out here."

Jhoen felt confused. "Our dad's not a noble."

"Really? Well, I must say I'm surprised. I just assumed he was, considering how you looked."

Azel and Johen didn't feel exceptionally noble at the moment. After doing chores for their mother in the morning and creeping through bushes with Jirus in the afternoon. They and their clothes were scratched, scuffed, and dirty.

The rich man noticed them looking at their clothes and, before the brothers could come to think he might be mocking them said, "Not your clothes, your faces. You both have the visage of a strong and noble line about you. I'm sorry if I confused you and let me say if my being here is something of a problem, perhaps we can work out a trade."

The old man looked around at his rich furnishings and tapped his chin as if he didn't already know what he was going to suggest. "Ah! That's just it. As I was saying when you first arrived, I've had something of a lucky day."

He gestured to a bow propped against a tent. It was as white as ivory, and the quiver next to it was full of arrows with gold woven in the fletchings. Jhoen and Azel came from the richest of all the local farmsteads, but in this small tent was more flagrant wealth than either of them had ever seen in their lives. The more they looked around, the more glory they saw in the old man's possessions.

"With my little toy," he said about the bow, "I killed a stag, which has given me more meat than I can possibly eat or save to take with me. Since I am only borrowing the use of a little dirt for a little while, do you think you boys would welcome a meal as fair trade? You look hungry, after all." His words came out smooth and sweet like honey and, even before the brothers saw what was being offered, the idea of the meal made their mouths water.

Then they glanced at the fire before them, and their stomachs rumbled in awe. Steaks fresh off the fire still steamed hot in a pan. Next to it, on a wooden plate, a fine loaf of bread packed with nuts lay partially sliced, still somehow looking like it was freshly baked. In a small jar sat a gravy that neither of them could fathom how the old man had managed to save or carry all the way here. The gravy looked sweet in perfect contrast to the steaks, and all either could think of was wanting to spend more time in the presence of this man's wealth and taking the chance to share in his meal.

"Su-sure," Azel agreed, trying not to seem half as desperate for the food as he was, but even his pride was failing at the sight of this meal. "We'll take a part."

"A part? Oh, well you see..." the rich man turned around and produced a plate with scraps of a meal already eaten, "I've already had my share. All that's left is for you."

"Really?" Jhoen asked excitedly.

The man laughed as richly as the gold around him. "Of course, my young friends. Come, sit at my fire."

The two sat down and, without any more words, the rich man produced smooth wooden plates and utensils, and served them the steaks from his pan, the bread from his loaf, and laid atop it all his supply of his honeyed gravy. The brothers sank into the food, their manners and pride having now finally failed. The more they ate, the more they wanted. They couldn't be sure how long they ate, but when they finished, the sun sat much lower in the sky and everything that had been offered was gone. They'd eaten it all and still wanted more. Both brothers looked down at their empty plates with steep disappointment.

The rich man, however, smiled. "How was it?"

"It was the best!" Jhoen said, taking a last look at the pans and bowls, hoping there was still something left, but there wasn't anything for him there.

"Then, I assume I can say we've had a fair trade?" the rich man asked with a laugh.

"Yeah," Azel said, wiping his mouth. Suddenly reminded of his manners, he corrected. "Yes, sir. Very fair."

The rich man stood with such poise that Azel found he was somewhat jealous. He wished to be like this old man. He possessed so much wealth and authority that his very being demanded respect and awe. Yeah, he was old, but Azel supposed everyone got old, eventually. Azel thought that, when he got old, this was how he wanted to be. Surrounded by his possessions, giving only because he had too much to keep, and demanding respect from everyone who passed without demanding anything.

Jhoen was feeling much the same way. Sure that, this is who he'd be one day.

Thinking on all that this rich man was, Jhoen turned to set his plate aside. Just as he did, Jhoen gasped and snapped back to the old man, half jumping in fear. Then Jhoen stared at his host.

The rich man looked unperturbed, with no threat, anger, or even surprise at Jhoen's sudden panic.

Azel's reaction was to smack his little brother on the arm. "What's wrong with you?"

"I... I just..." Jhoen paused a moment before trying to laugh it off. It was already dark out, and the coals of the rich man's fire cast writhing shadows on all their faces. "The shadows of the fire, they... I was imagining things."

Out of the corner of his eyes, what must have been a trick of the light, made the man's eyes appear dark and his face tattooed with strange long points. Jhoen felt like a fool. How could he ever be like that old man if he was jumping at shadows?

"Ah," said their host, "but whatever you imagined you saw was surprising. I notice that, instead of turning away, you faced the danger—or at least, what you believed to be danger. You are strong, and I can see your brother is just as strong. Clearly, you are both meant for great things, whether you are noble or not."

"I'm glad you think so," Azel said honestly. "Soon I will enlist in the Watchmen Brigade and—"

"The brigade, that's all?" The old man sounded disappointed.

That comment put Azel a little off balance. Jhoen, who'd opened his mouth to say he was planning to join the brigade as well, snapped it shut.

"I... I'd like to join the army instead," Azel said, trying to recover, "but, without a noble tie or something, they'll reject you. Our own father got rejected."

The older man looked relieved. "Oh, good. I worried you lacked the vision to see what you could be. I'm glad to see you are as worthy of glory and power as I suspect. That means you have a chance. Since you have the vision, the question is, do you have the other two parts you need to succeed?"

"What are those?" Jhoen asked.

"A title, idiot," Azel hissed angrily, hitting his brother again. "We aren't noble. So, we still can't make it in the army."

"Says who?" their host retorted.

"I... well..."

The old man spread his hand towards his lavish tent. "You may not guess it from what I have now, but I have never been a noble. In fact, I see a lot of myself in the two of you. I was probably worse off than you are now, but see the heights I've risen to." Both of the brothers were certainly doing that. "No, it's not a title you need. The first thing you need is an opportunity to show your mettle, and the second is the drive to see it through."

"Is that what you did?" Jhoen asked.

"Indeed, I was merely a son of any other man, but I had the vision to see in my reflection the great man who stared back at me. No one thought much of me, calling me a child and thinking I knew nothing of what I was about. Yet, I did.

"A lost beggar shuffled into town from far away coming to try his fortune begging elsewhere. The people of my home took pity on him and welcomed him in without a second thought, but I saw something they did not. I saw the danger this man was. Where they saw sheep, I saw a wolf under a veil of wool."

The two brothers were enraptured by the tale and by the way the light of the fire danced on and inside the eyes of the man of the inverted crown.

"That, boys, was the vision which I can see you have. He was my opportunity, now all I needed was the drive. I saw the danger, and it was my right to destroy it, so I did. Even as a child, I set a trap for this 'beggar' and killed him as he was leaving the town."

"Just like that?" Jhoen was shocked.

"What more needed to be done?" asked their host. "I knew the truth, he was a danger. The people of my town did not thank me, not at first. They thought me cruel and even a murderer, but they were sightless. It was not twelve hours after I seized my opportunity that a marshal rode into the town, telling everyone of a bandit leader from faraway lands who was sneaking into towns, pretending to be destitute and observing their defenses, before then leading in his troops and laying waste.

"After that, people for the first time began to see what I already had. An investigation revealed that the vagabond turned out to be the exact same bandit. From then on, while I may not have gained any royal title, I had a reputation. One that I lived up to, and that is all you need to really join the army or go even further than that. Vision, opportunity, and drive."

"So, your drive was killing the man everyone thought was a nobody?" Azel asked with an odd look in his eyes.

"No," said the wealthy man, to Azel's surprise. "My drive was doing what I needed to, even though I knew there were those who would believe I was wrong. I trusted in myself and in my vision. The same vision I see in the two of you. The question is, what will you do when your opportunity comes? Will you have the courage to trust in yourself, the drive, to do whatever is needed to seize your glory?"

"You know," Jhoen said, "talking about bandits from far away, there's—"

Azel clasped a strong hand on his brother's shoulder and squeezed.

Jhoen left his sentence unfinished.

The old man wasn't offended or in the least suspicious. He swished a cup of wine in a circle, peering into the swirling liquid, saying, "Maybe you have the vision and an opportunity, but I wonder about your drive. Don't miss it when it comes. I was once a servant of men who sought to lessen themselves and me with them. Now? I may not make the laws in this land, but in my way, I am a king."

At these last words, he looked up at them with fierce eyes. Azel and Jhoen felt the intensity of that glare and wondered if such an aura could come from one who was supposed to be so old. As they took him in again, however, something seemed different. Perhaps it was a trick of the day's dying light, but he now looked much younger and stronger.

"There's something I've been forgetting to ask," Jhoen said in something of a daze. "Sir, why are you here? This isn't the way people normally go through to get to... well, anywhere."

The old man drained the rest of his cup before replying, letting the crickets of the night interrupt their conversation with their dirge for day. "I have something of a rival in this world. I heard that one or two of his servants were doing something nearby. I don't care what they're doing, I just wanted to prepare."

"Prepare what?" Azel asked.

The man huffed, looking off into the distance. "I said it before. I may not be one in the way you understand it, but I am a king. I don't need to always interfere with my rival's designs personally. I usually task that role to servants of my own," his glance flicked toward the brothers "Tonight I've done just that."

Then he stretched. "Now, it has gotten quite late. I believe we have completed our exchange. Since this is your father's land, I have no doubt you can make your way home on your own. It is about time you were off."

The brothers had more questions, but the man was carelessly tossing his soiled plate into a bucket. Behind the tent, a black horse, the king's no doubt, huffed at the rattle of the bucket. It was clear that he was done for the evening and would not take many more questions.

Guessing this, the two brothers began to lift themselves to move on home, but the old man had some final parting words. "Oh, one last thing. I am a king, but you are only boys. That's because the world sees you only as boys and what it sees is all you are. Take the opportunity when it comes and make the world see you differently, or boys are all you will ever be. If you wish to be men, to be more than fodder, to be like me; then don't neglect what I've said. Do you understand?"

"Yes, sir," they both said with real respect and deference. Azel's pride, however, pushed him to ask one last question.

"Sir, you never told us your name. Who are you?"

The old man was half turned to his tent flap, revealing the signet of the upturned crown stitched onto the back of his coat. There he paused and seemed to consider.

"What should you call me? Hmm... I've had many names. How about Eznem, your King."

CHAPTER 6

GHEN ROCKED BACK IN a porch chair and pulled out his pipe, working at it until he blew out light wisps in the growing dark.

Em was finished thumbing through the later pages of his notebook. Ghen hadn't seen all that was in later pages, but he'd seen enough to guess Em had written down some instructions for training. Not that it was the kind of thing that could be learned from a book.

Em, however, apparently had a teacher in 'Nature.' Not that Ghen thought Em was learning much anymore. The way he held his tool, and how he stepped so lightly that even the rancher's careful ears lost track of him, meant Em had experience. This was closer to reminding himself of his skills than learning them.

With a flash, the longsword flicked out of the scabbard.

In barely a breath, Em flew into motion. Ghen quickly became lost in the blur of steel. He was only able to follow a few quick cuts from the lingering reflections of the dying sunlight. The quick flurry ended suddenly and Em glided back, retreating from his fictitious opponent.

Ghen blew a long stream of pipe smoke. "Now that was fast."

Stories always made swordfights sound like a dance, two fighters twirling and sparks flying as steel clashed. It was supposed to be beautiful along with deadly. Watching this kid, though, Ghen saw no beauty. Watching Em fight his shadow reminded him more of watching a snake than anything else. Slow and cautious, followed by a sudden, vicious strike, then returning to pause and wait.

When Em moved, the weapon blurred in a furious assault, but before Ghen could blink, Em was cautious once again. It was as if the many slashes were only something Ghen had imagined, and the careful fighter was all there'd ever been.

The rancher sat forward thoughtfully. Any lingering doubts about Em's possible skill were gone now.

The kid was too confident, too calm, and too cold. In festivals, there were always shows and contests where fighting was the height of entertainment. Ghen had seen a few of those and they were a dance. Lots of charging, spinning, flipping, shouts, and heavy clashes.

Even practicing, Em didn't charge, he prowled. He didn't spin, he glided. No shouting, Em breathed in deeply and exhaled with intentionality. Each breath pulled in strength and expelled weakness. Even in the flurry, he all but forced air into his laboring chest.

Em didn't do any backflips, he leaped forward but never with his feet more than an inch from the ground, hovering above it. Then slashed and slid back his feet, drifting over the ground with only the slightest sound coming or going. Em circled his unseen target with devoted intensity, one that put Ghen off slightly. In fact, it chilled the rancher, this predator on the hunt.

Ghen turned to make sure that Jirus wasn't peeking out of any windows. Seeing another lad only a few falls further along like this would send his wild dreams over the edge. Jirus already desired to live the adventurer's life. Uncle Grady had been Jirus's grandfather, and Jirus longed to do more than he ever had, which worried Ghen more than Jirus could ever know.

Jirus dreamed of joining the Watchmen Brigade, but Ghen was hoping to change his mind. It wasn't just that he feared the boy would get himself hurt. His fears were born from the same place as Jirus's inspiration, the boy's grandfather.

While Uncle Grady had come back and told some great stories of the world away from home, there was more he never said. Unlike many, unlike Jirus, Ghen had seen some of what Uncle Grady couldn't say. He put on a brave face, but Ghen recalled the difference in his uncle from before and after his 'adventures.'

By day Grady was a returning hero, but in the dark, the man had cursed himself for ever leaving. The same hero who laughed about past battles woke up screaming when he dreamt of them.

Ghen couldn't stop Jirus from dreaming and didn't want to either. Still, maybe he could just lead Jirus to a different big dream. There was time, Jirus was too young to join the watchmen for a few more falls, but his heart was already chained to the idea. When Jirus reached the right age, even if he didn't want him to go, Ghen knew he'd let Jirus join. It was his choice, but by the stars of the corsairs, Ghen did not want to see that boy broken or worse close himself off and become some thug. If Jirus was going to go with the watchmen, Ghen wanted to make sure the boy had a good head on his shoulders.

"I mean, look at Em," Ghen muttered to himself, letting out a big puff of smoke. Too quiet to be heard, he said, "Em, I wonder. Do you wish you could reel back the days like a fish on a line and stop yourself from learning to fight like that? You're still so young, I bet you didn't have much choice when you started, but still. Don't you think that path is what got you here?"

Em wasn't eight falls older than Jirus, most likely, but those skills were older than they should be. How early? How young? Could a few autumns really do so much to a boy? Why couldn't Jirus see that it could happen to him too, and end up like Em, who can't recall much before breakfast?

Ghen shook his head. "Think about that. You either end up an old man like Uncle Grady, afraid of the rattle of steel, or like Em, you swing it freely but don't know why you need to."

Em paused. "Forgive me, please say that once more."

"Huh? Oh nothing, I was just talking to myself. You're very good with that."

Em bowed his head thankfully and jumped right back into dueling his growing shadow in the fading light.

Sliding into step, Em circled his opponent and Ghen got a good look at his face as he unleashed another set of flickering cuts. There was nothing. Each brown iris in Em's eyes shined with life, but still somehow looked dead. He wasn't doing what he had to anymore, he didn't even look like he was having fun, he was just doing what he knew.

"And that's all he knows." Ghen shivered.

The rancher thought of the last line in Em's first note. *That is all we have to remember.* The first time Ghen had read that he'd taken it as something like 'that is all we need to remember.' Now, he wondered if it was, '... all we have left.'

But if all he had was this, where had he come from? He couldn't actually be a marauder, could he? How could a marauder have left Yongarad, and made it this far into Ifeldia without anyone stopping him? Also, from what Uncle Grady had said, marauders were chosen to join if they were cruel people. Em's eyes looked merciless, but not vicious.

No, a marauder just didn't fit this boy, or if it did, Ghen wouldn't believe it. How could anyone knowingly set a boy, girl, or anyone on a path like that and still sleep at night?

Sure, killing was part of a rancher's life. You raised calves, piglets, and more, knowing how they'd end up, but people? Ghen couldn't stomach the thought, but those eyes...

"Have you done it?" Ghen whispered. "No way you'd know anymore, but could you have done more than practice?"

Finally, Em finished, having either won or perhaps lost his battle with his shadow.

They didn't talk much as Em wrote his new notes and Ghen locked up the barn. Both were far too distracted by their own thoughts. As the lock on the barn door clicked shut, Ghen found himself alone.

Ghen heard his bed calling for rest, but now it was Ghen's turn to be hesitant to try to sleep. There was another voice still asking questions about Em. One that, even if Ghen went to bed, would keep him awake for a long time.

He turned towards the pasture instead of his house. Guiding himself by moonlight, Ghen trudged down to where the land sloped down towards his fields. Here he sat, looking up where the moon's pale face looked back. The nightly breeze danced through the grass, whispering stories no tribe could comprehend, and the grass offered soft applause.

"He looks different, acts different, is different from any kid I've met before," Ghen told the running wind. "Still, he's only a kid. Couldn't the world have waited till he was at least a little older? You know, ready?"

The rancher felt heavy. Weighed down.

"I guess no one's ever ready, huh."

Ghen had plenty of his own troubles. Jirus was Jirus, Kaddley didn't have a good place to learn anything proper, and Ghen and May had no time to teach. Amiria couldn't even cross a room without help.

Then there was the ranch. It always had something that was getting torn up or broken. Not to mention that Mr. Noren, burn him. The merchant had been beating at his door for many falls now, offering and bullying Ghen to sell what had been his family's home for longer than anyone could recall.

Then May. Long ago, Ghen had promised May he would work hard so that she wouldn't have to worry, but in the past couple of falls, he'd had to sell half his land to buy enough livestock and materials to keep the other half. She was always keeping him up straight, but Ghen knew she was disappointed at her patched dress and worn treasures. He always wished he could give May more. He wished he could give them all more.

"You know, when other people asked me about my life and any troubles I'd been having, I'd just put on a brave face and joke that, 'my troubles are better than nothing, so I think I'll keep them.' I guess I never knew how true that was."

Ghen shook his head. "Now here's someone who actually has nothing. How can anyone live like that?"

The shining moon peered down at him accusingly, as if this was somehow Ghen's fault.

"I'm doing what I can," he argued. "I've given him food, shelter, and I'll give him more too. I'm doing enough."

A freezing wind bit into him.

Trapped in the wind by his guilt, Ghen felt like the filth his cows left behind.

It made him furious. "I'm helping! Isn't that enough?"

The moon glared back, the unspoken word, 'Enough?' hanging in the air.

What was enough?

"Alright then, what should I do?" Ghen retorted.

The reply was silence.

Broad and empty, even the wind held its breath. No insects, no birds, no sound. At first, Ghen felt rather big, as if he'd stumped the night and was somehow justified. Yet as the silence stretched, Ghen saw how large it was, and he became rather small.

His eyes turned over fields of crops and fields of stars. Out in the dark, Ghen was very... alone.

"Alone." Ghen realized. "Em's alone. He's forgotten the world, and I guess it's forgotten him. That's it, isn't it? Em ain't got a soul to go with him. Every rancher knows that when cold winds blow, the herd groups together." Ghen turned back to look at his solitary barn and towards the young man who would be sleeping within. "But you're alone in the cold, aren't you, Em?"

Ghen bundled his arms as night's chill settled and the stillness remained around him. This was nothing and everything that Em must feel.

The moon's face bore down on Ghen once again, the silence of the night was permeated by the unspoken word.

'Enough?'

"I'll get him to Henaden, I've already said as much, but..." His words trailed off for a moment. "But I'll be there." Ghen continued, listening to the voice in his heart which heard his every word. "I'll be there for all of it, just like you want, Boss. Being there isn't much, but maybe that's enough. Leastways, that's what good folk do."

With that, the one who listened to all Ghen said allowed the rancher to go peacefully to bed.

CHAPTER 7

THE DOOR OF THE barn was strangely menacing as Ghen reached for the lock. He wasn't exactly sure what he would find when he opened the door. If Em was still asleep and Ghen woke him, how would he react?

"Maybe I should have asked Em to leave his sword somewhere else. Well, too late now." He eased it open slightly. When he heard a soft scuffle, Ghen flung the door wide and jumped back, expecting something like an angry bull to come dashing out.

Except, nothing ran out.

Ghen sat there for a moment, lifting his hat and scratching the top of his head before looking into the barn. The hay loft was empty. There was another scraping sound and Ghen recognized it came from the barn's lower level. Also, the sound brought back memories of the night before, when Em was...

"Oh, duh." Ghen shook his head. "He's practicing again."

Ghen caught him once more in action as he came down the steps, but the moment he reached the lower level, Em stopped swinging and sheathed his weapon. The young swordsman looked Ghen over cautiously. Even though the sword was back on his side, one hand remained on its hilt.

"You are Ghen-*sa*, yes?" he asked.

Ghen cringed at the honorific but let it slide. "That's right."

Em studied the rancher for a moment.

"Forgive my strange question, but how much do you know of me?"

Ghen paused to figure out how to answer. "Well, not much really. Now that I think about it, all your little note said is that I'd met you and planned to take you to Henaden. We didn't cover how much I know, did we?"

Either Em gathered the question was rhetorical or he refused to answer because he made no reply.

Ghen wasn't sure, so he decided to press on. "Anyways, yesterday you showed me your journal, that same one right there," he added, pointing to the small book.

"Oh, I thought... never mind." Em looked disappointed. He'd been expecting someone more familiar.

"Sorry kid. I can't fill in many of the gaps you're probably wanting."

Em seemed almost suspicious. "A note I left for myself states we made a deal. If you are the man Ghen-*sa* of who it spoke, can you tell me the deal?"

"Sure can. If you help me out for another two days, I'll take you to Henaden and help you find this mystic that you need."

That seemed to satisfy Em, as his hand left the pommel of his weapon.

Ghen took that as a sign to go on. "Listen, I'm sure this is confusing and whatnot, but if you're hungry, there's breakfast over the fire. I also brought some old clothes of mine you can wear while we work today so you don't tear up your own. Yesterday, I told you we'd seed one of my fields and while we did, I'd tell you about... well, really about the world."

For a moment Ghen wondered if Em would change his mind, like he was still weighing if Ghen could be trusted, but it only lasted a moment. "I understand. I will gather my things, where is the house? Is it far?"

"What?" Ghen asked, confused. "Oh! No, go out that door upstairs and you'll see it. Boy, you really do forget everything, don't you?" He was tempted to ask Em to leave his belongings behind but wasn't sure how well that would go over. "When you get changed, bring your clothes to May, that's my wife's name. We'll add your set of pants to our pile of things we want to wash tomorrow."

Em looked relieved. Ghen guessed Em had expected he'd be asked to leave his swords behind but felt more comfortable with them.

"Thank you, Ghen-*sa*." The kid bowed again. "If you do not mind my asking, you mentioned a wife, how many people live here?"

"On the ranch? You make six. Don't worry about being behind on things, by the way. While we eat, May and Kaddley will tell you all they know about you and probably everyone else, too." He chuckled. "You won't even need to ask."

Surprisingly, Em smirked at the joke as if he got it. Then, seeming to realize that he was, Em stopped and was both confused and embarrassed.

"My apologies Ghen-*sa*," he said, knowing Ghen had seen his grin. "This is all very confusing."

Ghen shook his head. "It is for all of us, kid. Yesterday you talked about your instincts doing things without your knowing why. My guess is that Ol' Instinct just showed you he's got a sense of humor to boot. They clearly know more than you do. Don't sweat having smiled, even laugh if you want. Jokes are meant to be laughed at. I'm not offended, if anything, I'm happy to see you can crack a smile."

As Ghen and Em continued throughout the morning, Ghen realized how much of a marvel Em was to observe. Some part of Ghen had still doubted Em's story. Watching him now, though, it all but vanished.

As they entered the house, he heard Em comment to himself about the barn looking 'short.' Then he looked at the house as if for the first time. All from how long the home was built to how 'strange' the fireplace was. Em listened with the same interest as Kaddley and May discussed a bunch of topics he'd heard the day before as if they were new because, to him, they all were. This boy was seeing the world with new eyes.

After eating, Ghen let Em change clothes before leading him around to the far side of the barn where he'd strung up yesterday's harvest of night root to start drying. He and Em needed to go through the same song and dance about why there was so little root, and how the trip was worth it for Ghen.

Despite the repetition, there was one difference in Em as they talked. It wasn't what Em knew or didn't know, but the fact that Ghen thought the kid felt more comfortable. He didn't hesitate as much to ask a question, not that he wasn't still a shy fella, but Ghen wasn't quite the stranger he'd been yesterday.

"Did some of your roots fall off of the end?" Em said, pointing to some of the drying roots.

The process of drying nightroot wasn't hard. T-shaped posts held twin lines suspended in the air a few feet up, almost like drying clothes. On the hanging wire, Ghen had spent time winding the root around the line, pinning it up in a few places. What Em was pointing to more directly were two thicker tap roots that were hanging slacked off of the line.

"Nope, I'm not going to dry those bits all the way. I can't cut them off till they've steeped a little, but I am going to snip those off soon."

"Is there something wrong with those roots?" Em tilted his head, "Are they bigger?"

"They are," Ghen confirmed. "That's why I picked them. See, nightroot doesn't have any seeds or the like. Next winter, when I want to grow more nightroot, I need a healthy cutting to start with. I'll take these bigger shoots, snip them off, and put them in a small chest I have. Really, it's just a box of dirt that shuts tightly, but it'll keep the root alive as long as I give it a little water every so often. Come next planting season, I'll pull the shoots out again and stick them in my planter so they can spread out a new crop."

Em nodded, but only partially understood. "Then the rest of the root will dry in the..."

"Oh, Gheeenn!" May called from out of sight. "We're all ready. How long are you boys going to be?"

"Uh oh. I'll fill you in on the rest later. We need to get a move on. Let's grab Bo as quick as we can. Keeping May waiting isn't a very smart thing to do."

"Ah, let us go then. But... your forgiveness, please. Who is Bo?"

Ghen sighed and started towards the barn. "This could be a long day."

Once Em got reacquainted with the mule, they led the old girl out of her stall and threw a bag of seed over her back. Unhappy as she was, she at least respected their time and didn't fight the halter. Without too much fuss, the two of them led her up the barn's ramp and they were soon ready to march down to the field.

May and the rest of the family were waiting.

"Everyone is helping?" Em asked incredulously as they arrived.

"Why shouldn't they? The field goes faster this way and scattering seed isn't hard. It just takes practice. May will keep track of Ami, so she won't cause trouble. Many hands make light loads, my friend."

Everyone took a small sack, filled with seed. With everything prepared, each took a row of tilled earth to seed for themselves, except Ghen and Em.

The rancher explained, "I'll help with the first row or two so I can show you how to spread the seed correctly. Then you should be able to go on your own from there."

"Understood, Ghen-*sa*."

Ghen still didn't like the whole *sa* thing, good folk could just be friendly and use names. He left it alone though, it wasn't worth the daylight trying to change Em's habits.

While making their way down the row, Em asked, "Ghen-*sa*, why does your son keep looking at me so strangely? Did I do something to upset him?"

"Son? Oh, Jirus. Man, this thing's hard to get used to. He's a relative, but technically he isn't my son. He's family, but we took him in after some stuff happened with his folks. You didn't do anything to him, he just got in trouble yesterday because of something he said to you, so I think he's sulking a little." Finishing that line of thought, Ghen figured now was the time to make good on his promise from yesterday. "You recall I said I'd tell you about the world today?"

"Yes, I want to hear what you can tell me. I dislike how little I know," Em said. "I am hoping that by hearing of the world that Instinct may give a clue where I come from. I read through all my notes this morning, but I know so little about myself."

Ghen paused. To have read all that... "How early did you get up this morning?" Ranchers were early risers, and he'd let Em out before daylight. Did the kid get any sleep at all?

"It was early, I do not know how long I spent reading. When I woke and could not remember myself, I... I had to know more. After I did, I had no wish to sleep again."

So that's why his eyes were so bloodshot, and why he always seemed so worn out. Probably went like that every day. Not a huge surprise, who would wake up without a clue who you are and decide to just roll over and go back to bed?"

Ghen decided not to press the topic further. "Okay, well go ahead and tell me what you already know about the world, then I won't waste our time on useless details."

"There is not much to tell. I read the names of cities, but beyond Henaden, I know nothing about them. There was a note about a group called Marauders and that they belonged to a Yongarad, correct?"

So, Em had made more notes yesterday than just about their deal? That was fine. "That's the wrong place to start. I tried yesterday, and we just ran into more questions. I'm going to start far back and go from there, sound good?" Ghen suggested.

"Yes."

"Right so, we're a country called Ifeldia. Now, I'm no scholar but I've heard that we are pretty special as far as countries go. Most have one ruler, but because of our history, we have eight, four kings and four queens."

"Eight?" Em froze and stared at Ghen in both wonder and perhaps suspicion.

"That's right, I doubted you were from here to start, so you being surprised makes sense. See before even my Pop was around—"

"Pop?" Em interrupted.

"Sorry, that's what my family has always called my dad's dad. Either way, before Pop was born, there was one king of Ifeldia. That king was named Roleius. I don't know many names of kings and such, but I know his name because he's famous and that. During his time, King Roleius conquered a bunch of his neighbors and made them all one big country."

"Ifeldia," Em guessed.

"Right again, he... Em, no." Ghen paused to point at the seeds he'd just scattered. "Don't just drop them. A pile is no good to me. It's in the wrist—fling it out. Kind of like skipping a rock, but not quite so hard." Ghen showed an example. "Your turn."

Em swished out his wrist, and it wasn't great, too much fell in their walking path. He tried again and did better.

"That will do. Back to what we were saying, where was I...? Right! King Roleius, he got all the places he took over and made it Ifeldia, that's where we are now. Next to us is Yongarad, and they're the ones with the Marauders."

When Ghen paused, Em pushed for more. "And what other lands are there? There are more than two countries in the world." It wasn't a question. Em knew that to be a fact.

"That's true, but like I said before, I'm no scholar. What I know is that Ifeldia is on one of those... what's it called...? Pel... pen... peninsula! That's it!" Ghen was proud he'd retained the word. He'd learned it from his uncle so long ago that he was impressed the word still rolled around in his head. "Ocean all around us, save for the mountains to the south between us and Yongarad."

Em was clearly disappointed.

Ghen tried to encourage him. "Don't give up kid, Henaden is actually a big city for trade. People are always peddling things from all over Ifeldia, and some from outside it. When we get there, we can find more country names than you can swing your swords at."

Em nodded sadly and then came up with a question to distract himself. "How did Roleius conquer so much of this land?"

"He won because he partnered with a bunch of other tribes to help him. Most of the other countries had a 'ruling tribe' and the rest were kind of second. He went around to those who were second in the country and helped them take out their own leaders."

"He instigated revolution," Em said thoughtfully.

"How much do you know about the different tribes, Em?" Ghen asked, suddenly curious if he had to cover that.

Em didn't hesitate, Instinct not even needing to whisper in his ear the knowledge being so innate. "I know them, the nine living tribes of man. Human, elf, usarumai, dwarf, and more."

"Good, just needed to be sure." This was going better than Ghen had dared hope, between that Instinct of his and Em's clear smarts, this was little more than storytelling.

Em paused, just before tossing more seed, with a new question. "Are then these eight kings and queens the descendants of your past king?"

Ghen chuckled softly, though Em didn't quite understand why it was funny.

"Not exactly," Ghen explained. "When he died, King Roleius didn't want his kids in charge. I've no idea why, mind you, but he didn't. Also, part of the deal he'd made with the tribes was that he'd give them some power to rule too, after he died. So, it came about that Roleius chose four kings and queens to rule his one country. He made it so that one king and one queen were each from different tribes."

"So only four of the tribes rule, and his family is not even in power?"

"Four tribes is right, but the other part isn't. Roleius picked the daughter of one of his friends or generals or something to be the queen of the human tribe. He didn't pick a human king and told the girl she could pick whoever she wanted.

"Because of that, all of Roleius's boys fell over each other trying to impress her. There are a lot of stories, plays, and comedies about the different sons trying to get her attention, some are pretty good, if there are any in Henaden maybe we'll catch one.

"Didn't matter though, 'cause she never chose any of them. That girl's daughter, the next queen, did choose one of the king's sons, though. He was Roleius's youngest son, born way later than the others, and became a king named Ordisus. He's still kicking, but people expect he'll drop off any day.

"That is confusing," Em said.

"That's why I know so little of politics, it always is. The rest of Roleius's family married into other families with power, so I can't say they aren't still running things."

"They just do not control this council of rulers."

"Exactly."

Em asked, "How do they decide anything?"

"Hang on." Ghen stopped him and looked around. "Hey May, we're about done with this row. Since y'all have the next few, Em and I are going to go to the far side of the field and start there."

May looked at the far end of the field and then back at Ghen. "Why? Can't you just go onto the next row?"

"If I do, Em and I'd get spread apart since he can't go as quick as we more experienced folk. I think it'll be easier if we just started over there and then we all met in the middle of the field to finish."

May scowled but nodded.

"She never likes going out of order. It's not in her nature," Ghen whispered to Em. Still, May would know there wasn't another option if Ghen wanted to continue coaching Em.

The two of them, the row completed, walked to the opposite corner of the small field and began to seed there. It took Ghen a second to figure out where he'd left off, but when he did, he picked it up again.

"So, uh... how does the ol' council of eight rulers make any decisions? Well, I don't really know, but I bet it's a hassle. I think they do have more rule over some places than others though."

"Why do you say that?"

"You know how I mentioned Ordisus?"

"The King Roleius's ruling son," Em said.

"The same, I know him because he made a bunch of rules for this area that the other kings and queens don't like. His wife is dead, and I don't think a new generation can take over till both the king and queen drop off."

"What law did he instate?"

"He put a bunch of conditions on how tribes who aren't human enter and leave cities locally. I think it officially has something to do with catching rebels who didn't like his father putting all the nations together. But that's a bunch of malarkey, I think he did it to make the rest of the rulers mad since they aren't human."

Em looked confused. "That seems strange for some reason. Are there many other tribes that live near here?"

"I hear there used to be more, but now it's kyate-siv, humans, dwarves, and not much else now," Ghen said. "Since the law, most of the others have gone elsewhere. Like I said, it's not everywhere, just a small patch of land."

Em opened his mouth, probably to ask 'why' again, but wisely held back, guessing Ghen wouldn't know. Instead, he said, "So then, what of marauders? They are with this 'Yongarad' to the south."

"I think so, people say they come from Yongarad, but the Marauders are like mercenaries too, I hear. It may be that they just work for them. We have something similar we call the Watchmen Brigade. The brigade drafts folk outside the army to fight where they feel is best and where it pays. Outside big cities, most of the town watches and guards have a connection to the watchmen. A difference between watchmen and marauders, though, is the kinds of people. The watchmen don't take on criminals and outlaws."

"But, the Marauders do," Em said nodding along.

"So, I hear. Works well for Yongarad, whether they own them or just work with them. That nation's another country that wants to be a conqueror, like ours was, but our people are fighting back hard to stop them. I saw Yongarad on a map once, I think they are smaller than us but growing. Stories say not only do the Marauders pick up scum and killers, but that Yongarad makes monsters with magic, and that their leaders are monsters, too." Ghen huffed after that and then his tone got lighter. "Of course, some people say our country makes monsters too, so that could all be hogwash."

"Monsters?" Em was curious about what these monsters might be like.

In Em's mind, he imagined an elderly hag looking down a hallway toward him. Next to her was an animal that might have been part hound and part lizard, with rows of needlelike teeth in its gaping maw. It was a strangely vivid daydream, and Em shook his head to get rid of it.

"You know as much as I do about that. That mystic you're looking for, Master D'gue, they may know more since it sounds like they know magic. I think most magic folk go study at some place in the east, then go fight against Yongarad with watchmen, the army, or the Guardians of the Blessed."

Em stopped and stood straight. "I am sorry Ghen-sa, but you pronounced their name wrong. Master D'gui's name ends with an 'e' sound, like that of your word eagle."

"Oops, sorry kid."

"Also, what are the Guardians of the Blessed?" Em added more sheepishly.

"Ifeldia has three militaries. A big regular one, the watchmen, which like I said are kind of mercenaries, and the guardians, which I really don't know much about. They're a small group of fighters, the 'best of the best' or whatever. I hear they use magic like sorcerers, but people count them separately. Not sure why."

Em simply nodded along as he scattered seed. He was getting better, the boy really was a quick study.

"You said that your people fight Yongarad. Is it a war?" Em asked.

Ghen shrugged. "Kind of."

Em looked confused.

Ghen stood straight and pointed to the south. "See far that way those hazy shadows just above the horizon?"

Em peered into the distance. "Yes?" He did not sound confident.

"That is the Borgiden Mountain range. Most here call them the Southern Mountains. That range stretches almost from east to west at our border. The mountains themselves are full of tribesmen who don't claim to be part of either country. So, they'll shoot at either side if they see someone invading. Between climbing mountains and being shot at the whole way, it's hard to be the one attacking. Since Ifeldia's not picking a fight, that works for us just fine. There are big openings far to the west and east at the range's edges. I hear that is where the fighting is.

"So yes, we are at war, but it doesn't feel like it out here. You won't find a soul in three days' travel who gives a whip about how things are going. The fighting's gone on too long for that. The war began when I was a kid and it's still going. Everyone backs off in the winter and there's been no fighting for a while, but with spring coming, I'm sure we'll start hearing war stories drift in again before too long."

Em considered all he'd heard. "Thank you Ghen-*sa*. I had hoped to recall something of my home, but it is good that I know all of this. I think it could be helpful. If you allow me the chance, I will later make notes so that I can keep much of this for tomorrow."

Em looked back toward the field gate where he'd left his bag and weapons. It was the furthest Ghen had seen Em from his stuff, but they were still in eyeshot.

"Don't sweat it, let me know if you get any more questions," Ghen offered. "I'm just trying to be helpful as good folk should."

Finishing another row, May stood to see where everyone was.

"Okay Ami," she told the toddler at her side, "I think we are at a good stopping place."

For her part, Ami only blinked back at her mother.

May waited until she caught Ghen's eye and merely held his gaze. Ghen looked around, up at the sun, and finally realized what she was hinting at.

"Alright everyone," he called. "It's about time for a break."

May was glad to hear he'd taken the hint. There were times she wondered if he would ever find a place to stop unless someone told him to. The girls would start making a fuss if they didn't get something to eat soon.

Their strange guest seemed to have learned how to seed now. Ghen did have to ask him to redo part of one of his rows earlier in the day, which had put him behind, but not as far behind as she would have guessed. They were still well on their way to being done with time left to finish pulling the nightroot.

As Ghen moved to leave the pasture, May caught a sneaky glint in his eye.

"What is he up to?" she asked the small child as she picked Ami up into the crook of her arm.

Ami again added nothing to the conversation, looking as bored as a toddler could.

"May and I will grab our lunch and fill the waterskins at the house, then we'll tow it all back here," Ghen announced. "Out here we can sit under the shade and rest, almost like a picnic. Then we can get back to it quick and finish this field by midafternoon."

She couldn't quite figure out exactly what he was planning yet, but May was sure she would soon. For now, there was no reason not to go along with it.

May walked quickly to catch up to Ghen, having to readjust the toddler in her arm when she caught up. By the time she did, they'd gained some distance away from those left behind.

"Now that we're away, what scheme is this?"

Ghen grinned. "One of my finest, May, that's what."

"Oh?" May allowed her tone to betray her curiosity.

"I think it will be a good thing for Jirus to spend some time with Em."

"And why is that? I don't know him well, but with his condition, I doubt Em has much to teach Jirus."

Ghen grinned. "He could teach our boy more than you might think. See, Jirus wants to go out into the world and fight monsters. Well, it's clear Em's been out among some monsters and Jirus is bound to ask questions. Em may not remember much, but he knows more than he thinks."

"You plan is to have Em inspire him?" May asked. "I think maybe you misunderstood what I said yesterday. What I said was—"

Ghen stopped her before she could continue. "No, no May. You're missing it. From what I see, Em has had a hard go of it out there. I think that by letting him talk to Jirus, the boy may figure out what my old Uncle Grady learned the hard way. It's not going to be all glory and adventure out there."

May wasn't sure she agreed. "I think it might be better if we sat the boy down and just told him he wasn't going."

"Well, I'd like to," Ghen admitted. "But at the end of the day, it has to be Jirus's call to stay or go. Otherwise, we'd have to tie him to our porch post when he gets older to keep him from running off on his own."

May relented the point. "Okay, play your game but be honest, do you really think it will work?"

"If not, I got a couple more plans," Ghen said confidently

The toddler began to struggle in May's arm, so she let her to the ground where she could waddle alongside, holding May's hand.

With her feet down, the small Ami finally decided to add, "Papa's smart."

"Thank you, girly. I certainly hope so." Ghen grinned at his young daughter.

While Ghen was in a good mood, May thought this might be a good time to bring up another problem that needed solving. "Ghen... I also wanted to ask, what do you plan to do this fall? We have time, but Mr. Noren is going to come back."

The cream of Ghen's smile soured quickly, and his happy voice became a grumble. "I don't doubt it."

"If we aren't ready for him again, we could be in trouble."

Ghen took a deep breath. "Well, I've only got part of a plan there, but I think that we can handle him this time. Who knows, this time I may even come out ahead. It has to do with the hay we're growing to feed the stock." Ghen sounded like he was trying to convince himself as much as her.

Mr. Noren was pushing farms and ranches all over to sell him their land. When a family did sell their land, Mr. Noren would hire the families as workers on the same property. They got to continue living in their homes and working on the same land.

There was nothing wrong with the offer itself. The families were paid for the land at a more than fair price, and when a harvest came, the families that worked on the land got nearly a third of the crop and stock to sell or use as their own and Mr. Noren got the remainder.

Of course, Ghen and a few others were stubborn. This land had been in their families for as long as anyone could recall. Sadly, Mr. Noren was equally stubborn, he wouldn't take no for an answer. One by one people were selling, and now most had. Ghen was one of the last holdouts.

To convince people like Ghen to accept his offer, Mr. Noren was pushing buyers not to buy stock from Ghen and those like him. Being a merchant, Noren leveraged a massive amount of inventory to influence the buyers. No one ever said they wouldn't buy from Ghen because of Mr. Noren, but they knew.

Henaden was the only place, aside from the small village of Marden Hallows, where Ghen could sell locally. However, that town wasn't large enough for him to offload everything he needed to. Sadly, Henaden happened to be the city where the illustrious Noren Trading Companies had their base operations, and Mr. Noren had all but a death grip on its sales operations. Since Henaden was a trade city, there were always foreign merchants who might buy this or that, but the official business would almost never.

Mr. Noren had the most stock to sell, so many brokers had to listen to him or go out of business. Those who could buy from Ghen safely still knew this penalty existed. Most of them only offered rates that were nowhere near market value, since they knew Ghen didn't have better options. To keep what he had left, Ghen had already been forced to sell parts of his heritage away to neighbors and to none other than Mr. Noren himself.

Ghen thought May didn't know that he had almost taken Mr. Noren's last offer. He'd tried to keep it secret, and she knew why, too. He was considering it because of her. May did often wish for better things, but she was proud that Ghen hadn't surrendered his home. She didn't want him to.

Mr. Noren was too wealthy and cared too little for the land itself to have any real reason to be so desperate to acquire it. May had followed Ghen out of the city world and into rural life, but before she left, she'd heard of too many offers like this one that had turned out to be a trap. She still wasn't sure what Noren's game was, but that was no reason to give in.

"Whatever you are planning Ghen, know I'm on your side. I want to keep this land as much as you do. I'm glad to hear you're thinking ahead and know that I am, too." May hoped her words would encourage her husband.

"Well now," Ghen said with a sly smile, "if that's the case, maybe I ought to send Mr. Noren a warning. Otherwise, you might take everything he has."

It was well known that, while Ghen was the heart of the ranch, it was May who always got her way when dealing with people. Not that it had gone like that these last few times, but they would come up with something to turn this around. May was sure of it.

Preparation being May's key to success, their party returned home to find that most of the midday meal was already prepared. However, it had not been prepared for travel, considering the expectation at the time was that they would all return home for lunch. At least, it was an issue easily remedied. May also decided to gather more supplies to change Ami, as she was going to run low before the work was done.

Minutes into their preparation, Ghen gasped.

"What the...? Oh, by the burned ashes!" he exclaimed furiously and burst out the door of the house.

"Ghen?! What is it?" May called too late. He was already running back out to the pasture, arming himself with a hay fork along the way.

Anxious, May stepped out and looked back at the field. Where they had left three people, May saw five. Figures ran at and around one another, kicking dust into the air. One of them was swinging a weapon at who could only be Em.

"Oh no." Fear jolted through her. "Kaddley!"

CHAPTER 8

EM SAT ON THE wooden fence that surrounded the field, adjusting the clothing he'd been loaned. They were Ghen's clothes, but being much shorter and slimmer, nothing fit right. To keep the pants up, Em had to borrow a thin rope to use as a makeshift belt.

"Who's that?" Kaddley asked.

Her words brought Em's gaze up from his baggy clothes.

There were two of them, closing in on the fenced field. They were too far for Em to make out much, but Jirus leapt to his feet excitedly as he noticed them. Climbing on the fence, he waved to the approaching figures. For a moment, Em wondered if Ghen had overlooked mentioning extra help.

"Those are my friends," Jirus said. "They're brothers and the sons of our neighbor. He was a big fighter in the watchmen, a ranking officer! Azel is the oldest and he's going to join the watchmen this summer, he's probably your age. Jhoen's younger, but he'll join soon too. I'll join later on."

"The watchmen? Why join the mercenaries? Why not the army?" Em asked.

"The army is too hard to get into. Plus, I think the watchmen are better. They go where they want, when they want. They don't have to follow all the rules the army does."

"That is why you wish to join them?"

Jirus huffed, annoyed at having to answer such an obvious question. "Kind of. They can go find adventure instead of just waiting to be ordered into it like the army. They can kill monsters and marauders."

Em was skeptical, though not sure why.

"Mama says you shouldn't join the watchmen," Kaddley said.

"Shut up, Kaddley. I'm not going to die on some farm or ranch having never done anything important with my life. Fighting with them, that's how you become a hero." Jirus's words sparked Em's interest.

What Ghen had said before about Jirus came to mind. Something had happened to his parents. His words depicted the thrill of the kill and a spirit of adventure.

Oh, to be so young, the elderly Instinct laughed loftily. *But is it a hunger for adventure or a fear of obscurity that drives him?* This was the second or third time today Em had heard Instinct's voice. While surprising at first, he was quickly growing used to it.

Em decided not to question him on this directly quite yet. "Ghen has said the Guardians of the Blessed are your... 'best of the best.' Would they not kill more of the enemies you wish to hunt?"

"Azel says those guys are all talk. Besides, you need magic for that. It's watchmen who do real work, I think."

"The words of Itōh, I think," Em accidentally said aloud.

"Huh? Who is, or what is an E-toe?"

For some reason, the word had seemed perfectly normal to Em, but he guessed he should explain since he'd said it aloud, accidental or not. "Itōh, maybe I should use the word... grunt? Yes, they both mean the same man. One who does hard labor."

"They aren't grunts! They're heroes!" Jirus was incensed at Em's bashing the Watchmen Brigade.

"I apologize," Em said with a bow. "I did not mean to be disrespectful. The watchmen are a militia and, according to Ghen, like mercenaries. I only meant that I doubt any soldiers of theirs are given much training. Or are hired for jobs the army cannot handle."

"Exactly, the army can't do what they can!" he said confidently.

Clearly, he had not taken it the way Em meant. "I did not mean jobs they are too weak for, I meant do not have the men for. Policing, and reserve forces."

"Oh, and what do you know about it? What do you know about anything?" Jirus jeered. "You barely know your own name!"

"You are right," Em admitted sadly, stung at the reminder.

Looking victorious, Jirus marched towards the fence where his friends were approaching. Em was surprised to see that the older one, or at least the taller one, strode with confidence as if this were his own home. Based on Jirus's description this must be Azel. The younger, Jhoen, had to walk fast to keep up with his brother's long stride but did his best to try to imitate Azel's confidence.

What Em observed next was that Jhoen held a wooden rod like a thin fence post in one hand, but with wrappings around one end like a sword hilt. Em wondered if it was a practice sword of some kind. It didn't look right to him though, but he couldn't say what was off about it. Materials or its shape, perhaps?

Then he considered it could also be a kind of tool. Em wondered if they were on some kind of hunt. Maybe the rod was used to scare an animal out of hiding? Yet the older brother's only weapon was a long dagger at his side, so maybe not.

The two boys climbed over the fence and, ignoring Jirus, approached Em and Kaddley.

Em had little trust in anyone, but at least he'd expected to meet Ghen and his family. These boys were complete strangers, and so Em kept a careful eye on them both. All the same, Em stood from his seat and bowed.

These were guests of Ghen's home and it would not be wise to offend either them or Ghen-*sa* by being rude. Hopefully, they would turn back to Jirus. Em would prefer it if they just ignored him. "Good day, I am Em. I am both guest and workhand for the next few days."

Both of them had curly hair and the older one was beginning to grow a beard. This one smiled at Em, but there was no welcome in it. The younger might have been a picture of the older from two or three falls before, they were so similar. They even bore the same green eyes and wide nose.

Jhoen leaned toward his brother. "He sounds funny."

Ironically, Em had been having the same thought about everyone else he'd spoken to this morning. However, he'd kept the thought to himself.

Now Azel, who'd been giving Em a very strange, hungry look, finally spoke. His voice was deep and blatantly condescending. "Ha, we thought you looked small from a distance. Now that I look at you, you're tiny. Aren't you, little foreigner?"

'From a distance', so they hadn't met. Em didn't respond to the obvious taunts. He simply leaned against the fence and met Azel's eyes without challenging him, waiting for these brothers to get bored and move on.

"Not a talker? That's fine. I think we already know all we need to about you."

"Azel? What are you doing?" Jirus asked.

"Looking at an opportunity," Jhoen said with something of a grin.

"That's right. We're setting up for where we want to be," Azel said. That hungry expression was back, and Em didn't like it.

"What? Like setting up to be in the Watchmen Brigade?" Jirus asked.

Azel scoffed. "Of course not, maybe being a watchman is something you'd settle for, but I've got drive and vision. I'll be going further."

"And me too," Jhoen added.

Confusion dominated Jirus's expression. By his own testimony, they had recently planned to join the Watchmen Brigade. So, the sudden change of intentions wasn't what Jirus had expected at all.

Em was beginning to expect something himself, perhaps they were on a hunt after all. He was coming to the conclusion these two had come here for him, and he guessed it was not to be welcoming. He couldn't even guess why they were targeting him, but Em wondered if they'd been waiting until Ghen was away.

Jhoen held out his wooden rod and made to poke Em with it, but as he prodded with the tip, Em swatted it aside.

"Whoa," Azel said with a dangerous grin. "Don't be rude little foreigner, we're just being neighborly. Otherwise, I'd think you were trying to start something."

The young man rose to his full height. Despite being somewhere near the same age, Azel stood head and shoulders above Em.

Em wasn't sure why, but he wasn't as intimidated as Azel wanted. He wasn't really intimidated at all.

A powerful form rose in Instinct's place, and a voice rumbled out, deep and resonant. *The path these brothers walk is not one of wisdom, but if this is where they chose to go...* Nature shrugged its thick, unseen shoulders. As Nature's heart beat faster, its words became choppy. The voice growled dangerously as he popped leathery, scarred hands. *Let them come.*

Em might have walked away, but he was not foolish enough to show Azel his back. That would be like asking them to strike. Instead, he braced a foot against part of the fence he'd been sitting on. He was ready to push off of it so he could dodge away or leap towards them as needed.

"Leave him alone!" a little girl shouted, cutting through the mounting tension.

All heads turned to Kaddley, who glared small pinpricks at the brothers.

"Buzz off Kaddley," Jhoen said, waving his rod at her. "We know what we're doing."

"Kaddley, it's fine. Just go away," Jirus said worriedly, not sure at all whether this was fine or not.

"No!" she said firmly. "You're just kids like me, but you're mean, and you break things. Everyone talks about it. Papa wouldn't want you here and you're bothering Mr. Em. Go away!"

Azel backed away from Em and took two long strides to tower over Kaddley, who shrank back. "You think we're children like you, little brat? We aren't like you, not like any of you. I can see what you can't. I have real *vision*. Don't you ever compare me to the likes of you ever again!"

Those... are not his words, Nature growled in broken speech.

"Hey Azel, what are...?" Jirus said, taking a step forward, but froze as Azel turned a stern eye on him.

Azel might have said something to Jirus too, but with his gaze off of Kaddley, she mustered her little courage. Sucking in a deep breath, she kicked Azel in the shin as hard as she could, shouting, "Go away!"

Azel leaped back, cursing. His proud composure shattered, and as it left, Azel's face twisted with rage. "You little..." He drew back his leg for a kick of his own.

Instinct's old voice sighed, shaking its head out of sight. *No helping it now, Little Em. Go!*

Pushing off the fence, Em leaped forward with unexpected speed. Azel had one leg raised to kick Kaddley, and the instant Em landed, he swept the other leg out from under the older brother. Caught off guard, Azel crashed to the ground with a heavy *thud*.

Practiced agility from days unrecalled took over, and Em leapt away from Azel before the small giant even hit the ground. Em stumbled slightly as he landed because of the baggy clothes, but other than that his execution had been textbook. Regaining his stance, Em readied himself for whatever came next.

He had more time than expected. Both brothers were stunned by Em's swiftness. But, as they regained their composure, Em pushed Kaddley away so she would not be caught as the brothers made their reply.

Jirus still stood gaping when Jhoen ran by him at Em, swinging his stick like a sword.

"So, it is a practice sword," Em muttered as he leaped back again out of the stick's range.

Jhoen stepped forward swinging again and again, pushing Em further back. Em's hand went to his side and groped for his sword hilt, but it wasn't there. None of his weapons were. He'd left them against the fence and could see them on the opposite side of the field.

Em groaned, longing to adjust the baggy clothes in order to move more fluidly. Em's face dropped to a stern but neutral expression, all the passion of the fight draining out, as the practiced survival skills Nature had drilled into him took command.

Jhoen swung deeply from left to right, but Em had a handle on the weapon's reach now. He was finished running. Backing off just enough to dodge the blow, Em leapt in, getting in too close for Jhoen to use his sword effectively.

Jhoen's eye widened at the unexpected attack, but instead of swinging back or jumping away, he spun in a wide arc to make a hard spinning strike. Em could have laughed at the maneuver. In the week and a half it took for Jhoen to spin around, Em took another step in and caught Jhoen's wrist.

The younger brother blinked, clearly puzzled at why the trick he'd seen so often in traveling shows hadn't worked for him.

Em didn't care. His freed hand curled and, bracing his back foot, twisted his body with a palm strike. The reward was a satisfying *smack*. He caught

Jhoen in the boy's unguarded face and the younger brother's expression went blank as he fell to the ground, completely stunned.

As he fell, Em took the training sword for himself. With a small break in the action, Em forced a deep breath into his lungs, giving him the strength to keep going.

A roar of anger heralded Azel's return to his feet.

Em spun on his heel, the wooden sword feeling comfortable in his hand.

Azel charged him like a bull, his hunting knife out. His intentions were plainly on crushing this 'little foreigner' and tearing him apart. The fact that Em was fighting back so fiercely only confirmed in Azel's mind that he was dangerous, just as the older brother had suspected.

There was no time to dodge the rush, but Em knew he needed to avoid the knife. Em gripped the wooden hilt with both hands. With a tight sweep, he brought the shaft of the tool down onto Azel's wrist, repulsing the knife. As Em hit, there was a *pop!* Azel's face pinched in pain, but he charged through it. He rammed Em with his shoulder, but the pain made Azel naturally pivot. Em was knocked off his feet, but Azel stumbled away, unable to follow up, the pain in his wrist throwing him off balance.

Em rolled to his feet and got ready for another charge.

Azel came around, but his offhand was clutching his other wrist tightly. Maybe it was broken. Even if it was, Em saw Azel still wished to fight. Jhoen's gaze was beginning to clear too. Soon, they could both attack him at once.

Instead of giving them a chance, Em decided to strike first while they were disorganized. Taking aim at Azel, he lowered the wooden blade. Even if the wrist wasn't broken, Em planned to snap any bone Azel put in his way this time. He dashed forward.

"ENOUGH!" Ghen bellowed.

Em slid to a stop and leaped back a pace in case his enemies did not respect the order.

"That's enough!" Ghen said again as he got to the fence, waving a hay fork. Ghen might have said more but had to stop to catch his breath.

Jhoen spoke first. "Look at this!" he said, showing Ghen a red stained hand.

It was only then Em noticed Jhoen's nose was bleeding. He couldn't help grinning slightly, that had been a good hit.

"Don't you see what that foreign freak is? Look at what he did! He's dangerous, maybe even a marauder! You just let him walk around like... like some free range chicken!" Jhoen continued.

"Marauder?" Ghen said, a sharp glance darting towards Jirus, who for his part was looking anywhere that wasn't Ghen's direction. "Jhoen, you're a fool. If Em were a marauder, which he's not, then you'd be a fool to pick a fight with him." Ghen finally began to catch his breath, and he even managed to grin. "Even though he's not a marauder, from what I saw, that 'free range chicken' just plucked you both."

"Don't start with us old man," Azel growled, holding his wrist still. "We know what we're doing."

Ghen wasn't impressed. "You trespass on my property without my permission, pick a fight with my guest, take a kick at my daughter. That's right, I saw that," Ghen said, his face reddening again, and this time it had nothing to do with any running. "Now what? You're going to threaten me? Quit this foolishness. Get out of my field and get off my land!"

Azel glowered back with equal fire, but Jhoen was starting to back away. Azel saw him.

"What!?" He glared at his brother. "Don't you have the drive to see this through?"

This was more than Jhoen had bargained for already, but the comment gave him pause. He seemed to teeter on a decision when a new voice broke the balance.

The tone was so icy that even Em flinched. "Didn't you hear my husband? It's high time you boys left. I don't know what inspired this madness, but it's not welcome here." She didn't shout, but May's menacing presence washed over all of them. It never wavered, even as she set down the toddler and basket in her arms.

"Mama!" Kaddley shouted. She clambered over the fence and sprinted to her mother.

May held Kaddley's hand as the little girl cried into her skirt, but the woman's piercing eyes remained on her unwelcome guests. Where Kaddley's glare at Jhoen and Azel had been pinpricks, May's were pikes.

"Come on Azel, let's go," Jhoen hissed, having made his choice.

Azel turned right and left as if looking for something, support maybe, but whatever help he sought, he didn't find it here.

"You're a fool, Ghen," Azel said before leaving. "Let that short freak stay on your land, for however long you have it. I hope he turns out to be as bad as one of those pad-handed usarame freaks and kills you in your sleep."

Jhoen looked at his older brother pleadingly, and Azel, for his part, finally relented. He knew he'd failed, it was over. Perhaps he could find a way to take some little vengeance, but no matter what he did now he'd always be a child in everyone's eyes after this. That meant that was all he would ever be.

Angry and defeated, Azel slumped away still nursing both his wrist and the chip on his shoulder. Jhoen, far less reflective, was merely happy to know he could get out from under the dangerous eyes of May Jarden. He walked as quickly as he could without quite breaking into a run.

Pad-handed 'usarame.' He needs to learn to say their name right. They're called usarumai. Instinct mocked in his mischievous tone, as they watched the brothers go. *No one ever quite lives up to the stories. The usarumai tribe is rarely as bad as we make them out to be, and the rest of us are rarely as good.*

Em's thoughts lingered on the tribe. The usarumai were rumored to be as vicious and terrifying as any tribe could be. They were like humans, but with hands as dark as shadow, their palms covered in thick pads, resembling those of an animal. Each of those hands would also be strong enough to shatter bone like the jaws of a wild beast, which was why the tribe was often called beastmen.

Kaddley's sobbing broke the silence and Em's train of thought. In the wake of the brothers' departure, the tears that had only come sporadically flowed freely. May bent down to embrace and comfort her daughter.

Ghen sighed deeply before lifting his hat so he could scratch his head. "Well, now what do we do? I don't figure there's a chance in the stars above those boys don't get home later, and..." Ghen didn't even turn to look at him "Jirus, you stay right where you are."

The boy froze in the midst of trying to make his escape.

He was hoping to come back when tempers had cooled. Now that he'd been seen, he decided to read the looks of everyone else.

Em didn't trust Jirus, and it was clear on his face. Equally plain to see, but far more passionate were Ghen and May. There was no doubt they would put their feelings into words very soon.

Letting his charge stew in his embarrassment and the idea of future punishment, Ghen returned to his earlier thought. "Ol' Mr. Colrage is no doubt going to ride in here by day's end and demand answers to why his two boys ended up all bruised. Probably after hearing a story that wasn't near enough to the truth."

Em bowed deeply. "Forgive me. I brought this on your house. It is clear to me that they came because I was here. After what the younger, Jhoen I think," Em purposefully left out the honorific, "said about my being a marauder, I have no doubt this Mr. Colrage will think the same." Jirus had said that both boys came from a big farm. If they were from a powerful house, then Em could be in danger if he stayed. He would also endanger Ghen and his family, who'd offered him shelter. "Perhaps I should be on my way to Henaden."

May scoffed. "I think not!" She patted Kaddley on the head and stood tall. "Those two hooligans came into our home to drive you off, or worse no doubt. If you left now that would only mean we let them win. I will *not* let that happen. Do you understand Mr. Em?"

Surprised at her forcefulness, Em reflexively lowered his head. "*Hai. May-se.*"

May raised an eyebrow at Em's unfamiliar response but made no more of it. May's talkative personality morphed into a commanding air. Friendly conversationalist no longer, now a general issuing her orders.

"Good. Now, Ghen."

The rancher straightened when called upon.

"You can take your lunch on the way to the Colrage farm. We're lucky that you used Bo to bring the bags of seed here today. Get your mule ready and set out quickly, so you beat those boys home. Considering which way they took off, they'll have to swing through the creek. You can make better time on the road. When you get to their farm, tell their mother first. She knows us better and she'll see to it that no more trouble comes of this. *Then* tell their father too, for good measure."

With her husband directed, May's attention shifted. "Em, this field will still need seeding. With just you, me, and Kaddley, it will take the rest of the day. Especially since it looks like your little scuffle undid some of our work."

Em looked down to see he'd made a mess of the seed that had been spread atop the ground where he now stood. There were visible boot prints where seeds were pushed down or kicked aside leaving bare patches.

He opened his mouth to apologize but May cut him off again. "I'm not complaining, just pointing it out. Now, I hope you've learned well this morning because we are going to have to eat quickly and work fast. That does not mean we will make allowances for shoddy work, I hope you understand."

Jirus noticed the lack of his name on the list of those working in the field but didn't need to ask. May was just getting to that. "Jirus, I have no doubt you knew those boys were coming here today. I don't think you knew why or how far they might go, but that does not mean that you aren't responsible. For the rest of the day, I want you to..." She paused and her head snapped back to Ghen. "Are you still here?" She pointed to the basket at her feet. "I brought everyone's lunches, take yours and be off before everyone from here to Marden Hallows is told you are working with marauders."

"Huh...? Oh!" Ghen jumped into action. He confusingly propped his hay fork against the fence, not sure what else to do with it, and then stepped up to the basket as commanded.

Having finished with Ghen, May turned back to Jirus. "Ghen and Em need nightroot to sell, so the rest must be pulled by today so that it can set out and dry. That will be your job, and don't skip cutting the shoots we need to plant for next season. When we are done here in the field, I will be stopping by the root planter to check your work, so don't think you can do half a job and get away with it. Once all the root is set to dry, you can come find me."

Jirus wore a sulky expression and was kicking up clods of dirt, which was an entirely unacceptable response to the matron of the ranch.

"Look at me Jirus," May snapped. "If I find out you've done anything else in between finishing your work and returning to me you'll wish you got what Azel and Jhoen did. Now grab your food and get to work, the day is wasting."

Jirus began muttering, trying to find some excuse or explanation, but couldn't.

May didn't say a thing, only shaking her head, *no*.

Deciding he'd better comply before May's glare turned him to ash, Jirus cautiously stepped forward to dig in the basket for his lunch.

As the younger boy ran off to start his work, May addressed her two girls and her guest. "Come on. Let's eat and then go back to work."

Em was forgetful, not foolish. Quickly, he bowed, saying, "Yes, May-*se*."

CHAPTER 9

"WHAT A DAY," GHEN thought aloud. He was tired.

He'd been forced to spend the whole afternoon at the Colrage farm. As May suggested, he'd spoken to Margren, the mother of the boys, but by the time he and Margren had gotten to their father, Ned, he'd already heard a cockamamie yarn from the boys. Ned had been ready to hunt a marauder at that point.

It hadn't taken long to prove they were lying, but Jhoen came up with one excuse after another, trying to explain it all away. When he finally coughed up something close to the truth, he tried to pin it all on a man they supposedly met the day before, who he claimed fed them the idea. No one had seen who they were talking about or knew anyone who sounded like the rich man they described, but it sounded close to the truth.

Ghen had passed where they said they met the man on his way to the Colrage farm and again on the way back. He hadn't seen any sign of a camp having been there, so he wasn't sure what to make of the story. Whether they got the idea from someone else or not, it was at least made clear to both of the boys' parents who was in the wrong.

Getting through that and the rest had taken far longer than expected, but by the end of the day, they'd finally got it settled. The boys were going to learn a hard lesson from both their parents. No matter how big and tough Azel thought he was, he still wanted his father's money.

Margren had also promised that they would not be able to leave the farm or have any visitors for a while. Good news for Ghen, since Jirus wouldn't run off to follow them into who knew what trouble again. He hoped he could use this time to try and get through to Jirus about this watchmen idea, but he wasn't sure that would work out. Ghen still had to apologize to Ned about Em beating up his boys, but Ghen didn't mind. It was fair, as it should be working with good folk.

When he'd been leaving the ranch, May had been talking about them trying to finish the field and seemed to already have a plan for Jirus. Ghen had a lot to thank his wonderful wife for. He hadn't had a clue how to handle all this. Not May, she'd been ready to say, 'Get to work!' Personally, Ghen felt she'd saved him from embarrassment and maybe worse. Yep, wonderful barely described his lovely little lady.

"The issue, Bo, is the nightroot," Ghen said to his mule as they walked back towards home.

Bo's head bobbed. Most people might have thought it was from the walking, but Ghen took it as a sign of agreement.

"If we can't get the root out to dry by tonight, it might spoil if we try to take it to Henaden."

As he gathered to leave, Ghen did hear that Jirus would be working on it, but he still worried it might turn into a late night of work to get everything done.

"The only other option is to wait another day, but I really don't want to do that to Em. Not only is the kid holding up his end of the deal, but... well you saw what he did for Kaddley."

Bo snorted.

"Yes, Azel is a snot," Ghen agreed. "But after all their trouble and then lying about it, those boys are in for a good load of trouble themselves. The thing is, with Em holding up his end of our deal, it isn't fair if I don't make a good effort to hold up to mine."

As Ghen and Bo approached the house, the sun was dancing along the treetops, with less than an hour of daylight left. Just as they pulled up, Em stepped out of the house, his sword strapped at his side once again. After the midday tussle, May would have told him to keep it on, no doubt. Not that the kid would need any encouragement.

Despite the earlier chaos, Em welcomed the returning rancher warmly. "Good evening Ghen-*sa*."

"Evening," Ghen said with a friendly nod. "Hey, would you run ahead of me and pull the back door of the barn open? Then I can ride Bo straight in."

His words were pleasant, but as Em ran ahead, Ghen got the feeling something was wrong with him. Had things gone poorly with the rest of the day's work, or was it something else? If Em was having problems, then Ghen figured he ought to help if he could, he owed the kid after today, even if that wasn't just what good folk ought to do.

The rancher pondered what it might be as Bo moved down the ramp and entered the barn. The mule hadn't been pleased with Ghen's hard riding, but there wasn't much that ever pleased her. At least she'd done the job. Dismounting, Ghen walked to a small drawer and snagged a bit of sugar for the mule. When she saw him go to the drawer, her ears perked up, and her eyes followed Ghen's hand.

The rancher grinned at her. "Yeah, you know what I've got, don't you? You're a pain sometimes, but you did good today. Here you go, girl."

The mule happily took the reward. Then proceeded to sniff at his other hand and his shirt to see if he had any more hidden. She got so close he had to push her head away.

"That's enough, I promise you got it all. The way you went at it I'm surprised you didn't take a finger too. Bo, off!" Another shove and the mule took the hint. Ghen led her to her stall and removed her tack. When he saw Em watching, Ghen gave him a sure nod. "Don't worry, Em, it took time, but I got everything straightened out with those boys."

"Thank you, Ghen-*sa*," Em replied distractedly. "Ah, and things went well with us, too. We finished with your field, according to the mistress, we finished in good time as well. I was able to spend some time writing out notes on what you taught me this morning."

'The mistress', huh? Ghen couldn't help smiling. "Good, how far did Jirus get on with the nightroot?"

"Originally, I was told we would not help him, but by the time the field was finished, May-*se* changed her mind. We traded off the work once the field was done. Whenever Jirus was not working, I believe he was in your wife's care. I believe she scolded him heavily."

She was a step ahead again. "Perfect. That's got me wondering though, if the roots are taken care of then what's eating at you?"

Em turned his head, trying to hide his face. He didn't respond immediately and when he did, he began to wander in a circle on the open barn floor. Pacing to clear his head.

"I do not understand your family. Jirus has shamed you, and his punishment is the labor that was already expected of him. May-*se* was harsh in her words, but has in many ways shown him mercy."

"By making him sit bent over all day, and then the rest lecturing him? Probably had him do more chores while she sat and lectured him too. I can imagine harsher things, but I'm not sure I'd call it mercy."

"Maybe you would not," Em said, "but it is still strange to me."

Ghen set Bo's tack aside and tossed some small feed in her trough for her supper. While she chewed on her meal, Ghen chewed on his thoughts.

"So then, this isn't about what May did. It's about how it makes you feel?"

Em did not answer.

"Alright then," Ghen said. "If it was you, and a kid you took in shamed you. What would you do?"

Em looked away. "I do not know."

Ghen sighed. He wasn't sure he believed that. "Even without much to look back on you still know a lot, but you don't know everything, Em. I think I can guess where you're getting tripped up. So let me ask a different question. What's Jirus supposed to do here?"

"I do not understand."

"You already know May and I took in Jirus and did that willingly. My question is, why? Why do you think we did that?"

"I suppose he needed a place to stay, and you needed help."

Ghen gave a loud snap of his fingers. "That's it, right there. It's a small thing, but it's important. You're right, we do need help, but that wasn't our 'why.' We didn't want him to do something for us, we took him in because we wanted to do something for him. Now, today, he messed up. So, to help him, May and I have to try and make it so he won't do it again."

"I understand that."

"I'm not sure you do," Ghen said calmly. "You've been looking at it as something we're doing for our benefit, not his. Where's that come from?"

There was hesitation on Em's face.

"I know you don't actually know," Ghen continued. "It's not your fault either. You've been dealt a bad hand, but I don't think this is your first."

Em's face became dangerous. "What do you mean?"

Ghen took a deep breath. "No kid your age, at least not around here, can fight like you can. Azel was twice your size and had you two on one, but that fight didn't go near his way. You didn't learn that just by hiking down the road or by practicing with Nature.

"Now you tell me a young man taken in by people who aren't his folks are supposed to act for their benefit instead of the other way around. That ain't coming from what you're seeing, my guess is it's from what you've seen."

Em's eyes drifted away from Ghen and he didn't turn back. He was silent for so long that the rancher wondered if he'd pushed too much.

"For him. You punish Jirus, for Jirus?" Em finally responded.

"Of course, I love the kid, he's family. I don't know what you expect, but whatever it is, do you think it would actually help Jirus if we did it? I need to make sure he knows his actions have consequences, but I have to do it the right way.

"Remember Em, I'm a rancher, my life is about raising things, whether it's a calf or a stalk of wheat. I'll switch a stubborn calf and I'll tear up the dirt in my garden, but I never do it without reason or limits. If I went around just trying to fix all my problems that way, one of two things would happen. I'd either ruin my crop by tearing up its dirt or I'd see that calf live to hate me. You gotta care for what you do, in all the things you do, Em. Otherwise, the things you care for won't grow right and, if we're being honest, neither will you."

Em's eyes flicked back to the rancher sharply. "And how do I grow?"

"Oh kid, I didn't mean..."

"And what did you mean?" Em hissed, his fist clenching. "I cannot grow right. Any attempt to improve my life is forgotten by the next sun's rise. Do you understand? I am trapped in every single day that passes."

"I know what you mean." Ghen consoled.

"Do you?" he shouted in jealous anger.

Looking at Ghen's surprised gaze, Em's features slackened, and he looked down, ashamed.

"Forgive me Ghen-*sa*. I wish you did understand, I wish anyone did. You talk of love and growth. Well, I have heard you, and I think I already knew where May-*se*'s mercy came from. Yet your fool boy, he is bitter while he has people who..." Em trailed off.

"Oh, kid."

"Do not pity me," Em said quickly. "I do not care anymore. I will forget it all soon."

"You should care," Ghen pressed.

"Why?" Em asked. "If I find Master D'gui, something I may never be able to do, what guarantee do I have that I will get back the past I lost? All the lessons, the people, the purpose I had, gone!"

Ghen noticed again how worn Em's young brown eyes were. Em sounded tired asking, "Is there even a point to going forward? My life is nothing, I cannot make anything from it."

Ghen stepped forward and put a firm hand on his shoulder. "Yes, you can."

"How would you know?"

Ghen shook his head. "Everyone has a point in their life where they have to figure out who they're going to be. Since you can't be sure where you are or have ever been, I admit you have a lot less to work with than most, but, Em, does it matter?" Adding quickly, "Not that none of it matters, but the fact is, neither of us could change your past if we knew it by blink and breath. You can't even start to try. It's who you are now, not who you were, that chooses who you're going to be."

"I don't know who I am supposed to be," Em said.

"Kid," Ghen said sternly, "don't start that. It's not fair to me or you. No one ever knows what they're supposed to be. Life is about finding out! No one can live up to 'supposed to.' Don't waste good daylight on the thought, as a rancher, I know how important daylight is."

"Then what should I do?" Em's voice rang out in desperation.

Ghen stepped out of Bo's stall and closed the door. He didn't reply quickly, taking time to think.

"Well Em, you seem to want me to offer you a life. I don't have a whole lot of those just lying around, but for now, I can help you remember. Not what you've lost, but at least what I know of you now. Then, when we get to Henaden I'll help you find your mystic. When we do, we'll get their help. After, when you can remember on your own, I'll help you at least find a place to start. All along that way, I'll tell you stories of this ranch, these people, and all I know of the world as many times as I need to. You are not alone, Em. Not anymore."

Ghen wasn't one to easily watch a man cry, but he understood what he was seeing. Em tried to speak, but all that escaped was a shaky breath.

"We'll find your way," Ghen assured him. "It's not like you don't have skills or that you're so old you can't learn new ones. You're not like me, destined to live in one place plantin' seeds. Mind you, I'm not complaining about my life. I'm just saying it probably isn't for you. I think we both already knew that much."

Em didn't reply, but Ghen knew he agreed.

"Still, you've got somewhere you're meant to be. If you want to find it Em, what you need to do is look. That's the point of going on. Look towards the sky and go down the road that brings you peace the way good folk do."

Em didn't speak for a long time, but now Ghen was willing to wait.

"You will go with me? All the way?" Em asked finally.

"I'll go as far as makes good sense to us both. Like I said, you're not alone anymore."

"Thank you, Ghen-sa," Em said after another minute of silence.

Ghen nodded, he figured it was best to leave the boy alone for now. Besides, May would begin to worry if he didn't turn up soon.

The rancher quietly dusted himself off. "Stay as long as you like, but be sure to come get some dinner. I'm sure May will have something soon if she doesn't already. If you decide to wait longer, I'll make sure to keep something for you."

Em nodded, and Ghen cautiously took his leave.

When he heard the door above close softly, Em sat down where he was and aired his thoughts.

Should I trust him?

Has he given you any reason not to? an elderly voice asked from the shadows above.

It is not my way to trust.

That does not mean that you can't. You trust me, after all, so you've done it before. Instinct had no visible form, but something in the older voice made it sound like Instinct was working on something. As if tuning an unseen instrument.

Were there better days? Days I could trust?

Oh, Little Em. It shouldn't be the day you trust, it should be the person. Instinct grinned at him.

Em ignored the attempt at humor, pressing his point. *What if I chose wrong? Ghen-sa has been good for now, but could it be a lie?*

It was an instrument, for with Instinct's voice, Em heard the sound of idle strings as the practiced fingers checked their tune. *There's always room for doubt. A chance things could go horribly wrong!* he said dramatically, then more grounded, *But do you really think that's what this is?*

No.

Then, as ironic as it is coming from me, have some faith, Little Em.

Ghen was a strange man, Em decided, but not a bad one. *Alright, I... we will trust him.*

With an unseen grin, Instinct lifted his instrument to his shoulder and began to play slowly a song that Em alone could hear. It was low and soft. A hum of familiarity to the forgotten.

Em stood slowly and crossed the barn, listening to Instinct's song. Taking up the quill and ink left for him, Em added a new entry in his notes that he would read every day.

When you are healed, Em, search for the path to go forward.
The purpose of our life is not over. Ghen, the rancher, will
help us start. Trust him, too. We can still grow, that too is

what we have to remember.
From the Em of yesterday.

His mind was still awash with thought, so he couldn't go to the evening meal just yet. Drawing his sword, Em stepped out into the open floor of the barn. Then, guided by lantern light, his long blade blurred. With each thumping step and whistle of steel, the music played along. A melody played to oppose and enhance every movement. Instinct's melody was a sound of peace for a dance of war.

Em's movements flowed seamlessly from one to the next. The prowl, lunge, flurry of blows, and finally retreat. Em practiced against the shadow of Nature. The strong unseen presence taught him as they battled with swords that never clashed. Each move Em made was in response to his invisible instructor. Despite how intensely he practiced with Nature's shadow, Em found it calmed him. The distance the fog of battle gave him brought unexpected clarity of thought.

Quietly, the voice of Instinct murmured with his music, his somber simple song. Like a pendulum, the verse swung in a low melody.

> *When I looked above, into the summer sky.*
> *Were you there, lost daughter of mine?*

Em heard the words distantly, but to himself, he asked, "What do I want? If I am healed, where will I go?"

> *Lovely heart, I left behind.*
> *Why do I sing if hope is lost?*
> *I made my choice and knew the cost.*

Straw fluttered under the wind of Em's passing. His blade stuck, slashed, and plunged with a deep lunge. "Could I come back here? If Ghen is good, then do I have to leave?"

But when the sun came down, and the
end drew near,
I was given a chance to once more hold
you dear.
So, hear my rhyme, lost daughter of
mine.
Now I seek to bring you this.
A boy needs your help, and you, his.

"No," Em admitted to himself. "This is a good life, but it is not mine." In that thought was a strange peace, but just because it wasn't Em's way didn't mean he didn't wish it were.

Darling child, now tall and wise.
Take heed my words, as your fears rise.
Unlike before, I'll be there this time.
The forgotten blade will burn red,
And we phantoms will do as we said.

If Ghen was true to his word, then Em knew he was in debt to him. No matter where that led, Em felt the bindings of honor to in some way repay that debt.

The fake shall fall, and the dread lose
heart.
The end of it all? No, but a start.
When the ever searching verse comes to
its last line,
forget not, fear not, the great worker is
near.
Find as I did, that things are more than
they appear.

Coming to the close of the song and of his practice, Em planted his feet. Gripping his sword with both hands, he raised it slightly, preparing for a last strong strike. Closing his eyes, Em took the time to focus. For this Em, it would be the closing act of his life. After this, his night and he too would quickly draw to a close.

"But I'm not alone anymore. Soon, I will remember and will go on to more..."

There *was* more. Just beneath the surface, it was as if Em could almost feel it. As if all that stood between him and his goal was a thin veil. He struck out once with his sword, to rend the veil, his eyes still tightly shut. Em felt a flicker of warmth and pain. He could have sworn that light too had touched his face, but when Em opened his eyes, there was only the lamp.

"Only my friend's lamp. A friend that..."

Em groaned and became distracted as pain filled his head, and Instinct's music faded away.

He rubbed his head with one hand. "A friend, who would tell me to eat so I do not get headaches like this one."

Deciding that was enough, he took the lamp and ascended the stairs to the upper landing.

However, something caught his attention. Holding up the lamp, Em looked down into the open basement landing. It was just like he'd left it, from lazy Bo to the rusted tools that hung on the wall. He couldn't see anything, but the feeling wouldn't leave.

"Surely there is... something."

It was on the lower level, but as he searched for it, Em felt as if, even from this distance, he could almost reach out and touch it. Then the sensation vanished, and Em wondered if he'd felt anything at all.

Maybe it had been a figment of his imagination or a delusion by his pounding head. Em wondered if he should drink some water, perhaps thirst was affecting him. Without another thought, he went to the house.

It was not long before Em returned and knew there were no more excuses to stay awake. Laying down, he set his journal by his side, took the separate note about his deal with Ghen, and slid it into his pants pocket.

CHAPTER 10

JIRUS WAITED LONG ENOUGH to be sure everybody was sleeping deeply before he risked slipping out. The full moon outside gave off enough light through the window slats for him to move about the house without much fear of running into anything. This wasn't the first time Jirus had stolen into the night, but this could be the last. If this worked, he should be able to come and go as he pleased.

The door latch slid as quietly out of place as his smile sliced across his face. None of them understood. They tried to force him to their way, as 'good folk' should. He didn't hate them for it, but they could never understand. They didn't know what it was like. Jirus could never accept living on a ranch all his life, only to die without anyone ever knowing his name.

Like Dad, he thought, but quickly squashed the negativity.

Jirus slid to the barn door. Jirus had overheard that the barn would be unlocked because Ghen trusted Em now. That made his job so much easier. Only May and Ghen had keys, and Jirus didn't want to risk searching for where they might be.

As for dealing with Em, he had sneaked past him once already when they first met. One thing Jirus was always good at was sneaking, he was a master and proud of it.

Getting to the barn was easy, and Jirus only slowed once he arrived at the barn door. Opening it softly, he let the moonlight soak in. There was Em. The man was fidgeting in his sleep. If he was a restless sleeper, then Jirus would need to be careful. Some of the barn boards could creek and he didn't need a forgetful Em awake, not yet. Jirus knew the squeaky boards by heart, so he knew he should be able to pull this off without a sound.

Then Jirus had something of a stroke of luck. All this time, he'd been worried he would have to dance around Em, searching for his goal, but the moonlight spilling across the barn floor revealed what he'd come to find. Right out in the open, next to the sleeping swordsman, was a small book.

Jirus hadn't seen the journal himself yet, and it was smaller than he'd imagined. He grinned. This tiny collection of paper was all that held Em together. To Jirus, it was so funny it was almost pitiful.

As he carefully navigated the creaky boards, he made his way toward the hayloft. He stretched out to seize the journal, but fate, ever capricious, turned against Jirus. The once bright moon was suddenly obscured by a passing cloud, plunging the barn into darkness. Jirus hesitated, his hand hovering somewhere near the book, but Jirus couldn't see it anymore. He considered waiting till the moon came out again, but who knew how long that would take?

No, I can't stay, Jirus thought, the weight of his decision pressing on him. *If Em wakes, he'll find me standing in the doorway, watching over him.*

Carefully, he felt around for the book and was rewarded with the touch of the soft small cover. Without the light, he had no time to search for anything else, and as far as he could tell, there was no reason to. Jirus pulled the little book into his arms and slowly moved back the way he came. Slowly shutting the door, he breathed a long sigh.

The hard part was finished, and that was the biggest risk to all his designs. He hadn't wanted to do anything like this, but now there was no choice. There was no way Ghen and May would ever let him see either Azel or Jhoen after Azel had tried to kick Kaddley like that.

It wasn't like Jirus thought of them as family or anything, they weren't always nice to him, but he'd needed them. The Watchmen Brigade was his dream, but Ghen and May would never take him to sign up. He had many a few falls before it came time to enlist, but Jirus knew he couldn't change Ghen's and May's minds. They were too set on turning him into another beast of burden for their ranch in the middle of nowhere. Azel and Jhoen had been his only easy chance.

The only nearby post to enlist at was in Henaden. On his own, it would take him five days to get there. Ghen would easily catch up to him before that, if something worse didn't find him on the road first. Rumor also said the road was getting more dangerous. Either way, he couldn't make it alone. That meant he needed people who would at least be sympathetic to his cause.

The other boys in the area often talked about enlisting, but to them, it was either a joke or a distant dream they knew they'd never realize. Azel and Jhoen were the only ones who were serious. Now, though, that option was all but gone.

Em was the only hope left, an unwilling hope but still a chance. Jirus knew that the future might hold another way to persuade Ghen, but there was no guarantee, especially in a rural part of the world like this one. So, Jirus intended to use Em while he was here, and in a way that would mean Jirus could apply for the watchmen when he was old enough.

On the surface, the plan he'd created was quite simple. Em would probably go wild when he woke up with no idea who he was and no way to find out. Em could easily beat Ghen in a fight and hopefully would. Em had been violent with Azel, after all. He just needed the right push, and he would go off.

Once Em went wild, Jirus planned to take control. Using his desperation to know who he was, Jirus would offer Em his notes in exchange for forcing Ghen to meet Jirus's demands. Jirus knew he'd be safe from Em because he'd never find the notebook without him.

Em was strong, but Jirus had careful ears. He'd stopped by the barn after Ghen had returned and overheard much. Em had whined all about 'finding his way' and how terrified he was of not having a clear path. Of course, Ghen and Em hadn't noticed, and Jirus had made himself scarce before they ever had a chance to find him.

Without his notes, he truly had no way, and Jirus could use that fear against Ghen. Jirus didn't want to actually hurt anyone, just set things as they should be. There was no other choice. After today, Ghen and May wouldn't let him out of their sight for a month or longer. Jirus knew that would be a month of the rancher doing all he could to 'help' Jirus. Well, he didn't want that man's help. Even if Ghen caught onto him, he didn't see how it could get worse, Jirus had nothing to lose. In his mind, this was his last chance to take control, he had to go for it.

Jirus was well aware that if he didn't keep Em on a short leash things could backfire. Once Em knew he had the book, though, he would be safe and in command. Personally, he felt that the plan was nearly foolproof. Ghen was too prideful to go back on his word, and if Jirus pushed him on how 'honorable' he was supposed to be, Ghen would comply with any deal Em forced him to make.

Back in the house, Jirus reset the latch silently in place and stepped noiselessly around the room. He had to hide the book somewhere smart. He wanted to hide it outside the house, but if the weather or an animal ruined the book, it could ruin him too.

Oh, right! Jirus remembered suddenly.

One of the two cushioned chairs in the house had an issue with the support below its seat. Ghen had nailed boards to the bottom of the chair to hold it together. He could hide the book between the cushion and the boards. It would never be found there.

The clouds outside passed, and the moonlight returned in a rush. Light flooded the dark home and Jirus froze.

One breath... two breaths...

Jirus waited, watching Ghen and May in bed. Neither stirred.

Jirus sighed before taking the journal and getting down to the ground. Laying on his back, he squirmed carefully to study the underside of the chair. The two planks of wood formed an X, pressing against the cushion. Pushing up on the seat, Jirus slid the book in place. As carefully as he'd crawled under, he wormed his way back out. Finished, Jirus turned back to his bed, where two open eyes followed his actions in the moonlight.

Jirus's heart skipped, and he almost jumped, giving the game away himself.

He caught his breath, it was Ami.

Still, if the toddler cried out, things could go very wrong. Jirus slowly lifted a finger to his lips in a shushing gesture. To his relief, Ami mirrored the gesture, but she kept watching him. She never made a noise as Jirus walked across the room and slowly slipped back into bed.

The deed done, Jirus breathed a sigh of relief. Ami was still just a toddler, she'd forget as fast as Em. If she did remember, she could barely speak or understand enough to mess things up. He would still win.

CHAPTER 11

BLINKING AWAKE, HE SLOWLY sat up and shook sleep from his mind.

Still waking up, he looked around. "Am I sleeping on hay?" Something was off. "Where did I fall asleep?" He couldn't remember.

Resting his head on his hands, he tried to collect his thoughts.

"I am... I do not know," he said slowly.

In his chest, his heart began to beat faster, and adrenaline boosted his wakefulness. A cold emptiness crept up his spine.

"I... I cannot think. I... I am here, but... What is happening!?" Taking deep breaths, he began to look around. "I need answers."

There were things near him, and they were his. He didn't know how, but he knew. The swords, the pack, and more were his. This barn, yes, this was a barn, was not his.

"Why am I here?"

He picked through his things, but there were no clues among the steel or supplies.

Something of yours is missing, a voice said firmly. It rumbled like thunder, dangerous but only if you were caught in its wrath. It was not a voice of anger, only intensity, and in this moment, this voice of Nature held a hint of worry. *It has the answers.*

Whatever this thing or these things were, they were important. Standing, he searched around his bed of hay and through his things but found nothing that fit his senses. The only thing that stuck out was a slip of parchment that protruded from one of the pockets of his pants. He unfolded it and read a short message.

There is a rancher, his name is Ghen. He is going to help us
get to Henaden. We made a deal with him to work for three
days and then he would take us there to be healed.

Healed? Was this void in his mind a sickness? Maybe it was, that would
make sense. This note could be for the owner of the barn instead of him,
but probably not.

You want to go to Henaden, a second voice, older than the first, agreed.

He noticed his clothes caught as he moved and were in many areas slack.

"These are not mine either. They are made for someone much taller and
larger. Did I steal them?"

Borrowed, Instinct corrected in the older voice. *There's no need to hide
them, the owner knows.*

"Yet, these are not what I am seeking." He took a last look around, yet
still nothing fit. "I need to keep searching."

So far, he'd only explored locally. This barn was quite large, so he needed
to expand his search to at least the lower floor he noticed below. He looked
at the door near the hayloft and saw through the gaps the outside beyond.

"I cannot go out yet. It's not out there. I must find it, whatever it is."

So, he descended to the lower level. On the lower floor was an animal, a
mule, that looked at him with disinterest.

"You know me, don't you," Em said. No animal should be so casual to
a stranger.

The mule only blinked at him.

He left the animal alone and returned to his search, sliding open drawers
and looking on and around tables. Nothing he found was his or filled the
void in his mind. Turning around, he spotted a long ramp leading up to the
upper doors. The light filtering through the gaps in their frame suggested
they would open to the outside of the barn.

Looking at the ramp, he wondered, "Is it hollow?"

Though he could not say why, he wondered if it was.

It is, Nature confirmed.

He saw no sign to indicate that it was hollow but was still sure it was. "So, I know this place. Yet, I do not know it. If this ramp is hollow, I must check it too."

Taking a few steps to determine how he could check inside, he stopped short as a knock rang out from the upper door. A second later, the sound of the door opening was chased down by a voice.

"Em, you awake yet?" The words were in a different language than the one he'd been using, but that barely registered over the panicked need to hide.

Leaping for the nearest cover, he rolled under a table and waited for the speaker to come into sight.

Am I Em? he wondered. *Then again, this mule could too be Em.*

"Em?" The man upstairs sounded confused. Em heard footsteps as the source of the voice stepped in to survey the area.

Now what do I do? he asked himself. *If I am Em, I should respond, if I am not, then I should probably not be caught.*

The tramping of boots on the stairs heralded the puzzled human who came down them. In the early light, there was little to make out beyond that he had a beard and curly hair. The figure looked one way and then the other before scratching the top of his head.

"Em, are you here?" he repeated.

Trust him, Nature said firmly.

I cannot, I don't know him.

You do, Instinct said with a grinning voice. *And, you already trust him, you just don't know it. If you don't believe me, step out and see.*

Still unsure if he was or was not Em, or if what Instinct and Nature said was true, he watched a moment more. Yet as he looked at the newcomer, his worry lessened.

Do I know him? he wondered.

Finally, he decided to risk it and slid out from his hiding place, taking a step toward the man.

At the obvious step forward, the new man jumped and put a hand to his chest, taking deep breaths. "Heaven's boy!" he exclaimed. "You startled me. Next time, just speak up." He laughed as he spoke.

Em did not feel like laughing. "Em. Am I Em?" he asked in the same language as the man.

The man's eyebrows went up with mild surprise. "Oh, well... yes you are. I'm sorry, I figured you... Well, I guess it doesn't matter. I'm Ghen."

Em remembered the name from the note he found upstairs. "Then... you are to take me to Henaden? For healing?"

Ghen tilted his head. "Have you read your book or not, kid?"

Em blinked. "A book... I... I could not find it. I have been looking for... something, it... it was a book," Em said to the rancher, also realizing it for himself. "All I found was this." He held up the note.

"Wait, you don't know where your book is?" Ghen looked right and left, holding high a lantern he brought with him since daylight hadn't fully broken yet. "You sure it wasn't upstairs?"

"No, I—"

Em cut off his words at the sound of soft steps on the stairs. Shifting slightly forward, he made out the small figure of a younger boy stepping down carefully.

You trust Ghen, but that one... Em's Instinct said mischievously, *he's a different story.*

Ghen turned too, and, seeing the boy, his eyes narrowed. Slowly he questioned, "Jirus, you didn't, by any chance, see Em's journal up there, did you?"

Jirus glanced at Em with an expression that might have been disappointment, but the look vanished as soon as it had appeared. "I wasn't really looking for it, but it might be up there."

Ghen's eyes narrowed and looked Jirus over carefully before turning back to Em. "Alright, well we need to find your notes for you Em, but first let's figure out what you know. Sadly, I'm guessing the list isn't long, but let's go over it."

Em paused, gathering his thoughts. "I... I know you say my name is Em, you are Ghen, this is a barn, and I am supposed to go with you to Henaden in three days. I assume that is the name of a place, but I do not know. There I am to get healing... for my forgetfulness?"

By the end, it was clear he was guessing. Knowing now what he was missing, Em's anxiousness to find this book was only growing. Even with his trust in Ghen, the vulnerability of not knowing was frightening.

Ghen nodded and spoke slowly, picking up on Em's anxiety. "Good, that's most of it. Of course, that 'three days' started two days ago. We should be leaving tomorrow to get you the help you need. Your notebook ought to explain all this and more. Why don't we start looking for it?"

"Yes," Em said, a little too emphatically.

For a moment Em thought he caught a slight smile on Jirus's face, but when he looked more directly, it was gone.

"Jirus," Ghen instructed, "run to the house and tell May that we're looking for Em's book. There's a chance it just got left behind at the house after dinner."

The younger boy nodded and dashed up the stairs, leaving Em and this stranger he apparently knew alone.

"Jirus..." Em asked carefully, "is he your son, Ghen-sa?"

"Em, you can drop the... oh, never mind. No, Jirus isn't my son, but he is a relative."

"Your forgiveness, but I do not trust him," Em admitted.

Ghen shrugged. "I get that. You may not remember, but he hasn't exactly acted as good folk should since you got here. May, my wife, and I are in the middle of trying to deal with that."

"I see," Em said carefully. He trusted Ghen reflexively but could not help being cautious around him. "I have searched through my things above and I have searched many places here as well. I was going to check under there before you came in," Em said, pointing to the hollow ramp.

"There?" Ghen asked. "I don't know why you'd put it in there, but if you want to check the planter, then have at it. I'm guessing you already searched the workbench, but I'll take another look if that's alright."

A planter? What could be grown within? Without another word, Em stepped around to the side of the ramp looking for a way in.

"The door is on the other side, kid," Ghen advised before Em had fully stepped around the right side.

"Eh? Ah, thank you, Ghen-sa."

On the other side, he did find a small doorway and opened it to pitch black. Quickly retrieving a lantern, he returned to find only dirt. Confused, he crawled in. Signs pointed that the earth was heavily disturbed. There'd been something growing here, but whatever it was, it'd been harvested. There was no point in his book being here, yet he stayed a little longer.

He knew so little. "I need something to fill the void." Em sought to fill his empty mind with something, anything. The emptiness was smothering.

Sifting through the upturned earth, he could find no leftover leaves or foliage. Feeling the air, it was dry.

"Dry winter air has not retreated yet," Em said naturally. So then it was past winter, but not by much. Did the lack of humidity rule out fungus? Em wasn't sure.

Deciding there was little more he could find, he started to leave. Turning, something caught his eye. As the lantern's light swept the soil, a small shadow did *not* move. Reaching out, Em grasped the shadow and pulled a small sprig of black from the ground—a remnant of the harvest.

Em's second voice of Nature recognized the small plant. *Nightroot.*

Em almost smiled. It was pointless information, but in a maelstrom of nothing, just knowing felt like finding a safe haven to cling to.

Glad we could help, Little Em, the older Instinct said kindly. *Don't worry, it will be okay.*

Steps echoing down the stairs drew Em from his discovery. Stepping out of the small planter, Em found Ghen looking down on Jirus and a young girl.

"Jirus, I want you to stick it out down here and keep looking. Kaddley, go on back upstairs and look in the hay where Em was camped out. If his book slipped into some crack in the night, maybe you could find it there. The pages didn't grow legs and just wander off, so it can't be far. I'll go talk to May and see if she has any other idea where it could be."

The little girl, apparently Kaddley, saw Em. She smiled and waved at him.

Not sure what else to do, he waved back as one did with small children.

Jirus followed the exchange, and his face darkened. "We'll take care of things, Ghen."

Ghen noticed Em peeking out. "Is it good with you if I go help out at the house while they search here?"

Em did not favor the choice of Jirus over Ghen, despite barely knowing either. By now, though, he'd guessed this was Ghen's home. While in his home, Em decided it would be disrespectful to reject his decision.

He nodded. "I will continue to search here."

"Good." he patted Kaddley's head as he passed by the little girl. "You keep an eye on these two for me."

She gave a childish salute. "Yes sir," and tromped up the stairs after her father to begin her search upstairs.

Walking toward Jirus, Em knew he was older. Even though Em wasn't too much greater in height. The more he thought about it the stranger it seemed that their height was so close even though he guessed his age was close to four to five falls greater. Ghen was rather tall too...

"Ah," Em said, looking down, "these are Ghen-sa's clothes."

Jirus snorted a laugh. "You really don't remember anything, do you?"

"Yes, were you not aware of that? Your relative seemed to be."

Jirus tilted his head one way and then the other, measuring Em and his response. "Yeah, well maybe I doubted," he said with a shrug. "I mean, if it were me, I wouldn't be so calm about it all. You know, with my only lifeline was missing and all."

Clearly, 'lifeline' referred to Em's journal. "If it is so dear to me, I do not think I would let it be far."

"Doesn't it scare you, though?" Jirus said unexpectedly. "The thought of what could happen if it's really gone? You'd be confused like this all the time. I don't think Ghen said it earlier, but you'll forget again and it's going to keep happening, too. No path to go forward, or back."

That struck a chord in Em, and he felt his heart shake under sudden turbulence.

What Jirus said felt frighteningly accurate. Since waking up he'd been desperate for anything, the idea of that going on forever was... unpleasant.

A cliff of panic was calling out to Em even now whispering the desire of watching him fall to despair.

"That is why we must search," Em said, fighting away the fear.

Jirus had one last comment for him. "You're right, you *need* those notes."

That was one comment too many.

Be wary child, he means to stoke your anger, Nature warned in a sudden growl.

"I understand, but why?" Em mumbled to himself.

As he and Jirus searched opposite sides of the barn, Em occasionally looked over his shoulder at Jirus. His searching was halfhearted at best.

"He does not care if we find the book." Em said to the voices in his shadow, but neither said anything back.

Em recalled how a moment ago, Ghen had said something about Jirus acting out. Had something happened to make Jirus wish to see him suffer? Em couldn't be sure. He tried to dismiss the thought. He had to find this book.

Yet Jirus had said almost the exact same thing. The more he thought of Jirus's words, the more anxious he became. His junior had definitely been trying to rile him up—and, sadly, had succeeded.

Em gritted his teeth but could hold in his bubbling apprehension no longer. His patience ran out, he was getting tired of not knowing. If Jirus held a grievance with Em, he would hear of it now. Em stood and turned, taking quick strides toward Jirus.

"Jirus," Em said powerfully.

Be careful, Instinct warned.

"Something the matter?" Jirus was unable to hide his subtle pleasure at seeing Em so emotional.

"Jirus..." Em started to say, but his anger and suspicion faltered. He was overcome with a very different feeling, curiosity.

Jirus waited, but Em didn't continue.

"Yes?" Jirus said finally, a little confused.

Em found himself peering at, well, at nothing. Nothing that he could see at least, but there *was* something. It hung in the air, between Jirus and

Em. Taking a step to one side and then the other, Em tried to find an angle where he might catch a glimpse of it. Disturbingly, he saw nothing.

Jirus's smile broadened for a moment before he caught it and closed it down.

Em didn't notice. "Jirus, is there anything here?" Em gestured to the empty air in front of him.

Jirus smirked. "No, and there aren't any books here either. You know though—"

"Em. Hey, Em." Ghen called down from above.

Em kept the supposedly empty air within the gaze of his peripheral view but tilted his head up towards his host. "Yes, Ghen-*sa*?"

"May says she recalls seeing your book at the house sometime yesterday. Come help us look there since, by this point, we've looked over the whole barn. Jirus, you and Kaddley keep on as you are just in case. You both are doing a good job, but if either of you have any idea where Em's book might be, just say something."

There was a long pause as Ghen waited for ideas. Kaddley and Jirus had nothing to offer. The silence stretched on, too long for mere suggestions.

He suspects Jirus has something to do with this, Em said internally.

Instinct didn't disagree.

With Ghen watching, Em no longer felt as motivated to interrogate Jirus. The idea of these notes had already become a symbol of hope to Em to help him fight off despair. Thus, he had to follow if there was any chance of finding what he'd lost.

Before following, however, Em looked back at the space where he'd felt the thing before. Its presence was less, but it was still there. He would ask Ghen about it later. If Ghen had a lead on his book, then he needed to follow it. Whatever this 'something' was, Em didn't get the impression it was dangerous. If that was true, it could wait.

Stepping up the stairs, he rubbed his temples as a slight headache was setting in. Em guessed this was another common symptom of whatever condition he had. If the book did not explain what his curse was, maybe Ghen knew. Em decided he should ask about that, too.

Em only stopped on the way out to collect the remainder of his things, including his swords. He'd lost one precious possession already and was in no rush to lose any more.

Once out, Em realized the barn looked much smaller than expected and that the lower floor was underground. The house was also built strangely, but he had little time to observe its features as Ghen quickly beckoned him in.

In the house, a woman waited for him and Ghen, a small child cradled in her arms.

Em lowered his head respectfully. "You must be May-*se*."

"Yes, and Em, I'm so sorry for what you've gone through this morning." Despite his fear, Em was comforted by her matronly compassion.

Em shook his head. "It does not seem it was any fault of yours. Still, I was told you might have seen where my book has gone."

"Actually," May said, hesitantly, "I'd like your help. Would you follow me to the washroom?"

CHAPTER 12

WITH GHEN AND EM gone, Jirus slowed down on the search, only picking things up when he thought Kaddley was looking. If she started to suspect, then she would say something. Kaddley couldn't help talking if she had the chance.

Minutes drifted by and Jirus found himself with the time to evaluate the situation. Things hadn't gone as originally planned, but that was fine. He'd expected Em to go wild a lot faster, but it still looked like he was beginning to fall apart. It sounded like he was even seeing things. There had been a moment when he'd feared Em had caught on and was going to force the journal out of him, but that had passed.

Soon Em would break, and Ghen wouldn't be able to do a thing. The only way to stop him would be with the book, and Jirus alone knew its location. The trick now would be making the right demands and getting the right assurances to make sure that Ghen did as he said after Jirus returned the journal.

Yes, that and—

A scream fled through the upper door and down to Jirus.

"It's started."

He raced out of the barn and to the house. Inside, it took only a moment to gather the situation, and it was perfect.

May was holding the young Ami in the kitchen. The moment Jirus ran in, she ran out past him to grab Kaddley. No surprise to Jirus, she would keep the girls safe. That was good, now Jirus knew they wouldn't get hurt.

Ghen was at the washroom door fighting to keep it from opening. A loud BANG against the door painted the picture of Em charging into the door to force it open. He was yelling inside in a language that Jirus couldn't even describe or begin to interpret.

Jirus guessed that, in a way, it was a good sign. Less reassuring was the fact that Em was small and even slamming into the door barely budged Ghen. He was supposed to be a fighter, was he even trying? Still, Ghen couldn't keep this up all day, but Em probably could.

Jirus could wait until Em got out on his own, but what then? What if it made negotiating tricky? What if Em was too tired to make Ghen do what he wanted? Still, he was a little impressed by Ghen and May.

Somehow, they'd convinced Em to put his swords aside. Jirus saw them lying on top of a small blanket thrown over the kitchen counter and some other things. They might have even tricked him in the washroom, too. Honestly, Jirus never would have expected the old rancher to betray Em.

The door shuddered as Em delivered a precise kick to its frame, and Ghen jolted as he felt the blow.

"Did you find the book?" Ghen shouted.

Jirus leaned one way, then the other. Should he start negotiating now, or wait until Em was free?

"What are you waiting for, boy?" Ghen said angrily. "Get over here and help me!"

Jirus felt a smile slide across his face. He was proud of how his little plan had come together. Why, he felt like the hero Jiffeil, from the stories he'd grown up on, who'd tricked the giant fox to steal its treasure.

This would be the first chapter in Jirus's own heroic story. Outsmarting a rancher wasn't a big achievement, but it would do for a start. From here to the watchmen, to the battlefield, and to the legend he would become!

"Why should I?" Jirus sneered, deciding that there wasn't any reason to wait after all.

"When Em breaks out, he could kill us all! You know that we have to keep him in here."

"He won't hurt anyone once I give him the book." Oh, this was so good. Ghen seemed a mix of angry and something else that Jirus couldn't quite read.

"You've had it the whole time, haven't you?" Ghen accused.

No point in hiding it now. Jirus basked in smiling down at the rancher. "Yes, and like you said, Em will hurt everyone. That is unless you do as I say and give me your entire ranch."

"What!?" Ghen asked in genuine surprise.

"Oh, don't worry, I don't want it. I'll give it back after I leave for the watchmen when I'm old enough, think of it as motivation to help me get in a little early. I just need to own it to make sure you'll honor our agreement." This hadn't been the plan, but it might work better than his original idea of just getting Ghen to promise to let him go to the watchmen. Either way, Jirus was riding high in the saddle now.

"Boy, don't be a fool, you—" Ghen started, but Jirus cut him off angrily.

"No! You're the fool! I warned you Em was dangerous when I first saw him, but you've taken in a freak. I told you I didn't want this life, and you made me look dumb in front of my friends. Then, you made it so I couldn't see them anymore! All so you could control me! Well, no more! I'm in charge, not you!"

Fighting the door, Ghen's face softened in pity, which only enraged Jirus.

How dare he pity me? Jirus thought. Was the rancher too dumb to see that he was the only one who could stop Em?

Ghen spoke in a pleading voice. "That book is his life in a way, boy. Do you think by taking them you've somehow gained something? You don't seem to..." Ghen stopped himself and shook his head.

Just then, Em bashed again and the distracted Ghen lost his footing. Em flew out of the door like a shadow fleeing the light.

Landing deftly, Em leapt to his swords and drew the longer blade with blinding speed. The flash of steel surprised Jirus, and he took an involuntary step back, drawing the young swordsman's attention.

"You have it," Em said with steel calm.

The voice was so lacking in emotion that Jirus faltered. Em's gaze was cold and Jirus shivered beneath it.

"Y- yeah and," Jirus stuttered, "and if you ever want to see it again, you'll force Ghen to do as I say."

He peered down at Ghen lying on the ground for a moment, but unbelievably the eyes came slowly back to Jirus.

"No."

What had he said? Quickly, Jirus tried again. "I'm serious..." Jirus tried to sound confident. "You'll never find it without me!"

Flicking his wrist, the steel blade wheeled around until its point faced Jirus directly. The blade swung so fast that Jirus barely noticed it was moving until it stopped and he was looking down its edge.

No, no! Em should be backing down. Jirus backed up until he found the wall of the house.

"Don't do it or... or..." Jirus warned, but Em only shook his head, taking slow steps toward the young boy.

What would he do? What could he do? This wasn't supposed to happen!

"Wait! Wait! I'll give it to you!" Jirus pleaded.

Em didn't respond but waited, his sword following Jirus as he rushed to the padded chair and flipped it over to retrieve the journal.

It wasn't there.

Jirus blinked, not believing his own eyes. "Where is it?" Jirus asked, nearly falling dead out of shock. Through the crossed planks, it was clear to see that the book was gone! "It was here. It was here!" Jirus repeated.

Where could it have gone? Little Ami? No, she was too small to have moved it, especially without someone seeing her. What could've happened?!

Jirus felt Em's shadow pass over him. All the color drained from his face, and he shrunk back. Sinking to the ground, Jirus crawled backward till his back met the wall again. He tried to say something, but all that came out were whimpers.

Em said nothing. Off of the clear steel, light glinted as the sword blurred in motion. Jirus clenched his eyes shut, unable to watch.

And nothing happened.

A slow scraping sound made Jirus open his eyes. Em was sheathing his weapon.

With the sword back in its place, Em strode back across the room to the blanket over the counter where the longsword had lain. He threw it back to reveal a small leather-bound book.

Em turned to Ghen and smiled keenly. "You flinched Ghen-*sa*. Did you think I was going to go back on my word?"

Ghen rubbed his face. "Well, there was a moment." When he let his hand drop, he was smiling too and shook his head. "You've got a mean streak, kid. The flurry with your sword at the end was a bit much."

"Even I agree with that," May said, stepping back into the house, pulling behind her two mildly confused children.

Em lowered his head in deference. "Your forgiveness then, please."

"You're forgiven," May said. "At least you made your point. Now, unless I'm mistaken, you've got a book to read. We've held you back long enough. Although I will ask you to step outside. We need to have a family chat."

He bowed again. "Yes, May-*se*. Thank you."

With that, Em collected his book, his second short sword, and the rest of his belongings from the kitchen counter. Before he was out of the door, Em already had his book open and was reading through it.

"Kaddley," May said sweetly, "please take your sister over there," she pointed to the far end of the house, "and play for a bit while we talk with Jirus. Okay?"

"So, everything is okay with Mr. Em?" Kaddley asked, sounding worried.

"He's fine now, dear." May shooed the children to the corner before stepping over to where Jirus sat in pants he began to realize were soiled. She picked up the overturned chair and sat facing him.

Ghen came alongside and grabbed the second of the two chairs and turned it towards Jirus as well.

"Y-you?" Jirus said. Everything was moving so fast.

"Me or rather Ami," May said. "I almost missed it while Ghen and I were talking about the journal. However, she said, 'Book' and I noticed she was pointing... well you can guess where." May patted her chair. "I really did almost miss it, but my little girl's a smart one, so I decided to do some looking. Tell me, did you know she saw you hide the journal or not?"

Jirus was too dumbstruck to answer, and May was too talkative to wait for him.

"No matter. The point is she did the right thing, and you most certainly did *not*. The moment we found the book, neither Ghen nor I held any doubt about how it got there. So, we came to a question. What are we going to do about you, boy?"

Jirus finally started to make sense of what had happened. He'd been set up! His fear and confusion quickly gave way to embarrassment, which then erupted into seething anger. "So, you tricked me? Tried to scare me into behaving like the good little brat you want me to be!"

"Trick you?" Ghen asked. "All we did was let you see how your plan would have worked out if it'd gone the way you thought."

"That's not what I expected, you made Em attack me!"

"Huh," Ghen scoffed. "Boy, did you forget I was in the room? He never touched you. You expected a scary marauder, and we asked Em to show you what that would be like."

"He wouldn't have acted like that!" Jirus said angrily.

"Oh really?" May said. "Then why didn't you catch on? We both know why. Em told us how you tried to drive him up a wall in the barn. You wanted him to go off, you just never considered he'd do it on you instead of us."

"I... I..." Jirus felt tears welling up, his anger failing him.

Ghen sighed. "Listen Jirus, we've warned you a hundred times that doing things like this could get you in trouble or hurt. We need you to understand. Do you think the watchmen would take some kind of joke like this well?"

"I'd be a hero with them," he mumbled.

"That, or the same dead nobody you're scared of being anyways," May said.

"What did you say?" Jirus had heard wrong, he'd had to. He'd never told them...

"Em," May explained, "yesterday he commented to me that he believed you were afraid of being a nobody and it was your reason for acting out. I wasn't so sure then, but after your yelling a moment ago I think I might have changed my mind. So now that you've seen what *could* have happened, and now that we understand where this all comes from, you get a choice."

"One I think you should take seriously," Ghen commented.

May nodded along. "Very seriously. Creative problems mean creative punishment, and this scheme with Em was very creative. Before that, though, we have an announcement to make. In five falls, you'll be able to join the watchmen by law and we will bring you to enlist ourselves."

Jirus blinked, confused all over again.

May wasn't finished, though. "That is happening unless you decide you don't want to join them after all. What happens when we get there, that's your choice. If you straighten up this foolish streak, then Ghen or I will go to whoever is enlisting and give them a great report of all you've done from this day until then."

Then her tone shifted. "On the other hand, this is your first and last warning. If you ever do anything like this again, I will personally tell every ear that will listen how you wet yourself when one of your little pranks backfired so that it gets around to everyone you know.

"Afterward, when we meet this official for registration, Ghen or I will tell this enlistment personnel how destructive, insubordinate, and lazy you are. Then I will pass you off to them without a good word on your behalf. That will get you notoriety and I'm sure they will be just thrilled to have you."

Jirus sat with an open mouth, digesting what he'd just heard and its implications.

"As I said, this is your *only* warning," May reminded him. "No need to tell me which you choose. How you act will say more than enough."

Promptly she stood and looked at Ghen. "Now before this began, we were going to break our morning fast. As it's been delayed, I'm quite hungry." Then she strode off to the kitchen, throwing a swift glance towards the two girls to make sure all was in order.

"Ghen, if you could get Bo and the cart ready," May requested after the late breakfast was finished. "I have a bit of finery I promised to loan to the Redgens since their daughter is getting married soon. Besides, I want to sit and catch up on the goings on with them. As they will be wanting to do with us." That last statement was obvious bait for a response, and she got it.

"You won't tell them what happened this morning, right?" Jirus sounded desperate. "I'm really sorry, don't tell them."

"Was that a request or a demand, Jirus?" May asked skeptically. "I thought you'd gotten all your demands out earlier today."

Ghen lifted his mug to hide his grin.

"I'm sorry, May, please don't tell them," Jirus pleaded.

"Jirus, if me talking about current events embarrasses you, maybe it's time that you look in the mirror and figure out why you seem to keep getting yourself into embarrassing situations. Don't worry though, a promise is a promise, as long as you choose to do as we talked about earlier, I see no need to mention any specific details you would find... awkward. That's despite how much I might be tempted." May smiled mischievously.

Jirus's eyes darted back and forth, trying to find the words. All he found was a solemn, "Thank you."

May sighed, dropping her gloating pretext. "I'm serious, as long as you hold up your part, I'll keep mine. For now, you have other matters you should be worrying about. This deal covers your problems today, but yesterday I told you that for your involvement in that scuffle, you'd have a little extra to do today. We need to get ready for Em and Ghen to leave. Gather all the linens and dirty clothes for a wash after lunch. Then you can..."

May was still instructing Jirus when Ghen leaned over to Em to quietly ask, "Would you mind coming with me as I get Bo ready? I want to talk for a bit."

Em had heard during the search earlier that Bo was the mule in the barn. He left the house with Ghen and took a moment to look back. May was finally finished giving instructions and Jirus appeared to regretfully accept.

Em wondered how much Jirus would learn from this experience. He didn't know the specifics of this deal, but it clearly meant a lot to Jirus.

Entering the barn, they descended to the lower landing.

Ghen wheeled out his cart as he spoke. "I think what happened this morning is my fault."

"I am not sure I would agree. You did not steal my notes."

"Yes, but he's my responsibility."

"You made it clear he was not your son. Why is he your responsibility?"

Ghen shook his head. "It's because I'm raising the boy now. I know you don't know why he's with us, but that doesn't matter, the point is he is with us and is our responsibility."

"It was his choice. He is old enough to suffer a consequence. I know little of your ways and heard little of this deal, but to me, I think he is getting off lightly."

Ghen looked at Em carefully and then shook his head. "You don't know it, but we had this conversation yesterday."

"Eh? I... my apologies," Em said, suddenly very aware of how foolish he might sound repeating himself.

"Nope, it's not on you, kid. All we really came to was that you've lived a bit of a different life. Though we also talked about setting you up for a better one after we get you all fixed up."

'We can still grow.' The Em of yesterday had left a message saying that. Em guessed that was what Ghen was referring to.

"Thank you." There was a short awkward silence and Em tried to clear the air. "Was there not something you wished to talk about?"

"Hmm? Oh, not really. I just wanted to get us out of the house and give Jirus some space. He's got a lot to think through right about now."

"I do not doubt that," Em said and stepped forward to assist Ghen.

As the rancher pulled Bo out of her stall, she fought back. Even with Em's help, it was a struggle to get the beast into motion.

"She's in a stinkin' mood again," Ghen growled.

As they tied her to the cart, the mule kicked it with a rattling *klunck*!

"Hey! What did the cart do to you?" Ghen said. "Keep this up and we'll see if I bring any extra sugar back with us from Henaden."

The mule snorted but calmed.

Em wondered for a moment if the mule really understood. Ghen did have a strange way with the animal, even when he complained about the mule, Em felt no sense of hatred. Annoyed perhaps, but to Ghen it was part of her personality.

He loves this place, these animals, Em muttered to himself as he watched the exchange. *He is as much a part of this land as the soil and sky.*

But he is in danger of losing his home, Nature speculated.

Could that be? Where was that thought from? Em, at least the Em of today, wasn't sure what evidence Nature had seen to suggest such a thing.

Yet he had to ask. "Ghen-*sa*, are you in danger of losing your home?"

Ghen went rigid with surprise but recovered well. He pretended to have some ache, and that the sudden motion was to relieve his back. "Danger, no. We're safe from dangerous stuff around here 'cause of the southern mountains and the woods. No one has reason to come through here and cause real trouble."

"Not physical danger clearly, but there is a threat. Is there not?"

Leading Bo up out of the barn's lower floor and the back doors, Ghen shrugged. "So, you heard about my troubles with selling and the land? Don't worry about it, we can handle it." Yet there was a shadow of a doubt in his voice.

"Yes, Ghen-*sa*," Em said, letting the conversation drop.

Yet, the forces beyond had brought Em to the door of one who'd been kind enough to aid him. As a matter of honor, it was only right to make some repayment.

What little he had of the common metal coins, halaks Em believed they were called, needed to be saved for the mystic. He did not know what Master D'gui would charge for their service.

Despite the lack of money, perhaps there would be another way to repay the rancher.

After May left to meet her fellows at a nearby crossroads for a small exchange of supplies and gossip, Em stole away to add a note onto the back of one of the last pages in his notebook.

After recovering his journal, he'd scanned all of its pages. If he did the same tomorrow after waking, that Em would find written...

> We have a debt to the rancher, Ghen, and his family. In our
> need, he gave up much for our aid. Yet, I fear he risks his
> precious home in aiding anyone.
> I do not know where this risk comes from, but we must find
> out. How can we find our lives and cost him his?
> From the Em of yesterday.

Fearing that the Em of tomorrow wouldn't be able to recognize the threat without more context about Ghen's family, Em made small notes about each family member. He wrote down facts about their relations and details Instinct brought up.

The moment he began to write the notes he became more and more adamant about writing down as much as he could about them all. Not just to learn more about what the threat to their home was, but to remember them.

Even if he only remembered on the page, every Em of a new day would know this family and that, somewhere in the world, there were still people worth trusting.

When he was finished, he looked at his notes and found he wore a grin.

It was odd, why should he care for these people? As far as he could remember, he only met them this morning, but he did care. Em could feel that part of himself did not want to trust them, but it was as if the decision had already been made.

"I am glad it is them. They will be the first people I remember in a long time."

CHAPTER 13

THE REMAINING DAY PASSED uneventfully until finally, night fell. As day rose again with renewed strength, Ghen found he was rather excited. It was finally time to get on the road.

Ghen stepped into the barn, somewhat more carefully than yesterday, after the surprise of that morning's events. However, much like his first morning in the barn, Ghen found Em practicing on the lower floor of the barn. Back in his old clothes, Em looked much like he had when they first met, except cleaner.

After the wash, Em had been pleased to reclaim his ragged clothes. Probably because they fit him much better than Ghen's had. The kid's gray and brown camouflaged coat was folded on the workbench as Em stepped and dashed around the barn floor, fighting shadows.

A board creaked under Ghen's foot as he stepped down the stairs, and Em's careful ears picked it out. Em stepped around and, coming to a rest, looked up at Ghen.

He didn't quite smile, but there was an extra light in his eyes. Ghen changed his mind, Em did look different from when they'd first met after all. He still looked tired and probably had gotten up far too early again, but there was more life in him than before. He wasn't as worn down. He was nowhere near his full strength, Ghen could tell. Still, Em looked better, and a little excited too.

His best guess was that Instinct, or whatever, knew the day's plans even if Em might not. So he was just as, if not more, excited than Ghen to be on their way.

"In case you haven't figured it out yet, I'm Ghen."

Em bowed. "Thank you Ghen-*sa*. As I suspect you know, I am Em Dér."

"That's right. Sounds like you've already read through everything. I guess that means you understand our little arrangement."

"Yes, but do you mind if I ask a question?"

"Go ahead."

"How long have I been here? My notes say that we are supposed to leave after three days, but Instinct tells me that we are closer to my departure than that."

The rancher grinned and stepped down the stairs. "Three days Em, that's how long you've been here." Reaching the boy, Ghen held out his hand and, when Em took it, Ghen gave it a congratulatory shake. "We're raring to go, kid."

Em blinked in surprise. "Ah, thank you again Ghen-*sa*. I will endeavor to make myself ready."

"I think you gathered most of your gear last night. If you go down and pull out the cart, you can go ahead and put your stuff in it. I'll collect the nightroot I'm planning to sell, and that should let us leave right after breakfast."

"Once more, thank you." Em bowed.

"That's enough of that, I'm just doing my part. Besides, the three days you spent here weren't the peaceful rest I'd hoped I could give you."

"Hmm, your relative Jirus, I assume."

Ghen blinked. "Huh? How'd you know that?"

"I made notes about your family. You did not know?" Em asked, surprised. "Apparently, I thought it wise. Do not worry Ghen-*sa*, the Em of yesterday also made note that Jirus was handled. Whatever trouble he gave me, I have no grievance against him."

Even if he did have a grudge, it wasn't like he'd remember it, anyway. What was with the notes, though? Ghen wasn't exactly mad or embarrassed, just a little confused. "Okay then, glad to hear it. Why don't you go on and start getting ready?"

Em lowered his head deferentially one final time before stowing his blade and making his way up the barn stairs.

Ghen walked over to Bo and patted her neck. "He made notes. How about that, girl?" He thought for another second before asking, "Do you think the boy we met on the road would have done that? All he seemed to care about was getting to Henaden or trying to figure out what he'd lost. Not that I blame him, mind you. I just don't think he trusted or cared about us."

Bo flicked her ears and blew a rush of air out of her nose.

"Yeah, I think he looks a little happier too," Ghen agreed and gave her a sidelong glance. "So, don't go and ruin his mood when he and I come to get you after we eat."

Bo snorted.

Ghen rolled his eyes at the mule. Opening a nearby barrel, he scooped out feed and tossed it into her trough. "There, now you're fed, too. So, no more complaints," he said with a wag of his finger.

Bo's reply was the heartfelt sound of chewing.

Leaving the barn, Ghen stepped around to the lines of root that still hung on the drying lines, the crop had turned out plentiful despite the early harvest. He still only collected two bags, but they were full bags. He'd had been worried at least one would only be half full, but it would seem the rancher had some favor after all.

Jirus had done the job of collecting and storing the shoots of root they would need to begin the next season's crop, so they were set to go. If, the heavens willing, the next harvest was good too, maybe he could fight Noren off without much effort this time.

Toting his bags back, he easily tossed them in the back of the cart with Em's things.

"You know, Em," he announced, "I think this is a pretty good... Em?"

Off to the side, Em stood on the dusty floor of the barn staring with intensity at nothing.

"Ghen-*sa*, do you see anything here?" Em was gesturing toward the open air.

"Nope. Do you see something?"

"I do not, but is there not still something here?" Em waved his hand out like he was trying to find something. He squinted for a moment before drawing his hand back to rub his head, nursing a sudden ache.

Ghen walked closer and glanced around. "Not that I can tell."

Em didn't look convinced.

"Could be that your head is playing tricks on you," Ghen suggested. "Maybe something to do with that issue you got, or you just need to get some water and food in you."

"That may be," Em said, halfheartedly still inspecting the nothing. "I cannot feel it at the moment, but it comes and goes."

"Well, let's get you some food. If it's just a hunger thing, it's easily fixed and I'm hungry myself. Unless you think it's dangerous in some way."

Em shook his head. "Instinct says it's not dangerous."

"Good, May probably has everything out by now. She's my wife, by the way, in case you didn't note that."

Em nodded. "I had, and I admit I am hungry." Em took one last look at the seeming nothing before moving upstairs.

Ghen held back slightly to make one last study of the area. He didn't see or feel anything.

All the same, Em might have a better sense of things than a rancher, Ghen thought. If he still felt something was there later, maybe Ghen would need to take more time with it. Rumors said that mystics and wizards were always letting loose strange happenings all over the world. Small chance those stories were ever true, but good folk could never be too careful.

Watching Em at the morning meal, there was little that was different from the other mornings. He observed the house with the same speculative glance, took a moment to inspect the fireplace, and listened to stories and gossip he'd heard at least four times in his three days without recognizing a thing.

What was different was how he acted around these 'new' things. What had been alien before was now only curious. Before he'd hidden in the talkativeness of Ghen's girls, this morning he accepted it instead.

Stepping up to May, Ghen whispered in her ear, "I think he's getting comfortable."

May rubbed her chin. "I'm glad, but that's sad, in a way."

"What do you mean?"

"It's a shame that right when he's finally figuring things out, he has to leave. Not that there's any other choice." She faced him. "That boy needs help."

Ghen nodded. "I'll make sure he gets it. That's what good folk do."

May rolled her eyes. "You know, I think I've heard that somewhere before. My point is, let's make sure we leave him better than we found him."

"Yes ma'am. I was actually meaning to say I figured I'd stay an extra day or two in Henaden if need be, to make sure he gets on with this mystic okay. The field needs to rest anyways, and while we've got Jirus willing to be helpful, might as well use it."

"You be careful too," May said. "I don't need to remind you that you've been ambushed on the road before, and dealing with magic sounds very... complicated. Come back safe." She looked at him sternly. "That's not a request, Ghen Jarden."

He smiled. "Yes ma'am."

No sooner did May step away than Jirus stepped up. He met Ghen's eye and began to shift from one foot to the other, working up the courage to speak.

"No, you can't come along," Ghen said. "I need you here."

Jirus sighed. "I know I've caused you trouble, but I can help out a bunch on the road. I promise I'll do what you tell me."

"On a normal day, that would be the best thing to hear, but it's still no." Jirus probably wanted to try to put his name in with the watchmen branch in Henaden. "You know our deal. We'll get you signed up in a few falls. It's too soon and think of this as a chance to prove you are committed to our agreement."

Jirus didn't give up. "The ranch will be fine, it's only going to be a few days, right?"

"I expect it could be a bit longer. So, show me you can handle it, and that you can learn. If you do, maybe next time I go on one of my shorter trips, you can come along."

"Yes sir," he said regretfully and then went over to the table to find any remaining slices of bread and sulk.

One day, Jirus would make something of himself. He had too much ambition for it to be any other way. The problem was, he had all that drive far too soon. If he could learn patience and maybe a little character, Ghen had no doubt he could go far at whatever he tried.

Over the next two hours, the sun clawed its way up the sky, stretches of light marking the ground where it had torn off strips of shadow. In those shrinking shadows came a good chance to get on the way. Goodbyes were brief, and well-wishes were kindly given. Everything in its place and ready to go, the cart rolled away from Ghen's family home.

Em was surprised to find that he felt like he might miss this place, despite not remembering any of the events the family had told him about. He caught Ghen looking back as well, the rancher wished he could stay too, but neither of them said a word aloud. The road called, and they would answer.

"The trip should only take five days for me," Ghen explained. "Two days there, a day to sell the root and make the purchases needed in Henaden, and then two days back."

"Then, why did your wife plan out what your family could do for up to two weeks with you away?"

"Oh, that... It's just a precaution. You never know with these things."

He didn't sound convincing. Yet Em made no comment, guessing it was for his benefit.

Deciding to change the subject, Em asked, "Ghen-*sa* why did you ask me if I could still sense anything in the barn?"

After breakfast, when they had finished loading the cart for the journey, Ghen had asked him to try to sense what he had before in the barn.

"Just being careful," Ghen said. "Too much this week has caught me by surprise already. You said there was nothing there afterward, so it should not be a problem."

"I agree that there is no problem. However, what I said was 'I am not sure,' not that there was nothing. There is a difference."

"If you think there might be something, how can you be sure it isn't a problem?" Ghen took another look back, but now with worry.

"Instinct and Nature," Em said as if that explained everything.

"Them again," Ghen muttered. He lifted his hat and scratched the top of his head. "Well, so far, they seem to be good at sorting out things like that. Since I trust you, I guess I'll leave it alone." Despite what he said, Ghen did try to sneak a last glance over his shoulder.

Bo led the cart down to the main road and they both finally passed out of view of the ranch.

"You said it should only be two days to Henaden. Then many mysteries may become clear," Em said. He tried to hide the excitement welling up in him, but it still managed to worm its way into his words.

"That's right. Two days of traveling, my friend, and we'll be there."

Em hoped desperately that this Master D'gui could heal his mind, but feared it could still come to nothing. All the same, he was so close now to where the master should be, he felt he could hold on to hope a little longer. He was *so* close.

Distracting himself from the fear, Em tried to enjoy the chance to travel with a friend. It was a surprisingly comforting idea. Instinct told him it had been a very long time since he'd last had the chance to do so. Repetitive amnesia made allies hard to come by.

Em leaned back as the cart bumped along and let his mind wander. The sky became his muse as the world walked by. Clouds passed freely overhead, and Em imagined each of the puffy shapes being watched by someone else far away, someone who knew him and maybe even missed him.

Bo paced down the road with a ready step as the morning passed. The cart could keep a quick pace since its supplies were so little and light. For this trip, they carried the travel supplies, Em's pack, the nightroot, Ghen's hunting bow, and a walking stick.

The cart bumped on a rock and Em was forced to sit up. While he was up, he spotted in the distance a home that could've almost been a copy of Ghen's own.

"I see it as a strange way to build a house, but I think I am, in fact, the strange one," Em said to himself.

Ghen was tempted to make a joke but wasn't sure how it would go over, so he let it go.

As the cart came down a steeper depression in the road, they both naturally rocked back to balance themselves. While on the rise, Em saw the way ahead. Quickly they were coming toward a wall of trees that only broke on the road itself. To either side, the forested hills grew thick.

"What forest is this?"

"Koen Forest," Ghen answered, "though this is just an edge. We'll be in it until we get close to Henaden, but it's longer than it is wide. That means we'll be out early the day after tomorrow. The rest of the woods flies out west."

Em reached into the back of the cart and from his bag drew out his notes. Thumbing through them, he saw no sign that he had taken much notice of either the strange houses or any forest. There was still so little he knew of this land. All he had about it were meager notes of its history and that of its neighbor.

Em thought of Ghen's bow, the rancher had said it was for hunting should they want more than bread to eat. Yet Em wondered if there was another reason. Before he left, May had pulled Em aside and asked him to watch out for the rancher, and now that thought came back to Em.

"Are thieves common in your country?"

"In the whole country?" Ghen said. "Dunno, probably not. We're supposed to be more peaceful than Yongarad, at least, that's our neighbor to the south, but I don't think there's a place in the world without any bad folk."

"And this road?"

Ghen rocked his head back and forth. "So May talked to you, I guess? Well yes, this road has had some unsavory characters in days past. Henaden's a trade city, which means there are people with nice goods coming in and fat bags of money going out. That can draw in some folk you don't want to meet alone in the dark.

"Though actually, this way used to be safe, seeing as not many rich folks use this road. Sad to say, I guess it isn't anymore. I got beat up early last summer on the road and lost a good bit of money, but I'm being smarter this time. Besides, even most folk who use this road to sell at Henaden won't come this way for another two weeks or more. That's a benefit of harvesting early, I guess. Thieves won't be watching the roads this early."

Em had a thought. "My notes say that there is a law by one of Ifeldia's kings, which makes it difficult for tribes other than humans to act in this part of your nation."

"That's right."

"Will Henaden be only humans, then?"

Ghen snorted a laugh. "Not hardly. I don't travel much, but in most cities that fall under the human edict, they check to make sure you're human before you can do anything. Henaden, on the other hand, is the exception. Since doing that would kill their trade they more or less ignore the rules. You could have feathers sticking out behind your ears, but if you tell the gate master at Henaden you're human, he'll let you straight in, no questions asked."

"They are exempt?"

"No, they just don't care to follow the rules. You know, speaking of that edict, Uncle Grady said that the area it covers is actually the old borders of the small country this area was before Roleius took it over as part of Ifeldia. That's probably part of how King Ordisus got away with making the edict cover it."

"Why here, what did this nation do?"

"No idea, maybe Ordisus just has more power here or maybe this old land did something. I only know that before it was part of Ifeldia, it was called En-Athen. Pop, my dad's dad, said that he knew people who still called it En-Athen even after Roleius took over."

"You say you have not traveled much, but I have seen you write even today, so you have been educated. Was there not some teacher to tell you more of these things so that you would not have to travel?" Em asked.

"No, the last real teacher in the area died when I was young. Others either learned in Henaden, if they had money, or from family. After that teacher passed Uncle Grady, Pop, and my parents were the ones that taught me." Ghen smiled. "I was lucky, actually. Uncle Grady was a common soldier, but he learned a lot while in the Watchmen Brigade. Do you have them in your notes?"

Em nodded.

"Good, well when he came back, what he'd seen had beat him up, but he had enough wit to share what he knew. He made sure as the day, none of his kids, nieces, or nephews would be fools. He'd seen enough people taken in just because they couldn't read or math out what their work was worth. Cons and cheats are everywhere, and he wanted us smart enough to be able to pick them out. So, I learned to read, write, and even count large amounts so I'd know what my work was worth."

There was a bitterness in Ghen's voice that Em guessed meant that other ranchers had not been so lucky. Em considered making a note about the sellers in Henaden not being trustworthy but wasn't sure he would have trusted them anyway.

A smiling seller is the first of many lies, Old Instinct said, equal parts amused and annoyed.

Em knew it was a quote but had no clue where Instinct was pulling it from.

"How are your cities managed? Your council cannot take on all their affairs."

Ghen shook his head. "No, the big old council of rulers picks out generals and governors to watch the military and cities. According to Uncle Grady, they can also be both. Those folks are second only to the council itself in their city, so they're a big deal."

"If your army is spread over Ifeldia, how can banditry be so common?"

"Ha!" Ghen laughed. "No, the leaders *can* be generals but aren't usually. Don't forget, we are at war too even if we don't see it here locally. The army is too busy to watch out for bandits. I hear most of the army is sent to the southwestern mountain pass near Old Yongarad."

Em gave Ghen a questioning look at that name. "Old Yongarad?"

"Oh right, so before Yongarad was the big bad it is now it was just a city. At least according to—"

"Uncle Grady," Em finished.

Ghen grinned "Told you I learned a lot from him. Now that city is called Old Yongarad, while the country just took the main part of the name."

"That cannot be Yongarad's capital if it is so close to your border."

"No, I don't think it is. It's just where the country started out, not that I have any idea where their capital is."

"How did it go from a city to what it is now?"

"See, I'm not totally sure," Ghen said. "Some say that when King Roleius... do you have him written down?"

"The conqueror who made Ifeldia so large," Em said, recalling from his writings.

"That's the one. When he was conquering what became Ifeldia a lot of people ran from the war. When they did, they went to Old Yongarad to build up an army and stop the king from taking more. Though I don't think they ever fought Roleius, so that could be hogwash. Others who don't believe that usually say that their leader got the dread together and used them to make it a country."

"Dread," Em said, with a chill.

It's a title, Little Em. One given to dark wizards of great power in Yongarad, Em's Instinct said, and then it changed. Instinct's place was taken by the deeper, younger, and gruffer voice of Nature. *They are dangerous, you cannot fight them directly. If you come to face one, flee.*

Ghen couldn't hear their voices, so Em decided to keep how much he knew to himself.

Not hearing the invisible voice, Ghen kept on. "Still, Yongarad got lots of fighters, however they grew. More people need more land. So, Yongarad pushed out and took the whole other side of the southern mountains opposite Ifeldia. From what Uncle Grady told me, they did that by offering rewards to thieves, killers, and troublemakers they helped the army conquer."

"Marauders." Em had no doubt that was who Ghen was referring to.

"Yep. Grady said Yongarad made three guilds that these folk could sign up at. My uncle said these groups even compete to see who finishes jobs first to get rewards. That's supposed to make them more ruthless since they each want to be the biggest and baddest. The army also picked up some powerful sorcerers and mystics. Those are people I mentioned called Dread, not sure why they're called that, but I hear their extra bad news. Less reliable folk say their sorcery makes a bunch of fighting monsters and other bad stuff. I think whatever Grady saw of those guilds and monsters is what scared him home."

"Hmm." Em tried to imagine what a dread with a monster might look like.

In his mind, he imagined an elderly hag looking down on him and next to her an animal that might have been part hound and part lizard, and rows of needlelike teeth in its gaping maw. The image was clearer than Em expected, and he pushed it aside as it came to mind.

"That's about as much as I know about them. In the end, Ifeldia's been able to keep them from taking our land for a long time now."

"How long have the two nations been at war?" Em asked.

"No clue, it's been on and off for as long as I can remember. Grady said there were a few small mountain passes where they could attack through. The only other place to get through is near Old Yongarad and Oredel."

"Where is that?"

Ghen thought for a moment. "Been a long time since I saw a map with it, but I think it's on the eastern coast. Really, on the opposite end of the mountains from Old Yongarad. I heard once that it's a fortress city. It's difficult for them to reach us, and for us to reach them. Because the fighting is so contained, it doesn't feel like what I imagine war to be."

"Most likely, they seek your capital. Actually," Em said after a sudden thought, "since you have many rulers, do you have a single capital?"

"We do," Ghen said as he leaned back to counter the slope of the hill the cart was rolling slowly down. "That would be the city of Roldea, named after King Roleius. It's east of us and a little north, basically in the center of everything, from what maps tell me. Of course, if you want to know more about important places in Ifeldia, make a note about Korodai. That's the place on the far eastern coast. Word is that all those who can use magic end up there to become a sorcerer or one of the Guardians of the Blessed."

"I definitely will."

In the silence that followed, an ominous wind blew over Em and his thoughts. His body retained some understanding of what it experienced, but nothing in the conversation felt in the least familiar. It was already clear

Ifeldia was not his home but what of Yongarad? According to what he'd heard his clothes did look like they belonged to a foreign military.

There was no answer from Instinct and Nature in clear words. There was a mix of emotions, but none that made any sense. Giving up, he looked at his journal and was going to read when all around them darkened.

Armies of clouds marched in rank to cut off the advance of the sun. Many bore a fierce countenance that was enough to make Em worry. "I fear it may rain. That could slow our pace."

"Oh no, not now," Ghen growled.

For a moment, Em thought he was talking about the chance of rain, but the rancher wasn't looking up.

Instead, Ghen had been looking at something that, in his opinion, might be worse than a bit of rain. "I'm afraid that weather may not be the biggest problem. They might." He nodded forward, down the road.

Approaching opposite of them was a small travel party. Three of the party were on horseback, and one drove a covered wagon with a banner sticking up above it. The banner was a deep blue, adorned with an image of a sleeping cat beside a sack of coins at its center. Ghen knew it well.

"Who is that?"

"That flag, is the symbol of the Noren Trading Company," Ghen said darkly.

CHAPTER 14

EM ROUSED HIS SENSES in response to Ghen's worried tone of voice. "Then you have met these traders before?"

"I've had the displeasure. If I'm not mistaken, one of those riders will be Dorig Noren himself, the company's owner. He's a rich metal merchant from Henaden who's been buying lots of land out here. Fair warning, he and I don't get along very well."

Em had difficulty imagining Ghen not getting along with anyone.

"Are the others also traders?"

"If that is Mr. Noren, then no. He usually has a guard or two with him. I bet that riders one and two are just that. The wagon driver is probably just someone who works for Mr. Noren. He prefers to handle all the dealings himself when it comes to those of us out here, any other traders would just get in his way." Ghen paused and tilted his head.

"What is it?"

"It's strange that he's visiting his lands at this time of the season. It's usually too early for him to pick up stock or crops and too late for him to bring seed, fertilizer, or other supplies to the places he owns out here. Also, he'd send someone instead of coming if it were either of those. That means he's planning to try and buy again, but from who? This is the wrong time for that. I guess it doesn't matter. If he wants to act like an idiot, I'll let him."

Em was surprised at the amount of disgust in Ghen's voice.

"You have said they may be a problem. How?"

Ghen hesitated before explaining. He hated that he was being forced to bring Em into this but there was little he could do to avoid it. "Short version is, he's been trying to buy my land and have me work it for a while now. Well, I'm not selling."

Em had a sense that this was the threat to Ghen's home his journal had urged him to seek. If so, this interaction could prove to be very revealing. Em kept his eyes open and tried to absorb every detail he could.

Two of the riders broke from the rest and picked up their pace to meet Ghen's cart. Ghen slowed the cart on their approach. As Em perceived the riders more clearly, it was easy to guess what role each one filled.

The lead man sported a neatly trimmed light brown beard and delicately combed hair. He was robust and garbed himself in an expensive green coat with golden stitching around the collar and cuffs. The merchant, without a doubt.

The other rider was a guard. To Em's surprise, she was a woman. Under her studded leather chest piece and leather strapped cap, it wasn't easy to realize until she was much closer. Her long hair was in a tight braid that went down her back. Her face was grim but calm, she didn't expect a fight, but Em wondered if she desired one. He made note of a shining broadsword on her hip and the bow she kept laid across her saddle.

"Greetings Ghen!" Noren face was etched with a broad smile. "How goes it on your land?"

"Hello Mr. Noren, things are going well." Ghen sounded polite, but it was obvious he hoped to avoid talking to this merchant.

That didn't put the man off. "Great to hear. Have you planted for fall yet, and how is your herd doing?"

"We planted all but one field, it's plowed and resting. The animals are good too. As always, it's nice to see you, but we need to get to Henaden and it's a long way."

Before Ghen could spurn Bo forward, the merchant broke in again. "Oh, don't be like that, Ghen. I haven't seen you since I purchased your northern fields last fall. Let's take a second to catch up and talk business. You haven't even introduced me to this young man yet."

Noren's tone was very friendly, but Em got the impression that Noren was gloating. All the friendly smiles in the world couldn't hide that neither man liked the other.

Ghen kept his eyes forward on the road and urged Bo to start moving again. "Em, that's Mr. Noren. Mr. Noren, this is Em. He's been helping me out a bit in exchange for a ride to Henaden. As for business, I thought I already told you how my business is doing. Besides, I'm sure you're as busy as we are. So why don't you move along?"

As the cart began to pull away, Noren called after them, "Be careful out there, Ghen. The roads have gotten dangerous, you know."

Once they had gained some distance from Noren and his traveling party, Ghen started to relax again.

"Your Noren-*sa* seemed friendly, but I do not think he likes you any more than you like him," Em observed.

"Good. He's tried hard to get me to sell my land, but May and I have held firm," Ghen said with pride.

"So, you dislike him just because he tried to get you to sell?" Em didn't really care who Ghen liked and disliked. His interest was in the reason, it was too odd.

"It isn't like that. Well, it isn't exactly like that. Listen, the problem I have is that after I told him 'No' multiple times, the man got mean. He's making it hard for me to work without him on my side, all to try and change my mind."

"He's trying to force it on you, then?" That made more sense.

"Right. That isn't all though, he's never said as much, but the way he looks at me and my family..." Ghen trailed off. "It's hard to explain, but it makes me want to knock him flat every time I see him."

"I am not sure I understand."

Ghen sighed, seeking the right words to explain. "It's like he doesn't care. Something in his eyes tells me he doesn't give a lick about the land he's buying. Probably cares even less about the people who live there. All that and then he smiles at us and pretends to be friendly. He hates everyone, and that isn't how good folk should act."

"He hates everyone?" Em didn't see why this merchant should dislike someone he'd never met before.

"Not you," Ghen said, misreading Em's words. "I think he hates ranchers, farmers, and that kind of folk. Oh, he acts like we're family, but

I'd bet my left leg up to the knee that he thinks we're all as good as the dirt he walks on." With that, Ghen spat off to the side of the cart as if he'd tasted something rotten.

Em struggled with the logic of it all. "Then why is he so friendly? Why buy all the land?"

"I don't know!" Ghen said with uncharacteristic anger. "He's a metal merchant! What's he going to do with a bunch of farms and ranches? And why should he care if I don't want to sell?"

Ghen was right, it didn't make much sense to Em either. "He has made things difficult, then?"

The rancher shook his head. "I'm doing all I can to keep from selling out at all, but especially to him. My problem is that my options are getting slim."

Em leaned back and whispered to himself questions he would note later. "Why *did* a metal merchant want the land, and want it so desperately that he would bully those who were reluctant?" This was indeed the problem Ghen faced. Now it was up to him to see what he could do to help.

In the distance, watching Ghen's cart roll away, Noren cursed it and its owner twice over. "How dare that seed-planting, cow-herding, wretch treat me like that! Dismissing me like a dog at his table. Who did he think he was speaking to? Dorig Noren is a name that he should be honored to know, not treat like a beggar looking for loose coin."

When the cart was gone, Noren spat disgusted on the ground they'd passed over.

Noren shook his head, Ghen was a fool who didn't know a good deal when he saw one. The two of them had gone back and forth about the land, and Noren had tried everything he could do above board and more below to get him to cave in. Still, the fool held on. Ghen and his wife were a real pain in Noren's side. No matter what they did, it was only a matter of time before he won. They should just simply give in!

They couldn't hold out forever, but that wasn't enough. Waiting until eventually was too slow. Noren needed them to sell sooner.

"You know Nedain," he said to his guard. "The Noren Trading Company now owns all of the region's farmland, save a very few parts. Colrage, Jarden, Erngen, and Milren are the four families I haven't gotten to sell yet.

"The Colrage family has too large a farm and is too well connected to put any pressure on them to sell. The Erngen and Milren families are just too far. I've worked hard and the Milren couple will sell out soon despite that, I can just feel it, but I'm not sure about the Erngen group. Then it's Ghen and May, they're close enough and small enough to push, but that family is just impossible."

The impassive Nedain huffed for a response.

Between those few families, Noren wondered if he might not get everything for another three or four falls. Much too long a time. Noren's math said that he would need just a little more land to get the right price for *him*.

When Noren had accepted the strange elf's deal, he'd had no idea how hard it would be to uphold his end. Not that there had been much choice during either of their meetings. Sadly, ignorance wasn't going to be a good excuse when it came to not paying the rest of his debt. He needed time to collect the rest of the "toil," a luxury Noren didn't have.

Noren couldn't guess why the elf wanted the land and didn't care. Whatever his "friend" wanted it for, the elf would likely drive all the farmers and ranchers out and Noren would be happy to see them go. The only reason he kept them there for now was that it made others more likely to sell and helped maintain the land's value. To get enough for the "Shepherd's Toil" he needed that value.

Still, he had to get the land in the first place for that to matter at all. If he didn't... he feared he might die, or worse be reduced to the same level as the wretches he was having to deal with now.

"Nedain," Noren said, bringing his mind back to the present. "I believe it may be time for more of those aggressive negotiations. Unlike before, I'm not going to ask you to hold back."

Of Noren's guards, Nedain was his most loyal and skilled. Adler, the other who he'd brought with them, was also one he trusted. Before joining

Noren's guard he'd been one of the watchmen, but even though he had skill, he was little more than a thug. Nedain, on the other hand, was a real talent. Noren had found her street fighting for a challenge. From there, she'd only gotten better and could toss grown men twice her size out a window without breaking a sweat.

Both had done work in these aggressive negotiations before. Ruining crops, roughing people up on their way to sell, killing stock. They'd done it all. None of that had worked on Ghen, though each had happened at least once. Noren couldn't risk trying the same tactics again. If he did, people might get suspicious—if they weren't already. The problem, Noren believed, was Ghen himself. That meant no more white gloves.

Ghen's wife was smart, no doubt about it, but she was only fighting because of Ghen and his stubbornness. Maybe she would negotiate better if Ghen wasn't around to be so stubborn. If Ghen was injured or dead, the family wouldn't have the manpower needed to work the land and animals at least. Then they would have to sell or collapse. Either option would work fine.

A smile blossomed on Noren's face, but then it faltered.

"Ghen's companion," Noren muttered, "what had he called him? Em. Yes, that was it."

He looked old enough to be called a man but not so old that he wasn't still a boy to Noren. The fact was, no matter his age, he owned a sword. Through the conversation, Noren saw the boy's careful eyes, and how he kept the hilt of his sword clear at all times. Noren knew those signs well enough to know a fighter when he saw one. The boy's face and clothes had also been strange. Noren might have wondered if he was from Yongarad, save that Ghen would never accept such a companion.

That meant if Noren was going to do this, he would have to send both his guards to see things through. The merchant didn't like the idea of being left without protection, but he liked the idea of failing his friend even less.

"Take Adler with you. I don't know who this Em is, and you know my policy."

"No mistakes," Nedain answered coolly.

"That's right, so you are both going. I want this dealt with tonight."

Nedain pulled off her cap and looked back down the road at the retreating cart. A knife edge grin split her tight lips. "Looking forward to it Noren, as always."

"No rain, that's good. We can get to Henaden without much trouble after all." Ghen said, as the clouds started to roll away and the late evening sun gave an orange glow to their fading undersides.

Even dealing with Mr. Noren hadn't been as bad as Ghen had feared. It was a good first day on the road and now it seemed to be a good time to set up for the night.

"If I remember right, there should be a small clearing nearby where travelers usually take a rest. We can set up camp there, and if anyone else is headed down the road we may have company too."

Em looked at the sky. "Do you think we could travel further? The sun will last for a while longer."

"I get that you're anxious to be in Henaden, but if we go on it will be harder to find a good camp. By the time we set up, there wouldn't be any time to hunt for a meal and I'd like more than our little bread if I can help it."

Em had to admit to himself that Ghen had a point.

"On top of that," the rancher added, "if we go too much further, Bo may get grumpy. We don't want to have to deal with that."

Bo turned her head and looked back at them as if daring them to push her on.

The clearing wasn't easy to see unless you were looking for it. A thin veil of foliage gave it a slight cover from unfamiliar eyes. Ghen, however, had been here before.

Noticing the telltale signs, he veered off the road and onto a narrow track that soon led into a much larger clearing.

"Well, maybe not large," he explained to Em, "but it's bigger than the road. Really, the clearing is a small patch of grass in a half circle tucked behind these here trees. Given time, I bet the bare patch would regrow and become just like the woods around it— that is, if we frequent visitors didn't keep trampling the ground, building fires, and guiding animals through it all the time."

As they came into view of the clearing, they were greeted by the sight of a man preparing to depart. Rocks were still piled into a small fire pit with some gathered wood alongside, but the man was just slinging his own bag over his shoulder and turning towards the road.

He had a solid expression that, even from a distance, was firm with his dark beard without being hard. He didn't wear anything distinguishing only the simplest of travel shirt and pants, yet the exposed arms were remarkable in their number of scars. They weren't the long scars from blades in battle, but obviously the many gashes made by ages of severe labor. Despite resembling a man who should seem burdened by his past he smiled with shining eyes and lifted his thin walking staff to them in a cordial greeting.

Ghen gave a friendly wave. "Evening neighbor, are you heading out?"

"Yes, but I'm glad you're here. This wood I collected won't help me anymore, so use as much or as little as you like. I don't like it when good things go to waste. I also managed to snare a few quail, I could take them all with me, but it wouldn't be easy. If you would be willing to trade, you can have the two I don't need."

"That'd save us some trouble finding meat for supper." Ghen thoughtfully lifted his hat slightly to scratch the top of his head. "What do you want for it?"

"How about a half halak and a loaf of bread? Do you have that to spare?"

Ghen chewed on the idea. They had a bit of bread to spare, and that would be a very good rate for two birds.

"Are you sure you wouldn't like anything more?"

The man smiled. "If you're willing to pay a full halak I wouldn't say no."

Ghen suddenly wished he'd accepted while it was still a half halak. All the same, it was still a good rate for two birds. "Sure, let me see what you've caught and if they look good, we can call it a fair deal."

Em had seen quail before and wasn't very interested in the trade. Still, he kept his eye on this stranger, and it wasn't just due to his natural suspicion.

There was something more, a stirring in Instinct and Nature, but neither said anything.

Em was tempted to ask the man if they'd met before. His guess was they might have. Ghen was being very friendly, so maybe they'd met on Ghen's land. Or perhaps the stirring had nothing to do with the man at all. Em wasn't sure.

As the negotiations finished, the traveler slung the remaining bird over his shoulder with his travel pouch and wished them well.

"I don't mind sharing a camp if you want to stay," Ghen said quickly. "Don't let us drive you out. I gotta say I'm a little surprised to find someone here since this isn't the usual time people do the trip to Henaden, but it's getting late and once it gets dark it'll be hard to travel."

The traveler laughed. "Don't worry about me. I've traveled further on darker nights than this one's going to be. I'm a workman, and I have many jobs to do and places to be. My job here is just about done, so I need to be on my way. Traveling at night can be dangerous, but there are times when it's the right thing to do. You should know that if you want to go on, the road will be safe tonight."

"Alright, well I figure we'll still stick around here but you have a good trip then, friend."

"If you are going to stay, would you take one last word of advice?" the workman asked.

Ghen shrugged. "Sure thing."

"All manner of strays have been passing through this camp lately. There is a chance something will come sneaking in tonight as well. Spread some dry brush around before you go to sleep, I spread a little myself when I stopped here. It may give you a much needed warning."

"Makes sense, we may do that."

The workman waved goodbye and nodded to Em, who was still sitting on the cart. Em bowed slightly in return. Then, without hesitation, the workman continued toward his next task.

Em gestured to the retreating form of the workman. "Do you know him?"

Ghen chewed the question a moment before replying. "I was wondering the same thing. He looked familiar, but I couldn't place him exactly. Not that I'm very good with faces, my guess is maybe I met him in Marden at one time or another. Still, seemed like good folk to me."

Em blinked, surprised. He'd fully expected that they'd met before. "Ah... I see. He at least appeared friendly. If you will not be offended, however, I think... I think I am glad that we will have the grounds to ourselves."

"Yep, looks like we get our pick of camping spots." Ghen gazed at the road again. "Don't be surprised, though, if someone else drops in before nightfall. That workman just goes to prove that anyone can turn up. Now, let's get Bo unhitched and set up my lean-to for the night."

Alone, Ghen and Em had their pick of where to camp. They surveyed the trees, where their many roots sprung up, where the shrubbery closed in, and where there was good space to build a fire. Somewhat unsurprisingly, it turned out to be where the workman had built his fire before they arrived. Near the remaining wood and fire pit, two stout trees made for great pillars to serve on either side of Ghen's lean-to he'd brought.

The lean-to itself was a rectangular lattice of logs that Em and Ghen tied into a strong panel. Leaning the panel against the two trees, they tied it to both of them and set up guidelines so that it wouldn't slide. When it was secure, they pulled out the thick tarp that laid over the panel, draping over the top and down the sides, making a quick and easy shelter for the night.

Since the camp was established earlier than they'd expected, and they didn't have to gather materials for a fire or meat for their meal, Ghen and Em discovered they had time to spare. Em spent it practicing, as was his habit, and Ghen decided he could use a bit of the same. Finding a good target, he pulled out his hunting bow and did some target practice.

Ghen wasn't too bad with a bow. He knew better bowmen, but not many. All his arrows scored his target with most of them near the center. After a few minutes, Em caught an interest and asked for a turn. Entertainingly, he turned out to be a surprisingly poor shot at first but picked it up quickly.

Ghen wasn't sure if this was a skill Em just had never learned but was catching on because he was a quick study, or if it was something he'd just forgotten and hadn't practiced in a long time. Of the two of them, Ghen was clearly the better, and the topic made for good conversation as they roasted the quail over the fire.

The whole event reminded Ghen of younger days when he used to go camping with some of the other boys on the ranches, like his cousin Mahden or Holland Redgen. Those had been good memories and seeing Em smile as they talked in the fading light, Ghen couldn't help feeling sorry for him. Ghen knew these would be good memories too, but they would be ones that Em wouldn't share. Tomorrow, Em wouldn't remember any of it, as if none of it had ever happened.

Not for the first time, Ghen wondered how Em ended up this way. And how was it that Em had to get this close to his goal before he found anyone willing to help? Were good folks just that rare, or was there something about Em that kept people away?

Em wasn't from around here, but was that enough of a reason for people not to help? He guessed maybe it was because Em looked a little dangerous at first. Ghen knew he'd thought, but now he was wondering if Em was really that dangerous after all.

"Will we be taking shifts to watch in the night?" Em asked, breaking Ghen from his reverie.

"Huh? Oh, I don't think so. Besides, it might be a little tricky with your condition. With the fire at our feet, I bet wildlife will keep away. I know there are rumors of bad folk on the roads, but I've never put up a guard or watch before, and I'm still fine."

"Be that as it may," Em said, looking around the camping area, "we should consider the suggestion that the workman made. The one regarding scattering some dry wood around the edges of our camp. Do you remember?"

Ghen nodded. "Sure do. We can do that if you'd like. I'm all for a little precaution."

When they finished eating, they set about scattering whatever dry branches they weren't going to use for the fire. The sky was already dark when they started and, personally, Ghen was ready for bed. He wondered if Em had suggested the brush because he actually wanted to be cautious, or if it was because he was afraid to sleep.

Em always talked about sleeping as a kind of death. Even his notes had it written out that way. In that light, Ghen could understand being a little scared. Whether it was a stalling tactic or not, it wasn't long before they were finished setting up and there was nothing left to do.

Ghen immediately settled down, and, after some idle wandering about the clearing, Em had to concede that it was time to sleep as well. They both settled down peacefully, unaware of the dangers that were soon to visit them.

CHAPTER 15

BLINKING AWAKE, HE SLOWLY sat up and shook to free himself from the mire of sleep. Awareness rising out of the depths of his mind, he looked around.

A campfire smoldered at his feet. Its shallow illumination breaking against the dark of the night. Trees shivered in the waves of the embers' soft glow. With deep shadows behind their trunks, the woods crowded around the camp and its light, to stay safe from the darkness behind them.

As the midnight riser woke, the dim firelight barely revealed the sleeping companion and the nearby animal, making it difficult to take in the scene. Yet, all he could think was...

"Where did I fall asleep?"

He couldn't remember.

Resting his head in his hand, he tried to collect his thoughts. "I am... I do not know."

In his chest, his heart trembled, urgency provoking greater wakefulness. A cold emptiness crept up his spine. Before it could take root, a voice spoke urgently into his head.

Listen! growled the shadowy base.

He did. Nothing... Not a sound in the night except the crackle of the fire, his breathing and that of the sleeping man, and... a distant rustling. Finally, a low dry snap.

Clarity trickled into his confused mind. That rustling and the snapping branch, yes, something or someone was getting closer. A sigh of moonlight revealed the vestige of the other beneath the lean-to. He lay motionless, buried in rest, of which there was no sign of his expecting anyone to raise him.

He's fine, you trust him, but you have to hurry! Another voice, old but just as urgent, said quickly.

Looking again, it was far from morning and the awoken sleeper knew that most things that come so late at night are not good company. A much louder crunch echoed in his ear.

Hurry, hurry!

Rushed by the voices, he reacted unconsciously. He, who did not know his name, reached to his side and closed his hand around a long scabbard by reflex. Taking it with him, he leapt into the deep shadows and moved behind a nearby tree.

He slid further and further into the dark, shielding his eyes so they would adjust more quickly to the lack of light. It wasn't long before, as he slid through the night's depths, he noted a shiver of movement. Practiced impulse guided his body again through shadow to yet another cover. Stepping carefully, he avoided a patch of dry branches that he somehow knew sat in his way.

Here he could see the other side of the lean-to and, more clearly, two distinct forms in the night drawing near to the shelter. The forms of people. These were not beasts of night, but the more common beast, the intelligent kind.

Survival intuition worked over mind, pushing him to determine which of the nine tribes of man these two hailed from. They were too tall to be from the dwarf or fae tribes and too short to be liome or most elves. One had hair, so at least that one was no wodjok, and neither walked with the stutter step of a satyr. The tribes of kyate-siv or usarumai were possible, but the forgetful watcher doubted that. That left humans as the last option and the most likely.

They're human, The voice of Instinct whispered. Sounding relieved, it added, *You should be safe for the moment.*

The fire near the lean-to gave off just enough light to see a reflection from the weapons the new arrivals wielded. It took little imagination to see that these people meant to do harm.

He, who did not remember, considered leaving the other person in the shelter to their fate, but there were a few problems with that. He'd been told by Instinct that he trusted that man. If that was the case, then he must be some kind of companion.

I do not wish to leave him behind, he told himself. Then, pushing his argument further, *If I leave, I also may never know who I am. I must stay.*

Good choice, Instinct applauded quietly.

He looked at the sword and considered.

Can I win this fight? I know this weapon, I can feel it, but these fights are meant to be won in an instant. A strike and then silence. If not, I should flee, but... He looked at the shape of his companion in the lean-to. *Can he run with me?*

The voices were silent, but their presence was still there, beyond some layer of the world. They were waiting, listening. Though for what, the small swordsman was unsure.

I do not know who or what you are, but can you advise me? Should I try to wake my companion or attack? Please, the newcomers round our shelter now. They will soon be at the opening. I need help.

Instinct considered his question. *It's not time yet for us to do as we promised, but ask for help, little one, and you may find it.* The presence shifted beyond sight, to turn and speak in unintelligible murmurs to something or someone unknown.

In seconds its presence drew near again. *You will have help*, Instinct assured him.

For a moment, even though he could not remember his own name, the forgetful swordsman had enough presence of mind to wonder if he was going insane. What was he even asking for? What aid could this voice even give? If he was going to act, he needed to act now.

He took half a step forward, ready to spring, when a firm hand gripped his shoulder.

Anxiously, the one who forgot turned, but no one was there. Still, he could feel it, a powerful hand that could break stone in its steel grip. Yet, despite its strength, it only squeezed gently to reassure him.

Wait, Nature chided, not unkindly. Forgetful as he was, the small form hiding in the shadows recognized that it was Nature who had told him to 'listen' before. Though now the voice was slightly different. It was closer or more real. The voice of Nature had been allowed to step into this layer of the world. With a thrilled heart, Nature was forced to focus on his words to make them clear. Each one fought to be a bestial growl or a roar, but they were tamed. *Calm... your heart. This is...* another growl, *... battle, but we... Grr... We can win. I trained you... Move like it!*

He understood immediately what the voice wished him to do.

Creeping back along his path, the forgetful one placed himself against his original hiding place nearer to the lean-to. He drew his sword cautiously, keeping the blade under his long coat to stop it from reflecting the firelight. Holding the drawn sword, it felt natural in his hand. He gave himself over to his practiced intuition.

Crouched low, there was no time to plan, other than deciding who he would strike first. He decided it would be whoever moved to attack his companion. As the newcomers rounded the lean-to, glowing embers revealed more of their frames.

Instinct was right. They are human, he said without breath, observing them.

One was thin with a short sword and a weaved buckler of hardened leather. He thought the thin one might be a woman, but in low light, it was hard to tell. The other was big, very big. This one kept a dagger on their belt, but a hammer in their hand. The head of the hammer was thick, but the handle wasn't long. It was a common tool for smiths, but that made it no less deadly a weapon.

There is something strange about them, he thought. *They are masked, but it is the dead of night, and their intentions appear to be final.*

They have... rrrrr... something to hide, Nature agreed.

They both wear finer leathers, and their clothes have no patchwork I can see, yet their weapons are mundane and common. Are they thieves who stole armor from victims?

Nature's quiet laugh rolled like distant thunder. *It fits too well... See how they move, too good for... bandits.*

Both intruders rounded the shelter on opposite sides. As they peered in, he without name coiled to pounce, aiming for the larger one while his back was exposed. Yet, once again, the strong unseen hand of Nature kept him back.

The people paused. Instead of attacking, they looked at one another. The woman signed with one hand, and they both began to look around carefully.

It wasn't long before the one who forgot deciphered what it meant. *They are looking for me. Then these are not random attackers. They expected to find two people in the shelter. Instead, they only found my companion.*

That explained the mask, if there were witnesses perhaps, they could be identified. Good weapons might also lead to who they are, which explains why they wield common ones now.

What... will you do? Nature asked.

He considered. *With a target missing, they could attack my companion, search for me, or retreat to attempt again later.*

Even as he said this to himself, the thin one signed again. She stepped back into the shadows of the lean-to and began peering around. The larger one instead began to patrol, moving slowly past the fire.

So that is their plan. The thin one waits, watching my sleeping companion, and the hulking man searches for me. If my companion wakes, he will be killed in a moment.

I ask... again... child. Nature's words became even more of a labor as the moment approached. *They move... what will... you do?*

Wait, he decided. *If they are willing to search, then they will come to me soon enough.*

In the shadows, Nature nodded unseen. Its hidden face became a menacing snarl that permeated through its invisible presence.

Where the forgetful swordsman was hiding, the little light given off by the campfire's dying embers put him in a dark shadow. The contrast of the dim light and the pure dark rendered him all but invisible.

My sword is not too long. It will be faster than the hammer and nearly as dangerous. Besides, they do not know where I am yet. However, he hesitated, *in the dark, judging the distance will be difficult.*

You asked... for help, Nature reminded him. *I provide it. Close your eyes... and prepare.*

He did as Nature commanded and, without his sight, his ears painted the scene around him. The wind rustled through the trees as if a powerful animal was taking a deep breath. Smelling the night air and all it held. Then the wind faded into silence as if it too were holding its breath. All that was left for the swordsman to hear was the soft crackle of the fire, his own quiet breathing, and the low thump of the big boots that were getting closer and closer.

He comes... Wait for my... signal, the voice warned. *Hold... hold...*

The moment the invader's boot hit only an arm's reach away, the signal came.

A terrifying bestial howl split the night, booming through the camp. Both attackers snapped up in surprise and turned away from the small swordsman's ambush to look for the source of the cry. The one who forgot leapt from the shadows, his large enemy jolting in surprise, and the battle began.

There was no time to aim, so the small swordsman's blade flashed recklessly as it came free from under his coat. Striking in the firelight, the one who forgot slashed twice quickly. The large invader was close enough that the blade cut the large invader twice under his left rib. Sadly, the cuts were hardly damaging, they were stopped by the man's thick armor.

Down! Nature bellowed.

Hearing the command, a third attack was directed downward. The forgetful swordsman's blade plunged into his enemy's leg. The invader gasped and groaned in pain, and he tried to keep the lances of pain from rioting his body.

Before the big man could even finish crying out, he without name turned his attention to the other invader. To reach her, the forgetful swordsman braced his feet on a tree root and leaped forward. The force of the leap ripped his blade out of the big man's calf and helped the small fighter escape the large man's desperate hammer swing. The renewed pain of the new cut sent the attacker stumbling as he missed, and he was left clutching at his wound.

The little swordsman cleared the fire in his agile bound and landed already with his next steps in mind. Sucking in a powerful breath, he struck quickly with an upward slash.

His opponent's instincts seized command, and she stepped back, despite the utter shock that showed in her eyes. The tip grazed the leather jerkin she wore, but nothing more. Making quick strikes, the forgetful fighter tried again to capitalize on their surprise, but his opponent was fast. She recovered, caught the slash on her buckler, and countered with a lunge of her own.

Well trained, Nature growled.

Of the two of them, Nature's student had judged the larger attacker as more dangerous, but now he wondered if it was this woman.

The forgetful fighter parried the lunge to his left and rammed his right shoulder into the buckler. The unexpected force made the woman stumble, and she startled the mule who was resting nearby. The stirring of the animal distracted the woman, making her turn to see what was making all the noise behind her.

That gave the swordsman a moment to act, and he wanted to pursue her, but Nature growled dangerously. *No... flanked!*

The voice was right, he realized. If the larger man recovered, the small fighter could find himself attacked on two sides at once. Just like when he'd moved back to the camp, the swordsman got an impression of what Nature wanted him to do.

Instead of leaping at the distracted woman, the one who forgot used his enemy's inattention to circle to her side. By the time he'd finished moving, the woman was ready to face him again, but that was fine. Blurring slashes like the roil of rapids fell on her from the small swordsman's blade. She blocked most with expert grace, but the blows fell with far more skill than she expected, and she was pushed back. She tried to gain the momentum and counter, but as she got ready, she left an opening that cost her.

When she lowered her sword slightly, the forgetful fighter pretended to make a high strike at her side. She lifted her shield to block, but in doing so, exposed her lower side. As planned, the swordsman pulled back the feinted strike and kicked under the shield.

The invader gasped as the wind was knocked out of her and did the best she could to stay upright. She tried to raise her shield in a weak defense, but it wasn't enough.

Circling to her left flank, the one who forgot lunged over the shield. The blade should have plunged deep into her back, but his opponent's reactions saved her again. The woman caught on and shifted her shield to turn it away. However, she was too late to stop it completely. Her shield knocked the blade up near the hilt, which saved her life, but the sword still dug into her opposite shoulder, cutting a gash into it.

She groaned and the skin around her eyes pinched in anger and rage.

Before this invader could counterattack, the little fighter kneed her in the same spot he'd kicked before. She spun away to abate the force and backed towards her ally. Unwilling to let her escape, he without a name stepped forward to reengage. When he swung a short testing slash, she parried it easily and took another step back, closing ranks with her more severely wounded ally. The big attacker had slowly turned around but wasn't able to move well on his injured leg.

"Em!" The one who forgot turned to see it was the man, his companion, rising from the lean-to with a staff in his hand.

"Em? Is that my name?"

For now, Little Em, the older voice of Instinct said quickly, but the voice was soon lost as Nature roared a command.

Back!

Em leaped back, avoiding a cut from the woman's short sword. The moment Em avoided the blow, both he and the invader took another step away from each other. Then, for a brief instant, both parties froze, facing one another.

Surprise has been lost, Em said to himself.

Nature's voice rumbled menacingly. *For both sides.*

Thoughts, as trained by Nature as any of Em's sword techniques, analyzed the situation as the pause stretched out.

The woman is skilled, but her wound is slowing her down. See how she faces me holding the shield further out and her weapon back. She cannot attack anymore. If she did, it could be the end of her. Her companion can still swing his hammer, but it will hurt to do it. His ability to move is even worse. Even in the low light, the leg wound looked awful. *He is nearly immobile.*

This battle draws to... its end, the growling voice in his shadow agreed.

Now they face equal numbers, and I am not wounded. They are already finished. Em thought excitedly. The two groups observed each other for another moment, when the bestial voice spoke again to Em.

They weigh... retreat. We will help them... grrr.... decide. Em felt as much as heard the long scrape of steel as Nature drew out an unseen weapon. Then, the creek of leather and cord as two powerful scarred hands gripped the hilt of the weapon with frightening strength. *Follow me.*

What happened next, Em could never have described clearly even if he'd remembered the event well. He was overcome with a duality of purpose, vision, and power. Like the wind blowing a leaf through the air, Em was ushered by Nature's force. Even though he could in no way see Nature's weapon or the hands that held it, Em's movements matched those of his phantom guardian.

Aligned, they charged together.

With each blow, their swords struck like lightning, the strikes raining down with surprising strength for one whose stature was so small. Em followed his shadow in a step to the right. It put the smaller fighter's shield in his way, but he soon saw it meant her ally was on the opposite side and couldn't reach him. Any attempt to get around her and at Em would be excruciating for the deeply injured invader.

Now! Nature roared.

Following his lead, Em was able to attack with a flurry of strong blows to keep up a constant pressure with unusual ease. Perhaps this was an illusion, some trick of the mind, but Em felt Nature. Strong, untiring, and even while Nature was ferocious, he was not wild.

Yet, in the excitement, a forgotten violence began to build up in Em. The echoes of the past secretly filled the sides of his vision, obscure but dangerous.

The bestial Nature maintained focus, he parried and countered whenever their opponent tried to break the assault with attacks of her own. Bit by bit, they broke through her defenses. Nicks and scratches cut through onto his opponent and it became clear to the invaders their hopes of victory had fled, and it was time they did the same.

"This is a bust," the smaller invader called out. "Go!"

Then she made her first real mistake. Whoever this woman was, she was familiar with battle, but not with retreat. The moment she called to run, she spun about and found her own ally in the way of her escape. He was too big and too slow to get away quickly, and when she turned around, she'd turned her shield away from Em and Nature. Without that defense, she was exposed.

The battle… is won, the shadow of Nature said with finality.

Em's sword blurred, but not to end her. Nature guided the steel, deftly cutting across her back and shoulder near the same place Em had wounded her at the outset of their battle. A final warning, and farewell.

Nature lowered its invisible weapon, but Em resisted doing the same.

The echoes of the past now covered his vision, and he no longer perceived the woods around him. All that was clear was that someone was fleeing before him and, in the echo, a familiar voice was shouting, *Don't let him get away!*

Em attacked on his own, fighting off Nature's attempts to hold him back, but the brief struggle gave the invader time to realize her mistake. She spun around again, knocking Em's reckless attack aside.

She winced. The effort to keep Em away seared through her shoulder like a raging fire. The smaller invader stumbled to her left, taking a longer way around her ally to escape, but at least kept her shield toward Em. This saved her from further punishment but left her ally defenseless.

The large man left behind tried to run as well, but he was too slow.

The vision of echoes refocused on the remaining enemy, and Em sprang after him.

STOP! Nature roared.

"I have to." Em wined in a small voice. "To survive."

In a moment, he caught up to his prey. Em slashed at the man's unwounded leg and the cut nearly brought the man to the ground. Yet, despite shuddering knees, he still stood and kept trying to escape.

Switching his grip, Em's sword stung like many wasps, with steel jabs aimed at any unarmored points.

The large invader had barely escaped past the lean-to into the clearing, but now he slowed to a stop. It was too much, and they both knew it. Even if he escaped, this man was finished. The big man stopped and gritted his teeth. Screams of pain became a final guttural roar. If he could not escape, he would take this little wretch with him!

Or he would try.

The hammer came around with powerfully morbid intentions, but before the mallet was halfway to Em, he slid to a stop and reversed direction. It passed near enough that Em felt the rush of air as it swung by with a bone crushing force but never touched him. Since his sword was too short to reach the large invader, Em took another step back.

Of all the wounds this man bore, the worst were on his legs. Now that Em stepped back, the large fighter had a choice. Charge on his slow weakened legs, or stand where he was and wait to die. It was an awful choice, but an easy one. He took a weak step toward Em, wheezing through the pain, then another step, and then... it was too late.

Em could back away, a thing which Nature pleaded him to do, but instead, he gave into the vision of forgotten echoes. They threw him forward, closing the distance between Em and his prey. Em stood inches from the man's chest, and, from that position, he lunged deep and high. The enemy stiffened, and there was a thud as the heavy hammer dropped to the ground.

As the enemy collapsed Em's sword came free and he was left standing on a bridge over a river with snow on each bank. That echo's familiar voice was saying, *We had to. We had to, to survive. You did the right thing. Say it, 'I did the right thing.'*

Tentatively, Em repeated. "I... did the right thing."

Then his vision cleared. There was no bridge, no river, and no snow. He was in a clearing surrounded by trees, where Em's companion stared at him and the body at his feet in absolute horror. Slowly shaking his head, tears began to run down his face.

Ghen, the companion, dropped to his knees. "What... did you do?"

CHAPTER 16

THERE WAS A GRATING of metal on earth as Ghen planted the small shovel in the loose soil once again.

"Why? Why... and... and how did...? That was *not* right!" Ghen growled angrily, knowing Em was too far away to hear.

Ghen looked over to be sure. There he was, sitting calmly on the bed of the cart. A lamp illuminated the pages of the journal he read tenaciously. His longsword, freshly cleaned, by his side with his short sword.

Ghen wiped the sweat from his face and shook his head.

"That's it, then? You're just done, kid? Just like that, as if nothing happened? That's what another tribesman's life is worth? A rag and some oil to get the stains off?" There was nothing in the boy's posture that showed a hint of mercy or guilt.

Ghen looked back down at the body at his feet. It was Adler. The shock of his identity had taken Ghen a moment to get over, but now that he had, thinking about it only made things worse.

It wasn't like he knew Adler well. To him, Adler had been the quiet bulk of a man who walked in Mr. Noren's shadow. That Adler, big and strong, and Em had torn him to pieces. Beneath Ghen's quickly fashioned shroud, using his own blanket, the man's clothes had been flayed off in ribbons and his eyes were unbearably vacant.

Ghen tossed the shovelful of earth into the small hole where the shrouded body lay. He was nearly finished. The shroud only showed through small gaps in the loose earth. Adler had never been a friend and, in the end, had turned out to be something like an enemy.

"That doesn't make it right, though. Does it?"

The sound of steps behind Ghen made him spin, afraid.

He let out his breath. "Oh, it's you. You scared me, Bo."

The mule bent her head low, looking into the shallow grave now nearly buried.

Ghen patted her neck. "What do I do, Bo? I'm so confused. I... I just don't know. I've killed pigs, cows, deer, a mess of bugs, and things that tried to get at you or the stock, but girl, I've never killed another man of any tribe. I've never really wanted to."

Bo lifted her head and looked at him mournfully.

"I just feel lost, girl," he said as he tossed another shovelful on the grave and spread it out over the top. "In a decent world, good folk should never have to do anything like this."

Bo snorted.

"So, what if the world isn't decent? It ought to be," Ghen said, bitterly.

Bo looked up as Em shifted in the back of the cart, and then she looked back at Ghen expectantly.

"What? Do you expect me to go over to him? He doesn't even know me. That kid... is he even a kid?" Would anyone who'd... Could anyone do something like this and still be so young?

Staring off into the dark of night, Ghen was reminded of a very similar image of someone slightly different.

"Is this what broke you, Uncle Grady?" Ghen asked. "All those times you gazed into the dark like it would bite you, were you seeing boys like this one?"

The rancher sighed with a mix of sadness and anger. "Yeah, whatever he's done, or however many times, Em *is* still a kid. But you know..." Ghen shook his head. "I just don't know, Bo. I mean, I knew he'd killed. Well, I guess I didn't know, but I was pretty sure. It's just... I hadn't seen it, not for myself. You know, maybe we should..."

Bo looked at him sorrowfully, but intently.

"What? Don't tell me it doesn't scare you. He doesn't remember a thing. Is it so odd to think things could go wrong? Maybe he would be better on his..."

Bo shook her head and let her eyes bore into Ghen until he understood.

"Oh," Ghen said, reaching a realization. "So that's it, then. That's what happened."

Bo snorted.

"You know what I mean, or maybe you don't. I guess I ought to explain," Ghen said as he rubbed the mule behind the ears. "I've been wondering why Em was the way he was when I found him. How did someone walk as far as he must have, and no one chose to help? There were a bunch of things I thought it might be, but now I bet it was something like this." Ghen gestured at their feet where the shallow grave sat.

"I'll bet he did get help along the way, two kinds. One where people wanted to take advantage of Em, and learned the same lesson Adler did. The other might have been genuinely kind but saw what we just did. '...did what was right', huh? Maybe he thought it was."

Ghen went back to shoveling dirt and, when he finished, patted the earth down. Now what? He couldn't go back to Em, at least not yet. So, unable to think of anything better, he sat down next to Adler's grave.

Bo turned her head and nudged him.

Ghen patted her head. "He killed him, Bo. He did it right in front of me! It's not right! It shouldn't be this way. I get it, that Em was fighting for us, but did it have to end this way? When Adler was finished, we... we should have helped him, you know. It doesn't make sense! Weren't we supposed to help even if... even if...?"

Ghen looked up angrily. He glared past Bo, past the trees, past the clouds, and past the light of the moon beyond.

"This is *you*, isn't it?"

The night said nothing back.

"Why me?" Ghen whimpered. "Why couldn't you have brought him to someone else's door?"

There was a long silence, and then Ghen recalled the silence he'd felt before.

"Yeah, I know he's lonely," Ghen said to the still night. "I heard it before, but Boss there's something dead in that boy. That look he got in that fight, like he couldn't even see me. There's something broken in that boy, but... C-can't he take it on his own? At least till Henaden?"

There was no reply.

The rancher had the idea of walking straight over to Em and telling him to get off his cart and get out of here. Then Ghen could just drive on to Henaden without him. If he did, then at least Ghen figured he could feel safe, and... No.

Even as he thought about it, Ghen just felt plain wrong. As if he knew he was about to make a mistake. "I just want to be done with all of this, but..."

As Ghen trailed off, the night gave no reply.

"Why?" Ghen asked one last time.

But the silence remained around him, and his loneliness mounted, but Ghen fought back. He felt the press of the loneliness, and sure it didn't feel good, but was it really so much worse?

Bo pressed her head against his shoulder.

For an instant, her push broke the feeling of being alone in the world, and then Ghen was thrown quickly back into the loneliness, and he felt it. Ghen was faced with the full contrast of the silence. It was only for a moment, but being alone and having company always changes in an instant, and despite how quick the change was, the difference between them was night and day.

Ghen didn't like it, but he understood. "Em can take it, but that would mean I'd be throwing him into the worst of it and doing it because he chose to protect me. I don't agree with what he did, but that'd be a poor way to pay him back. I still think he was wrong." Ghen sighed. "But that's no reason not to act like good folk should. If I did toss him away, it wouldn't matter if what he did was right or wrong, I'd be wrong for sure. I can't leave him." Ghen kicked the dirt. He wasn't even sure who he was mad at anymore. He looked up at the night again. "I gave my word to you and to May that I'd help him. I'll be all kinds of messed up if I break that promise."

Bo took a step, pushed him with her nose, and then she pushed again.

Ghen pushed her head away, but she brought it back and pushed hard.

"Alright! I get it," he told her.

Bo drew her head back and snorted.

"I'll go over to him," Ghen said. "Just... give me a minute."

Bo looked at him. Then, tossing her mane, wandered toward the cart.

"Know it all," Ghen muttered, picking up his hat from where he'd set it.

He turned back to the sky. "Is this going to get easier?"

Ghen barely finished the question before he was shaking his head.

"No, of course it won't. I knew that from the second I read Em's book, didn't I?" He let out a long sigh and looked inside himself.

There was still a nagging part of him pushing to turn away from Em, but Ghen had chosen his course now and, thinking about his choice, had peace with it. He knew the right way.

"Let's get to it then." It was only a moment more before Ghen made his way back to the cart. Not much happier, but he felt more whole.

"Ghen-*sa*," Em said when he got closer.

"What is it, kid?" Ghen asked, feeling suddenly very tired.

"I am sorry." Em bowed. All that blood and emptiness was gone, and he was just Em again. "I do not know why this man's death has made you unhappy with me after he attacked us, but I had no wish to hurt you. I... I..." Em sounded like he wanted to explain something more but never did.

Ghen sighed. He couldn't decide if he was annoyed or relieved that Em sounded more like the kid he'd been traveling with so far. "I'll admit, I don't like what happened, but it's not right of me to blame you like I've been doing. I'm sorry too."

Em stayed with his head lowered.

"Oh, for heaven's sake, get up," Ghen said, shaking his head. "Adler might have come on his own to cause us trouble, but I'll bet that woman was Nedain. I don't think she'd have attacked if Mr. Noren hadn't told her to. That means they may come after us again. We'll have to go by lantern light. That's not usually smart, but that workman seemed to think the road would be safe tonight, so I figure we can make a good go of it."

Em raised his head. "Ghen-*sa*, before we leave, there is something I wish to know."

Ghen raised an eyebrow at him.

Em hesitated, but managed to ask, "Why do you help me? I can see from my notes you have treated me well even though there is little I can do to repay you. Now, even after I've upset you, you sound as if you still mean to help me. Why?"

"Why?" Ghen could've almost laughed, hearing Em ask the same question he'd posed to the night a minute ago. The rancher set his hat in its proper place and even managed a small, genuine smile. "'Cause Em, that's what good folk do."

This could be a problem, Noren thought.

"He surprised us," Nedain explained.

Yes, a big problem. "I understand that Nedain. Where I struggle in my understanding is that I sent two of you instead of just one to make sure something like this didn't happen. Also, I've seen you walk up to an army platoon looking for a fight because you were bored. I don't see why him jumping out of the bushes meant it was time to turn and run."

Nedain tried to explain again. "You weren't there. When he jumped out, he hit us both before we knew he was there. It burns me to say it, but he hit us hard and fast. It was over before we knew it started." Nedain ground her teeth. "Whoever this Em is, he's an experienced fighter."

"So were both of you!" Noren shouted before taking a deep breath to calm himself. "Do you have any idea how bad this could be?"

"Don't kid yourself, Noren. They probably don't even know who hit them," Nedain said dismissively.

Usually, Noren found a certain charm in Nedain's lack of respect, but at the moment it was just annoying.

"Why? Because you had your faces covered? Adler didn't return, remember?"

The woman glared. "I know that, but like *you* said, he's experienced. I took the horses as a precaution, but he should have made it out."

"And if you're wrong?"

"Then they have Adler, but he'd never say anything if that foreigner even left him alive. They can't prove our attack was tied to you or that I was even the other person there."

Nedain winced slightly as Noren's driver sowed another stitch in her shoulder.

Noren shook his head in disappointment. "They wouldn't need proof. The people of Henaden would believe me over Ghen any day."

"Then what's the problem?" Nedain countered.

"Do I look like I care what he says in Henaden?!" Noren yelled, face burning red. "I am working *so* hard to get these mud-grubbing cow herders to sell to me, but if those country oafs catch a whiff of a rumor that I am attacking their neighbors, they'll..."

Nedain shrugged. "Then they'll know you mean business. How is that going to hurt you? And who cares if these leftovers sell, anyway? Didn't you say you already have most of the land around here?"

Noren, so far, had kept his reasons for buying the land a secret from everyone. Even Noren's wife and son didn't even know about his elf 'friend.'

"I still need those hicks to stay where they are, they make the land more valuable. You've worked for me for a long time now, haven't you been paying attention? I need, desperately, to keep the land at its current value or higher. They cannot find out about this."

"Like I said, they will never know it was us. Or at least that it's connected to you."

Noren had known this would be a risk, but he'd expected better from his people. He might be fine, but he might not. When Adler returned, if he did, he could be more confident of his anonymity. Until then, he needed to make a contingency plan.

If Ghen did know who'd orchestrated the assault and had any shred of proof, then he could not make it home. It would be Noren's life or Ghen's, and Noren knew which he favored.

The driver stepped back from Nedain, showing he'd finished his stitching. He had minor skill in sowing, so his stitches were well made, and he'd been careful to clean the wounds. With time, she would heal well.

Noren waved him away. "Go. When Adler returns, bring him straight to me. If he isn't back by morning, we are going back to Henaden."

Nedain nodded but wasn't nearly as concerned as Noren felt the situation warranted.

"He'll be injured, but I doubt they killed him," she said.

Noren wasn't convinced. "Ghen wouldn't kill him and wouldn't want him killed, I agree. This Em, on the other hand, has surprised you once already. If Adler is not back by morning, we assume the worst and deal with it. We will deal with *all* of this."

Nedain smiled hungrily, like the beast she was.

"Wipe that smile off your face!" Noren commanded. The nerve of her, to smile after so royally botching affairs. "If it comes to it, and you fail your next task, you may find yourself in another fight you can't win. This one, however, you won't be able to run away from."

CHAPTER 17

"ARE YOU SURE YOU don't want to sleep?"

Em shook his head.

"Alright then," Ghen said, as he took back the reins of the cart.

After the burial of Adler, both Ghen and Em agreed that, despite how little they'd slept, it was better to move on. Getting on the road, the anticipation of another attack kept them awake for a while, but as the miles dragged on, their nervous energy faded. Before long, they began to feel sleepy again.

Ghen had offered to let Em sleep in the bed of the cart while he drove, but Em refused. So, after consideration, Ghen offered Em the reins and took the rest himself. Now the rancher was happy to be back, leading his trusty cart. In the east, dawn's first light made a blue haze in the sky. An amber glow announced the rising sun.

"The back's more comfortable than you might think," Ghen said a last time. "If you sit back there now, I'll bet you'll be down before the sun gets up and you'll get some good shut eye."

"No, but thank you Ghen-*sa*. I... I do not want to forget."

Ghen nodded as if he understood, as if he could.

An awkward silence stretched out and was becoming deafening before Ghen broke it with a long whistle.

"Would you look at that?" he said, pointing to a stream. "Either Bo got a move on, or you pushed her last night. This has got to be the other end of Degen Creek, I see it every time I come this way, but if we're here already... Well, we made more progress than I thought."

"Your mule did what it wished. I never pushed her to go faster."

"Hear that, Bo? You've been a good girl."

The mule snorted.

"Yeah, yeah, don't worry. Since you've been so good, I'll be sure to pick you up something in Henaden. And why don't we get you off the cart a bit, and you get a drink from the creek and take a break?"

Bo flicked her ears, and Em wondered if she understood the rancher.

Ghen pulled the cart alongside the dip in the road that marked the crossing of the creek's subtle waters. In the dim light, he could just see the flickering edges of its bubbling ripples and hear the soft gurgle of its laughter. As the rancher stepped down to unhitch Bo, Em hopped down and walked to the water's edge.

Sitting by the side of the stream, Em peered into the glossy surface. His reflection was little more than a shadow that looked back at him. Em couldn't see any more of his face than he could remember of it.

"What are you thinking about?"

"I'm not sure Ghen-*sa*."

But that wasn't true. Many thoughts crowded Em's mind. Last night, he'd read his notes. Em had seen that he'd been close to this rancher, his family, and his problems. His journal made that clear. But, when those strange echoes called him to do what appeared 'right,' it'd broken Ghen's trust.

That was part of why he'd apologized, and Ghen seemed to have accepted it well. The rancher was feeling better and was trying to be friendly with Em again. He got the feeling Ghen wanted them to be close and friendly, and honestly, Em desired that too. He just wasn't sure that was possible.

You can trust him, Little Em.

Maybe I can, but, Instinct, does that make it better?

It wasn't that Ghen didn't seem like a good person, if anything, it was because he seemed so good that Em was unsure. Em couldn't help but wonder if *he* was the problem. Em could barely remember what he'd seen or felt in those echoes, but if they led him to do what a good man thought was wrong, what did that make Em?

Em just shook his head. This was the same circle his thoughts had run through all night. All he was left with was more confusion.

Instinct seemed to understand Em's hesitation. *You'll never find answers if you aren't willing to ask questions, Little Em.*

"Ghen-*sa*?" Em asked, after a little more consideration.

"Yeah, kid."

"Who are you? I know you are a rancher. I read that in my notes, but who are you really? Why are you doing this? What is your goal?"

Em couldn't see Ghen clearly in the dim light, but he could hear the man's deep breath as he considered. "I guess I'm a person who's just trying to live like good folk should. Which kinda answers why I'm doing this. Like I said last night, I'm doing this because this is what good folk ought to do."

"You say that like it makes everything clear, but what does that mean? How do you know what 'good folk' would do? How does it help you?"

"It helps me because it's right, and doing the right thing is good for everybody." Ghen chuckled. "You're acting like it's complicated, but I think you're the one trying to make things difficult here. I'm not a complicated man."

"Because it is right?" Em looked up at the dark silhouette of the rancher. This was what he wanted to know. "How do you know what is right?"

Ghen lifted his hat and scratched the top of his head. Then he nodded confidently and tapped his chest with his thumb. "The world is full of voices telling us all kinds of things. Right about here, though, is my heart. In there, is a voice that I've always known to know what's right. So, when I'm not sure what to do, I listen. When I feel the peace that voice gives me, about one way or another, I know that's what I gotta do."

"So only you know the right thing to do in the world?"

"No, no!" the rancher said quickly. "That's not what I meant. No, I'm sure everyone's got this voice, even you, most folk just don't like to listen to it. That or they listen to any other voice in the world and fool themselves into thinking that it's the one I'm talking about. That whatever they choose to listen to is telling them what's right, even if it isn't."

Em peered back into the shadowy reflection on the water, and there was enough light now that he could begin to see something of his own face in the water.

"How are you so sure everyone has this voice that knows what's right?" Em asked aloud "How do you know I have it? Even when I listen to what sounds right, it does not feel right."

Em heard more than saw, the rancher walk over and crouch down next to him. "Em, like I said, there are a bunch of voices in the world. Some things are natural, but that doesn't always make them good. Even when you do the right thing, some voices will shout at you, saying, 'You did a bad thing.' The voice I'm talking about, though, is a special one.

"I like to call it the Boss. It's easy to miss, but if you choose to listen you can hear it. When you listen to the Boss, there's just a peace about things. If you're wondering how I know everyone has it well..." The rancher touched his chest again with an outstretched thumb. "I've got peace about that."

There was a pause as Em thought about how to reply, but he didn't need to.

There was a rattle as the mule lifted her head and then shook her mane.

When Em didn't pick up the conversation, Ghen walked towards the animal. "I think Bo's ready to get on the road again."

Bo snorted.

"Well, Bo," the rancher replied, "I didn't say you wanted to get on the road, I just said you seemed like you were ready to."

The mule stomped, and Ghen shook his head.

"Don't mind her, she's got a problem with everything. How about you? Are you ready to hit the road again, or would you like a moment?"

"I... I'm ready, but can I rest in the back of the cart now? Not to sleep, I want to keep remembering, but I need to think."

There was just enough light to see the rancher smile. "Sure kid. Just do what you know is right and hop in whenever you're ready."

The cart pulled away from the creek within the hour and, as planned, Em sat alone in the back, reclining against their rolled-up blankets and bags, watching the stars disappear beneath a veil of blue.

"Are you there?" Em quietly asked the voices in his shadow.

The moment Em asked, Instinct's unseen presence appeared. He couldn't see it but knew the old voice sat hooded on the end of the cart with his legs dangling over the road. As his presence came to the forefront of Em's thoughts, the forgetful traveler began to hear music. Instinct strummed an instrument beyond sight, keeping the music in tune with the dawn.

Good morning, Little Em, the old voice said kindly, as he continued to play.

Eh... good morning. Em felt very foolish talking to someone he couldn't see and wasn't even sure was real, but last night he'd felt the presence of Instinct and Nature so strongly that he couldn't help but wonder if maybe they were.

Em had to ask, *Are you the voice? The one Ghen talked about.*

'The Boss?' No, I'm not him. Instinct laughed. *I mean, I guess I work for that voice, in a kind of way.*

So there is a voice then?

I'm only saying, Little Em, that there is something out there inviting you to good, whether you know it or not.

Me? Why me?

I know why I am helping you, but that's a story for another day, Instinct said with an unseen wink. *What you're really asking is, who are you to be helped? Or, even more accurately, who are you at all?*

The question brought the echoes back to mind. *Was that my past?*

I don't know. Instinct admitted. *Does it matter? Even if it was, would you suddenly want to quit your journey and go on as you are? All you have to remember, contained in a little book?*

No, Em thought quickly. *But what if that was my past? What does it make me?*

Instinct shook his unseen head. *You are who you choose to be. Ghen said something like this before, but nothing that has or is happening to you makes you who you are. It's what you choose to do with the past you've been given and the future you want to build that makes you, you. That's what Ghen was trying to tell you before, and I think it's what he was saying a moment ago, too.*

How? The only thing he spoke of was this Boss.

A voice that tells him what 'good folk' ought to do. A voice that helps him be the person you know and know you can trust. Would I be wrong to say that, even though you barely remember him, you find that you admire him a little?

When Instinct said it, Em had to admit that he did admire Ghen a little. Ghen had been so angry about that enemy's death, but he hadn't given up on Em. Em wasn't sure he wanted to be like Ghen, but Em couldn't help but marvel at what Ghen was.

I guess I do admire him. I think he sees some future for me that I cannot see myself.

And you want to see it too. Listening to the Boss is about being who you can be. That's how what he was saying ties together. It makes you so curious, doesn't it? If listening to the voice helped him find a way that fits him, you wonder if it could do the same for you.

Em, still staring up at the sky, nodded slightly. *If... if I wished to learn to hear this voice, do you know what I have to do?*

And what would you do if it was not so easy? Nature said, once more beyond this layer of the world. His strong voice took Instinct's place, but the music kept going even without the older voice present. *Ghen-so gave you a hint of what you can do, but he warned you that there are distractions. Is it so important to become what that voice can make you, that you would be willing to listen? Even if the instructions are not easy for you to hear or obey?*

Is the Boss that hard to hear?

No, but hearing is not the same as listening, Nature said, firmly. *I never heard the voice in my heart as Ghen-so does, but I see that there was a voice. It spoke through dreams, people, and whispers in the wind. All of which I ignored as I was coaxed down a different path than the one the Boss would have had me walk. As a teacher of great warriors, I had much responsibility but little recognition. So, I dismissed the words of the wise and was led to think I could build my own way to greatness.*

Your own way? How?

Nature growled dangerously, and Em could almost hear the creaking of his hands as the primal voice clenched his fists. *The cost of greatness was to* betray those I was meant to teach and protect. I did it, and I long enjoyed the rewards I had hoped for, but they did not last. The voice that calls to you called to me also, with many warnings of my road's end, and I did not listen.

Em was a little taken aback by the story. Once again, he wondered just what these voices really were.

Do not follow my way, Nature warned. I suffered for my deceit. By the time I tried to change, it was my last chance. A chance for one good act before the end, and to achieve it I faced great challenges. I battled men and monsters, persevering through great pain. Despite these threats, that time was a gift. In it, I was given a new life I did not deserve. A life where I could be loyal once again.

Em felt the unseen eyes of Nature turn toward him.

A life where I could save a final student I nearly let slip away. Failing them would have been my greatest disgrace.

I am not sure I understand. What do you mean? But by the time Em asked, Nature was gone.

Once again, Instinct sat on the edge of the cart, playing his tune. It rose to a crescendo as the musician neared the end of his song. Em worried that Instinct would vanish back into his shadow too, and decided to speak before he did.

Please stay. I still do not understand. All of you talk of paths and decisions, but what is it I have to do?

Instinct laughed brightly as the new sun rose over the horizon. Ah, Little Em, none of us came to live your life for you. Then the voice paused and became more serious as his song concluded, and he lowered his instrument. I can tell you're still scared, Little Em. Take comfort in knowing that, no matter how it speaks to you, the right way will always speak loud enough for you to hear when you need to.

Em had many more questions but could tell that they would only answer one more for now. So, taking a moment to consider, he decided on his question.

I am still unsure what you are or what you know. But knowing whatever you do, how would you try to find the right way if you were in my place?

Instinct grinned as he turned toward Em. *I guess there are three things I would do. First, consider your options as they come to you. Each one, no matter how silly or tough they seem. Second, trust the advice of those you know you can rely on. Lastly, and Little Em, most importantly...* Em couldn't see it but felt an unseen hand touch his chest just above his heart. *Listen.*

CHAPTER 18

RETURNING IN THE DAYLIGHT revealed much that had been hidden by night. One of the first things Nedain noticed was the abundance of dry brush around the campsite. It took only a moment for her to realize they'd walked straight into a noise trap.

"So that's how he got us. He heard us coming."

The most obvious thing to see in the daylight though, wasn't the trap. It was the sign of where the fight had taken place, and why Adler hadn't returned.

The grass and earth were stained with blotches of red where their team had been injured and bled as the fight continued. Yet those small stains paled in comparison to the variable pool of stained grass on the path of their escape. Between the morning dew, and the grass soaking it in, the stain would fade in two days tops. But for now, it was clear someone had died here.

Nedain grimaced.

Noren noticed the large stain as well, and Nedain knew he'd guessed its meaning.

He wasn't an idiot; if he had been, Nedain never would have worked for him. She couldn't stand idiots or arrogant pigs. Noren was arrogant, but could at least take some of her lack of grace. Even his name was an example, Noren was his last name after all. Nedain would call him Dorig, but Noren hated his first name and refused to be called it by anyone but his family.

Usually, he preferred to be called 'Mr. Noren', but Nedain refused to call him 'Mr.' anything. Titles like that made it sound as if the man or woman she said it to were somehow above her. Nedain tolerated some who thought like that, but she hated to think of anyone as her better.

In Nedain's mind, might made right. Status came from one's ability to destroy the other; equals were simply two people who hadn't yet discovered who was superior. Noren was teetering on the edge of being too much. Beyond his respect for her, Nedain tolerated him for two reasons. The first, of course, was that he paid well, but the second was that he recognized her strength.

Growing up, Nedain often felt belittled by others, either because they were physically bigger or because she was a woman. Even though in Ifeldia, women could join the military, the Guardians, or become magicians, there were still some tribes and men who thought of them as weaker. Nedain's favorite pastime was finding people with that view to correct.

Noren had always been different. From the beginning, he'd given her the chance to prove how much better she was than those who'd spent so much time looking down on her. The merchant was arrogant, but Nedain respected him, if nothing else, because he respected her.

"So, it seems Adler did not make it after all," Noren stated.

"No, he didn't." Nedain sighed. The 'I told you so' was written all over Noren's features. "Should we search for the body?"

Adler had been strong and useful, but Nedain wasn't exactly mourning him. She only suggested the search out of something like courtesy.

"Don't waste your time. What would the point be?" Noren wasn't any more torn up by his loss than she was. His employees might as well be numbers on page, save a select few.

"Should we just go then?"

"In a moment, Nedain, take some time to look around first and see if you can learn anything about our friend, Em." With a piercing smile, he added, "Oh, and try not to run if you see a shadow in the trees."

Nedain glared.

Yeah, she'd had to run, but she'd trusted Adler to be competent enough not to die. Noren seemed to think she was afraid, and that burned. She didn't fear anyone!

This Em had ruined her reputation with one of the few people who respected her the way she deserved. In her mind, Nedain marked it down as yet another reason, adding to the growing list, that she would deal with that little whelp when the opportunity arose.

"Don't be so quick to judge Noren. When we met him on the road, I thought he might be some watchman washout. I underestimated him, but I won't do that again. I know what he can do now, and how he fights. Next time, he bleeds."

Noren turned to her, looking amused. "I hope so."

Nedain wasn't sure what he found so funny, but his mocking attitude was quickly beginning to strain her patience. Not that there was much she could do. She technically could kill him whenever she wanted. He was a fat merchant, after all.

The problem was that would mean she'd have to leave Henaden or be hunted down by the company and the bounty it would no doubt place on her. That would be way too much trouble.

Nedain settled for grinding her teeth and growling.

Nedain consoled herself in knowing that when she killed Em, it would not only make her feel better, but she could earn back the respect she'd lost. Noren would forget everything, and the mocking would end. Everything would be right again once Em was dead.

Turning her mind away from vengeance, Nedain inspected the camp. From the state of the fire, the two campers had left a long time ago. Her best guess was that they left soon after the attack. That was fine, even if they got to Henaden, it wouldn't matter. According to Noren, it only mattered if they got back home. There was little left of the rest of the camp. They must still have taken the time to clean up before leaving. Adler's body was nowhere in sight, but that could be from wildlife or the two travelers. It was possible that—

Noren gasped suddenly and his face went deathly pale.

Fearing Em had returned, Nedain spun about, her hand on her sword hilt.

Someone was in the glade, just on their side of the tree line, but it wasn't Em. It was an elf.

He stood with his arms crossed, patiently waiting for something. Nedain's senses were sharp, but she hadn't noticed him approaching. He'd arrived soundlessly, despite the dry brush that had given her and Adler away last night.

Tall, like most elves, he was dressed completely in black. Everything he wore, despite the lack of color, was finely made without a stitch or a speck of dust on any of it. He was covered nearly completely, wearing a cloak, riding pants, gloves, and a shirt with a tall neck. Only the flesh above his chin was exposed to the sunlight, and every inch of that skin was so pale it looked sickly.

Despite that, the elf and his expression showed no sign of weakness from sickness or anything else. The contrast of his pale face against his jet-black hair made his sickly complexion appear almost ghostly. His elvish heritage was clear not only from his tall height but also by the long, stark white, pointed ears that protruded from the long locks of hair that flowed over his shoulders.

Nedain looked around and saw no sign of a horse. Had he just wandered up to them?

Not likely, she realized. No one so richly dressed, or looking so sickly, would wander through the woods alone. To be sure, she scanned the trees again but caught no sight of anyone else. He seemed to be alone.

The more she looked at him, the less she thought he was sick despite his complexion. The elf stood with an indescribable air of dangerous authority. The hairs on the back of Nedain's neck stood tall and goosebumps prickled on her skin. Something about his posture was unnatural.

She gritted her teeth, and her body tensed. Something in her mind began to scream at her to run! Either that or draw her sword and die fighting! It was a carnal feeling of being cornered which crept up in her chest. It kept growing until she couldn't hold it back any longer. She drew her blade and stepped in front of Noren.

Her movement broke him from a surprised trance. "Nedain, stop."

"Noren, do you know him somehow?"

Instead of answering, the merchant pushed past her and raced forward to prostrate himself before the monstrous elf.

"My lord, I was not expecting you for another season," Noren babbled.

"I have no time for chatter," the elf snapped. "I am here to collect on the favor you owe."

Noren tensed at the elf's voice but seemed somehow relieved when he heard this was about a favor. Almost happily, Noren asked, "What can I do to serve, my lord?"

"It is good that you know your place, but sadly, your servant does not." The elf's fierce eyes fell on Nedain.

Noren's head whipped over his shoulder and gave Nedain a look of both terror and rage. In a terrified screech, he yelled, "Nedain! Get down and beg for your forgiveness."

Noren had money, but Nedain wasn't going to bow down to this pointy-eared pale freak. Her pride demanded more, and if this was how she was going to be treated, then maybe both Noren and the elf needed to be corrected.

"Now that's too far Nor..."

The elf barely flicked his eyes toward her, but Nedain felt suddenly... blank. All sensation vanished for an instant, but when it returned, it was even worse. Everything was just wrong!

Dizzy, she collapsed in a heap as if the earth had given way beneath her feet. Sweat began to trickle down her face. She felt her nose pouring blood, but barely noticed as she heaved unexpectedly. Then again, and again, until her stomach was emptied. When her stomach had no more to give, she coughed and spluttered. Nedain tried numbly to rise, but the twinging in her stomach was small compared to the vertigo that clouded her mind. She only collapsed again, writhing on the ground. She tried again, working carefully, but found she could rise no higher than her knees.

The feeling of being cornered came over her again, only worse. As a cold shiver ran up her spine, Nedain's thoughts spun with visions of being crushed like a bug under a boot.

Now that Nedain was subdued, Noren's lord ignored her entirely, and she was allowed to remain gasping on her knees.

"My apologies, my lord, I have told none of you. She did not recognize your station," Noren explained quickly.

"I shall let this pass. So far, you have been a fruitful investment. Fate says you may continue to be."

Noren only bowed lower as the elf continued to speak.

"However, we are wasting time, and I am in a hurry. I have long sought to reclaim the sylwerd. The threads of fate and other signs concur, it is near." A greedy light burned behind the elf's stony expression. "I will have it back. What I require of you is to use all your resources to seek out the sylwerd and return it to me. You will focus your search on the nearby city of Henaden, as I find you have authority there. Should you find what I seek, you will bring it to me without delay. Am I understood?"

"Yes, your lordship," Noren answered quickly, then paused. "But... uh... please forgive my ignorance. I don't know what a sylwerd looks like or even is."

Nedain was starting to recover from her sickness and visions. She was just lucid enough to know she had no idea what a sylwerd was either. Despite her fear and dizziness, she found herself somewhat fascinated by the mystery of the unexpected lord with the strange request.

"I would not expect that you do. This time, your ignorance is forgiven. Treat the sylwerd like a person, its form is like that of a human male like yourself, only younger. This will give you further description." The dark-clad elf dropped a small scroll in front of Noren.

Noren reached out without raising his head and took the scroll, quickly reading it, his head still bowed.

The lord turned to leave, but stopped and without turning asked, "How long have you been tied to me now?"

"My lord, we met over twenty and three falls ago."

Was this elf really from that long ago? Nedain could barely believe it, that was before anyone had ever heard of the Noren Trading Company. Nedain hadn't even heard a rumor of Noren having connections with someone like this.

"I see, such a short time, but from your graying hairs, you humans must see it as an age. I have cared little for you in the past, but remind me, what is your name?"

"I am Dorig Noren, my lord."

"This favor is greater than you know, Dorig Noren. Succeed and you will find yourself greatly rewarded. Fail, and you will regret the moment you took in the breath of life. Do you understand?" The elf's tone was as solid as granite.

"Of course, shall we bind it in contract?"

At Noren's words, Nedain felt the change in the air. For the first time, the elf paused, considering, but about what she had no clue. He glanced upward, his eyes tracking something she couldn't see.

She could have sworn the elf chuckled before turning back to the merchant. "An unexpectedly useful investment you are, Noren. Stand."

Noren bolted up.

Both the elf and Noren spoke too quietly to hear for nearly a minute. The only thing Nedain caught was, "Is that alright, my lord?" from Noren.

"I accept," the elf said, his eyes watching Noren with careful interest.

Without another word, the elf then took his leave, simply walking into the opposite tree line across the road. Nedain didn't see where he went from there. Her body was still too weak to rise any further than her knees.

She remained where she was until, after another minute lost in a daze, it passed. Whatever had pinned her to her knees disappeared, and the fit left as suddenly as it had come. At first, she stood slowly, worried about falling again, but found she was completely fine. Groaning slightly, she began to wipe off some of what she'd unintentionally rolled in during the fit.

When she looked around, her employer was alone, there was no sign of Noren's lord. The merchant's eyes were again scanning the scroll the pale elf had left behind. Had it not been for the scroll, Nedain could have imagined it was all some very bad dream.

Whatever that elf was, he had magic, no doubt about it. She'd never met a true magician before, only the ones who played at having power. They were nothing to fear, but that elf... Nedain shivered. That magic was unreal, she'd been helpless against him. She wanted to be angry, but she couldn't muster the fire. There was nothing she could do. Nothing at all... What was that elf?

"Noren?" she said.

He snapped up, nearly jumping at her voice. A strange light in his eyes. "Nedain, where is the driver?"

"He went into the woods to relieve himself."

Noren scanned the woods impatiently. "If he isn't back soon, we depart without him. We're going back to Henaden."

"What about Ghen and Em? If they're moving slow, we may catch them."

"No matter, if we succeed at finding the sylwerd, I may not need Ghen's land anymore. Even if I do, this may allow us to be rid of that annoying rancher even more easily."

Nedain wondered if that meant all this farmland was for the elf.

"Who was that Noren? How do you know him?" Nedain expected Noren to be cross about her demanding tone, but he cackled gaily.

Noren looked in the direction the elf had wandered towards. There was no sign of the black-clad figure. "Oh, my 'friend?' I know almost nothing about him, not even his name. As to *how* we met, that is a long story. The shortest version is I scammed him once, and he found out. Now let's go get the horses, I want us to get to Henaden as fast as we can."

"You what?" Nedain said, shocked. The meaning of the words registered slowly.

Noren only laughed again.

Nedain wasn't sure if she should be horrified or impressed.

CHAPTER 19

"YOU KNOW HOW I said we made good headway in the night?" Ghen asked when Em shifted back to the front seat of the cart.

"Yes Ghen-*sa*, I remember."

"Well, originally, I figured we'd get to Henaden tomorrow morning. Thing is, since we went through the night, I think we might make it to Henaden before half the afternoon is gone."

Em had still been in a quiet and thoughtful mood, but this made him jolt upright. "So soon?"

"If I was riding alone on Bo, our time would be about normal," Ghen said. "With a cart and passengers, I thought it would take longer. It might have if we hadn't gotten that early start."

"Good, I want to get to Henaden as soon as I can."

Ghen grinned, hearing Em's anticipation. "We still have another few hours yet, but we'll be leaving the forest soon. Then we'll start passing by all the small towns that surround Henaden."

Em nodded and peered ahead. If the city was as close as Ghen hinted, he hoped to catch a glimpse of it in the distance. Yet, while the foliage was beginning to thin, there were still too many trees to see very far in any direction, and Em wasn't even sure which side of the road Henaden would be on.

Then a new thought struck him. He really didn't know anything about Henaden. His journal had no details about it other than that it was a trade city and that Master D'gui was supposed to be there. So he decided to ask more about it.

"Is Henaden large?"

"According to my uncle, Henaden isn't big compared to some other cities. Not that there are many cities around here, so it's big for locals. Personally, I've only been to one other place that could actually be called a city. That would be Cobaden, and it was *way* bigger than Henaden."

"Do you often travel to many different places?" Em asked, having no idea that Ghen had explained this before.

"Not me, really these places are everywhere I've ever been. My father and uncle took me and my two cousins to Cobaden for the big festival that's held there every sixth fall, to celebrate Roleius making Ifeldia what it is. It's a big deal, but the trip takes two weeks from home to Cobaden. That's not a trip any rancher can make lightly, so we only went to the festival once. I still went there a few times after that when I met May there, but that is still the furthest I've ever been from home."

"Do they always hold the big festival in that city, or is that only sometimes?"

"It's held in most cities in Ifeldia. They just make it a bigger event in Cobaden because, before Roleius took it over, it was the capital of En-Athen. Also, probably because Old King Ordisus's estate is out that way too."

"He is on your council of rulers," Em recalled the king's name from his notebook. "How long has King Ordisus ruled?"

"A really really long time," Ghen said. "He was the 'old king' when I was a kid. People have been waiting for him to drop off for probably twenty to thirty falls now. You may not remember, but before you ask, I don't know how the change of rulers works. I have no idea who will be next, or if it will change anything." Ghen added guessing Em's next questions exactly.

The two traveled for a while, talking peaceably, mostly about facts Em had heard before. Yet Em's mind wasn't entirely on the conversation, it reminded him too much of his curse and his actions from the night before. So, he distracted himself by listening to the rhythmic rattle of the cart and by looking behind them at the pattern painted on the road by the spring sun and the shadows of the woods. The designs of the forest were a network of light that wove across the simple and yet came alive as each glimmering line shifted in the wind. He watched the road this way until the light around them brightened and the trees thinned as they left Koen Forest.

Breaking free of the walls of foliage, small towns and pastureland were revealed in the distance. Over time, the small towns grew larger as Ghen's cart closed in on them. The main road never passed through any of the towns, so neither did they, but the cart did pass closely by two such villages on their way.

Em found them strange, but interesting to look at. Mainly, his fascination was with the buildings, because in both towns they had two distinct types of architecture which were very different from one another. The first time he saw the two types of buildings, it just left Em confused, but when he kept seeing the same differences in the second town they passed, he realized that the difference was based on age.

Older buildings, houses, and structures, like wells, were formed of stone and clay. Each of them was shaped like large blocks in one way or another. Most of these had stairs on their outer walls granting access to the flat roof. Atop many of these were furniture or clay pots filled with family herbs, turning their roof into an extension of their living space. The newer structures were made more of wood with only a little stone at the corners. Their roofs were slanted and their ends were either more rectangular than the square design of the older homes.

When Em considered why they might have changed, he recalled what Ghen had just been telling him about King Roleius. The change must have something to do with the exchange of rulers Ghen had said took place centuries ago. Perhaps, Em guessed, it was based on a development that Roleius had brought with him to the land, or the opposite, in which the technique to make the old homes had been lost in the war.

He was still considering this, and trying to guess what the king could have brought with him to make these new buildings better than the old ones when he spied a large white stone building on a far distant hilltop. At first, he thought it might just be a rock, but even in the distance, he could see it had edges too distinct for nature. To be seen from so far away, it must be big and, therefore, Em assumed, important.

He opened his mouth to ask Ghen about it, but the question halted on his tongue.

As they left the second town behind, Em could see it more clearly. Now, he could tell that what he was looking at wasn't a building at all, it was too long, and there was an extra depth to it. Em could see now that most of what he was seeing was a wall, and the rest was behind it since the wall wasn't very tall. In the midday light, the wall's white stone shone like a beacon, and Em slowly guessed what he was looking at.

"Is that Henaden?" Em asked the question in a whisper. As if he feared, by speaking too loudly, he would frighten away the city and never see it again.

"Yes," Ghen said softly, "that's it. Henaden."

Em slumped in his chair so quickly that Ghen half tried to catch him, but the forgetful swordsman caught himself before he toppled off the cart.

"Are you alright?"

"Yes, Ghen-*sa*. It is just that I find I am suddenly tired." Exhausted might have been a better description. At that moment, Em felt it all wash over him. All his efforts... Em could not remember a day of it, but now, seeing the city, Em felt how long the journey had been.

"It was so long," he whispered.

It felt so strange to see Henaden. Even stranger was how emotional he felt, even though Em only remembered reading the name of that city for the first time not so long ago.

"How many first times has it been?" Em asked no one in particular "How many days did I wake up for the first time and, day after day, seek Henaden? There it is." Leaning back, with the cart supporting him, Em felt tears well in his eyes.

Em bore scars, healed from forgotten wounds. He wore shoes, torn from so many forgotten steps. Then, his eyes, worn down from how many forgotten lives? But now, finally, he was here.

"It was worth it. We did it. It *was* worth it," Em told them. He said it to each of them, all who were gone, every Em from the forgotten days.

Somewhere, Instinct and Nature both smiled broadly.

Well done, Little Em. Well done. Instinct said proudly.

At the sound of Instinct's words, exhaustion faded to relief.

Em laughed softly, not with abandon, but with a deep, peaceful joy. His laughter lingered, flowing until tears welled up and traced down his cheeks. He wiped them away, only for more to spill, unable to contain either the tears or the laughter.

"I did it!" Em yelled so loud his voice cracked, and he fell back again laughing even harder.

Ghen, at his side, marveled. Em had grinned, smiled, and maybe even chuckled once, but hearing Em laugh, really laugh, was entrancing. There was so much in it. Ghen could hear Em's pain, exhaustion, and even fear as it all washed away under his laughter. All that misery was being replaced by relief, a bubbling joy, and the wonder of so much more!

Later, when Ghen tried to put what he'd heard into words, all he could say was, "It was a good laugh. I wish I'd heard it sooner. It showed me how much the trip was really worth."

CHAPTER 20

FAR LATER, AFTER EM'S mirth at the sight of Henaden had faded to a subtle beat that drummed in tune with his heart, Bo and her cart towed Em and her owner up as the road inclined near their destination.

"We've already covered that you know the different tribes, and, while most of this land is full of humans like us, Henaden is a bit different. There'll be people from all over so. Try not to offend any of the tribes here, some of them can be a little short on patience for humans," Ghen warned.

Em knew he'd met some of the different tribes before, he just didn't know when. Luckily, he wasn't sure it mattered. He could identify and recognize something when he saw it.

An example being a mule, like Bo, when he looked at her, Em knew that she was a mule and that meant she was a cross between a horse and a donkey. He knew they were used as beasts of burden or mounts, but he had no memory of any mules other than Bo.

It was the same with the different tribes, each tribe represented the different peoples of the far world. The human tribe, the satyr tribe, the dwarf tribe, the kyate-siv tribe, and more. The odd tribe out being cross-tribe. While they weren't common, they were not quite a rare sight. Cross-tribes were the living result of two tribes bearing a child together.

"I believe I can be careful enough," Em assured him. "What I am more concerned about is how you plan to find Master D'gui, or do we first sell your root?"

Ghen shook his head. "Selling the root isn't as easy as it sounds, we'd better find your mystic first. Lucky for us, I know where the city offices are. If your sorcerer is here, I bet they can probably point us in the right direction."

Considering Ghen's words, Em began to wonder if Master D'gui was human. If not, would they be less willing to help him? "If no tribes beyond humans live here, why do any of them trade in Henaden?"

"Well, in Marden there's a dwarf family I know. So, it's not like no other tribes live here. Just not bunches of any other tribe. They come because I guess this is where trade is or has been for as long as I can remember. Usually, if you aren't human, you still need special papers to enter most cities. Henaden doesn't care a wit about that, though. So, it's just not a problem for them here."

Em opened his mouth, but Ghen shook his head and cut him off.

"Before you ask, I've only got guesses and rumors as to why this law was made. I gave them to you before, but since you didn't write them down. I'll bet you found them as useless as I think they'd be."

"I see," Em said, dropping his unasked question.

"You know," Ghen said, having an idea, "if you ask someone who ain't human and has to put up with the law, maybe they'll know more about why King Ordisus made it."

Em considered this. "If I get the chance I might, but I think I have enough to do already. I understand enough for now, despite the laws, other tribes come to Henaden because it ignores the law that annoys them, and because of Henaden's trade."

"More or less," Ghen said.

The cart rolled up the slope to Henaden, and Em's thoughts turned to how the city was built. The city was built on a short plateau with a sheer edge circling the southwest side of the city, while its landscape tapered down to the east with a steady slope. Bo pulled her load uphill on a more rigid slope to a smaller southeastern gate. According to Ghen, the city had been founded as a trading post on the top of the hill and, early on in its history.

"When they started getting lots of trade though and became a city," he said, "they got too big to just stay on the flat top. So, they expanded in waves. To grow, they built on the gentle downturn of the east side. It's kind of funny, as they went down, the area they could build on got wider.

Now, when you stand on the top and look down, it sprawls out like a cup of spilled milk towards the east."

"Why does the wall seem so strange?" Em asked, referring to how on the western side the top was flat, but at a random point, it began to stutter step down. Tactically, it made little difference, but it looked disjointed and out of place.

Ghen snorted. "That's 'cause someone got cocky. See, I remember when they started building this wall. All the talk was about how they'd make it, so the top was flat all the way around the city. At the city's highest point, since the cliff keeps anyone from getting in, it was and is little more than a rail. Seriously, the stone blocks are shorter than the fences I keep my stock in, but on the opposite side it was supposed to be super tall to keep the same height all the way around." Ghen shook his head. "Problem was, no one really thought about how big that would actually be until they started making the wall." Ghen pointed to the same spot Em had, where crude wooden posts sat around some of the blocks of the wall. "That is where they realized how stupid they were, and decided a smaller wall would be just fine. They don't expect any fighting to go on here anyway.

"Henaden and our lands are far from where the war's going on and even when things drift our way the Koen Forest is between us and that part of Ifeldia, so we aren't in any real danger. The wall is more decoration than defense."

"So that is where they changed their building style," Em muttered to himself.

When he compared the walls on the opposite sides of the awkward joint, he could see it clearly. On his left, the wall was uniform and flat with firm blocks, with only the occasional support showing itself. On the right, the wall would continue for a little more than a house length before it met another joint, these less awkward than the first. After which, the wall continued as before, only slightly lower down.

The walls surrounded the city for as far as Em could see. As they climbed and the wall sloped down, Em began to see the tops of roofs and spires of buildings peeking above the wall. Much like the towns they'd passed, each one seemed a haphazard blend of designs. Yet, there was an underlying order to it all—one Em couldn't quite grasp with his limited perspective.

A small clatter drew Em's eyes forward as a wagon ahead of them jumped over a loose stone. It had joined the road pulled in front just as they'd started up the slope to Henaden. Em guessed it was another person on their way to try to sell items as Ghen was. Looking at the wagon, Ghen began to smile, and Em could not fathom why.

"Do you know that driver?" he asked.

"Huh?" Ghen said, with a raised eyebrow, puffing on his pipe.

"The wagon driver, do you know them? You seem to enjoy watching them travel ahead of us."

"Oh, that," Ghen said. "I don't recognize the wagon, but who knows, maybe we've met. I'm just smiling at the fact we're moving at all, and thinking maybe I ought to sell early every season. Entering through the small gate up ahead instead of the bigger one out east is faster, but I usually get stuck waiting in a long line, so it feels like it takes forever. I've seen people backed up from hilltop to bottom, but right now, there's only that one."

Looking back over his shoulder, Em could see two riders on horseback with a cart in the far distance. They might have been on their way to Henaden, but they were still far away and might divert before arriving. Nothing like the numbers Ghen was describing.

The ground began to level out as the cart reached the top of the hill, and Em detected more of the small gate they were coming toward. The gate was built into part of the strong level wall that Henaden had begun with. The tall wooden doors were ornate in their designs, but not overly rich or gaudy. The surprising thing was their thickness. The gates were open, so Em could see their depth, and it was surprising how thin they were for outer gates.

Ghen had mentioned these weren't the main gates, and that Henaden cared little for defense, but Em was still surprised. Then Em took another glance at their height. Although the doors were tall, they were not huge. The wagon in front of them was barely small enough to fit through on its own.

"It is a good thing that no one else is leaving from this gate," Em said.

"You're telling me. I can't tell you how many times there's been a hold up with us all trying to get in and two or three carts trying to get out. The hoplites occasionally have to get involved to break up fights, and that only slows things down more."

"Hoplites?" Em asked, unfamiliar with the word. From its usage, he assumed they must be a kind of soldier or men of law.

"You don't know that one? Well, around here we use it the same way we use the word guard. Not that many outsiders use it. It's probably something left over from the old days. Still..." Ghen trailed off, only shrugging his shoulders.

Thinking about these guards, Em looked for them.

As Ghen had suggested, they were nearby, but woefully inattentive. They were dressed in foreign armor, and were technically at their post, but sat lazily off to the side of the road. One even with his back to them. Em shook his head disappointedly as he noticed the twin spears and round shields propped against the city wall, far out of reach if they were needed.

There was also an attendant who circled the wagon in front of them before waving it through. As Ghen ushered Bo forward, Em saw exactly what these hoplites were doing. They sat at a rickety wooden table with an empty spot where, no doubt, the attendant belonged.

Clearly they didn't expect any real work, since the hoplites were holding cards, with an extra hand laid aside face down in front of the attendant's spot. The only reason the guards even looked Ghen's way was because they were impatient for the attendant to get finished so they could get back to their game.

"No, defense is not something this city concerns itself with," Em muttered to himself.

Ghen pulled to a stop as the attendant held up a hand.

The attendant lifted his pad, ready to make notes. "Business?" he asked, his voice betraying absolute boredom.

"Trade, selling two bags of nightroot, and planning to visit some folk here as well to get some medical work done," Ghen answered happily.

"What tribe are you from? If you are of mixed tribe, please state both." The attendant spoke as though this question was well rehearsed, and he was ready for this to be over.

"I'm human, no mix." Ghen then looked at Em.

"Human, no mix," Em answered truthfully, at least as far as he knew.

The attendant noted it all down on his pad and then gestured through the gate. "Fine. Please..." The attendant's words trailed off, and Em found himself caught in the man's gaze. The attendant looked to the guards who were chatting among themselves, then back to Em and the clothes he wore. "I... uh... You said you are here to sell nightroot?"

The attendant was looking at Em, but it was Ghen who nodded and said, "Yep, and to talk to someone about helping my friend."

"The medical work?"

"Yep."

The attendant's eyes flew around, and his mouth worked without words for a moment. He looked like he was on the edge of saying something, but a glance toward Em's swords made him pause. After another moment of internal dilemma, the attendant waved them through nervously. "Well... um... cause no trouble." Quickly adding, "Good day." He stiffly walked back towards the game table, constantly glancing over his shoulder.

Curiously, Em noticed that the attendant hadn't checked their cart to verify their supplies, even though he had checked the wagon before. It was as if he wanted to ignore Em and anything to do with him. Was it out of fear?

"But why would he be afraid of me?"

Ghen hadn't noticed and whistled as he flicked the reins, the cart rolling into Henaden.

Rolling into the city, Em soon dismissed the strange encounter. He had to blink as light from the afternoon sun shone off of the cobble. The heat rising off of the stone paved roads warmed his face and Em surveyed the place he'd sought after for so long.

"We're in Hilltop Proper, the part where Henaden was started," Ghen explained. "It's a nice part of town on the outside, lots of old buildings, and where the city has the governor's office."

Indeed, the buildings in this part of the city were old. Each was made of carved stone or shaped from clay, but Em wasn't sure. Whatever it was, it gave an appearance like natural stone. Unlike the villages outside the city, some roofs were tiled around the edges in a combination of both the old and new styles of construction. In the distance, taller and more important buildings formed a circle, all made of shining pale stone. Even at a distance, they were clearly ornate, with large pillars and carved designs, even if the designs themselves were too small to make out at a distance.

Em was watching them, wondering if that was their destination, when he asked, "The governor, will he be the one we need to speak to about the master in the city offices?"

"Not exactly, but they're close by. I've never seen the governor, but I doubt he wants random folk like us just wandering into his office. There are other buildings for records and things like we're hunting."

Before reaching these monumental buildings, Ghen turned off the street, crossing through a tight alley to a parallel road. Then he continued toward the center of the city again. However, this path led further east, away from the old monuments.

Now that they weren't going towards them, Em was about to ask about the buildings, when a low din began to echo down the stone walkway towards them.

Ghen made another turn and directed Bo out of the back roads. The din grew far louder, and Em saw its source. A bustling square was ahead of them with a fountain in its center. Many figures, some riding, some walking, and a few in a run, flowed around the circumference of the square, each on their own errands.

Ghen nodded toward the square and raised his voice to be heard over the din, "This was where the first gates of Henaden would have been, but they were long gone before my lifetime. Now it's where the old city ends and the steps begin."

"The steps?" Em shouted back.

"You'll see," Ghen said, with a wink. "The important thing is it's also where the main road of Henaden, Buyer's Road people like to call it, starts. That's where this trade city gets its business."

Em thought they were already where the city got its business. All around the outside of the square stalls lined the road, but these weren't foreign traders. Em was starting to understand. These were local market men, and their stalls matched shops that either stood behind them or weren't far away. The only purpose of these vendors was to advertise the glories within their true store. Many of the other buildings around the fountain did not seem to be businesses at all. They were formal and rigid, little more than large parlors for rich housing.

Ghen turned Bo around the north side of the fountain and slowed her pace as they walked by the largest opening in the square. The resounding din became a roar as Em got his first look at the main road of Henaden. The gate they'd come through was misleading. Despite only a single other wagon entering in front of Ghen, business was already booming.

Henaden's famous Buyer's Road ran from the fountain at Hilltop Proper into the far reaches of the lower steps, where it came to meet the main gate of the city. The road itself lived up to its name as a variable bazaar even in this slower season of the market.

The roar of it rolled over them at the head of the road like crashing waves, thousands of competing voices fighting to be heard. The city was alive with the clamor of "Sales!", "Deals!", and "The finest!" shouted from the mouth of every vendor crowded shoulder to shoulder on the busy street side. The echoing uproar carried in its tide more than the sellers, though, it brought hints of music, chatter, and laughter as warm as the sun above.

Em was overwhelmed by the size of it all. The road expanded out for miles, weaving down the descent of Henaden's plateau. Yet every visible cobble was cluttered with traders, shoppers, and salespeople of all types. The road was so wide that few people or wagons in the press disturbed any of the clusters of shoppers that lined the roadside. Instead, they made up a mass within the mass of the Ifeldia's trade bastion.

The small parts of the streets that were visible were alight with dancing colors, as a rainbow of banners, overhanging stall covers, shook in the wind and bright light of early afternoon. Between shifting forms and flowing colors, Henaden's marketplace was as alive as any of the people that moved through it.

From their seats at the top of the plateau, Em was able to see the rest of Henaden. The city sloped down from Hilltop Proper, leaving his view of the road all but unobstructed. Off of the main road, many side roads jutted out perpendicular to Buyer's Road.

Despite the changing elevation, each of these roads remained flat. Each sat atop a lattice of scaffolding, keeping aloft the roads and buildings on its level. Further down Buyer's Road, the next road jutting out was built on a scaffolding a step lower than the first. The same trend repeated all down the hillside of Henaden. It reminded Em of standing at the top of a...

"Ah, a staircase," Em realized. So that was what Ghen had meant by, 'the steps.'

Each step was slightly wider than the last until the ground was level enough that the scaffolding was unnecessary, and all the land could be used. Even at the end of the city, the walls bustled with as much movement as the city streets. They were still unfinished, and Em could make out the builders along the top of the wall, bustling like ants on a mound.

Em wished he could see more of their progress on the walls, and what they were going to be like when finished, but it was all too far away. The construction was on the opposite side of the city, and he knew it was a testament to his eyesight that he could tell it was still being worked on at all.

As Bo sauntered past the open street, Em was a little disappointed that Ghen wasn't taking them down Buyer's Road and its colorful stalls. Still, he consoled himself, knowing that he might have the opportunity soon. Henaden was not a city he expected to leave very quickly.

Clearing the attractive sight of the bazaar, Em turned his eyes back to the part of the city closer to his person. Ghen was right about more than Henaden's appearance. Its population was as diverse as the colorful banners in Buyer's Road. Already Em spied various tribespeople, more in a moment than he'd seen throughout the entire rest of the day.

Em spied the cat-eyed kyate-siv, with their long hair and lithe steps. The prancing satyrs, whose legs more resembled those of goats than men and whose heads were crowned with twin horns. The regal, long-living elves strode through the mix with proud postures, their slender features and pointed ears marking them unmistakably. The dwarves, small and stocky, had ever-calloused skin and faces shaded by robust beards. And of course, prolific humans surged through the crowd in abundance, with neutral forms and features they were similar to many of the tribes, yet never quite like any of them. In this city, all the tribes came in every height, weight, and complexion imaginable.

"A liome?" Em asked, astonished, looking at the tall figure in the distance.

"Where?" Ghen asked, and then he saw the immense figure. "Well, I'll be, even here we don't see those giants very often. In fact, I think that big fella might be the first one I've ever seen with my own eyes."

I would think so, Nature said, as the giant passed out of view. *This city is too close to the mountains for many of their tribe to like it, but that one seems to be alone, which is odd in itself.*

Em could feel knowledge of the tribe well up within him even though he could not remember where he might have learned any of it.

Sometimes called plains or coast giants, the liome tribe was a more reserved group that was well known to largely keep to itself. They preferred the company of their own tribe and flat open spaces over almost anywhere else.

"They certainly are big," Ghen breathed.

Em nodded with silent agreement. The titanic figure of the liome looked in almost every way like a human except for their size and bright eyes. That one had been at least twice Ghen's height, not to mention how much taller it was than Em with his short stature.

Do not be fooled. Nature said as Bo continued to circle the fountain. *Your tribe and that of the liome may appear similar but your tribes are very different in how you act.*

When the cart reached the opposite side of the square from where they'd entered, Ghen turned off onto a side street. Then he altered course again a moment later, leading them back towards the more official buildings. Yet they'd barely started in this direction before they pulled into a much smaller and less ornate little square. It was full of dusty buildings, all clearly older than either Ghen or Em.

At first glance, Em thought they were old stores. Many large windows were cut into them to present wares and bold signs hung above the doors. However, there were no wares in any of the windows, and, when he read the signs, he realized that these weren't stores after all.

Ledgers of Rights and Management, read the first sign. Another, *Office of City Appeals.* In front of this one, a surly dwarf sat rubbing his temples.

Looking around at the rest of the signs, Em noticed all of them seemed to be official offices for the city. Ghen took the cart to a small opening between two buildings, where there was a rail for tying animals.

"I see these are the offices, but were they stores before that?" Em asked as he got down from his seat.

Ghen hopped down after him and scratched the top of his head as he looked around at the offices. "I guess so, but after Henaden grew, it looks like they became the offices of all the city and its bookkeepers. Doesn't matter what they were though, now they're how we're gonna hunt down this Master D'gui." The rancher rubbed his hands together excitedly. "Let's find ourselves a mystic!"

CHAPTER 21

SAUNTERING INTO THE *OFFICE of Housing and District Assignments,* as the door claimed, Ghen was pleased to see the chairs set beside the entrance were empty. He'd been in this office only once before. It had been a small experience, but a memorable one. At the time, he'd come to ask about what inns were in the city after the one his family regularly visited had closed down. Three hours of waiting later, he was ready to set up camp in the office itself.

The city could take forever to get its act together, and there wasn't a thing to do while waiting. The chairs were for waiting folk and, Ghen recalled, they were downright uncomfortable and got worse the longer he waited. Ghen remembered that way the back rested, he couldn't really lounge, and it made his rear hurt. Since his last time here, the chairs and the office didn't look like they'd changed a bit.

The office itself was small and cramped. Over half of the room was taken up by a large desk that went from wall to wall. Ghen guessed that was intentional, since behind the desk was a back room they kept locked. It was the same room where they kept all their records for the city and was not a place where just anyone was supposed to wander into. At that moment the door was open, and Ghen could see the little room had cupboards down each wall and shelved boxes where scrolls were kept on everything.

Ghen could read, but thinking of that much writing hurt his head a little.

Today, a young kyate-siv girl sat at the front desk. Not that 'young' wasn't a relative term between tribes. Kyate-siv tended to live only slightly over fifty falls at best. Their tribe thought of each other as adults after about ten falls, and this girl appeared to be around twelve.

Their tribe always had the unique trait of growing small whiskers along their cheeks, giving them six to eight dark lines sprouting out the sides of their face. In the dark, you might think you were looking at a human. But once you turned the lights on, the whiskers and the tuft of hair on the tops of their slightly pointed ears gave away their kyate-siv heritage.

Ghen spoke to get the girl's attention. "Good afternoon."

The girl looked up from whatever she'd been writing to meet Ghen's eyes. While the eyes of a human might come in blues, greens, and browns, a kyate-siv's were either bright green or orange. From the look in her orange eyes, she was probably nice, but not the type of young lady you wanted to make angry. She seemed like she might hold a grudge.

"Hello. Is there something we can help you with?"

Ghen decided to get straight to the point. "We're looking to meet with a sorcerer."

"In Henaden?" She sounded surprised. "I've heard of them passing through, but suffice it to say that there aren't many of those here. Depending on the work you need done, I know some people who might be able to help you. It would probably be easier to get help from them, than anyone who truly practices magic."

"That's nice of you, miss, but I think this one may actually live here, or at least I hope they do. A Master D'gui."

The girl leaned back in her chair and tapped her lips with her quill. "Hmm, I don't know the name, but let me check the records." She got up and turned to go into the back room, her waist-long hair flowing behind her.

That was another thing about the kyate-siv, be it on their chin, top of their head, or anywhere else, they always had hair that grew *very* long. There was no rule in their tribe about their hair or anything, but a shaved kyate-siv was about as common as a purple horse.

Ghen turned to see that Em had silently slipped in behind him and seated himself in one of the chairs. "So, Em, what do you think of Henaden?"

"I am not sure what I expected if I am being honest. The city is impressive, and I would very much like to explore it for myself, but it does not match what I imagined."

"How so?"

"From the way you described it, I imagined it was smaller."

Ghen shrugged. "Well, like I said, I haven't seen many cities in my life. Of the two I've seen, this one's the smaller, but I guess it's closer to medium-sized... well, I don't know about that either. Maybe we should leave how big or small it is to those more traveled."

Em smiled just slightly. "That is fair." Then he adjusted in his chair for the third time since sitting. "I also imagined the seating to be more comfortable."

Ghen grinned. "It gets worse the longer you sit, believe me."

"Don't blame me for the chairs, I just work here," the kyate-siv said.

Ghen jumped a little in surprise. The girl had come back, and he hadn't noticed as he talked to Em. "No problem, miss. Were you able to find our mystic?"

"Well, I was able to find a 'Master Ida D'gui' in our records. They are registered in the city, but I should let you know that the lady Master D'gui is registered as a researcher and scholar. If she is a mystic, she hasn't informed us."

Ghen winced, fearing he might have accidentally gotten the master in trouble. "Is that a problem?"

"Hmm? Oh, no. We don't require it or anything, I only mean to say she isn't advertising magic if she can do it at all. If you want her help, she may not be taking requests. If Master D'gui is a sorcerer, then I fear the lady will turn you away."

"Wait... she's a lady?" Ghen asked, finally picking up the pronoun.

"Yes, she is." The employee smirked.

Ghen was glad he'd learned that before meeting Master D'gui herself, it might have made for an awkward introduction.

"If it's all the same, we'd still like to know where she might be. She might even be expecting my friend here." He thumbed over his shoulder to Em. "Is her home public?"

In Henaden, houses were marked as public or private when occupied, that way the city knew if the residents wanted people to be able to find them or not. The worker tapped her lip with her quill again.

"It isn't, but she has a public place marked as her research office. Though why, I don't know. See, the truth is, her home and office are at the same address. So why she has one private and one public is beyond me."

Ghen wasn't sure the office worker was supposed to tell him that, but she didn't look ashamed. This girl was probably like May and Kaddley, they would talk about anything they felt like, and no one could tell them differently.

If the girl was going to offer it though, Ghen wasn't going to say no.

"That'll work," he said, wrapping the top of the desk with his knuckles happily. "So, where is this research office?"

In the odd-shaped house on the eighteenth step of Henaden, Master D'gui sat next to the open window watching her apprentice in the backyard and silently rooted for him. The backyard wasn't large but was quite peaceful. It was the perfect place for Ceahan to clear his mind.

"You can do it," she mumbled in hushed tones. He needed to project the flow perfectly to complete the test.

She heard the magic pulsing in the air around the bubble of water suspended in front of Ceahan by his innate power. He was sitting on the ground, staring fixedly at the bubble and the plate floating in its center.

The plate exercise was simple, yet challenging. Master D'gui was proud of having devised such an ingenious test. Her apprentice, in theory, would set the cheap clay plate in a water pail and, using magic, influence the water to make a bubble. Then he would lift the bubble and plate into the air above the ground. After holding the bubble up for two minutes, he then would bring it down without damaging the plate. That was the test, and it was just what Ceahan needed to learn.

The young man had excess in spades but in the matter of control... Well, saying Ceahan had a problem controlling his magic was like calling a forge fire 'frosty.' It was beyond an understatement.

Ceahan wielded a sea of power, but when it came out, it was either a trickle or a flash flood. This test forced him to meet in the middle and stay there. Too much power and the plate would crack from the water pressure, too little and the plate would fall out of the bubble. This was a test all about control.

She sighed. "If only Ceahan could learn to manage that tempest he's got. He could be very strong, maybe even one of the strongest."

He'd learn eventually, but eventually wasn't going to cut it. The problem was that the human of fifteen falls could no longer afford his fatal flaw. Time was against them, and now he needed to learn how to control it himself. Master D'gui hated to push her apprentice, but if she didn't, she knew the foolhardy boy would only be worse off.

"Very good, Ceahan, that should be the right amount of power. Now keep the flow steady."

He didn't need support, but Ceahan did appreciate his master's guidance. "Yes, master." He had just passed the first time marker and was quickly approaching his record for the tests.

The bubble began to ripple, and Master D'gui bit her lip in apprehension. Just a little longer!

"Stop... knocking... please," Ceahan said in a labored voice.

"Knocking?" she said.

Master D'gui listened for a moment. There *was* a knocking sound, someone was at the front door. "Sorry, Ceahan, but that isn't me. It, uh... seems we have a visitor."

Ceahan didn't reply, doing all he could to calm the growing fluctuations in his power.

"How strange," Master D'gui said to herself. "We almost never get visitors."

While she and her apprentice could utilize magic, she worked hard to keep that fact secret. It made people either nervous or needy, and she wanted to deal with neither. Even those who did know about her art had learned by now that, unless it was interesting, Master D'gui had better things to do than answer silly requests. She entertained the idea that Ceahan might have invited someone, but soon dismissed it. Ceahan rarely went outside and, despite her efforts, didn't seem very interested in making friends.

She heard Ceahan take a quick breath. His plate slipped halfway out of the bubble, his power falling away too much. Quickly he pulled, increasing the pressure to pull the plate back in.

Tink! A hairline crack divided the plate and part dribbled out of the bubble. With the plate cracked, Ceahan gave up. The water splashed back into the bucket and the remains of the plate crashed down with it.

Master D'gui sighed. She made no comment. She knew what had happened and trained Ceahan too well for him not to know too.

Trying to pull the plate back into the bubble, he'd added too much power too quickly. The pressure increased beyond what the hardened clay could handle.

"That makes it an even forty," she muttered, too quietly for her apprentice to hear. "I'm going to run out of plates again."

Ceahan's gaze snapped toward her after a moment, he was angry. "Why did you do that? I had it that time, master!"

Master D'gui looked from behind her glasses at the boy. She hadn't done anything, hadn't he been listening? And why was he so upset? There was still time enough, he could just try again later.

"I told you, Ceahan, I'm not the one knocking. We have visitors. Now you clean up while I see who is at our door."

"Visitors?"

She rolled her eyes. "Yes, that would be people who are not you and me. They come from outside the house."

Ceahan made a face somewhere between pouting and nervous.

"Oh, come now." Master D'gui laughed. "My guess is it's just a neighbor, now please start cleaning up. This is a good stopping place anyway."

Sighing, the apprentice stood, stretched, and bent over to pick up the pail of water.

Master D'gui got up and moved to one of the front windows to peek at the door. Ceahan was her pride and joy, but he had his flaws.

"He's always making a big fuss over nothi—" She froze.

The figure at her door was no neighbor.

Master D'gui's mind raced. It had been a long time since she'd seen one, but the uniform was unmistakable. A Yongarad Marauder was at her front door!

How had he gotten this far into Ifeldia without someone catching him? On second thought, most in this region had never seen one, and those who had probably would be too afraid to do anything. But how did he get *here*? Did he know? He couldn't, could he?

"No... wait... there is something wrong with this marauder." Her eyes narrowed.

The uniform looked right, from the marsh camouflage coat to the thick leather boots. The problem was his features didn't appear Yongardian at all. Also, he wasn't wearing a marauder's guild signet on his chest. That was a huge cultural anomaly, and she should know, considering her specialty.

As an expert in foreign and historical cultures and societies, she knew the sociological structure of many foreign communities, and she knew more of the marauder community than even she liked, thanks to her source.

For anyone else, the small metal signet would be insignificant, but it put the master off slightly. The small metal pin was more than a marker of allegiance, it was a lifeline. A marauder wouldn't be caught dead without wearing a sigil. If he was, he could very quickly die in a sense more than the metaphorical.

Then she noticed his manner, this 'marauder' was quite relaxed. He certainly didn't seem to be hiding or expecting a fight. If he really knew anything, then any marauder should know she would be very uncooperative.

The marauder reached out and knocked on her door again. After he did, another man walked up the steps to her house. This one was *definitely* not a marauder. In fact, he looked like he belonged in a field somewhere tending sheep.

"An interesting pair."

Well, she liked interesting things. Except that she did not enjoy the overtly dangerous. To be safe, she would prepare a little magic for easy use. She decided to prepare her spell before even walking to the door, so she could gauge their reactions.

As she whipped up a slight whirl of power, neither guest so much as flinched. It was a small chance that they had the art to begin with, but if either had any magic in them, they would have felt the spell and reacted. At least, even if the one in uniform was a marauder, he at least wasn't one of the ones with the art.

Carefully, she moved to the door and opened it slowly. Neither of the men at the door reacted hostilely. They seemed, if anything, curious.

"Good afternoon, miss," said the rural man. "Would you happen to be Master D'gui?" He sounded genuinely polite, and surprisingly pronounced her name correctly. Most locals misspoke and said 'D'gue'

Master D'gui kept her voice level as she spoke. "I am usually not so coarse, but... and I am sorry, but I would like to know who you are before I tell you who I am."

"I get that, miss, and you're right, I should've given my name first. Didn't mean to be so rude," the rural man apologized. "I am Ghen Jarden. This is Em."

Master D'gui watched them through careful eyes. "Your name," she said, pointing to Ghen, "means you're a local, but I doubt that you are Mr. Em. Where are you from?"

Ghen looked surprised that she'd guessed he was local. While this historical loss was maddening, she didn't need to know cultural history to tie him to this region. One look at this man and anyone could guess he was a local. Em, on the other hand, seemed almost saddened.

Em bowed. "Forgive me, but that is why I have come here. I do not know where I am from. I seek the help of Master D'gui."

"Help how? Explain."

The man named Em reached behind his belt and Master D'gui prepared to release the coral of power she hid behind her back. Then, he drew out a book. Em opened the journal to the first page and held it so Master D'gui could read it.

You go by the name Em Dér.

I know you are confused, and I know why. You have forgotten again. I am writing this message to warn you. If you sleep, you will forget. I know this because I am you, a you that has been forgotten. That is what our life has become, living for a day to die in our sleep. Then, a new Em rises tomorrow with no memory of who we were.

Em, even as I write this to you, I wonder how long we have been this way. I do not know who we once were or who we are supposed to be now. All I know is what I have been told, which I will pass on to you. We forget everything each day, but there is a chance to be whole again. This curse or sickness we have can be cured, Em.
In the city of Henaden is a master of magic known as Master D'gui. Our guides told me Master D'gui will help us. I do not know why, but this may be our only chance. Trust Instinct and Nature, they will see us to our goal.

Also, you should know that whatever has been done to our mind has not affected everything about us. You will find that our body remembers much of what our mind cannot.
Seek Henaden, find Master D'gui, and find who we are supposed to be.
That is all we have to remember.
From the Em of yesterday.

She read it twice, then thrice, and had to stop herself from reading a fourth time. She inspected Em, and her gut twisted. It was a totally unnecessary risk. One, that clearly, she should not take.

But... 'You go by the name Em Dér', even this first phrase lent itself to the validity of the story. Why else choose it? It would be a strange but clever lie if it was one. Also, there was Em himself, she'd never seen such features on a human's face, if that was his tribe. Marauders were mostly from Yongarad lands or Ifeldian, Em's heritage didn't look like either as far as she knew. That was not definitive, but it was more evidence to his benefit.

The message said he remembered nothing, but that in itself was equally inexplicable. It was a strong cover for a liar, but a dangerous one that could be easily disproved in the right circumstances.

Yet, what if it was all true? Could she actually turn away such a mystery? There was so much opportunity in it. Couldn't she at least hear them out? But the risk, and Ceahan. He wouldn't like this at all. Drat! Double drat! True or not, it was so very... *interesting!*

CHAPTER 22

WATCHING HER EYES SWISH back and forth from behind her glasses, Em could see she was rereading the words of his notes. As she went over the page of Em's journal, her green eyes sparkled with an ever-burning fire of curiosity.

The woman seemed to be of the human tribe. Her gray hair was gathered into a bundle on the top of her head. She wore a long velvet robe, that was made to be scholarly and refined, but there was a wildness in the way the belt was tied tightly around the waist that belied its haughtiness. She was thin and slightly taller than Em, but the second was unsurprising.

Em had noticed many of the people they'd passed by were taller than he was.

Yet, something in her manner held Em's attention. She was almost... familiar. Something in the tilt of her head or the swaying of her step was forcing Em to feel like he should know her in some way. She, however, clearly looked at him suspiciously, having never seen him before.

The only thing Instinct said upon seeing her was simply, *Hello Ida*.

"You have acceded to my request, so I guess it is only fair to admit to you that yes, I am Master D'gui. Now, you say your name is Em Dér, is that right?"

While she looked older there was strength and authority in the voice of Master D'gui, however much like her clothing her voice of authority held an undercurrent of verdant rhythm.

"As far as I know," Em replied.

The woman searched Em's face and smiled. Then her smile faltered, she squinted, smiled again, finally scowling before shaking her head aggressively. "Oh, bash it all," she muttered. "Fine, yes, I will... see about you. As long as you are here, you should continue to refer to me as Master D'gui, it's only proper. While I've agreed to take a look at you, I should tell you that I haven't the faintest idea what to do with you yet. What I will say though, is that you, Em Dér, are either a foolish liar or telling the truth."

Ghen laughed to himself. "I think I had something of the same thought when I met Em."

Master D'gui sighed and smiled. "I doubt for the same reason."

Neither Em nor Ghen understood her comment, but she didn't give them time to ask about it.

"Mr. Ghen, is that cart yours?" She pointed at Bo.

"Yes miss, and please lose the Mr., I like being called Ghen."

"Very well, Ghen, please take your animal and cart through that alley." She pointed to an alleyway on the right side of the house. "I will have my apprentice meet you there. His name is Ceahan. I have a small pen in the backyard with a horse of my own. It may be a tight fit, but both our animals should be able to stay in there for now. You, on the other hand, Mr. Em, please follow me."

Ghen nodded to the master and gave Em a slight push towards the door.

He only took half a step. Em's heart was beating like a festival drum in his chest. So many things could go wrong. He couldn't risk this chance, he had to make a good impression. He'd looked for so long and she was nervous about them both. What if...

Em felt frozen, unsure.

That's her, Little Em, Instinct said almost wistfully. *Don't worry, Ida will take good care of you.*

"Are you coming?" Master D'gui asked from inside the door.

"Ah, yes master." Em forced himself up the two stairs and to her front door of the odd house of Master D'gui.

While the other homes were reminiscent of those seen outside the city being square or rectangular, Master D'gui's was built in a large U-shape. The front door sat at the base of the U, the doorway was of the squared clay design but with a slanted roof similar to the old style of construction, however hers was newer. It looked like she or whoever had built it had ignored the modern way of construction entirely. Behind the square doorway, the sides of the home rounded out into tunnels that arced back to the wall of the step. Yet each of these rounded arms of the U were interrupted by short cylindrical spires that were topped with points tiled like the entryway.

Em wasn't sure if its unique shape made him want to marvel or laugh, it was so different than everything else around it.

Stepping into the building, Em had the sudden urge to remove his shoes, but didn't. One reason why was the master was wearing shoes in her own house, the other was there was nowhere to put them.

The entryway was in absolute disarray, Em immediately felt cramped by the piles of books and strange devices that cluttered her entryway. It got no better as he moved further into her house. He stepped into a living space that had a fireplace and what looked like at least a tapestry on a wall, but it was hard to perceive its design considering the mounds piled in front of it. What might have been an oak dining table was to his side, like everything else it was overtaken by books, loose parchment, scrolls, and dishes that were yet to be cleared away from a previous meal.

The rest of the house was much the same. Stacks and stacks of material lay on chairs, side tables, and in various places on the floor. One stack went from the floor and was piled so high, Em was sure the volume on top must graze the ceiling. The house held more documents than Em might have believed existed in the whole world.

Finally tearing his eyes away, Em looked for the curving hallways of the house. He found them quickly. On his right, one hallway led to a surprisingly neat kitchen whose floors glowed green as the sun lit it through the ivy that covered the kitchen's small window. To the right another that led a passageway lined with bookshelves which were decidedly not neat. The shelves overflowed with an incomprehensible amount of knowledge as cluttered, if not more, than the rest of the house.

The cleanest place, however, Em could make out through the rear windows of the house was a small yard or garden that was protected by the odd shape of the master's home. Sadly, much like the decorations on the walls, it was hard to see clearly considering the mass of junk between Em and the windows.

Despite the impressive amount of knowledge Master D'gui had at her fingertips, and the air of freedom and discovery that lingered in the home's atmosphere, all Em could think of was how much of a mess it was!

There was no order that he could make out to tell what was where or why. Master D'gui looked at it all and navigated the clutter without a second thought. She was a fish in her reef, the expert of her own personal chaos.

Without issue, she reached the back door and began distributing orders. Em couldn't see who she was talking to, but from what she was saying, Master D'gui must have been talking to her apprentice.

When she turned back, she addressed Em directly. "Please take a seat wherever you can find one. I want to hear everything you can tell me." Then Master D'gui moved to one of the few empty chairs not overtaken in the pursuit of knowledge, sat, and looked at Em with hungry expectation.

Em awkwardly made his way to a table chair that was free of any piles of material. "I apologize, Master D'gui, but I know little more than my notes have told me. Ghen-sa told me that when he met me less than a week ago, I had next to nothing with me other than my notes and my swords."

"Intriguing. By any chance, do your notes give you any hints to your origin?"

Em shook his head. "My journal mentions many names of places, but none are listed as being my home or where I began my journey."

"That's disappointing. You must come from a very different and intriguing culture. Perhaps we can discover it with time." Master D'gui sounded more like she was consoling herself than Em. "Is there any record of how long you have had this condition?"

"No, or not in my notes. But..." Em hesitated.

"Go on," Master D'gui encouraged.

"I... I am sure it has been a long time. I can feel it."

"I'm sorry to hear that. I know..." She paused, her gaze turning to her back door.

"Master D'gui?"

Her eyes flicked to him, then back to the door. "Oh no."

Em looked out the back window and saw that Ghen was following someone up the small steps to the back door.

Master D'gui's hands circled each other quickly. Wisps of air whirled, drawing dust off shelves and fluttering nearby pages in time with the master's hand. The winds gathered together atop her palms just as the back door opened.

A young man stepped in. He was human, or at least appeared to be, and Em guessed they might be similar in age. His hair was dark brown, matching his eyes, but that was almost all the color he had. His skin was pale and his body thin. He looked as if he'd spent nearly all his life indoors. He wore a shirt dyed a slight blue with brown trousers. However, the most distinguishing item he had on was a broad black band tied tightly around his forehead.

Em guessed correctly that this was the apprentice, Ceahan.

The moment Ceahan's gaze fell on Em, his expression, which had been perfectly bored when he entered, went stricken with panic.

"Marauder!" Ceahan screamed.

Em recoiled as a jet of fire sprayed from Ceahan's hand.

Trained reactions took over Em's body. He flipped over the back of the chair, lifting as he did to make a crude and pointless defense against the powerful hungry flames.

Thankfully, the fire never made it halfway to him and his flimsy shield.

FWHOOSH!

Even as Ceahan started his attack, a blast of wind blew out the fire and knocked the apprentice back out the door. He landed, sprawling, at Ghen's feet.

Em blinked before realizing that the fire wasn't going to engulf him. Master D'gui had saved him. She really did have magic, and so did her apprentice!

Angrily, Master D'gui stood and marched to the back door. "Ceahan! You dare to use fire in my study! What if you'd burned my research?" Master D'gui stopped at the back door and, glaring down at her charge, tapped her foot testily. "I know how our guest appears, but if I was in any danger, don't you think I would have dealt with it myself? It's that hot head of yours that keeps you from control."

Ceahan sat up, looking confused and disoriented.

"You had absolutely no control over that spell, I felt that power. If I hadn't stopped you when I did, you would have blown a hole through my house! Worse, I barely had time to stop you before you used more power than I could compete with, and I was casting before you came in the door. Ceahan, do you know why I was casting before you came through the door? It's because I knew you would overreact!"

As Em heard Master D'gui yelling about her research, he noticed a square of parchment on the ground that had a small flame licking at its edge. Anxious to avoid any blame, he quickly stamped it out.

He picked up the page to inspect it. Only the corner was burned, and all the words were still visible. Hopefully, Master D'gui wouldn't be too upset. He desperately needed her help.

Em was relieved to realize, after reading the page, that its contents were ingredients and instructions for putting together some soup or side dish for an evening meal. Em had no clue as to why Master D'gui would leave this lying on the top of so many books, but whatever the reason, the recipe was saved.

"Master... I." Ceahan started to apologize.

"Stop! Come inside, listen, and say *nothing*. Not... one... thing," she said precisely. "You may comment if I ask you a question, and then only answer the question. Do you understand?"

"Yes, master," Ceahan said, thoroughly chastised.

"Good." She then gave an embarrassed glance at Ghen. "I'm sorry about that, my apprentice has a problem with temperament."

Ghen stood gaping for eight to ten ticks of the day before he shook his head and tried not to laugh. "I won't hold it against you, miss. I happen to be taking care of a boy with a similar problem myself. Though mine doesn't blow holes in walls or anything like that."

Master D'gui rubbed her temples. "Count yourself lucky then."

As the three of them stepped in, Ceahan gave Em a wary look, but Master D'gui led him aside before he could do much more than that.

There, she whispered instructions and a minor explanation that Em could not completely hear.

Ghen stepped up to Em. "Not exactly what we expected, is it, kid?"

Em shook his head. "No. Yet, if they can help, I see no problem with how they are."

Ghen nodded. "Well, I think we figured out that there really are mystics in Henaden."

Em nodded, then to pass the time while the Master spoke to Ceahan asked, "Were you able to get your mule settled?"

"Yep, they have a nifty little gate hidden back there and a paddock where they keep a nice little brown mare that Mr. Ceahan there called Lena. Like the master said, the fence is a little small for both of them, but it's not too bad."

Em nodded to the whispering pair of academics. "What do you think of this Ceahan-*so*?"

"He's nice enough, I think he ought to eat more," Ghen said, "he's skinny as a fence post."

"I meant his sudden attack."

Ghen shrugged. "You, him, and Jirus. All you young boys tend to be aggressive every once in a while. Think of last night. Also, you won't remember, but you kinda fought Jirus the first day we met. Then, you got into it with two neighbor boys the next day. So, if I were you, I might not point too many fingers. He's just young like yourself, nothing more to it. Looks like his master is sorting him out. Though she seemed more worried about her papers than herself." He looked around. "Wow, she's got a lot of stuff and..." he whispered, "it's a mess."

"You are not wrong," Em said in a hushed tone.

Ghen gestured to Em's hand and the partially burned parchment he was still holding. "What do you have there?"

In the conversation, Em had almost forgotten the recipe. "Eh? Ah, yes." He stepped around a pile of books, and the master and apprentice looked up as he approached. "A small flame caught your instructions. It was fortunate that it did not spread far before I caught it. I do not think it is ruined."

Master D'gui took the recipe and looked at the corner. Seeing there was no real damage, she glanced at the words and her eyes widened. She looked from the page to Em and back again. "Instructions you say?"

"Yes... for preparing food," he answered carefully. "Why?"

She turned it so it faced him. "You can read this?"

Em thought he understood now. "Ah yes, I can read it. My memory loss has not affected many skills. I can still read and write."

Master D'gui kept her focus on the page as she spoke. "I have very few things like this one." Her voice rose with excitement. "All of them are written in the same language, and I don't even know what language it is. I haven't been able to decipher any more than a few numbers."

"Eh?" Em said, confused again, but then he thought back.

He quickly realized this recipe was not written in the same language his notes were, but the meaning was just as clear. Em began to feel slightly nervous. Reading it had been so natural he hadn't even noticed the language was different. "Ah, I see now. To speak honestly, Master D'gui, I didn't even pay attention to how it was written. I won't be able to tell you what the language is."

Master D'gui's excitement was electric, and she shook her head quickly. So quickly she had to push up her glasses afterwards. "That hardly matters at this point, you can read it! That means I can decipher all I have written in this language with your help." She paced back and forth, muttering to herself before spinning back to Em suddenly. "How about this, Em? In exchange for your help with my research, I promise to do what I can to aid you with your condition. I'm still not sure what I can do, but I'll do what I can."

She sounded and looked surprisingly desperate. It was so unexpected that Em stood stunned for a moment. He'd come expecting to be the one begging for *her* help, not the other way around. Once the offer caught his mind, Em knew immediately how he should answer.

"*Hai!* I will do it!" Em said quickly before she could change her mind.

"Perfect! Let me go find more and we can begin right away. You say this one is a cooking instruction. I wonder what for? No, never mind, if that is all it can wait." She bustled towards her bookshelf.

"Miss." Ghen's voice wasn't rude, but he was loud enough to make sure he was heard. "Shouldn't you see about Em first?"

Master D'gui froze like a child caught with her hand in a jar of sweets. "Oops, I'm so sorry. I can get... *excited* about my research." She thought for another moment, then nodded to herself. "Yes, you are more than right, Mr. Ghen. Oh, I'm sorry, you said that you preferred to be called Ghen. Either way, my apologies. Besides," Master D'gui rambled on before Ghen could reply, "if his memory issue brought about a loss of his ability to translate in the middle of our research, it could be detrimental to our efforts. We will just have to see what we can do about Em's memory first."

Em wasn't sure that had been Ghen's point, but the result was at least the intended one.

"Master D'gui, before your apprentice came in, you were going to say something, were you not?" Em reminded her.

Master D'gui paused. "Yes, I was. Now that I think about it, however, I see that most of what you know you learned from your notebook or Ghen. Anything else would only be to see if you were telling the truth about your condition. Of course," she said thoughtfully, "I already think there is much evidence for believing you."

"Because I could read that language?" Em asked, confused.

"No, but there are multiple reasons to believe you. First, you may not realize it, but you are wearing something akin to marauder garb in the home of people who are their enemies. If your condition was mere make-believe, that would be a rather odd thing to do. Another thing is your name. The last clue is your focus, you truly seem intent on getting my help and nothing and no one else's. All this leads to my belief in your story, at least so far."

Em understood two of her points easily. It wasn't even surprising to hear his garb was from a marauder, even if he was still sure he was not a marauder himself. His journal mentioned that people had compared him to a marauder while he had stayed on Ghen's ranch. However, hearing his name was one of her reasons came as a surprise.

Ghen appeared to be as confused as Em was. "What's this got to do with his name? You said earlier that you knew I was local by mine, are you saying our names tell you something?"

"Oh, this is so irritating." Master D'gui sat heavily down in her chair, she almost looked like she was pouting. She pushed her glasses further up on her small nose. "To explain everything, you need a brief lesson in history."

"Master, I think just telling them whatever you know will work. No need for a lecture." It seemed Ceahan hoped to be spared from many things he'd heard before.

"Ahem! Ceahan, I don't recall asking you a question." Master D'gui said. "As I was saying, Em, do you know about King Roleius?"

"Yes, I wrote notes about him. Ghen also explained more on the ride into Henaden."

"Perfect, then maybe we can make this quick. So, Roleius took over other nations to make what is now Ifeldia, that's where we are, did you know all that?"

Em nodded.

"Excellent, well after he did, Roleius ran into a problem. Countries don't always like the changes that come with a new ruler, I should know. My expertise is cultural and sociological study." She seemed rather proud of this. "Nevertheless, Roleius *did* want to change things, so he came up with a few solutions. I won't drone on and on, but one of them was to make it so everyone spoke the same language. Any and all documents made in a language other than Ifeldian were said to be invalid. Not that Ifeldian is the language's original name or that it's only spoken here, but it is what the king decided to call it."

Ceahan twitched, fearing his master was going to get off track, but she caught herself and shifted back to her main topic.

"Everyone was to speak the language and all announcements and discussions were to happen in this language. So, everyone was forced to learn Ifeldian, unifying the mass of people somewhat. That was bad enough from my perspective as a researcher since so much culture is held in language, but Roleius wasn't finished. He needed the people to accept *being* Ifeldian instead of their past nationality. This is when he enacted a move to influence the learning in his new nation.

"Educated individuals in conquered countries were offered large sums of money to move to what had always been Ifeldia before the campaign had begun. There, they were taught a new history and new ideas that the king liked. That way, these people taught very little about their original country's history, and it progressively died away.

"At the same time, Roleius also paid educators from what was Ifeldia, before expansion, to go out into conquered places to teach them their new history. Of course, there weren't enough educators, so this has made teachers hard to find everywhere except in the old borders of Ifeldia. That squashed even more history and heritage in its native lands. All of this made it so that, in only a few generations, the nations of the past faded from the minds and hearts of those who should have inherited them. Thus, they became Ifeldian through and through."

Ghen raised a hand like a child in a schoolhouse. "No offense, miss, but what does that have to do with our names?"

"I'm getting to that," she said. "For you, it's everything about your name. Where we are now was once the nation of En-Athen. Did you know that?"

"I've heard that, but it doesn't mean much to me," Ghen said.

"Then you know more than most already, Ghen. Did you have an actual teacher in your life?"

"My father and uncle taught me most things."

"My point exactly. It's now up to either parents or teachers of Ifeldian propaganda to educate the following generations. It ruins good history and knowledge. I've spent my adult life trying to dig up a past less than five hundred falls old, and these decisions have made it exceedingly difficult." Master D'gui's tone was bitter. "Back to the point, you said your name is Ghen Jarden. In En-Athen, it was considered a necessity for the people to end their surnames with 'en' to reflect their allegiance to the country. Many also did this for first names. Of course, not all people with 'en' at the end of their names are from En-Athen, but you look like you are from here as well. It was a safe assumption."

"I know other folks that have been around a long time whose names don't end like that," Ghen said.

"King Roleius also encouraged people from every country, conquered or from old Ifeldia, to move across borders. Stipends of money were given to those who moved, and the fact that there were a ton of refugees made it easy for him. So, the people were shuffled all over the land. Of course, this buried all the old cultures even deeper. My guess is that these people you know either married some of these foreigners or are descendants of them."

That made sense to Em. A mix of cultures would water down all the cultures involved. That still didn't answer the question about Em's name. "That explains Ghen, but what about me?"

Master D'gui grew a large smile. "Your name is a different story, but still similar. It's a name that seems to be based on a phrase using the native language of what used to be the country of Gophlan. Before you ask, I don't think that is where you are from. Please don't take offense, but you don't look like you are from anywhere in Ifeldia that I know of. Also, your accent when speaking our language is very unique. I'm familiar with Gophlanite descendants, they are very different. I'm descended from that group myself through my father."

"I do not see how this helps you believe my story," Em said, only more confused.

"Like I said, most have lost their old language, but there are still a small few who still can recall it. I suspect that 'Em' is not your real name. I noticed that your notebook says 'You go by the name Em Dér' not 'Your name is Em.'

Em paused, and pulling out his journal, reread the first line.

You go by the name Em Dér.

She was right. He hadn't noticed that when he read that this morning.

Seeing his reaction, Master D'gui smiled. "My guess is you must have forgotten your name while passing through the part of Ifeldia that was once Gophlan. Then maybe someone might have told you that your name was Em Dér to... well I'm sorry, but it might have been to mock you."

"Mock me?"

"Yes." Master D'gui pointed to the book. "Even the first page of this book praises your instincts, they probably gave you the impression that this wasn't your real name. If you suspected they might have been mocking you, that might be why you wrote down the name the way you did."

Master D'gui was intelligent, but based on her guests' reactions, she was losing her audience.

Ghen finally brought up the question Em had been getting at. "Sorry miss, but how is his name mocking him? You said it was a phrase in that language you talked about. What does it mean?"

"Oh, well, that's simple. The word 'Em' in their tongue means 'I,' and 'Dér' loosely means 'lost in the mind.' Do you see?" she asked expectantly.

None of them did.

The master of the house rolled her eyes. "Think about it. What it means is that every time Em was asked 'What is your name?' his reply was, in a sense, 'I forgot.'"

At first, the room remained silent, until Ghen began to chuckle to himself. Em could not help but smile either.

Well, it fit, didn't it? Instinct's old voice said mischievously. Em couldn't see it but, beyond the pale, he felt a knowing grin cut broadly across an aged face.

Seeing that they understood. Master D'gui clapped her hands. "Now! Before we begin our new project, I need to bring Ceahan into the fold on the details. We are going to have a quick private conversation. Then, I'd like to review your journal for clues. Is that alright?"

Em cringed at the idea of handing over his journal again but knew there was no choice. He'd come to her after all.

Em nodded slowly.

"Perfect. Oh! I would also like to eat something since the evening is drawing near. Luckily for me, I've recently learned I have a new recipe. I must admit I'm excited to try it out!"

Master D'gui straightened her glasses, her eyes alight with anticipation, and then she faltered slightly. "Oh, well, that's assuming we have the ingredients, of course."

CHAPTER 23

"CEAHAN, PLEASE CARRY THE jar down into the backyard. It's too heavy for me." Master D'gui had many strengths, but physical prowess was not among them.

The jar contained the mapping sand they were going to need. It would be a great help for getting a better understanding of what was going on in Em's mind.

During dinner, she'd risked questioning Em further, though Master D'gui had known that her questions would likely be met with an answer of, 'I don't remember.' She asked anyway, her hope was to get information out of *how* he responded instead of *what* he responded with.

That way, she might determine the origin of this mysterious young man. Despite her assurances that she trusted his story, there was a need to be careful.

His clothes suggested Yongarad, but he did not have the physical traits of the country and most of the people from Yongarad she'd met during her research had shared a propensity for curses. Em, so far, hadn't said anything of the sort.

He was actually very polite, so much so, that Master D'gui was now convinced it was a cultural staple. Ifeldia had manners, but this was to a far greater degree. His origin wasn't from Ifeldia and probably not Yongarad.

That didn't mean he wasn't a marauder. The Marauders took recruits from any country or village. Em might be from a remote village in the southern mountains, unlikely but possible, or even from one of the uncharted nations on the other side of Yongarad.

Other things that Master D'gui gleaned about Em were things like how he carried himself. Em peered around as if there was always danger nearby, at a sudden noise he would jerk slightly. His observational skills and reflexes were as keen as the edges of the two swords he always kept near at hand. Em had seen combat or lived near it for a long time.

He was protective of everything he had and, when they were cleaning up their dinner, Em even tried to save tiny scraps for himself. She knew that was the sign of an impoverished upbringing. Which also explained the distrust she occasionally observed in his eyes. Working with him, she guessed, would have been difficult had Ghen not softened him up or if he hadn't come to find her in particular. Under the circumstances, he had no choice but to trust her.

That doesn't mean there isn't good reason to tread carefully, she thought.

Then there were 'Instinct' and 'Nature,' which she was surprised to learn were voices Em apparently perceived and spoke to. She guessed these were a product of what some of the mystics and academics who studied the mind referred to as the subconscious. What that implied was that Em's character was probably a product of his life, not a recent development, but there were flaws in that theory. Clearly, more study was needed to understand him fully.

What she knew now told her both a lot and very little about Em. At least he seemed genuinely forgetful about his past, it made the story far more believable. An actor would have a hard time not accidentally letting slip some fact they shouldn't have been able to remember. Em was consistent, but that meant she learned nothing about his family, origin, or how he'd come to be this way.

Ghen had provided some interesting facts. For one, it seemed true that Em's amnesia was tied to sleep specifically. He never forgot before falling asleep. Also, even when Em's notes had been out of reach, he'd remembered trusting people, even if he did not know why.

Truly an interesting case. I wish Master Kimble was here to study this, she thought, reminded of her old teacher. Lost in thought, Master D'gui nearly tripped down the step of her back door. Stumbling into her own backyard, she stood straight and looked around. Luckily, no one seemed to have noticed.

Em was already lounging in the reclined chair she'd asked him to bring out and settle into. They would need him to fall asleep to see the full effect. It would be awkward if he fell out of his chair when he lost consciousness. Thus, she'd opted for this one.

Of course, he was fully awake for now and probably nervous. To make sure he could sleep, Master D'gui prepared tea with a light sleeping agent for Em. Also, on hand, she would keep a mixture to wake him up if needed. Experimentation required repetition, so chances were good that Em might be up and down many times throughout the night.

A rustle of feet signaled the coming of Ceahan and Ghen behind her, each with a hand on a handle of the jar of sand, carrying it between them.

"Perfect. Now Em, please turn the chair so your head points toward the door and your feet towards the back wall. You two, please dump the mapping sand somewhere in front of Em."

All three complied, but Ghen looked vexed. "Miss, it's going to be a mess to clean all this dirt up after, isn't it?"

Master D'gui smiled at Ghen's ignorance. "Ceahan, please explain the mapping sand."

"Yes, master. Mapping sand is magically infused, it makes it easy to move and shift. Either of us can gather every grain up and put it back in the jar easily."

Now that she'd explained the full situation to her apprentice, Ceahan was behaving much better. He was still keeping an extra half step away from Em, but that was better than trying to roast him alive. As for their two guests, neither acted like they cared at all about Ceahan's earlier outburst.

Master D'gui could see Em trying to listen in on the conversation between the other two, as curious as Ghen about the sand. Ghen continued his questions. "No offense, but what do we need magical dirt for?"

Ceahan rolled his eyes and explained. "Because mapping sand can be moved easily and can change color depending on how you control it. We can use it to show what's going on in Em's mind. Many armies use sand like this if they have a sorcerer with them, they use it to get an accurate map of terrain and display it to everyone."

"So, Master D'gui is going to be looking in Em's head and this stuff will let us all see what she's looking at?"

Was that not what Ceahan had just said? Then again, Ghen had said he was just a rancher taught by ranchers. Still, she'd better take over the explanation from here, Ceahan might get impatient if the conversation kept on like this.

"Actually Ghen," Master D'gui said, "Ceahan will be the one searching. Don't worry about what I said about his tempering abilities. He will only be using his magic to search and project as one spell. More power only lets us see more. It's actually better since we will see more than I could show with my abilities. As for showing it in the mapping sand, there is only so much magic you can put into the sand, so there is no worry there either."

"I've got no complaints, miss. I can't do magic, but even I can tell young Master Ceahan here is a special one. I'm interested to see what he can do."

Ceahan looked surprised and maybe even a little embarrassed at Ghen's comment. Personally, he'd expected Ghen to doubt his abilities.

"Now then, are we missing anything?" Master D'gui asked, before working her way down the list. "Sand is in place, I have our herbal tea, our patient is in position, everyone is accounted for, but... Oh yes!" Quickly setting the tea down on an outdoor table, she skipped back into the house.

Entering, she paused, looking right and left. "Now I know I saw you just the other day." Her eyes scanned the various loose piles of materials. She knew it was messy but cared little. As disorganized as it seemed to everyone else, the placement of everything spread about always helped her to... "There you are."

Gliding through the forest of research, Master D'gui came to a pile of books on the far side of the room and ran her finger down the spines of each tome. She ignored the scrolls and loose pages on top because she knew it was a book. Just the other day, she had seen it while looking for a record of elvish poetry.

"A fascinating little book in its own right, in fact..."

Master D'gui shook her head to keep herself from getting distracted.

Her finger stooped on a spine that was a lighter color than the others and, lifting the books on top, she drew it out. Opening to the title page, she knew she had the right one.

Mangorin and Sebliah's studies on the structure of the mind.
Vol. 3 Humans and Kyate-siv.

Perfect, she only owned volumes three and four, so she was fortunate to have one of the ones that covered human physiology. Working her way back outdoors, she was already thumbing past the sections on the less physical aspects of the research. If Em's condition was psychological and not physical, there would be little they could do, so it was best to ignore that to start with.

"Now we have everything," she announced her nose still in the tome. "You'll forgive me if we go by the book for this one, my expertise is in sociology, not psychology. I haven't the slightest notion as to why your notes point me out specifically, Mr. Em, but Ceahan and I will surely give it our best shot."

"Ma'am," Ghen asked, "if you aren't an expert, why do you have the book?"

Master D'gui looked up disappointedly. "Books do not make one an expert, but I consider it a moral obligation to collect knowledge for the sake of my studies."

"You certainly have many things to study," Em said.

"True, but my focus is on cultures, Em. A single culture has more depth than any one person may ever know, and you never know what can hold an interesting detail about a society. So of course, I collect knowledge wherever I can. Besides, I'm proud of my collection."

"You know," Ceahan commented, "so few people collect documents like the master does, that this little house holds more research than most places within leagues of Henaden. It really is a feat."

"Thank you, Ceahan," Master D'gui said warmly. "Still, that's enough chatter, it's time we began."

"How do we start, master?" her apprentice asked.

"Go ahead and take your position, Ceahan, and let's begin to look at Em's mind while he's awake. It's not a perfect baseline, but we may see something without endangering his memories. Ghen, the representation of a mind in mapping sand may seem strange since it won't be what you are used to.

"This is going to be complex, and I may not have time to explain everything as we go along, but another set of eyes could still be advantageous in our research. If anything looks out of place, say something. I will tell you if it is worth looking into or not."

Em reclined back in the chair and Ceahan moved around so that he could place a hand on each side of Em's head. Ceahan closed his eyes, and Master D'gui could feel the magic begin to flow.

The experience of perceiving magic was different for everyone. Ceahan described it as something like a smell. Master Kimble had felt it as a special tingle in the tips of his fingers, but for Master D'gui, it was music.

The sound of Ceahan's magic as it searched through Em was a warm but plucky melody, like a babe awakening its first awareness of the world around them. It was a song Master D'gui knew well, because of how close curiosity and exploration were to her heart.

Only the master of the house could feel the power and hear the song that flowed off of her apprentice. The empty yard was flooded with his power in the dimming evening while Ghen and Em were left totally unaware. All they could feel was the stillness in the fading light of day.

Until, with a low *thrum*, the mapping sand rippled.

A moment later, it rippled again, flickers of color sparkling. Then, another wave and another, the waves came slowly at first, but the mapping sand soon began to pulse in a quickening rhythm. Small ripples flowed over the shimmering grains like a cup of water in a tremor. Each wave rolled higher and faster than the last, the crest of each one starting to glitter with a rainbow of color.

At the center of the rippling sand, a pocket began to rise out of the rest. As it floated up, the sand began to take on a new shape. It swirled up like an hourglass flowing in reverse. Soon all the sand lifted itself up and danced in the air.

Like players on a stage, each grain of sand dressed itself in bright colors and sprinted to its position. At Ceahan's direction, the sand settled to form a rippled mass that Master D'gui knew to be the human mind. The picture of sand was large, so large that it wouldn't have fit through the door of the master's house. With the dusty impression complete, the lights began to shine with a new purpose as each grain played its part in the illusion. Lights raced hastily around the mass, in a pattern and regulation which were the actions of Em's mind.

Between the sight of the rising sand and the song of curiosity, Master D'gui's excitement was nearly boiling over. Her passion was for the culture and history of different tribes, not their physiology, but this challenge reminded her of her younger days and her time as an apprentice in medicine long ago.

"This is going to be fun," she whispered with an eager smile.

"By the Stars of the Corsairs!" Ghen exclaimed as he gawked awestruck at the glittering sand.

Em could not even manage that much. He was speechless despite looking at what was technically a part of himself.

"Is this the first time you've seen a brain, Ghen?" Master D'gui asked.

"Not really, but kind of. On a ranch, when you're young, you get curious about things. After hunting or something, most up and decide they'd like to see what's under the lid. It's nothing like this, though." Ghen said, still obviously amazed by the mapping sand.

Master D'gui couldn't help but laugh. This rancher knew more than most she'd met since moving here, but he still knew next to nothing at all.

"What you see isn't some dead animal brain, but it is alive and working. Allow me to show you." She stepped up to Em. "Do you mind if I pinch your arm?"

"I... eh. I guess that is fine." He held out his hand, and she pinched him behind the wrist.

The sand sparkled as mental lanes brought word of painful sensation.

"Fascinating, isn't it?" she asked her patient.

"Yes," Em agreed, feeling dumb at his underwhelming reply. But he was still at a loss for anything better.

That was enough fun and games. Master D'gui turned to the research volume again and decided on a starting point. "Ceahan, please inspect that area on the right closer." She pointed to the place on the sand representation. "Ghen, so you know, a common misconception is that memories are stored in a mind like you would store objects in a box. In truth, memories are all over and are controlled by tiny messengers, called impulses, that run through the tunnel-like passages of the mind. Or if it's easier think of impulses like your cart moving down a road."

As Master D'gui spoke, Ceahan edited the view for a closer look. A light coat of the mapping sand moved out in a bubble that surrounded all of them. The view zoomed into the flesh of the mind to show millions of tiny lines. Changing shape, the lines grew, following what Ceahan felt. The result was a network of sandy lines in a pattern more complex than any spider web. A three-dimensional map of byways that no shoe or hoof had ever tread upon, nor ever should.

"These are our roads," she explained. "Let us see if there is any obstruction or if any have been ruined in any way."

"I'll keep both eyes on your 'roads' then," Ghen assured her.

"Good. Ceahan, your sense of this will be better than ours. Search for any abnormalities in the pattern and move along the areas. The mind is vast and even the greatest experts still do not know and understand it all, but let's try to map around large portions for now just to get an idea of how things should be."

"Yes, Master." The pathways began to scroll by quickly, a blur, as the sand scrolled through images of the glittering inner workings of the mind. The passing images were a breeze to Ceahan who felt them more clearly than any mapping sand could hope to show. To Master D'gui and the others, the quick images only gave them a glance at what they saw, but it was enough for the time being.

The group continued their inspection like this, occasionally slowing to look more closely at where any of them thought they might have seen something. Every so often Master D'gui paused the search and requested Ceahan move to completely different sectors of the mind, searching for abnormalities based on what she read in her book. She was trying to find the various quadrants that the text mentioned, but everything was too similar and her knowledge of the mind too little to be sure of anything. Despite that, she was confident they were either in or near the various areas where the research depicted most memories came from.

Minutes drew into hours as the search continued, yet none of them detected any areas of damage so far. Ceahan's senses should have been able to tell if there were any major, and even most minor, breaks in them due to his strength.

"I think we have gone on long enough with this. We could spend our whole lives like this, many have," Master D'gui commented briefly. "I think it is time Em goes to sleep."

Em's face showed acceptance and worry. He nodded somberly. "I know there is no way to avoid this." He laid a hand on his journal. "I am prepared for what happens when I wake. Good night, and... goodbye," he added, not sure if he, the current Em, would ever see these people again.

Master D'gui herself couldn't imagine losing all her memories and didn't want to. All that knowledge, gone. This was torture and a cruel kind she detested fundamentally. For that alone, it would be worth finding the answer to this mystery. Knowledge should never be lost, only gained. That was how she always had and would continue to live until the day she died.

She handed him a drink of the drugged tea. Without complaint, Em drained the cup and leaned back. It did not take long for the tension in his face to relax. Soon after, Em fell asleep.

"Ceahan, his mind will change as it prepares for sleep. Be careful to watch that transition," Master D'gui warned. "It will only come as he goes in and out of sleep. If the key is in that change, we may have to go back and forth a bit."

As if on command, the impulses in the mind changed color. The roads of the mind took on new travelers as signals went on their living highway to errands all of their own. In some areas, the impulses grew more frequent while in others they lessened as Em transitioned to the different stages of sleep.

"I think he's settling master," Ceahan said, with a nod towards the sand.

Master D'gui narrowed her eyes. "The mind changes many times in sleep, so stay vigilant. Let us begin back near where we started, I want to go over familiar territory and see what's changed."

"Yes, master."

For better or worse, the changes were few. During sleep, the sandy paths had travelers of new colors and shades, but their travel flowed freely. As Em drew deeper and deeper into sleep, they pressed on. Switching zones and coming back as the cycles of rest peaked and then relapsed. There was little Master D'gui found of interest.

Multiple times, Ghen called out something he thought looked out of place, but so far all had turned out to be items he just didn't understand. After more than two cycles of sleep were completed, Master D'gui had a thought.

"There is a chance that sleep itself has nothing to do with his loss, maybe it is something in waking that causes Em to lose his memory. We should consider..." She never got to finish the thought.

Bright flashes burst to life and signals of red and pink danced across the sand in hurried flight. The flurry of impulses was so bright in the now dark night that everyone had to blink their eyes at the sudden illumination. Alarmed, Master D'gui turned to look at Em, yet he barely even twitched as his mind lit up like a city on fire.

CHAPTER 24

"IS THIS NORMAL FOR sleep, miss?" Ghen sounded agitated, perhaps sensing the worry in Master D'gui at the flurry of fleeing impulses in Em's mind.

Ceahan's senses, partially attuned to Em's mind, didn't even need to ask what the many signals meant. "No, that was pain."

"Find the source!" Master D'gui ordered urgently. "I want to know where the impulses started, they all would have spread from there. For as many as we just saw, we can't be far off."

The mapping sand shifted rapidly, seeking... seeking... Then the sand suddenly formed into a new image. The view was of another network, but these roads were different. Parts of the network looked as if they were incomplete, or maybe... broken.

"Someone's torn up the roads here," Ghen observed.

"The rancher's right master, much of this area is heavily damaged or destroyed altogether. Is that why his mind lit up like that?"

"That is a likely conclusion, but..." She stated carefully. Her first impression had been wrong. It didn't take her trained eye long to notice while most of the mental passages were damaged, some showed signs of healing. Other wounds were fresher, yet there was still no sign of what caused the damage. "How odd. Get a wider view of the area, let's see if we can spot any more of this damage occurring."

Ceahan altered the mapping sand. The image expanded, thick clear paths becoming part of the large web of thin spidery lines as if viewed from a regular map.

Still, it was clear enough that the damage was contained. Only a few of the mind's crossroads showed signs of destruction, and all were in one area near together. She took a step closer to the sand and squinted at the slightly paler area. Without realizing, Master D'gui began to mumble to herself.

"The new damage isn't on the outside. Then, it's not spreading from the inside out like a disease. That can only mean that this is targeted damage. Is it intentional then, or is it some tendency of these specific clusters to cause harm to themselves? That's unlikely, how would a mental path destroy itself? Some rogue bodily defense, perhaps? Possible, but why here, and where are the attackers? If it's not that, then what caused the damage?

"Wait a moment! This shouldn't be enough to erase all of Em's memories, the damage is too localized. Actually, the damage isn't even in the part of the brain where most memories are." She rechecked the research volume to be sure but saw nothing to indicate she was incorrect in her swift glance. "Why would this section be damaged at all?"

"There!" Ghen shouted. He was pointing to the edge of where the mapping sand showed, but Master D'gui didn't see anything.

"I don't sense anything," Ceahan said doubtfully.

There was nothing else to go off of, and Master D'gui believed it was better to be safe than sorry. "Move the view to show more around where Ghen saw something."

Ceahan shrugged. "Yes master."

The new view showed no damaged clusters, though Master D'gui did note this was slightly closer to where they'd been earlier and where memories moved more frequently. Observing the connection to those areas, she suddenly saw small flickers of purple in the sand. That color hadn't been used so far, that could mean something was different over there.

"Ceahan, move that way." Master D'gui indicated the area where she'd seen the purple sand.

"I saw it too this time." Ceahan brought the view in close, but just as the view started to settle, it shifted again. "I sense it now. I think it's only an impulse. As far as I can tell, it's just a fast one, but that's it."

"Fast one?" Master D'gui remarked skeptically. "It's faster than the others?"

"Yes."

"Follow it." Master D'gui commanded quickly, her eyes narrowing.

Ceahan jumped into action, zooming in and following the purple blur in the sand, but was a little confused as to why his answer had gotten such a response. "Is something off, master?"

Master D'gui explained as the scene began to change, tapping her book. "You may not have noticed this, but all impulses, no matter what they are doing, move at the same rate. This research agrees that all should only move at one speed, yet you say that purple light is moving faster. The volume is incomplete in its subject, so this may be something new, but I won't risk it. Faster is wrong."

Understanding blossomed in the young mystic's face, and Ceahan pursued with new vigor. "I'm sorry, I would have missed that. I messed up," Ceahan said as his senses registered their quarry before the sand could reflect it.

"Nonsense," Master D'gui said with a wave of her hand, as the image cleared. "Discovery is all about mistakes. As long as you learn from it, I see no reason for you to apologize."

The sand stabilized, shifting with regularity to follow as Ceahan directed. With a better view it became apparent that what they were looking at was not an impulse after all. It certainly appeared to move along the road like one, but while they watched, it displayed a very different behavior.

It stretched, without stopping, across the empty space between the mental highways and latched onto a new one, leaping over. This entity wasn't inside the mental paths like an impulse should be, it was on top of them!

"I know I already asked this," Ghen said, "but that isn't normal, is it?"

To the rancher's surprise, Master D'gui giggled like a child. The excitement of discovery taking over. "No, no, not in the slightest!"

Master D'gui pushed up her glasses, and her foot tapped with an excited twitch as she stared at the unfolding scene.

The thing, whatever it was, surely wasn't an impulse. However, it certainly spent a lot of its time imitating one.

As they observed, another light entered the picture. This one was clearly an actual impulse. The thing altered its course until it was on the same road as the real impulse. Faster, and faster, the strange being sped up until it caught up with the real impulse.

They all watched with a morbid fascination as the sand showed *it* overtaking the real impulse and slowing to latch onto it. The impulse impersonator covered the real one and the light of the true impulse faded from the mapping sand. When it finished its meal, the lasting purple glow picked up speed once more. The imitating entity moved on as if nothing out of the ordinary had occurred.

"It's stealing the carts off the road!" Ghen gasped. Despite the poor analogy, Ghen was at least able to follow what was happening.

"It's more than that." Ceahan focused on the creature so that it took most of the view in the sand. "I'm looking at the pathways it's traveling over. I think it's warping them somehow."

"Fascinating. This fake impulse is not only feeding off actual impulses, but it's warping the passages too. Now, why would it do that?" Master D'gui pondered for a moment. "The impulse is likely how it keeps on, the natural current used as food. The warping though, hmm.... Maybe that is how it keeps the mind from registering that anything is wrong. I imagine losing impulses isn't healthy in abundance. Thus," Master D'gui said, warming to her theory, "the mind can't combat this thing effectively."

"I didn't follow all of that," Ghen admitted. "Can you tell me straight if that little thing is what's hurting Em?"

"It could be, but it's hard to be sure at this point. Em's memory may only be a side effect of the, shall we say, faker's diet and its effects on the pathway. Of course, one may have nothing to do with the other."

The faker swallowed a new impulse as they spoke and hopped roads again to chase another one.

"I think it sounds reasonable," Ceahan agreed, "but I have a hard time believing this little thing could do this all by itself."

Master D'gui's glasses flashed with the reflected light of the sand as her head bobbed. "You're right, it may not be alone. Though seeing how fast it's moving and considering that makes three impulses gone," she pointed at the sand, "maybe even going for a fourth, I don't think it's impossible this creature could do this alone."

"How so?" Ceahan asked.

"First off, notice the sand, so far, all the impulses it's eaten are of the same color, meaning they carry similar signals. Something about those signals must interest our little friend since I think the faker is ignoring others. This could explain some memory loss. Then, all it has to do is eat more than one day's memories each night. Eventually, that would get Em to where he is now."

Ceahan looked as if he was still trying to catch up, so Master D'gui tried again.

"Think about it, if it ate a week's worth of memory every night, then it would barely take two months before Em had nothing at all. The mind doesn't keep every memory we store to begin with."

"Oh, I get it now. I wasn't thinking long term."

"No need to worry and I doubt its appetite is quite that large despite its speed and plainly avaricious nature."

"Can you two kill it with magic or something?" Ghen asked.

The master chewed her lip. "I don't know. If possible, I'm not sure we should. Remember, we can't even be sure this is the cause. Even if it is, I would like to find a way to extract it for study."

"How are we going to do that?" Ceahan asked skeptically.

Master D'gui laughed. "Why, I haven't the foggiest idea, but isn't that the fun part?"

Ceahan rolled his eyes.

"Oh, you're no fun, Ceahan." The master pouted playfully before laughing once again. "Whether we decide to kill it, catch it, or leave it alone, we first need to know more about it. So, Ceahan, what can you tell me?"

"Yes, master." Ceahan closed his eyes and focused on the information his craft poured into his mind. "At first it does feel like nothing more than a part of Em, but the more I study it, I can feel something different from it. It's... no, no it's not a part of Em, there is some kind of foreign nature about it and... I think there may be some magic to it. Every now and again I think I feel something, but it's slight if it's there at all."

"Well, it is a small thing." Master D'gui stepped over to her apprentice. "Now, Ceahan, I'm going to use your senses to guide me. I trust you and since you've declared this isn't part of Em, let's give it a jolt and see how it reacts."

Master D'gui laid one hand on Em's brow and the other upon Ceahan's headband he used to hide his scar. Working together, Master D'gui and Ceahan became in tune and she began to feel the faker as he did.

"Interesting." To her, the presence of the faker felt ferocious. A foreboding, ominous song that rattled with an urgency and ugly rasping that was eerily familiar. The strong aura of the entity washed over Master D'gui and for a moment she was overcome by unease. Her objective pulled her back however, and she kept her focus on the faker.

"Master, do you think there is any chance this thing will attack Em after you provoke it?"

"It could Ceahan, but that is why I am going to be using a very small amount to start with." Master D'gui sent the smallest trickle of magic she could manage as a shock against the faker. Excited, but still slightly nervous as she once more tested herself against the unknown.

The mapping sand flickered with the tiniest amber bolt as she targeted the faker.

It didn't react.

"Well, that's disappointing," she said sullenly.

"Was that you, miss?" Ghen asked.

"Yes, but our friend there didn't seem to notice. Let me try a little harder." She sent a second jolt, stronger than the first by a near fourth.

The amber reflection hit the faker and for a moment she thought it ignored the hit again, but right before she spoke up, she noticed through her connection with Ceahan that it began to slow.

"I think it felt that one master, if only slightly."

"Yes," she agreed, "but I don't think it did any damage. Now, what will it do?"

The faker moved on, still at its slower pace, but made no other changes.

"Will you increase the power again, master?"

She sighed. "Yes, it seems we may have to. If we want it to stop attacking, then it will need more incentive. Since it seemed to only just sense my last shock, I will use twice as much as my first strike. That should get its attention without severe damage."

There was no sound as she attacked, the sand giving no effect other than a slight rustling as it shifted, the image only flashing with brief light.

Master D'gui expected it to either pick up the pace again in a run or change directions, but instead, it stopped. Instantly and without hesitation, it froze completely in place. The faker simply sat atop the mental passage, as if waiting.

"What's it doing?" Ceahan questioned.

Master D'gui was as curious as her apprentice. *Why stop?*

"I think I get it," Ghen said.

Ceahan cocked an eyebrow. "No offense, but how is a rancher finding insight while we are still thinking?"

"Be silent Ceahan," Master D'gui chided. "Sorry Ghen, please continue."

Ghen seemed pleased to be heard out. "I may not know half as much as you two, but I have hunted before. When a wolf or predator like this thing first gets light shined on it, the animal sits a second. It's trying to figure out if you know it's there or not. If nothing happens, it will slowly start to move again, but if you show you know it's there, it'll run."

So Ghen is seeing predator behavior in the faker, Master D'gui thought.

It was a fair theory. "It does hunt like a predator would. For now, we'll wait. If it starts moving slowly, that will be evidence of the predator hypothesis. Then if it moves, we'll let it know we've seen it. If it runs, that is more evidence, and we can watch where it runs to."

After a few minutes, the faker slowly began to move, just as Ghen had predicted, it seemed to be trying to imitate the behaviors of a normal impulse. It did not stretch from one passage to another, instead following in a manner like any other impulse would. Even through Ceahan's powerful sense it almost felt more like an impulse should.

"Well, we're not convinced of your little act," Master D'gui said, giving it another shock.

The amber bolt made a quick flash in the sand. Even before the light had fully cleared off the sand, the purple speck raced off at a speed greater than any they'd seen.

"Whoa!" Ceahan exclaimed.

The act having failed, the faker abandoned all pretense. It skipped from road to road, stretching across gaps and cruising past like a monkey swinging from one vine to another. Moving almost as quickly over the gaps in the roads as it had on the roads themselves.

Not that it could escape the view of Ceahan and the mapping sand. "It seems you and the master were right about how it would act, rancher."

"It comes with experience," Ghen said, shrugging off the compliment. "Don't pay it too much mind."

Personally, Master D'gui hoped her apprentice might pay it 'much mind', it would be good for him.

The faker continued to run in as straight a line as it could, likely heading to wherever the faker rested during the day. Until, without reason, it began to veer off of its direct path.

"Why is it changing direction? Ceahan, is there anything you sense?" While she was in tune with him, Ceahan still possessed a clearer and wider view.

After a moment of silence, Ceahan replied. "I think it sensed an impulse."

Soon enough, the faker caught up to an impulse of its preferred color and quickly enveloped it. Then, it continued straight in its original direction once again.

Ceahan shook his head. "I guess we didn't scare it enough, it stopped for a snack."

"Or maybe it needed one," Ghen mumbled.

"Well, Ceahan if that is how it is then... Wait a moment, Ghen what was that?" Master D'gui pivoted as his muttered words came to register in her mind.

"Nothing, ma'am," he said quickly.

That was odd. Master D'gui watched the rancher intently for a moment before turning back to the sand, yet his comment remained in the forefront of her thoughts. She would need to ask him about it later.

"Master, our faker is veering again," Ceahan said, drawing her back.

"Yes, well, as I was saying let us see if I can't encourage our little friend to leave his quarry alone."

A new bolt thudded against the purple speck of the sand, and the edges of the faker's image shuddered as the faker quivered. Despite the hit, the faker powered through the jolt and quickly came atop its prey. Another light of Em's spirit faded to darkness under the purple intruder.

"Interesting," Master D'gui said but found her eyes drawn back to the rancher.

His lips moved in some phrase too quiet to hear, and he nodded slowly. He wasn't talking to them, but Master D'gui suspected whatever idle words he was saying were a clue to some theory the fuzzy-faced man had yet to reveal.

"Do you have something to add, Ghen?" she asked.

Ghen shook his head as his deep thought was broken. "Huh? Oh, uh not really."

"This is a time of discovery, Mr. Ghen. No thoughts are unwelcome and it's clear you have something in mind."

"I don't know if it's good enough to bother heads like yours yet, miss. Only thing I can say is, I'd bet that even if you hit this thing three or four times your faker won't care as long as he's after food."

"Is that so?" she said carefully. She turned a thoughtful glance on her apprentice.

Ceahan shrugged. "That's easy enough to test I guess."

"Then let's," the master agreed.

And so they did, and not once but twice more the faker veered off. During each small hunt, Master D'gui attacked with various strengths and different forms of power, all she was sure would not harm Em. Ceahan had a clear view of the faker and confirmed, along with the mapping sand, that the faker had felt most of the hits, but it never altered course until its meal was done.

"It seems you were right Ghen, but now we have something else to speculate on," Master D'gui said.

"Which is?" Ceahan asked.

"Look at where we are. Our little friend moves fast, the mind is a vast plane and memories drift in many places, but unless I miss my guess we are moving out of where the memories are more frequent."

Ghen scratched the top of his head. "Where are we now?"

"I'll need to check the book." Master D'gui stepped away from Ceahan, breaking their connection. As she thumbed through the book, she passed out instructions. "Ceahan, is there any way you can slow down? I'm no expert on the mind of humans, or any other tribe for that matter, and it's difficult to find any signs of our position with things blurring past."

"I'm sorry, master, but if you want me to keep up with the faker, I'm afraid this is our pace."

"Ugh," she growled. "How inconsiderate of it. Well, there's no helping it, keep up with the faker, Ceahan. Ghen you keep an eye out too. If the faker was going to go anywhere, I would've expected the faker to return to the damaged area where we first found it. I thought that the damage being so contained might have been because it was using it like a nest or a place to run in circles, pretending to be an impulse. That way, the brain wouldn't try to fight it off."

"And that's not where it's going?" Ghen asked despairingly. "I honestly thought that's where we were. I'm sorry, this all looks the same to me."

"Don't feel bad rancher," Ceahan said. "I can see in Em's head clearer than the sand and it all looks the same to me too."

"Me as well, that's what the book is supposed to be for. Despite how similar all the paths seem, though, I can tell from its overall position in the brain it's not near the earlier damage." Without realizing it, Master D'gui's explanation began to blend with her thoughts, and she began to ramble about their position in terms so advanced even Ceahan couldn't comprehend them.

"Plain speech please, master," Ceahan said tersely.

"Hmm? Oh, we aren't near the damage anymore."

"What should I do next?"

Master D'gui shrugged. "If those impulses it's been feasting on were responsible for Em's memories, then it won't find many more here. The hunt seems to be over. Until we know more, let's sit back and observe."

The faker moved on quickly for a while longer until it reached a large web of roads. At this cluster, it circled the cluster in a devolving spiral. With each pass worming its way deeper into the web of thought. Achieving the center point, it slowed until it came to a stop. Curiously, the mapping sand sensed some change in the faker because the purple hue of the little faker faded to a smaller speck of black in the dancing grains of sand.

"Is it still moving?" Ghen asked.

Ceahan shook his head. "No, it's paused completely."

"Is it dead?" the rancher pressed.

"No, I don't think so, but it is harder to feel. Master, do you know why it stopped here?"

Master D'gui tapped her chin and took time to think.

In the small paddock at the back of the garden, Master D'gui's horse flicked her tail as she and Bo tried to sleep through the goings on. On the roof of her home, an owl hooted as he scrutinized them all, silhouetted by the waxing moon.

This must be where it was going, but why? Master D'gui flipped quickly through the pages of the old research. "Oh, I'm afraid I'm still somewhat lost. Clusters like this are everywhere in the mind. Even worse, for all I know the faker's arrival here could be the most important clue, or it could mean nothing at all." Frustrated, she closed the book with a *klump!* "Burn the thing."

"What do we do?"

"If our faker is trying to hide from us, then it has failed, whether it knows it or not. I can still reach it there as easily as on any other pathway. The issue is, it's coming here might have a different meaning entirely."

Ceahan gestured toward the book his master had set aside. "Shouldn't we have another look then at the research?"

Master D'gui sighed. "Sadly, this book is only part of a larger research endeavor. One that, I might add, was still ongoing the last I heard. Even the researchers who wrote this book might not know any more than we do about the faker or this part of the mind than we do. That being the case, let's not jump to any action, especially since our faker isn't moving. It doesn't seem to be causing any problems at the moment, so let's take the time to think. Ceahan, what would you say our options are?"

The sand's image became unfocused as Ceahan's attention shifted. Thinking, the apprentice began to click his teeth. "We could shock it again, see how it reacts. Since it's at rest, we can also just leave it alone until it moves again. Also," his words lightened as a new idea came to mind, "we could try to think of a way to contain the faker."

Master D'gui considered the proposal. "Hmm, I like the idea, but we may want to wait on that last option." When she noticed Ceahan's disheartened expression, she quickly added, "As I said, it's an excellent idea, and one I think we should pursue, just not yet."

"Why not?" Ghen asked. "If you can seal it up, wouldn't that be a good fix for now?"

"The mind is complicated," she explained. "It has many parts, and all of it must continue to flow freely for it to work properly. Finding a way to catch our faker and not kill Em in the process requires a skill I haven't practiced in a while. We would also need more information about the faker. We don't know what will work on it and what won't."

"Then we're back to two options," Ceahan said.

"So, it would seem. With our options on the table, it's time to choose. Wait, or prod? I know you will both want me to decide, but I became out of my depth the moment Em knocked on my door. Everyone gets a vote this time. Ceahan, we'll start with you."

The sand cleared momentarily as Ceahan's focus returned to the faker, then blurred as he turned away again. "Could we do one prod, then wait if it doesn't move?"

"Why that?" Master D'gui asked, intrigued.

"Well, we need information, right? You ought to sense the faker now, master, it's gone dormant. I can barely feel it at all, that's not odd if it's hiding or sleeping, but there is something else too. I can't quite describe it. If we shock it one last time, I think we may learn something. If it starts to run again, we can, of course, follow it. If it stays, we can just leave it be."

"I think I'd rather leave it to start with," Ghen said. "I don't know much about all this magic, but to me, it looks like you've cornered a predator. Those things bite when you poke them."

"You say that but, are we sure we've cornered it?" Ceahan countered. "It's got plenty of room to run, and it might do just that if we prod it."

"And that'd be a good thing?" Ghen said, irritated. "It could tear up more of the kid's head."

"Are you joking? I'm not the master, but unless I miss my guess, it's been in his head for months or longer. What more is it going to do in one night that it hasn't done in that time?"

Ghen wasn't put off. "But you can't be sure it won't do worse."

"Of course not, that's the whole point!" Ceahan said, exasperated. "We aren't sure of anything, and it's not like I'm suggesting we try to blast it to pieces. I just want to find out what it's doing now."

Ghen opened his mouth to retort, but Master D'gui cut him off. "Both of you, that's enough!" She waited until she was sure neither would argue before continuing. "There's a risk no matter what we do. As researchers, we must embrace that fact and be willing to take risks. Therefore, I agree with Ceahan. We can at least try to learn a little more before we stand by to watch." Noting her apprentice, she added, "Though, also as researchers, we don't make smug faces just because our master agrees with us."

Ceahan quickly wiped the expression off his face and focused back on Em, the image in sand sharpening deftly as he did so.

"Good," Master D'gui said. "And Ghen, don't worry. I have an idea." She stepped back over to Em and placed her hand back on his head, preparing to deliver another shock. "I don't want to chase this thing all night, so I'm not going to try to make it move. In fact, this next jolt will be less than the previous ones were. I merely want to show our faker that we know it's there, nothing more. That will at least let us learn if it's trying to hide or if this dormant state is something else entirely."

Ghen sighed, and the argument ended.

The matter settled, Master D'gui began again without hesitation. She used Ceahan's sense to make sure she would not miss, gathered the correct amount of power, and released.

The next moments were eternities in seconds. Master D'gui's small jolt flickered on the mapping sand, it hit the faker and the picture of sand burst into bright light! Ceahan recoiled, throwing both himself and Master D'gui out of sync.

"Em!" Ghen yelled and ran forward.

Blinking the flare of light out of her eyes, Master D'gui looked at her patient and gasped. Em writhed and contorted, seizing, his eyes open but unseeing as his body shook and mouth went slack.

"By the... hold him down! We need to get him settled before he chokes! Ceahan quit gawking and grab him now!"

CHAPTER 25

FRACTURED DREAMS TORTURED HIM who the voices called *Em*.

Emptiness, pain, and longing ground his mind like lodestones in a mill. Visions of cities, marshes, fields, castles, and dungeons flew through his mind. Shadows of people and beasts prowled through his states of fitful waking and sleeping. People yelled and screamed. Sights of dueling lights and dreams of people holding him to a chair came and went in instants. The sound of distant singing was challenged with snarls and growls. Yet all these sensations were overwhelmed by two distinct and constant roars. One was accompanied and melodious, the other was alone, yet with a tenacious passion that would not be denied.

"What are you waiting for, Little Em?" came an old raspy voice, cutting through the confusion. A sly kind smile tugged at lips hidden from view. "Today's a big day, so I think you ought to get up."

"Are you going to come with me?" Em asked, all the sounds and images beginning to fade.

"In a way, but I've got to go for now."

For a moment, the vision cleared completely, and someone was sitting by his bed. Gray curly hair, with curving horns poking through it, and an instrument on his lap.

He was leaving?

"Don't go! Please, Silas, wait!" Em pleaded urgently.

He fought violently to sit up, to stop him. It was too late, it was gone, all gone. The confusion, the images, and the voice slipped away.

Em was sitting up in the reclined chair of the backyard once more, breathing hard.

A woman watched him curiously sitting where... he wasn't sure. It felt like someone *else* should have been sitting where she was. Not that he was sure who or why.

"You're awake," said the woman, still peering at him from over the rim of her glasses. "I'm glad to see it, you gave us all quite a scare last night. We took shifts watching over you."

"I... Something is wrong." He rubbed his head trying to tighten his frayed thoughts. "I... can't..."

"Remember?" she suggested.

He nodded slowly.

She pointed to a small book next to the chair he sat in. "I believe you will find that journal quite enlightening. Once you've read it, I will gladly fill in what gaps I can."

"Thank you," he said, but picking up the book, he hesitated before opening it.

The woman saw his pause and her eyes narrowed. "Is something the matter?"

"Eh... Did I say a name when I got up?"

"A name? I don't think so. Why?"

"I think I meant to."

Curiosity flared behind the lenses of the woman's spectacles. "Fascinating, and what name is that?"

It was there, on the tip of his tongue, but he could not bring it to mind. "I forgot." He shook his head in disappointment.

"Equally fascinating. I wonder if the desire to say a name is a recurring factor, or something new," she muttered to herself. "No matter, please continue with your notes. I have my own book to peruse." She lifted a weighty tome from her lap.

Reading the first page of the journal, Em found it surprisingly familiar. Yet, as he continued to read, there were a few things that he began to find odd.

You go by the name Em Dér.

I know you are confused, and I know why. You have forgotten
again. I am writing this message to warn you. If you sleep, you
will forget. I know this because I am you, a you that has been
forgotten. That is what our life has become, living for a day
to die in our sleep. Then, a new Em rises tomorrow with no
memory of who we were.

That fit what Em was experiencing, but something was strange. Chiefly,
he already knew he was Em. The way these notes were written and how he
felt made that fact somewhat surprising.

Em, even as I write this to you, I wonder how long we have
been this way. I do not know who we once were or who we
are supposed to be now. All I know is what I have been told,
which I will pass on to you. We forget everything each day,
but there is a chance to be whole again. This curse or sickness
we have can be cured, Em.
In the city of Henaden is a master of magic known as Master
D'gui...

Master D'gui! The moment he read the name, Em connected it to the
woman who sat next to him. The details were strangely vague in his mind,
but clearly, he had already made it to Henaden. He read on.

Our guides told me Master D'gui will help us. I do not know
why, but this may be our only chance. Trust Instinct and
Nature, they will see us to our goal.

Also, you should know that whatever has been done to our
mind has not affected everything about us. You will find that
our body remembers much of what our mind cannot.
Seek Henaden, find Master D'gui, and find who we are
supposed to be.

That is all we have to remember.

From the Em of yesterday.

Was knowing his name part of what the message meant by, 'our body remembers much of what our mind cannot?' Maybe recognizing Master D'gui was, too. That made sense, but part of Em couldn't accept that. It felt wrong.

"Master D'gui?" he asked the woman.

She looked up and blinked in surprise for a moment. "You mean me?" she said, pointing to herself.

"Yes, you are Master D'gui, are you not?"

"I am, but I find it surprising that you realized that."

Em nodded. "Then this is not normal. Is remembering my name strange as well?"

Master D'gui sat up straighter. "You knew your name as well?"

Again, he nodded. "It did not seem right to know it, yet I do. I am Em. As my notes say, though, I remember little else. But, whatever you have done has had some effect."

"Interesting, it's not as if we did very much. Still, if it has had a positive effect, it was well worth our efforts." She tapped thoughtfully at her chin. "However, as I hinted at earlier, not all went as planned and we will need to be more careful before we try to do more."

"What happened?"

Master D'gui shook her head. "No need to cover that now. At breakfast, everyone will come together and compare notes so we can make a proper plan. During that, you will learn all that there is to know. For now, I'm interested to see if there is any connection between what you know and what you don't. Is it alright if we do a little test?"

Em wanted to know what happened since it had 'given a scare' as the master had phrased it, but clearly, he would get no answer out of her at this point.

"What is the nature of the test?"

"Simple," she said with a smile. "I'm going to ask you things you should know the answer to, and we will see if you do. Ready?"

Em nodded.

"Then let's start with an easy one. Where are we?"

"Henaden," Em said confidently.

"That doesn't count," Master D'gui said, wagging her finger. "You could assume that from what you read in your notebook. Either be more specific, or less specific. Like, where are we in Henaden or where is Henaden in the world at large."

Em paused. He hadn't the faintest clue where Henaden was in the world, the first page of the journal said it was a city but gave no hint where the city was. As for the other option, he looked around. They were in a back garden or small yard.

At the back of the garden was a pen where a horse and mule were. They seemed tightly packed and clearly one or the other didn't belong, but that gave no hint of where he was. The garden was surrounded on three sides by a building and the fourth side was hemmed in by a wall that stretched up to where there was a railing that looked down into the backyard. Clearly, the top of the wall was some road or battlement, but again no clues.

He looked more closely at the building. There were windows. He couldn't see into them, but there was a small planter box on the outside of two of the windowsills. The building, while larger, could still not fit more than six to eight individuals of a medium size. All this led Em to his conclusion.

"Is this your home?" Em asked.

Master D'gui had been watching Em very carefully. "It is, but did you remember that or solve that?"

"Solve," Em admitted.

"Then it doesn't count," she declared before a new thought struck her. "Both your name and my identity are matters of people instead of places, so let's change directions. Have you ever heard the name Ghen?"

Em felt a jolt of excitement. "Yes, I have."

Master D'gui grinned. "Excellent, who does that name belong to?"

Em's energy faded as he floundered to answer. "It is someone who... they have..."

"Don't worry about giving a full description, just say what comes to mind," Master D'gui said.

Em tried his best, but it felt less like knowing than taking wild guesses. It was Instinct that spoke in his ear, and he only relayed the answers. "Ghen-*sa* is a he."

"Correct."

The boy, whispered Instinct assisted with an unseen wink.

"There... there is a boy who is not Ghen-*sa*'s son."

Master D'gui blinked. "Interesting, I think he did mention that a boy lived with him, but I don't recall if it was his son or not. My guess is that is the connection."

"He works on..." Em struggled to find the word, "roots?"

The woman smiled. "Yes and no, he owns a ranch. On that ranch, he has grown roots and has come to Henaden to sell them. Now, how are you connected to Ghen?"

You trust him, Nature said in a simple rumbling bass.

"I trust him," Em repeated.

"That's not very particular," Master D'gui said.

Em shrugged dejectedly. "It is all I have."

Master D'gui leaned forward and patted his arm. "Don't worry. Ghen is a friend of yours, who brought you to Henaden. I think he will be quite pleased that you remember as much about him as you've already said. Now let's see if you can remember someone you haven't known for so long. Are you alright with that?"

Em nodded.

"There is one more person who lives here, my apprentice. Do you know anything about them?"

Em searched his mind but found nothing pointing to this person, even Instinct held its tongue. He shook his head.

"That's too bad. Well, he won't be offended, you only met yesterday after all. His name is Ceahan and he—"

"He hides a scar under a headband," Em said, interrupting unintentionally. He hadn't even realized he'd said anything at first, but the words tumbled forward the moment he heard Ceahan's name.

Master D'gui sat very still and spoke slowly. "That he does. Did you happen to see the scar?"

"If I did, I do not remember it, only that he hid it. My apologies for interrupting. When you spoke his name I just suddenly knew, and I wished to say it."

Master D'gui relaxed. "No need to fret, I understand what you mean. It's positive to know you remembered anything about him. You may not have tied the fact to him being my apprentice, but it was clearly tied to his name, which means at some level you remembered it."

Em's spirits lifted slightly. It was true, which proved this was progress.

Then the master's voice became more serious. "However, I would warn you against bringing up that scar. It's an old wound, and he is very sensitive about it. It may be better if you pretend to only have recognized his name." That topic covered, her voice lightened again. "I think we have a good idea of where your head is at now. Even for Ghen, who you should know the most about, you know very little. Here and there facts seem to have remained about multiple people and probably other things too.

"With that in mind, please finish catching up on what is in your notebook. Ghen and Ceahan are still asleep, I think. When they wake up, we will break our fast with a discussion of the night's events." Her eyes flickered with a light all their own. "I'm excited to see what we have all learned."

"Nightroot is an odd little plant," Ghen was saying as Master D'gui led Em back into the house a little later. "Very few places can grow the stuff, but our soil is good for it. Considering how valuable it is, it's a right blessing to us who grow it."

Despite herself, Master D'gui couldn't help laughing.

"You know Ghen," she said, "in Yongarad most people outright refuse medicines that have a mixture of nightroot in them. It's no blessing to anyone in their mind."

"Why's that?"

"Oh, it has to do with old legend. I'm sure you are aware that the root grows in the dark and looks like black veins on the ground." She sat down at the smaller kitchen table.

She owned two tables, a larger dining table that was always covered by one thing or another, and this small round table made for two. Usually, this was where she and her apprentice ate most of the time. Four could probably fit at the table if they sat cozily.

"I do, miss," Ghen said skeptically about the nightroot.

"Well, there's an old superstition that it's a cursed plant."

Ghen stared with wide eyes. "Is that true?"

Ceahan laughed. "No way! It's just a myth."

Master D'gui grinned. "Yes, the 'Black Veins of Death's Bane' is its more superstitious name, though I admit I don't know why. Still, it is interesting considering nightroot itself was thought a myth not too long ago."

"It was a myth?" Em said confused.

"That's right. No one is sure who or why, but the oldest histories record that nightroot was totally extinct. A generation before Roleius took over, farmers in En-Athen found small patches of the root and were able to cultivate it. It was only after that people found that it held medicinal properties. All of a sudden, the scary black root became far less scary and far more desirable."

"And the curse?" Em asked.

"Likely fiction," she said, "or based on something else, or an event that occurred but was blown out of proportion."

Ceahan brought a hot pan holding toasted bread to the table.

"Real or not, I still need to sell the root," Ghen said.

"You won't have a problem doing that here. The war is heating up again, so medicines are on the rise," Ceahan said grimly.

"Is that so? I thought that might happen since the fighting always heats up in the spring, but isn't it still early? Winter only just broke."

The master and her apprentice both shrugged.

"That's just the local word," Master D'gui said. "I study tribal and historical cultures. These wars won't interest me for a few generations."

"Hey Em," Ceahan said. "Do you know me?"

Em nodded. "In part. You are Ceahan-*so*, Ghen-*sa*, and Master D'gui." He pointed to each in turn.

"And," Master D'gui added excitedly, "last night was a partial success! He even remembered some facts about each of us after hearing our names."

"Really?" Ghen said, looking happily at Em.

Em raised a hand. "Do not rejoice yet, I recalled very few details."

Ghen slumped. "That's too bad. Still, it's a step down the road."

"We need to be more careful about the faker, though," Ceahan said.

"Faker?" Em asked, but he wasn't heard as Ghen accidentally spoke over him.

"That's what I said last night."

"Hey, we had to try something," Ceahan said defensively. "We didn't even know it could fight back, if we hadn't tried something we'd be wondering if it could or not *right now*. With what we know, we can make a good plan and try again."

"You want to try again?" Ghen said, raising his voice. "After what happened to Em, you want—"

"Of course, we're trying again!" Ceahan yelled back. "Would you rather just leave that thing in Em?"

With a bit of magic, Master D'gui brought her hands together in a deafening *CLAP* that rattled the shutters of the kitchen window.

All three boys recoiled slightly, and Master D'gui glared over her glasses at her apprentice and the rancher. "It was too long a night and is too early in the morning for this."

Ghen looked down bashfully. "I'm sorry miss, May would have my rear if she knew I'd shouted like that while I was a guest."

She turned her gaze on Ceahan, who wilted. "Sorry master."

Having the table back in order, she nodded. "Now, you both clearly missed that Em asked a question just as you two began your little spat." Both looked at Em, but Master D'gui continued. "He asked what the 'faker' was. I'll explain—

"Last night Em, you may or may not remember, we began to probe your mind. After you went to sleep, we found something unexpected. We found a creature we believe could be a virus of some kind. It pretended to be part of the regular workings of the mind, which is why we called it 'the faker.'

"We messed with it, the details of that will come up later, but the important part is that we came to a point where we had it more or less cornered. As you might guess, Ceahan and Ghen disagreed on how to go forward. That's what their fight was just about. Unfinished business, you might say. The point is that when we pressed on, it fought back."

"It was able to strike you?" Em said, astonished.

"No," she said, "it was able to strike *you*. This thing is clearly no normal virus you picked up from drinking out of the wrong river. For one thing, it has magic. As far as we know, only the nine tribes have even the slightest chance of having magic. Nevertheless, we felt it. It blew out a burst of power when we cornered it, not much, but enough to send you into a seizure."

"This was the 'scare' you spoke of before."

"Quite right, and after that we decided it was best to call it a night. Each of us took shifts watching you and doing what we could to learn while you slept. That catches you up generally. Did I overlook anything?" Master D'gui asked the other two.

Surprisingly, both hesitated.

"Actually master, there were the previously damaged mental lanes," Ceahan said.

"Mental lanes?" Em asked.

Ghen tried to explain, "Those are roads in your head."

However, that only confused Em further. "Roads in my head?"

Master D'gui shook her head. "Yes and no. Listen, before things get more confusing, I'm going to leave it at this. Mental paths or lanes are part of your mind like the arm is part of the body, if we try to go into specifics, we'll cover many things we have before and lose half the day doing so. I'm sorry, Em, but you may have to learn on the go."

"Yes, master," Em said, confident in his ability to do so.

Master D'gui was surprised at his quick answer until she realized that 'learning as you go' was something Em was forced to do every day due to his condition.

"That's very good. Anyway, we don't know enough about the damaged pathways at the moment. We suspect the faker attacked them, but we aren't sure why. I noted there was some healing, but I'm not sure what to make of that yet. Do we know anything else?" She focused on Ghen.

The rancher caught the glance and opened his mouth to speak, but then closed it again and shook his head.

Master D'gui looked at her apprentice. Ceahan watched Ghen, then meeting her eyes, nodded. He too thought Ghen had more to say. Well, her burning curiosity would get through whatever self-conscious debris was holding him back one way or another.

"If that's all, then let's get down to details. We will go around the table and all four of us can say what we think we know or learned from last night's experiments about Em's condition overall or the faker in particular."

Catching that she'd said 'four' Em dejectedly reminded her, "I fear I will have little to offer, master."

"Actually, you may have the most to offer. You can tell us not only anything you remember but also offer judgment of what you learn from what each of us has to say. You have a sort of objective perspective. For that reason, you will go last. To start with, why don't we go with you, Ghen?"

"Me? Well, I don't have much either." Ghen said squirming in his chair. He looked at Em to dodge the master's delving eyes. "After we quit, I was the second shift to watch over you. Ceahan here started, and then Master D'gui went after me. Since I can't use magic, I just kind of sat around and checked on Bo, that's my mule out back. The horse out there is the master's."

"Her name is Lena," Master D'gui commented. "But what about the faker, Ghen? Was there anything you noticed about it?"

"I..." Ghen hesitated.

Come on! Master D'gui thought. *I know you have something.*

"Well, it looked really hungry to me," he finally said.

Ceahan sighed disappointedly and rolled his eyes. "That's all?"

Ghen shook his head. "No, I mean it was starving, you know?"

That was an odd choice of words. "Starving? Why do you say that?"

"It just looked it."

"How so?" Master D'gui pressed.

Ghen ran a hand through his curly hair. "Well, it has to do with something that happened when I was a kid."

"Do tell." Master D'gui leaned back, taking another bite out of the toast Ceahan had provided.

Ghen finally picked up that he wasn't going to get out of speaking his mind, and with a sigh, started his tale. "See, when I was a boy, the Redgen family, they're neighbors of ours, were trying to catch a fox they'd spotted a few times trying to get in their hen house. I came to help because it sounded like fun.

"Now, something you ought to know is that it was a bad season everywhere. Too dry after a hard winter. All that was really bad for the land and wildlife. Many things were going hungry at the time. When the fox showed up, you could see its bones with how thin the villain was. What makes this all come to mind is that the fox acted just like your faker, start to finish."

"Be specific," Master D'gui said. She could feel that there was something in this. "How was it like the faker?"

"Well, it stopped when we first got nearby hoping we'd pass it by. After, when it knew we were onto it, the fox made a break for the trees. Odd thing was it ran wide like your faker did and did it twice."

"For food?" Ceahan said.

Ghen nodded. "Once because a hen had got loose, but the hen flew up and the fox missed it. The other time, the thing spotted a field mouse, it caught that one on the run. You know when I said that hitting the faker when it was hunting wouldn't stop it?"

"I do," Master D'gui said.

"What told me your faker wouldn't stop was the fox. When that fox chased the hen, one of our slings broke its leg with a well-aimed rock. Even hobbled, it kept on for the chicken. Then after it kept on running. Holland Redgen stuck the vixen with an arrow, but the fox didn't seem to care till after it caught its mouse. The fox died from the arrow, with the mouse still in its mouth. If the fox had given up on the mouse, it might have gotten away, but it was too hungry to give up."

Master D'gui narrowed her eyes. "Fascinating, that does sound similar."

"It might also explain what I found," Ceahan said, thoughtfully.

"Oh?"

Ceahan looked at Ghen to make certain he was finished speaking, and the rancher nodded.

"During my shift of watching over Em, I kept checking on the faker. It stayed still, ready to attack for a long time, but eventually began to move again. It went back to hunting Em's memories and fed like crazy."

"Another indicator of starvation. It was willing to risk being attacked again to feed." Master D'gui surmised.

"Yes, and after studying its signature carefully, I went over Em's mind and body on a larger scale. Do you know what I found?"

Master D'gui was on the edge of her seat.

"Nothing," Ceahan declared.

"Fascinating, so you are saying there is only one faker."

"I checked more than once for any magic like the faker and found nothing. Think about it though master, if there were more, and they all needed to feed on Em's memories to live, then there might not be enough to go around."

Master D'gui nodded, seeing Ceahan's logic. "It would be strange for a virus not to replicate. However, if it's on the brink of starvation, it wouldn't have the energy. If one starves, two or three would all die together. Then again, there would have been enough food when the virus first infected Em."

"Well... you know," Ghen said, emboldened by his last idea striking such a chord, "it could be that the damaged roads we saw were because of an old contest between two fakers."

Master D'gui's face twisted. "Sorry, but no, that doesn't come out right."

"Why not?" Em asked. "I do not remember ever seeing it, but I am sure both animals and tribesman fight for less than food."

"Because some of the mental passages were damaged by the faker last night. It was actually how we found it to begin with. It would be a very big coincidence for the faker to kill its last rival the day we begin our study. No, I think there is some other reason. I do like the starving faker theory. Until we know more, let's pursue this line of logic. We will operate under the assumption that the faker needs to eat as much as it can to survive.

"For my part, I spent the majority of my shift reading the research on the human mind. I focused my reading on what diseases they found, but sadly none matched the faker. Beyond that, I focused on how they conducted their studies, and in doing so, I have thought of some ideas on how we can handle the faker."

"Handle it?" Em asked. "Could we not starve it? Put it under a kind of siege?"

"How would we do that?" Ghen asked.

"Rest, would that not work?" Em suggested.

Ceahan tilted his head thoughtfully. "The faker does seem to only be active when you're asleep. If you slept more, you wouldn't make new memories to eat, and it could run out of food quickly." He chuckled. "A strange new disease and the cure is extended bed rest."

"Don't jump to conclusions," Master D'gui warned. "There is one other lesson we learned last night that makes that plan difficult."

All three looked at her, confused.

"The lesson is the very one Ghen was arguing about. The faker is willing to fight back. For all we know, the faker could commit to killing Em before it starves to death if it feels it has no other choice. Clearly, it has enough natural intelligence to know when it's cornered. Since an attack could wake Em up, it could shock him if only to stir up food. Even if we forced Em to stay asleep, I would fear what the faker might do."

"I hadn't thought of that," Ceahan said. "In other words, the faker is holding Em hostage."

The mood of the table darkened, but Master D'gui was not so easily put out.

"That's right, but all that means is that we need to find a way to contain the faker."

"Contain it? Not kill it?" Ghen asked.

"Too risky," Ceahan said since he could guess the answer. "If we attack the faker with too much power, we could kill Em without meaning to. If we attack with too little, the faker might decide to kill Em itself."

Master D'gui nodded. "Yes exactly. Luckily, despite being able to do a lot of damage, the faker is quite small. If we can put it in a trap, one that won't hurt Em but will stop the faker's attacks, it won't matter what we do. Whether the faker starves, or we intentionally kill it, Em is not at risk."

"Is that possible?" Em asked.

Master D'gui smiled weakly. "This is where I remind you that I am a researcher of tribal and ancient cultures. I think it is possible, but I need to study more before I'd be willing to try."

"Could we get help?" Ghen suggested. "Are there other mystics in the city?"

Ceahan snorted derisively, but it was his master who answered.

"No, and even if there were, I wouldn't count on them."

"Why not?"

"Rancher," Ceahan said, "there are two types of magic users. The kind that stumbles around stupidly and those that are educated in how to use their power."

"Don't be rude, Ceahan. Just because they didn't follow my approach does not mean they deserve to be insulted."

"Sorry master."

"To Ceahan's point though," Master D'gui began, "healing is particularly tricky even for those with training. See, using magic as medicine is a delicate thing. One mistake and you can make things so much worse. Trying to regrow flesh, you can make a tumor. Try to fix it by destroying the tumor and you damage an organ and so on. I know some of the details because I went to the Korodai Institute."

"That is a school for those of magic, yes? It was in my notes," Em said.

"Then rewrite your notes, it's not a school," Ceahan corrected. "There are no classes or sessions. It's a research institute. The only way to learn there is to impress someone who will be your master, learn from them, and then strike out on your own."

Master D'gui nodded. "My master was a scholar of medicine. I wanted to be the same when I started, but I changed directions while learning from him. It was through learning the herbal remedies of lost cultures, and learning how medicine was different between the tribes, that I found what I really wanted to study."

"So not all magic people go to the institute?" Ghen asked.

"No, we 'magic people'," Master D'gui said with a wry smile, "are very rare. That means we can come from anywhere and Korodai is a long way away, so not everyone can afford to travel so far. It's also the case that you have to be impressive to start with to get the attention of a master if you want to be an apprentice.

"A fact you may not be aware of is that the amount of power we wield differs from person to person. One wizard might make a hurricane while another will struggle to lift a drop of water. There are those with the art who have so little they don't even know it."

"Could I travel to Korodai for help then?" Em asked. "I do not wish to, but if I need to..." he trailed off.

Master D'gui considered the idea. She and Ceahan were going to leave for Korodai in only days, or had planned to, but considering Em's marauder uniform Ceahan would not accept Em's company on the trip easily.

One look at her apprentice and she knew she was right. He'd guessed her thoughts and was shaking his head.

"It's a long trip," Master D'gui finally said. "Considering your condition, it might take you forever to get there, and if you weren't careful in how you phrased things in your notes, you could end up back here or not knowing where to go at all. Then there is one other thing to consider, the faker. If it is starving now, then is its life running out? If so, will it kill you before you get there?"

Em couldn't think of an answer to that.

"I'm sorry," Master D'gui said picking things back up in the silence, "but I think Ceahan and I are your best chance for the moment. We need to learn more, but if we find some way for you to make the trip to Korodai maybe we will consider it again. For now, I think you are in the right place."

"So, then, what do we do?" Em asked.

"You get to translate some documents, Ghen gets to go sell his root, Ceahan and I on the other hand..." Master D'gui smiled, and Ceahan rolled his eyes knowing what she would say. "We do research!"

CHAPTER 26

WHEN EM WAS TOLD he needed to translate documents in exchange for his treatment, he was afraid he wouldn't be able to do it. He had no memory of other languages. However, after being handed two pages written very differently, Em found, at least with these tongues, he could read both easily.

It was long after everyone began their work that Ghen finally stood from the small breakfast table. Em thought he looked rather down. He kept looking at the stacks of research and then turning away.

Em guessed he was upset that there was so little he could do to help. He didn't remember the rancher, but the man did seem to have a vested interest in Em's recovery. Out of all of them, however, Ghen had the least to offer.

It had arisen in conversation as they finished their breakfast that Ghen could read but was slow and that big words still confused him. Master D'gui had guessed as much, which was why she recommended he leave to sell his root. The rancher lingered though, but not just because he wanted to help.

Ghen wasn't looking forward to wandering Henaden to find someone who would buy his nightroot. Mr. Noren's pressure made it hard to sell anything, even something as valuable as nightroot. Ghen knew he had a friend who might buy some but wasn't sure he could get all the bags sold just by going to Ol' Roger. Those two things made him slow on his way out of doors.

When the rancher finally got up and passed through the entryway, he was greeted with the sight of Master D'gui leaning over Em's shoulder, and pointing to multiple lines of text.

"You sure put Em to work fast," Ghen joked when Master D'gui saw him.

She smiled. "Of course, who knows? Maybe the answers we seek for Em's curse are in one of these pages and I just can't read it."

"What do you think?" Em asked, showing Ghen the text he was in the middle of translating.

Taking a step closer, Ghen looked at the page. His face twisted. "I guess those are words, but I can't read a one of them. They all look more like a bunch of badly drawn houses than any word."

"Some are words, some are more of ideas," Em tried to explain, but Ghen only shook his head.

"Don't bother, kid, reading Ifeldian is hard enough for me. That looks way harder."

"I find that very strange. If anything, I find your words more difficult," Em said.

"It may be your native tongue or something closer to it then." Master D'gui suggested.

Ghen only looked at the large stack, still to be translated. "I sure hope it's easy for you, 'cause boy you've got a lot to do. Honestly, it's hard for me to believe all the stuff is something somebody out there wrote down." He looked at the room covered in manuscripts, loose pages, scrolls, and books. "I didn't know there was this much to read in all Ifeldia. Did you know that even in her guest room, there are piles of this stuff?" he asked Em.

"I have two guest rooms, Ceahan's chambers, and my own, and yes, they are all the same," Master D'gui cut in. "It's not my fault my house isn't large enough to hold it all."

"Do all sorcerers keep such collections?" Em asked.

"Not even close!" Ceahan shouted, his voice rebounding from around the corner of the hallway. "My master is a hoarder."

"A collector," Master D'gui corrected icily, "and I am proud of my collection."

"That's right," Ghen said. "Last night, Ceahan said it was bigger than most folk nearby."

Master D'gui shrugged. "Did you know that almost no one looks into cultural histories? They are seen as near garbage to many, a travesty in its own right, but it was that flaw that allowed me to amass this knowledge. I'd guess my research contains more about the various tribes and histories than anyone else outside of Roldea, because of the collections of the noble houses, and Korodai itself."

"If you don't mind my asking, miss, is all your family as excited to learn this stuff as you?" Ghen asked.

"My family? No, my father might be, but I don't remember him. My mother was never curious about anything. The only risk she ever took was trying to marry a satyr, but he disappeared chasing after his own tribe, and she stopped trying new things after that. My mother just sewed for a living until she learned of my ability to perform mystic arts. From there we went to Korodai so that I could study and support her. Not that her plan worked out as she hoped."

"Did you struggle then, master?" Em asked.

"Actually, I was quite good," she said. "The issue was that my master specialized in medicine, and I went into studying history. The Korodai Institute is a wonderful place where discovery is the only true king of the realm, but they have little care for anything magic cannot influence. As you may have guessed, the mystic arts do not aid me as much in history as they might in medicine, combat, or some other discipline. I became somewhat of an outcast and set off on my own after about eight falls at the institute."

Ghen looked the master up and down. She'd changed her robe but had wound her hair in the same tight bundle atop her head, and to all appearances, looked human. "Pardon, but you said your father was a satyr?"

Master D'gui raised an eyebrow. "I did, and yes, that means I am cross-tribe. Do you have a problem with that?"

"Uh, no ma'am. I'm sorry I didn't mean it like that. I just didn't realize. You don't look much like the last guy I met who was cross-tribe."

She brightened. "Oh, we are a rare breed. Tell me, what was the last person you met a cross between?"

"He was a dwarf and kyate-siv fella who was passing through Marden Hallows." The little fella stuck out in Ghen's mind as a walking ball of hair. "He has a relative on the dwarf side there."

"Ah, I see. Both of those tribes are more common locally and have historic roots in the area, but that is still a strange cross. Kyate-siv usually avoid dwarves fairly avidly."

Em looked at the master with curiosity. "I was not aware of any enmity between those tribes."

"Enmity? Oh, nothing so aggressive. It's not personal, or even mutual. Dwarves don't care where the kyate-siv live."

"Then why do the kyate-siv avoid them?"

"Fleas," the master said. "Kyate-siv have a natural inclination for lots of hair, and dwarves do too when it comes to their beards. The difference is that many dwarf clans tend to go underground and pick up fleas and bugs. The dwarves aren't as bothered by the bugs, but things like that will throw kyate-siv into a panic. Aspects like this are what lead to there being so few cities where all the tribes live together."

"I thought that was due to some law?" Ghen said.

"King Ordisus's little jab at the other rulers?" The master guessed. "That is a local cause, but not the only one. Tribe specific cities exist in many places. Though, in each of those 'one tribe cities' there are usually still two or three tribes, just with one more dominant than the others."

"I didn't know that," Ghen said thoughtfully.

"Lucky for you, that *is* my expertise, unlike small brain invaders."

"I see," Em said. "That explains something in my notes that seemed strange. It mentioned this law, but it never felt right, as if it was pointless."

"Not exactly," Master D'gui said. "The reason most tribes separate is because other tribes can't stand their neighbor's natural habits. However, the human tribe is very flexible so there really aren't any 'human only' cities outside this land. That makes the law quite novel historically, even if it is both annoying and slightly offensive to people like me."

"How can that be?" Ghen asked. "Shouldn't elves be the same way? I always heard they were like humans, except they don't age."

Master D'gui giggled until she laughed.

It took her a moment to collect herself, but when she did, she lifted her glasses to wipe away a tear. "I'm sorry, Mr. Ghen, but that is... shall we say, off the mark in a few ways. Besides maybe the wodjok tribe, the elf tribe is the most likely to try to live only among their own kind. It's true they are only slightly taller on average and have few physical differences, but that is the end of their resemblance. As for aging, I guarantee you they do age, just differently than other tribes."

Well, for one thing, they can't eat meat, Instinct agreed offhandedly, and Em repeated it aloud, agreeing that elves were very different from other tribes.

"True." Master D'gui said. "It upsets their stomachs and makes them the only herbivorous tribe. Not that they won't kill animal life, they just won't eat the meat afterward. That's why it's so rare to find elves where vegetation is sparse, they need it for food."

"Huh, well that's something. You know, I'd heard they had a cow's diet before, but I never quite believed it." Ghen said as he made his way to the back door.

"I doubt they would phrase it that way," Master D'gui pointed out. "Yet it's not completely incorrect. It's not uncommon for them to snack on certain types of grass when traveling if they don't have anything better to eat. However, they don't like to talk about it."

"I won't bring it up if I try to sell to an elf then," Ghen said with a grin. Then, stepping out, he waved back. "Until later, I'll do what I can to be back quick so I can help with whatever you need."

"Excellent, see you then," Master D'gui called back.

The moment Ghen closed the door behind him on his way out, Master D'gui turned an odd glance on Em.

"Yes, master?" he asked.

"Did you know I was cross-tribe?"

Em hesitated. "I... I do not know. In a way, I might have."

"Interesting, I noticed you didn't react when I brought up the fact. What gave it away?"

Em observed her once again. "I do not know. It is not as if there is much to give it away."

"Not obviously." She leaned down to where he was sitting and, taking his left hand, placed it higher on her forehead. "Feel that?"

The moment his hand touched her bundle of hair, he did. There was a patch beneath his hand that was unexpectedly firm.

"You have horns."

She pulled his hand away and stood back up. "That's right, small things, but if I let my hair down, they would be clear to see. If I wore the more fashionable shorter skirts instead of my robe, anyone would know my tribe instantly."

"Is your heritage something to be hidden?" Em asked.

She scrunched her face. "Not quite, it's not as if I'm pretending to be human. I am registered as a cross-tribe in the city. I do this because there are people who find speaking to a cross-tribe member awkward."

"I was under the impression that people of both tribes would accept you."

"A common thought, but not always. Even if we are, being accepted is not the same as being a part of the group. We are still outsiders, 'the half breed', or something of that nature.

"Considering I was lucky to get most of my mother's more human features, I usually pretend to be of your tribe. There are those with satyr blood who are far too obvious to hide. Other than my horns I just have muscle in different places along my legs, more along my father's heritage.

"That means I do have some advantages of being cross-tribe, I'm more than twice your age, but I could probably outrun you. Of course, there are... disadvantages as well." Master D'gui's expression turned somber.

A silence hung in the air, and for a moment, Em wondered what she meant.

Ceahan poked his head around and gave a weak smile. "She means the shedding." His smile broadened. "All satyr's shed in the spring, fur everywhere."

"You little brat!" Master D'gui tried to sound irritated, but she was smiling. Snatching up a book, she spun around and hit him on the shoulder with a thump.

"Ow!" Ceahan laughed as he rubbed his shoulder.

"Go back to your studies, before I really give you something to complain about." She was still trying to sound angry, but couldn't manage it.

Despite Ceahan's joke, Em knew that shedding was not what Master D'gui had meant. She'd been too serious about it for something so trivial. Her apprentice was trying to break the sour mood this 'disadvantage' brought on the master. Em respected him for that but found that he envied Ceahan too.

He cared deeply for his master, who in turn cared for him. They introduced themselves as master and apprentice, but Em could not help seeing them as family. Ceahan's lack of satyr traits made it clear they shared no blood, but this was still a mother and her son. They were happy, but the light of their joy cast a shadow over Em.

Where is my family? Do I even have one?

Oh, Little Em, Instinct said. *Closer than you think.*

Em wasn't sure what to make of that, but it and the progress Master D'gui had already made with the faker gave him hope. Maybe he could go back or go forward to something new.

Em opened his eyes and turned back to his work. He was only distracting himself with it, but it was better than listening to his fears. There wasn't much hope, but there was a little voice that gave him peace.

CHAPTER 27

"YOU KNOW BO," GHEN said to his equine assistant, "there's a lot I like about the city, but those crowds make me wish we were going home already." He led her off the Buyer's Road and out of the constant press that was Henaden's shopping highway.

Bo snorted and shook her mane as if dusting off the crowd.

"The open land is just better. Both of us can go whichever fair way we please. Well, as long as we didn't go over a field, it's no smart thing to tromp down sprouting crops. Still, we need to come into town every now and again." He sighed, and said, "For all that our open fields have, they don't have a place to sell nightroot."

The mule stomped.

"Yes," Ghen said, "I know I could have left you behind at the master's house, but two bags of nightroot would have been a might cumbersome for me to carry for who knows how long. Since it isn't quite so hard for you, you'll have to do it."

Turning off onto a step with a few shops he recognized he began to count them off. "There's the farrier, but the guy in Marden saw you the other day. Here's that little watering hole we tried last time, it was good." Ghen chuckled and patted Bo on the neck. "I might bring Em here for a drink once he's all better."

The next shop had a distinguishable splash of green against the grayer masonry and dark wood posts that supported every other storefront on the step. Clay pots lined the open windows where ivy grew up and over to a lattice. A network of vines ran up and over the front of the store, making a variable spider web of green leafy threads. A small wooden sign swung in the wind over the door, announcing it as *The Potted Post* with a small subtitle reading *Trading and Selling of Growing Goods*.

"There's Roger's spot," Ghen said happily.

He pulled Bo over to the tie post off to the shop's side. The building was bare of ivy and there was no mystery why. The moment Ghen finished tying his mule to the post he saw her straining to reach a leafy green branch that had been bold enough to round the corner of *The Potted Post*.

"Now you behave," he warned Bo as he lifted off the two bags of root.

Bo ignored him, as she found she could just tickle the leaf with the edge of her lips and was grasping at it.

Ghen shook his head and went around the corner. He'd sold nightroot to Ol' Roger a few times. *The Potted Post* usually only sold spices and herbs for regular folk to use that Roger grew on his rooftop. He couldn't grow nightroot and a few other little plants since he didn't have the space or right earth to care for them. So, he would usually buy some stock.

Last time Ghen had sold nightroot in Henaden, Roger had given him a fair price for the root all in one go, a rare thing indeed with Mr. Noren's pressure. Ghen wasn't so hopeful to expect a repeat, but maybe he could at least offload the lighter of the two bags.

Stepping in, Ghen was greeted by an earthy smell that reminded him of home. The store was small, lined with shelved planters that Roger had brought down from his garden. He let folk cut what they wanted straight from the planters to buy. Of course, if you cut the wrong thing, Roger wasn't so generous that he didn't make you buy it anyway and he had little black stenciled signs announcing that on every shelf. Despite the warning, Ghen had heard it from Roger's own lips that it still happened often enough.

Ghen looked at the coal dust lines on the dark wood sign and smiled. "He ought to paint it brighter or something."

Ghen took a peek down the aisle and spotted a woman at the counter talking to the owner himself. Luckily there was no rush, so Ghen paid them little mind and decided to patiently wait his turn. Taking a gander at the array of little plants, a funny looking one caught his eye. It had a green stem, but the leaves were all sorts of colors.

"I wonder what you are," Ghen asked the little plant. "Maybe I'll ask Roger, you certainly are interesting looking."

He looked back at the counter and, turning his head, caught part of the conversation between Roger and the woman.

"Listen Roger," the woman said, annoyed, "I know you don't work for Noren, but he will still pay you as long as you let us know if you see this guy, okay?"

Suddenly more aware, Ghen took another look at the woman.

"Mrs. Nedain," he gasped.

Hearing her name, Nedain turned and locked her viperous eyes on the rancher.

Ghen wasn't sure what to do, as he was almost sure she was with Adler when they were attacked. He took a step back, and Nedain smirked at the nervous gesture. Roger was no friend of Mr. Noren's though, so Ghen held his ground from there. He only wished his heart wasn't beating so loudly.

Nedain broke the silence. "Hello Ghen. I haven't seen you in a while."

Ghen's expression hardened. "Did you forget, Nedain? You and Adler saw me the night before last."

Nedain's eyes narrowed, but she smiled after a moment. "Oh, that's right," she said innocently. "By the way, is your little friend with you? I owe him for his hospitality the other night."

That confirmed it. Now that Ghen was sure it was Nedain, he could be sure the order had come straight from Noren. Nedain wouldn't have attacked without a reason. The reason this time must have been Noren.

"I don't think I ought to put you two together again," Ghen said. "I'm not sure what would happen."

Her smile stayed the same, but her umber eyes sharpened to knife edges. "I can tell you what would happen."

The threat was obvious, and, behind Nedain, Roger shifted nervously.

"Well, he isn't here," Ghen said. "Now, unless I heard wrong, you're looking for someone. That wouldn't be me or Em, would it?"

Nedain laughed. "Oh, I'd like to think so. Still, while Noren may not care about you anymore, pass a message to your friend. 'Next time, you won't be so lucky.' You got that?"

Fearing Nedain might follow him back if Nedain thought she could find Em, Ghen said, "Sorry, I drove Em to Henaden, but who knows when I'll see him again." Which was more or less the truth. "You'll have to find him on your own."

"Too bad. Well, good to see you, Ghen. Who knows, maybe we'll see each other again soon." With that, Nedain left the shop.

"Not if I can help it," Ghen muttered when she was finally gone.

Ghen stepped up to the counter, and Roger looked at him like a stranger despite having known him for ages. "What was that all about, Ghen?"

Ghen ran a hand over his face. "I think it means my troubles with Mr. Noren are worse than I thought."

"How bad did you think they were? I thought he was beating you up bad already."

Ghen nodded, very tired suddenly. "I thought so too, but I guess he wanted it in more than just words."

Roger blinked in surprise. "Are you serious? He had you beaten up? When?"

"On my way here."

Roger leaned over the counter so that he could see all of Ghen clearly. "You don't seem that much worse for wear."

"That's no thanks to them, I'll tell you. This time I came with a friend who... well, let's say he's got some military experience." Ghen guessed Em did anyway, or something like it. Ghen thumbed over his shoulder towards the door. "Anyways, she and Adler showed up at my campsite armed and in the dark. They weren't expecting my friend though, and they all got in a fight."

"Is your friend alright?"

"No worse than when I found him," Ghen said with a shrug. "But... well, in the fighting, Adler died."

"He killed one of Noren's guards?"

Ghen wondered if he should have left that out, but he was an honest soul at heart. He nodded. "You heard Nedain, sounds like she's ready to settle the debt. I'm going to have to keep as much distance as I can and tell Em to do the same."

Roger paused a moment to take it all in before letting out a long whistle. "That's quite the tale, Ghen. I wouldn't go spreading that around while you are in Henaden if I were you, lots of people know Mr. Noren better than they know you. Not to mention how many of those people work for him in one way or another. I might not have believed you if I hadn't just listened to Nedain there."

"I'll be careful, but she wasn't asking after us, was she? Didn't I hear her say she was looking for someone?"

"She was," Roger confirmed. "I don't know if it's your friend, but the person she described definitely isn't you. Human, but a younger guy."

Ghen groaned. "It really might be Em, then."

"I thought she said it wasn't," Roger reminded him.

Ghen wasn't convinced. "She wasn't extra clear on that, but even if she was, do you think I should trust her?"

Roger made a face and shook his head. "I wouldn't. To tell the truth, I'm kind of glad that someone stumped Noren like that, but he isn't the kind to forgive and forget. Neither are the thugs he hires for bodyguards. Watch your back."

Ghen nodded.

With that, Roger waved a hand between them both. "Now that's enough about this whole mess, I doubt you came all the way to Henaden to get ambushed and tell me about it. What can I help you with?"

Ghen smiled. "Yeah, let's turn that corner. Are you still buying nightroot?"

He asked, lifting his two bags.

Roger eyed them. "Why'd you pull your crop early?"

"I had other reasons to come to Henaden, and I didn't need two trips that close to each other," Ghen said.

Roger's smile weakened. "Well Ghen, I... I want to. Really, I do, but... I can't."

"What happened? I thought this was a good sale for your store."

"Oh, nightroot sells well enough, but I picked up a deal with the herbalist down the way since you were last here. If I stopped selling nightroot, he would stop selling melblooms. We were getting in each other's way and both of us were losing out. I want to help you, but I can't buy something I can't use Ghen."

He looked ashamed, but they both knew it made sense.

"No need to look so down, Roger. I know you're one of the good ones. Hey," Ghen brightened, "where's this medicine man's shop? I'll see if maybe he'll take it."

"You can try," Roger said doubtfully, "he's on the next step down, right next to a weaver. It's called *Urdlen's* something. I wouldn't get your hopes up though, he works for Mr. Noren on the side."

If that was the case, Ghen couldn't expect a coin from this herbalist. He didn't want to make Roger feel bad, so he tried to put on a brave face. "Thanks, Roger."

Roger tried to think of some lead or idea to help, but all he got out was, "Good luck, Ghen."

CHAPTER 28

NOREN'S OFFICE WAS ONE of lavish taste. Only the finest lamps, tables, and couches were kept. Deep varnished wooden inlays with designs of the finest craftsmanship covered every surface that would accommodate them, breathing an air of elegance into every aspect of the room. The cushions were richly adorned and, on the wall, hung tapestries of fine historical scenes that told the story of Ifeldia's founding as King Roleius and his cohorts swept over the land. Over the marble fireplace that burned warmly hung a pair of expensive dueling swords, which Noren had never held a day in his life. All this, and more as Noren saw fit. What else could be fit for the illustrious Noren Trading Company?

Noren only wished that his employees would respect the furnishings more. He was going through some of the reports on his desk when Nedain returned.

"Any news on our quarry, Nedain?" Noren inquired without looking up.

"No, but Noren, I ran into a friend of ours in town," the guard began, and Noren paled. He dropped what he was doing right away, and half rose from his chair. He expected to see the tall, dark shadow of an elf behind his guard. "I saw Ghen," Nedain finished.

Noren furrowed his brows and sank back. "You had me worried you meant... someone else."

Nedain's face showed she suddenly understood he'd thought she was talking about the pale elf. "Oh, no not him. Ghen was trying to sell something. It looked like nightroot. Would you like me to have someone find him and tail him?"

"No, we can't spare anyone right now," Noren answered dismissively. "We need them all searching for the sylwerd or keeping up the normal business."

He went back to his papers. What had he been doing again?

"Noren, do you mind if I ask you a question?"

He sighed. "You've already made me lose my place, so why not?"

"Why are you searching so hard for the sylwerd?"

That was an odd question. "Really? You usually aren't one to question my methods."

"*I'm* acting out of character?" She raised an eyebrow. "Noren, you're throwing everything you have at this. That isn't your usual method at all."

"Point," Noren said.

"I don't usually care what you do or who with, but that elf was..." she paused, "...different."

Noren wondered if she was frightened, that would be a first, but he couldn't blame her considering it was *him*.

Well, Noren had been planning to have this conversation with Nedain, eventually. Now might be a good time for this talk. "I suppose this is a fair place to pause my work." Pushing back his chair, he stood and walked around his desk. "Let's you and I have a quick chat. Know that this may take some explaining, and time to do it right. So, please take a seat."

Noren gestured to a sitting area with a small table he kept in the corner of his office, where silver goblets and a jug of wine sat on the table. He picked up a cup and poured himself a drink, before walking to stand against the hearth with his fireplace burning low behind him.

Nedain sat in an opposing chair and set her feet on the small table. She had mud on her shoes.

Noren cleared his throat. "Please respect my furniture, Nedain."

Nedain rolled her eyes. She removed her boots, but then put her dirty feet on the table. "Better?" Her voice was full of mock concern.

"Hardly."

Nedain only smiled in response.

Noren sighed. There was no fixing some people. "Anyway, what do you know of my acquaintance you met the other day?"

"Nothing, that's my point. All I can tell you is that he was an elf, and I think some kind of magician."

"Magician," Noren scoffed. "If he is a magician, I'm a street peddler. His power is beyond any I've ever met, and I don't just mean magic."

"I thought you didn't know much about him either," Nedain said. "When we saw him, you said—"

"I know what I said. And you're right. I know little, but I know more than you, and guess even more that I think is quite right. To that point, there is much about him that I wish to share with you. However, before I go on, though, I have two questions. First, do you plan to tell anyone about him?"

Nedain gritted her teeth. "Something tells me it wouldn't be good for my employment."

"Or for your health."

Nedain's eyes narrowed at the comment, but Noren didn't give her the chance to respond. "Don't look at me like that, it's not me who I think you should be afraid of. If that elf is half the person I believe, you running around talking about the 'elf in all black' would not make him happy."

"I get the point," she said. "I'll keep it to myself."

"A choice well made. For my second question, what do you know of the beginning of the Noren Trading Company?"

Nedain looked confused, how quaint. "Your dad started it, right? He some friend of your father's then?"

"No, I don't think my father ever crossed paths with my 'friend,' but I did inherit the company from my father. Long ago, the Noren Trading Company was little more than a small hole in the wall shop for metal trading. We were out of a small little building on the south side of Henaden's fourth step. Back then—"

"Wait," Nedain said. "Does that mean you were based out of that little shack you have there for storage?"

Noren shrugged. "What can I say, I'm sort of sentimental."

"It's falling over," Nedain said dryly.

"I guess not that sentimental. Of course, it was run down in my father's day." He waved his hand around his lavish office. "Still, from humble beginnings, and all that. I must admit my elven friend was a large part of my rise to these heights."

"Okay. So how did you meet? Did you really scam him?"

"Indeed. My father was never a good merchant. I knew he would run his business into the ground before I could stop him, so I was pulling money from many places to try to save it myself.

"My 'friend' happened to be strolling through Henaden looking for a meal. I offered to sell him fresh fruit I borrowed from a street vendor. He bought it, and I made myself scarce when the vendor saw an elf walking away with his wares while I took the money. A simple scam, but I had done it many times before."

"But the elf caught you this time."

Noren nodded. "That is the rub of scamming someone with magic, they have ways of finding you. I was cornered before I even knew he was on my trail. I remember it vividly, him standing at the head of the alley, my head whipping back and forth looking for any way out. When I saw none, I made a mad dash to knock him over and get out."

Nedain snorted.

Noren cringed at the memory. "Yes, it did not end well for me. He thrashed me as no one ever had or has since. When he was finished with me, he didn't need magic to keep me from rising. I would later have to literally crawl home. Suffice it to say, I was quelled."

"I'm surprised he let you live. He didn't give me the impression he was very forgiving."

"He isn't," Noren said darkly. "I too thought that was my last day, but instead of finishing me he merely watched me. Cruel, I thought at the time, but now I think I must have done something that caught his attention or impressed him. He spoke to me."

"Boy, do you wish to live?" the imposing elf asked those many seasons ago.

"Yes... my lord," the young Dorig Noren groaned, now that he'd been beaten into submission.

There was a pause before the elf asked, "What else do you wish?"

Noren didn't understand, and his only answer was to cough from a broken rib.

"Hmm..." the elf murmured. "Your thread can go far, but how far I wonder?"

Slowly, the young Noren at least rolled to his knees but feared to rise any higher if he even could.

"Boy, I will make you an offer." The elf had no humor in his voice. "Acceptance is the only way you will survive this meeting."

"Of course, my lord."

There was a clinking sound as a bulging pouch landed near Noren.

"Take this and take your life. They are yours but for a little while. In return, you will owe me three things. You will repay this gift with its value in coin, a favor you cannot refuse, and..." the elf paused and for the first time, there was humor in the sick complexion of the elf's face "... and in a shepherd's toil. Do you accept this?"

"Yes," the small Dorig Noren said, too dizzy to understand half of what was happening.

A gloved hand was laid atop his bent head and Noren felt a strange warmth outside himself, and then a resonance within. His pain drew back and, for a moment, the younger Noren felt utmost ecstasy, until that joy was quickly bound in cold steel beyond imagination. He felt heavy, as if a lodestone was chained to his heart. The light in his chest faded, and he returned to his brokenness. The stone, however, remained. Ever weighing him down.

The accord made, the darkly clad pale elf left with a final word of caution. "When I return, it is best you be ready. Fate has saved you today, but do not count on it to do so again."

Noren drained his goblet and set it on the mantle as he finished recounting his tale. "That is how we met."

"He gave you money?"

"More than 300 halak gold."

Nedain gasped. That was a small fortune and more than she made in eight seasons as the chief guard of a highly profitable merchant.

Noren grinned. "If you think you're shocked, imagine how I felt when I finally got home and counted out what he gave me."

Nedain thought for a moment. "So, is that why you got all jumpy when we saw him? You thought he wanted you to pay him back."

Noren shook his head. "I already paid him back the halaks in full."

"What? How? I thought..." Nedain was completely lost. "I'm only a guard, but I've been here a long time. I would have heard of you making a payment that large."

Noren grinned. "Would you, now? Oh, actually I don't doubt it, you've always been one to keep your ear to the ground. The reason you never heard is because nearly two-thirds of the coins I gave him back were the same ones he gave me."

"You didn't spend them?" She sounded incredulous.

"Oh, I was tempted to many times, but no. See, the moment I saw the fortune I also saw the trap."

"Trap?"

"It's obvious," Noren said. "He never intended to have me pay him back."

"So, he just gives up a small fortune, for what? Laughs?"

Noren shook his head. "He intended to have me in his debt. He gave a tempting amount he expected me to squander. I was fortunate enough to catch onto that quickly. I also realized that if it was a trap, then my investor had surely put in place some insurance to find me should I try to escape. That meant I needed to instead be wise. So, I used the money, yes, but never much. I drew from it slowly, at most need, or only when I knew I could add it back.

"That much was enough for me to wrestle the Noren Trading Company from my father and to put it back on track from his awful business sense. From there, the business grew on its own merits and my skill. Instead of taking money out, I was able to slowly put it back in."

"Then he came back for it all," Nedain said, but then paused. "Wait, if you paid him back what does this have to do with Ghen then? After you got his message, you said you might not need Ghen's land, so obviously that ties into things. I get that this sylwerd is the favor he said you couldn't refuse, but what's the land got to do with anything?"

"You're right," Noren said, grinding his teeth at the mention of Ghen's name. "He did come back. Three falls ago I found his dark figure in this very office."

"Here?" Nedain said, looking around as if expecting to see the pale-faced elf standing behind her.

"Yes, here. If it was anyone else breaking in without being noticed, I would have been disappointed in you, Nedain. Obviously, he is a special case. He'd indeed come to collect, and I was happy to surprise him by being able to hand him his very coin purse back full to bursting. Save that I was missing something."

Nedain leaned back, obviously trying to figure out what. It took a moment, but Noren saw the flicker of insight on her face when she caught it. Yet clearly she was still unsure.

"Noren," she asked, "what is a shepherd's toil?"

"An excellent question, one that I did not know the answer to myself for too long a time. I remembered the term but had never found out what it meant, at least not yet. I guessed it meant a bonus, so I had added an extra third to the coin pouch and was oddly close to what it actually meant."

"Which is?"

"It means whatever the debt was, and an extra fourth *in land*," he finished, emphasizing the condition.

"Oh."

"Oh, is right," Noren agreed. "I hoped he would accept the extra money but, since he wants me in debt, he accepted the extra halaks but gave me no credit on the land."

Nedain snorted. "And you call him a friend?"

"He called it interest." Noren groaned. "It had been over twelve falls, so I guess it wasn't completely unfair. Even if it was, I wasn't in a position to argue, and I think that interest saved me."

"How?"

"Well, I actually could have paid the debt there and then, it just would have destroyed the trading company. He saw that too, and what would that mean?" Noren paused briefly for effect. "It would mean we both lose. I go out of business, and he gets land he doesn't actually want.

"Luckily, by creating the situation, I proved I was a profitable investment. Instead of forcing me to ruin myself, he amended the offer. Remember, he wants me in debt, and that can only be so that he can use me. Better to wait and get a useful tool than get useless trash on time."

"Okay, and it was this new offer that involves Ghen?"

"Not him specifically," Noren said, with a wave of his goblet. "He gave me an extension on paying the toil, but I had to get him more land and get him farmland specifically. Farmland is harder to buy because the farmers who live there have personal ties to it, so if the land is worth thirty copper halaks, they want sixty to eighty. At the time, I didn't know that. I deal in metals, remember? But I am painfully aware of that now."

Nedain nodded. "He must have known, and that's how he wants to trap you."

"Exactly, and he may still get me. All my buying and I'm still short, too much of the land is wrapped up in bigger, harder-to-buy farms or land owned by the royal families."

Nedain tilted her head thoughtfully. "I didn't know the royals own land here."

"They do, and more than you might think. The proceeds don't go to the government but instead to their pockets, meaning they hate to sell. I can buy other land that isn't owned by anyone really, but for it to count, I have to make it farmland. That takes time and money. It's too late to even try that now, I waited too long."

"Sounds like you're in trouble," Nedain said without much concern.

"Yes." Noren glared at Nedain, but his smile returned quickly enough. "Or rather, I would be. This favor has given me an opportunity. See, every deal he's made we've bound with magic."

"I remember your detail of how you felt, all that talk of 'warmth' and 'stones.' I guessed that's what that was. That makes me wonder though, can you do magic?"

Instead of answering directly, Noren walked over to a candle hung on the wall and held out his hand. He focused on the wick and pushed. He kept pushing with all his might until sweat dotted his brow. Slowly, smoke drifted up, and the wick caught alight. He turned around.

Nedain looked unimpressed. "That was a lot of effort for a candle."

"And you wonder why I didn't bring it up before now. That," he said, pointing at the candle, "was a chore for me. I have almost no talent. I've done some reading, it's rare to have the skill at all but among those who do, my situation isn't uncommon. I have no training at all, but in the end, that doesn't matter. All that matters is that I have it."

Nedain leaned forward with interest, finally pulling her filthy stockings off Noren's table.

"As for how it matters, all you need is a pinch of magic to be able to do two things," the merchant explained. "The first is to feel magic used around you, I'm not good at this and since magic is so rare, I get almost no practice. The other factor is, you gain the chance to be part of a very special kind of contract. One bound in magic. I can't instigate the pact because I have no idea how to do so, but my 'friend' does."

"Now you're in the pact," Nedain guessed. "Let me guess. Break it, and magic breaks you?"

Noren cringed. "That wasn't how I was going to say it, but that is more or less the case. I could be cannibalized by my own little power if I tried to escape the deal. Even if I could survive my small power turning on me, it would be..." he hesitated, "... unpleasant."

"So where is the advantage?"

Noren was relieved at the change of subject. "The conditions, the deal needs strict rules. Any ambiguity makes the spell weaker. Did you hear what he and I spoke of near the end?

Nedain contemplated. "Yeah," she said, unsure. "You and he whispered, and you both agreed to terms. Those were your rules?"

"Basically, though all we really said was that I would contact him straight away, and I made an offer. He mentioned that his favor could get me a great reward, but I asked if my reward could be that he would consider a new deal that would partially release me from our former contract, but that he would still find most profitable. He agreed. In that way, this favor has finally given me leverage over my friend."

Nedain looked thoughtful but then her features betrayed worry. "Wait. Are you planning to find this sylwerd and blackmail him with it? If you do, I recommend you rethink your plan. He will kill you or worse."

"Oh, I wholeheartedly agree," Noren said, not perturbed in the least. "He can easily kill me to get out of rewarding me. That is why I want to present the sylwerd to him as soon as I can. All he agreed to do was to hear out my offer."

"Which is?"

"First, to either release me from my debt or let me pay out the rest of what I owe in regular halak coins. Second, to be given a reasonable position in his service."

Nedain's mouth gaped. "A what?" she said blankly, sure she'd misheard her employer.

"I want to work for him," Noren said slyly. "For a time at least, but I do not wish to be a slave as I think he hoped. More of a..." he took a moment to consider "... a lesser partner. He won't release me no matter what, but if I still work in his service there's no need for us to be ugly about it.

"Accepting my deal, he doesn't have to risk me getting away free, which is possible. I, on the other hand, don't need to worry about defaulting on my debt. I'm not one for forced servitude, but working under him willingly might not be so bad. If he can throw bags of money at a random boy on the street, then imagine what I can accomplish as a partner, even a lesser one. He gets what he wants, and I get what I want."

"Okay," Nedain said, having gathered herself. "I think I get what you want and why, but do you even know who this is you're dealing with?"

Noren breathed slowly. He wanted Nedain on his side, but this was going to be the trickiest part. "I believe I do. I've met him a few times now and between his wealth, magical power, and trend towards secrecy, I believe that he might be a, shall we say, noble of our country's neighbor."

It took Nedain a moment, but her gaze became dark. "A Dread?"

He nodded.

"That's a big risk, Noren," Nedain said, gritting her teeth.

It didn't take much to understand her hesitation. Dread was the title of the highest and most dangerous class of people in Yongarad, the same nation Ifeldia was currently at war with. Dealing with this dread was dangerous because not only was the elf a threat, but Noren and anyone who worked alongside him risked charges of treason in Ifeldia.

Noren could almost feel her looking for a way out. That was bad. Luckily, Noren knew Nedain very well. "I'm not afraid. Are you?"

She scoffed, all thoughts of backing out suddenly dashed by her pride. "Of what? You're supposed to be on his side right, I might worry if he was an enemy."

"Exactly my thought. If one of these dread can get into Ifeldia so easily, then I'd rather be on their side than against them."

"One last question," Nedain said.

Noren bent down and refilled his cup. "Ask away."

"Why tell me? You could have gotten away with saying a lot less than all this."

"An excellent question, Nedain. Probably the best one you've asked since walking into this room." Noren felt another smile grace his face, and he took a long sip of his drink. "Realize Nedain, this is not just an opportunity for me, but for you, too. We've already discussed how my relationship with my 'friend' can't be public, especially if he's what I think he is. That means I'll need more work done in the less public forum."

Nedain suddenly understood. "And you'll need someone to manage that part of your business." A greedy smile tugging at the sides of her lips, she began to relax again, overcoming some of the shock of their potential partner.

"Precisely, I know you well enough to know that you dislike having a superior. In this way, you will be less under my control and more your own master. You will simply work as a middleman, or more accurately, woman, between me and our 'friend'," he said, including her in the relationship. "I already manage much of Henaden's dark and light, and under him, I may do more of both. In this, you will be a ruler of shadows."

Nedain said nothing, but Noren knew his sales pitch had struck home. She would not refuse anymore.

"What do you say? Will you become the Dark Arm of Henaden?" Noren asked, reaching out a hand.

She clasped it. "Sounds like fun."

Releasing his hand, Nedain kicked back and put her feet back on the table. Her eyes stared up, imagining things that could be.

"Pleasure doing business with you," Noren said mollified, peering disappointedly at her feet back on his furniture. "Now if you mean to make this dream a reality, I think it's time you go back to searching for the sylwerd. All this will go to waste if we fail to locate it. Also, when you go, wipe off the mud you left on my table. You are not out of my employ *yet*."

CHAPTER 29

"Nedain," Em murmured to himself. "I do not remember her at all. If you were not telling me otherwise, I would think the name is new to me."

"Well, she remembers your name," Ghen replied. "I recommend you steer clear."

"I shall try, but even if I see this woman, would I recognize her?"

"Good point," Ghen said. "Just steer clear of angry women in armor for a while."

"There's a joke in there somewhere," Ceahan commented offhandedly. With a smirk, he took another bite of their midday meal. It wasn't much, but it would tide them over until dinner. "Something about picking fights with angry women in armor never being a good idea."

Ghen and Em sat at the same small table where they'd shared breakfast while Ceahan stood against the far wall, from there he had a better view out of the back window. Master D'gui was elsewhere in her home, reading from some of Em's translated works.

Ghen grinned. "Yeah well, just you mind, that Nedain's a cut above the rest."

"Oh, I know. Her reputation is no secret. How did you manage to get on her bad side?" Em shrugged and opened his mouth, but Ceahan spoke first. "Never mind, you forgot."

"Yes," Em said.

"What a shock," the apprentice said sardonically.

"It has to do with who she works for, a Mr. Noren," Ghen explained. "You know how I said he and I don't get along, because of that, Em and Nedain got into it a night ago?"

"Yeah, you said that merchant killed your chances of selling the root today. What did you do to get on his bad side, rancher?"

"I told him no. He isn't used to hearing that word, and I don't think he likes it."

"You aren't kidding. I've heard rumors that he could make it hard to sell if you didn't go through him first, but what you're describing is a step up," Ceahan said.

"Yeah, I'm not sure what to do. I spent most of the morning going to the few folks who aren't under Noren I know, and they couldn't buy a sprout off me."

"Why don't you ask Em to sell it?" Ceahan suggested. "Noren's people won't have a grudge against him."

Ghen brightened at the idea, but an instant later his expression fell. "It might have, but if Nedain is back in Henaden, then you can bet Mr. Noren is too. He met Em and probably told everyone to treat him the same as me. What about you? Would you be willing to lend me a hand?"

"Um, I don't go out much," Ceahan said nervously.

"I'll give you a little for your help if you can get me a fair price."

"No!" Ceahan said firmly, and far louder than he'd intended.

Ghen and Em gawked at him, stunned.

Ceahan turned crimson with embarrassment. "I'm sorry, I just... I prefer to stay here. I don't like crowds."

Em and Ghen looked at each other across the table and then back at Ceahan.

"Fair enough, I don't like them much either," Ghen said, dropping the subject.

Em, on the other hand, wished to know more. Ceahan was very forceful for simple nervousness around crowds. There was more at work, but he could not guess what it might be.

"Are there not shops on the edges of the city where you might find smaller crowds?" he asked, probing.

Ceahan hesitated in answering.

"It has to do with his training," Master D'gui said, trotting into the room. "Ceahan has a lot of power but is still working on its management.

It's embarrassing, but it could be dangerous if something went wrong. Smaller shops make little difference, I hope you understand."

Ghen and Em nodded. Ceahan's power could certainly be dangerous, so Em let the subject drop. Yet, he did not fail to notice that Ceahan looked more relieved than embarrassed when Master D'gui explained the situation.

"My apologies, Master D'gui, I was not aware." Em rose from his seat to bow slightly to Master D'gui and then to her apprentice. "I will go in his stead. Even if this Noren-*sa* is back in Henaden, I disagree that he could spread my description so quickly. From Ghen-*sa* I can learn what I need to sell the nightroot."

"Actually, since we disturbed the thing in your mind, I'm not sure it is safe for you to be far from me or Ceahan either," Master D'gui added.

Ghen sighed. "She's right Em, I'm glad you're willing to help, but you're in no shape to do this. I'll find a way, I always do."

"I never said you couldn't get help." Master D'gui said. "I was already planning to go into town to purchase some ingredients. I'd like to try that recipe Em translated, but we're missing some things. If you move the nightroot to my horse instead of your mule, I can leave in a few minutes. I can even collect a fair price for it all. I already know its worth, and where it can be sold.

"I'm somewhat of an oddity to begin with, so no one will question how I acquired nightroot, especially the few who know I wield magic. We mystics are too strange for them to know what we can and can't do. That and most people are superstitious and afraid to anger a mage. They fear I'll turn them into a mole or something," she said, amused.

Ghen nearly leapt to his feet. "Would you miss? I mean, sell the nightroot, not the mole thing. It'd be a big help and I'd be very appreciative. How much will I owe you for this?"

Master D'gui shook her head. "You brought me one of the most interesting subjects of study I've seen in ages, who can also translate languages that have puzzled me for far too long. That is worth quite a lot for me, but also, I may want your help if you are willing to give it."

Em still was not sure how he felt about being a 'subject of study', but he was pleased that it benefited Ghen.

"With what? I can't imagine what I can do for you," Ghen said, scratching the top of his head.

"You live nearby, don't you?"

"A few days out, but not too far."

"Well," Master D'gui said with a cautious look at her apprentice, "in the next few weeks to months, Ceahan and I expect we will go on a research expedition. Of course, we will have Em more settled before we leave, but our plans are already made. After we leave, someone should come by here occasionally to ensure no one tears apart my home or moves in while we're away. I want a nice home to come back to after all.

"I understand that you don't come to Henaden very often, but if you would check on my home whenever you do, I would very much appreciate it. Just step inside to make sure all is in order."

Ghen grinned. "I'd probably have done that for nothing, miss, but if that's what you want for selling my root for me, I'll see if I can't make an extra trip now and again so that I can be sure all is well."

"Excellent." Master D'gui beamed. "Whenever you come by, feel free to stay here those nights. It will be good for the house to be lived in now and again. If you can keep them from getting into my research, you can bring your family as well."

Ghen's face twisted slightly, unsure how anyone could even walk through Master D'gui's house and not get into her research, but a short family trip to Henaden would do the girls and maybe Jirus good if he could swing it.

"Sure thing. By the way, do you have any books kids can learn from?"

"Um..." Master D'gui didn't quite understand.

"Well, I'd be willing to buy them off you if you do," Ghen explained. "See, my girls are getting to the age I'd like to start teaching them more. May's got my oldest trying to read, but it's not like we have almost anything to read from. There's nowhere around for her to learn good stuff like you have, so I was thinking—"

"Absolutely!" Master D'gui interrupted excitedly. "Didn't you hear me say I hated this societal gap in knowledge? Come with me." She grabbed his arm. "We'll find some great books to start on and a few for higher learning. When Ceahan and I leave, I'll make a nice big stack of them for you."

Her voice trailed off as she led Ghen out of the room and back into the deep forest of cluttered knowledge.

Ceahan shook his head. "That rancher has no idea what he just got himself into. There is no way that Master doesn't go overboard with this."

Em smiled and shrugged, he agreed completely. While the master and Ghen weren't around, Em turned his thoughts towards the apprentice. "Ceahan-*so*, how long have you been training under Master D'gui?"

"More than a few falls now, I'm not even sure exactly how many, probably five or six by now," Ceahan said, still looking into the living room.

"How did you meet her?"

Now Ceahan looked back at Em and the marauder uniform he was wearing. "Why?"

"I am just curious," Em said. "Did she discover you by your great power?"

Ceahan's eyes darted nervously toward his master's direction before returning to Em. "Not exactly. I was... on my own, kind of. When Master D'gui found me, it was because we just kind of ran into each other, nothing special. Then she noticed my talent and said she would make me her apprentice. Like I said, I was kind of on my own, so..." Ceahan trailed off.

Em nodded. "I see. If you were on your own, where did you meet? Were you already living in Henaden?"

Instead of answering directly, Ceahan said, "Listen, I need to get back to trying to learn more about the faker. You get how important it is, and the quicker we learn things, the better. So, we can pick this up later. Alright?" Without waiting for Em to reply, Ceahan got up and left the room in a hurry.

When Ceahan was gone, Em was left with only Instinct, Nature, and his own confusion for company.

"Did I say something wrong?"

CHAPTER 30

"THIS IS ALL WRONG," Sicyen complained.

With his left foot over the edge of the step's wall, Sicyen sat where his leg hung high up over the yards and homes of the step below. His right foot was otherwise occupied, being massaged by his hands to work the aches out of it. He looked over the city and the darkening sky as a few clouds gathered for an overcast afternoon.

"I walk half the steps in Henaden, and for what?" He groaned. "Some brat, who may not even be here."

Sicyen didn't work for the Noren Trading Company, but the company occasionally passed down odd jobs open to anyone. The pay was attractive and for many, it meant a nice bonus, or sometimes a week without missing meals. For Sicyen, it meant he could go to see the doctor again.

Not that he was ill, he just needed more of his 'medicine.'

Thinking about it, Sicyen became aware of a tingling itch. He scratched at the many wounds in the crook of his arm. He wanted more and would get it. For even a hint of this brat the merchant company was after, they were willing to pay enough that Sicyen could afford his medicine for a while. If he made the money stretch, he could be in for a month of bliss.

Sicyen couldn't admit to himself his habit of gorging on his medicine. Yet somewhere in his mind, he knew the stockpile he could afford with the reward would only last him two weeks at best.

The addict rubbed his bloodshot eyes. "Wrong or not, I need to do it anyway. Alright, time to get back to work."

Slipping his sandal back on, he walked down the step, his head turning left and right. Since this hunt was an open contract like this, everyone was already searching the lower roads and understeps for this kid.

The lower steps were for the poor or those who wanted to slum it for whatever reason, and the understeps weren't much better. They were small hidden places in the city built under the buttresses that held up the steps' roads. Being in the understeps at all was illegal due to the danger, but that didn't stop businesses from setting up there. Of course, those shops were never any more legal than being in the understeps itself.

Sicyen, being such a regular in both places, was pretty sure he'd never seen his quarry there before, so he took a slightly different approach.

He'd made his way up Henaden's hill and was now working his way back down. As he walked on down the step, he kept peering over the walkway's edge, which was flush with the wall, to spy into the houses below. If anyone caught him, they'd be angry about him spying and run him off, but it wasn't like there was a law against it.

He caught sight of a boy carrying a load of crates onto the flat roof of his home below.

Sicyen stopped walking and peered down intently. "He looks about the right age."

For a young fella, he was strong. His hair was longer than how the company had described the boy, but that happened over time. The teenager below turned his head and Sicyen spat in disgust and disappointment.

"No mark. You aren't him," he muttered to himself more than the boy who was too far below to hear. "Why'd you have to go and get my hopes up?"

Despite his own words, he double-checked. His cravings made it hard to think, but he couldn't afford to be wrong.

Sicyen pulled out the scrap of leather that he'd scribbled on with some coal dust. Sicyen couldn't write exactly, but he could scribble little pictures. For him, that was just as good.

A crudely drawn figure had a line slightly to the side of its head. A reminder to Sicyen that this kid should be half a head shorter than he was. Next was another drawing of a stick man with an arrow pointing at his head. Sicyen's sign that the target was human, like Sicyen himself. Another little crude drawing made it clear he was looking for a boy.

"Looks like me, but you're marked, little sylwerd," Sicyen said with a grin spoiled by rotting teeth.

The last picture was a rough copy of what the man who'd let on about the job had shown him. Four wavy lines came in from the top and met at the bottom, where they curled in on themselves like a swirling flame caught in the wind.

Sighing, Sicyen started forward again, looking at his little strip of leather. When he reached the end of the step, he took a side street near the city wall that would let him climb to the step below.

"You can't be local, you'd have been found already if they'd known a brat who was branded like you," he said to the little drawing.

On the next step, he made his way back towards the center of the city.

"Maybe you don't know anyone here either," he said to himself. "I'd have thought you'd avoid the lowers since you weren't found quick, but maybe I was wrong. I guess you could be a little rich brat, but then I haven't got a chance to find you."

Sicyen laughed to himself. "Fat chance of that. Why would the Noren people ask us in the understeps to search for this kid if he's going to be a rich one?"

He stopped and put his little pictures back in his pocket. looking over Henaden.

"Where are you?"

The crunch of splintering wood and the sharp cry of an animal made Sicyen spin around from the city's sights.

"Well, there's a fun show," he said in sick amusement.

Outside of an oddly built house was a man of middle age with a wide brim hat. The fun was that the fool seemed to be having a bit of trouble. He gripped a halter in each hand, one was for a mild-looking horse, but the other was attached to a mule with the temperament of a thunderstorm. The clatter of wood was a bucket the mule must have sent flying with a strong kick. Sicyen saw it still rolling down the street, doing what it could to escape its abuser.

The mule bucked and kicked, the man fighting hard to calm it down while not losing hold of the horse that was starting to get nervous at the mule's thrashing. If something didn't change soon, the horse might become as bad as the mule.

Sicyen was hoping that was exactly what would happen. He laughed at the unfortunate fool and his animals until he was out of breath. He nearly doubled over with mirth when the mule rushed and knocked the man to the ground. The horseman lost hold of both sets of reins and the mule kicked even more once it was free. The horse was nervous and tramping, it was going to bolt any second.

Or would've, if the commotion hadn't drawn three people out of the odd house to help. Two young men were the first out, followed by an older woman. The moment the woman took in the commotion, she raised a hand.

"Enough!" she commanded forcefully. The word chimed like a bell, and even though she didn't shout, her voice carried far.

The instant he heard the words, Sicyen was overcome by an unseen wave. He felt pressed down as if a weight had been placed on his heart and his laughter crumpled under the weight dropped on his emotions. Sicyen saw the same slowing in the rage of the mule, panic of the horse, and spluttering of the man.

"A witch," he gasped.

Sicyen didn't want to be near an angry sorceress and was ready to get on with his day. The only problem was that they were in his way. If he was going to search this street, he would have to walk right past them.

Taking a brave breath, Sicyen ducked his head and shuffled quickly forward, doing his best to simply avoid their gaze. He got by the house without a problem and was ready to hurry on and get as far away from the witch as he could until...

"Hold up a second," someone called.

Sicyen froze and slowly looked back. It was the man who'd lost control of the mule. He was dusting himself off and kept a hold on the mule's reins again.

The man pointed past Sicyen. "Would you mind grabbing that for me?"

It was only then that Sicyen realized that the bucket the mule kicked at the start of the commotion was basically at his feet. He was tempted to kick it away, but they were looking at him now. Not just the witch, but all of them. Sicyen's eyes went over each of them.

Of the three that had run out, Sicyen was most scared of the woman. Luckily, she looked to be more amused than anything else. The other two were older boys or young men. One was short and had strange features. Next to him was a taller one with a slightly younger face who had caught the horse's reins.

The speaker was a grown man, clearly some farmer by his clothes, and he led the mule closer to either get the bucket or take it from Sicyen.

Slowly, Sicyen leaned down, picked up the bucket, and held it out to the farmer.

"Thank you. Ol' Bo here has a temper that's none too friendly."

"No trouble," said Sicyen, his eyes darting from the farmer to the mystic and back. Anxious to leave, he turned and quickly walked away again.

To his relief, no one said anything, and he got away cleanly. He was glad to be away from that house.

"I didn't even know there was a witch in the city," Sicyen grumbled, "but I'll never set foot on this step again if I can help it. Now I can go back to finding that..." The addict stiffened as if turned to stone by the witch's magic.

He whipped around and focused on the little group. He was further away from them now after trying to get away so fast, but he was close enough. They were still outside the house, just standing around talking about something.

His prey was supposed to be shorter than he was, but the odd looking one was too short. The other one, though, could be about right. Sicyen racked his brain, had he seen the brand on the taller boy? He'd been too distracted by the witch to check.

Sicyen scratched his arms nervously. He decided he had to go back, but couldn't bring himself to take a step in the house's direction.

It was the witch. Sicyen wanted, needed, the reward, but he hadn't signed up to deal with one of their kind. Sicyen sat, waiting, trying to decide what to do.

Then the woman in question leaped onto the horse.

"She's leaving!" Sicyen said, his heart lifting. How lucky was that? Then he squinted. "She made that in one leap, that's a big jump for someone that old. Either that was more magic," Sicyen shivered, "or she has blood that isn't human."

She'd looked human, but...

He gasped. "The cursed breed."

He didn't mind different tribes for the most part, but crossing them was just unnatural. Having magic only made it more so.

The farmer led the mule around the back and the shorter one followed him. With them gone, the mystic talked with the boy who held Sicyen's interest. When she was finished, she spurred the horse in Sicyen's direction.

The moment he saw she was coming his way, Sicyen whipped about looking for a place to hide. The rumors said that witches could read minds. He didn't want a mystic, a cross, or, worst of all, something that was both, rummaging around in his head. Running to the nearest two houses, Sicyen squeezed into a tight gap between them and waited.

Minutes passed with Sicyen sitting with only his own reeking breath to keep him company in the thin alley. He waited anxiously for the rider to pass by. Finally, the clop of hooves drew near and Sicyen clenched his eyes tight, trying to block her out of his head. Sicyen waited for the inevitable digging to start as she pushed into his thoughts, but then the clopping began to fade away as the rider passed him by.

He was surprised he hadn't felt anything. The stories said witches could burrow into your head, and that meant he should have felt something, shouldn't it? Maybe she just hadn't noticed him.

The addict let out a long sigh of relief. That gave him another nose full of halitosis, and he quickly decided to work his way out onto the street again. It was harder to get back out than it was to get in but, eventually, Sicyen pulled himself free of the alley. Taking in a gasp of fresh air, he looked for any sign of the witch, but the woman and her horse were nowhere in sight.

When he looked back towards her home, the boy he wanted another look at wasn't around either. He wasn't sure if that was good news or bad, but it was probably bad. "I'm sure it's always bad news with a witch around," he muttered.

If he was going to peer into the house, now was the only time he could be sure that the mystic was away. Quickly, he crept down the now empty street toward her home. When he got near, Sicyen noted there were a few windows with their shutters drawn, and that one near the door had slits of light that gleamed through in the cloudy afternoon.

Getting closer, Sicyen picked out voices trickling through the window. "... a big help." a man said. It sounded like the same man who'd asked him to get the bucket. Apparently, there was a back door the farmer had come in through. That meant the short fella was probably in there as well.

Sicyen stood on his toes and worked his head back and forth until he could peer through the small gaps of the shutters. There were many things in the way of his view, but he could catch flickers of movement.

"Yeah, and while I'm glad you can get what you need Ghen, I think we need to turn our thoughts back to the faker," a younger man said. "Night will be here before we know it."

"I agree," said someone else with a strangely accented voice. Sicyen guessed it must belong to the boy with the odd face.

That would make the one talking about some 'faker' the one he was looking for.

"Do we really have to prod that thing again?" the farmer asked.

"I don't see another choice that isn't just avoiding the problem."

Homing in on the voice, Sicyen squirmed to get a view of where he'd heard it from.

"Maybe not," said the foreigner. "Master D'gui suggested to me earlier that she had a new idea. She tried to explain it, but I became lost. Since I do not remember all that occurred last night, I could not grasp it very well."

"If it's less dangerous than the faker, I'm for it," said the farmer.

A little motion helped Sicyen finally get a glimpse of the boy he was looking for. The teenager was shaking his head. "I'm all for a new angle, but should we really let the faker run loose?"

He was the right build and was about the height of the description. The symbol of fire was supposed to be a brand on his head or somewhere near there. This boy had a broad headband above his eyebrows that covered most of his forehead.

He really could be the one.

Sicyen thought he saw something around the headband, but then the boy shifted, and the addict lost his view. He squirmed back and forth, trying to get a view again.

"You are right Ceahan-*so*, I would prefer if..."

"Prefer what, Em?" the farmer asked.

"Eh?" the boy called Em said, returning to the moment. "Ah yes, I only mean to say I wish this over with. Excuse me, I will return soon." Footsteps clumped on wooden boards as he obviously left.

"That was strange," said Sicyen's prey.

There was a rustle as the older man possibly shrugged. "I've only known him for a few days, he's still a bit of a mystery to me too. He's got a lot on his mind though, so don't give him grief about it."

"I get that," the boy said. "I'll be back in a second, too. I need to relieve myself of something other than troublesome thoughts."

There was an amused snort from the farmer. "You do that. Oh hey, while you do, think if there's anything I can do to help. I'm not a fast reader, but I know you and Master D'gui have been doing research all day. If there's something I can go through to help, I'd like to."

"Sure, I'll find something," said the younger man as he retreated.

Sicyen bit his lip. He considered trying to find another window but decided against it. He didn't want to push his luck where magic was involved.

This might be enough, though. He scratched his arm again, and then his neck. He needed more medicine soon. This boy might be enough for Sicyen to get paid if he reported him now, before anyone else. Possibly, paid enough for a small trip to the doctor.

Sicyen nodded to himself. Desire breeding confidence, the idea of getting medicine made him surer that he could get paid for his information. He hadn't seen the scar of the brand, but it was a lead. He backed away from the window. "They pay for leads, pay good." He licked his lips excitedly.

A gust of icy wind blew into Sicyen's face as the clouds darkened above. When he began to walk away a chill up his spine made him spin around.

He looked around but only saw an empty street and received another blast of cold wind.

"Time to go," Sicyen said worriedly.

This was a sorcerer's house, and he'd stayed long enough. Not only that, but he might have found the one the Noren Trading Company was calling the 'sylwerd,' whatever that was. He bounced on his heels, twitching with excitement and a bit of something else. This meant he could collect the big reward, right? Oh, how he craved the clarity of his sweet medicine.

Already basking in his bounty, he set off at a brisk pace to give his report. He was unable to wait, and thus completely unaware of the second shadow that paced his steps.

CHAPTER 31

EM'S EYES SHOT TO the window. He could have sworn he'd seen something move. Watching for another moment, there was another flicker of movement.

Listeners, Nature's voice growled dangerously.

"Prefer what, Em?" Ghen asked.

"Eh?" Em said, as he realized he'd stalled in the middle of his sentence. "Ah yes, I only mean to say I wish this over with. Excuse me, I will return soon."

Ceahan and Ghen traded confused glances but didn't stop him as Em walked with intentionally loud steps towards the rear door. Once outside, he ran quietly.

Bo snorted at him as Em ran past her at the rear of the yard, but he ignored her, going for the gate on the northern side of the yard. He reached the back gate in seconds. It wasn't locked and stepping out, he jogged down the alley, only slowing as he reached the edge of the house. Peering carefully around the corner, Em saw him.

It appeared Nature was right, there was a stalker. The same man he'd seen when he had gone out to help Ghen with Lena and Bo. His clothes were ratty and unclean, and his skin was stained in various places. Along his neck and arms, light patches of flesh made pale blotches.

"One of the kanmana," Em whispered under his breath. He had a feeling that kanmana wasn't the Ifeldian word for someone like this, but if there was a word for them in that language, he didn't know it.

It meant an addict to a small poultice that left calloused and scarred skin where it was placed. Even though the mixture burned the skin, its users never cared because it had certain other effects they salivated for.

Why would this man have come back to spy on them? Before, he'd only had eyes for escape, clearly fearing Master D'gui.

Em waited, watching.

The addict backed away slightly and turned towards the main road. Em was about to follow when the man froze, and Em ducked back into cover. The addict looked around but didn't notice Em. When he was comfortable, the stranger walked away quickly toward the end of the step.

Curious, Em slipped after him. He kept a reasonable distance between him and the stalker. Reaching the end of the house, Em slipped into the alley between Master D'gui's house and the next. There he watched again.

The man paused again, shaking and looking around. He muttered something and then began to walk again, his pace speeding up into a jog. Despite the man being taller, with a longer stride, Em kept up easily. He paced through the growing shadows of the homes as the sun darkened under cloud cover.

Forgotten training from Nature guided Em's feet to silent padding that left him unnoticed. His eyes flicked up and down to track his quarry and to watch where he stepped so that he wouldn't stumble. It was good that he did. A doorstep snagged the edge of his foot, but Em caught himself before he fell. His boot scraped and it was too loud for Em's liking, so he paused. The addict, however, was too much in his own world to pay attention. Seeing his quarry was oblivious, Em took up the chase again.

Reaching the end of the step, Em waited. Someone creeping out of the shadows might draw eyes in the crowd they were approaching. The addict, on the other hand, only slowed enough not to careen into pedestrians.

As the stalker settled into the flow of the crowd, Em stepped out confidently and walked swiftly into the current of people going uphill. Ghen had mentioned that the main road of Henaden was a busy street called the Buyer's Road and Em correctly guessed that was what they were traveling on now.

Despite having fallen slightly behind his prey, Em was able to follow the man easily. The addict was far from clean, and so the crowd parted slightly as they came into contact with his aromatic aura.

With a quick step, Em kept close enough not to lose sight of the man as they made their way further and further uphill. Em noticed as they climbed that the buildings got older and some more ornate.

"Where are you going?" Em muttered quietly. "You walk with too much purpose to be wandering, but this is clearly not your home."

They crested the hill and Em found himself in a square with a fountain in the middle. Strangely, it seemed familiar.

I came here with Ghen, Em thought, unsure if he was right or not. Perhaps he would ask later, but there was no time to ponder now.

The addict ignored the flow of traffic, cutting almost straight across. He walked briskly along the edge of the fountain and then once more pushed through the crowd.

Em gritted his teeth, knowing he couldn't make such an obvious maneuver without risking being seen. Instead, he fell in with the other few people walking around the fountain until he came to the far side of the fountain where the man had exited.

Stepping onto the road the man had gone down, Em was just in time to see the addict disappear around a far corner. Em had to run, drawing many eyes, to make sure he didn't lose his quarry.

When Em rounded the corner, he immediately spun back toward the way he came. The addict was right there. Only two doors down from the turn, he was banging aggressively on a gate. His head whipped this way and that anxiously.

Em kept his back to the addict and pulled up the hood on his coat, pretending to watch the street they'd just come from while he instead peered from the corner of his eye at this strange spy.

The rapping on the gate was answered by the drawing of a bolt and a stern man quickly stepping out the door.

"This is a private office. Off with you!" the man shouted loud enough for all to hear.

"Wait... wait," the addict begged. After that, his voice dropped too low to hear.

He said only a few more words before he finished, and the stern man looked him over carefully before leading him in and shutting the gate behind them. Em didn't hear the bolt this time but had no doubt the gate would be relocked. A moment later there was a *thunk* as a wooden door behind the gate opened and closed.

Hesitating a moment, he turned and strolled toward the building. The building had a short wall around it with the gate that the addict had been pounding on. The office was rectangular and stone, like many other buildings around it. Em could see the office because it was far larger than its wall and was built with outcropping blocks of rooms with tall windows. Also, unlike the less ornate structures lower in Henaden, this one was tiered with two more floors. It was no castle, but it was impressive.

The gate was short enough that Em considered climbing it, then he could listen in just as the addict had.

Don't stay here. The enemy is watching you, Nature said.

Em wasn't sure whom Nature meant but checked his surroundings. He stood out from the local crowd so there were a couple of people looking his way. An armored man who looked like he was a city guard, a few richly dressed gentlemen of various tribes, and one woman by herself. For a moment, Em imagined the woman had a strange tattoo on her face like a black crown worn upside down, but when he looked directly at her, there was nothing.

Em reconsidered his plans. The guard inside the building had called this a private office and, clearly, this was not the kind of place just anyone would stop at, and definitely not one someone should spy on. Em guessed that Nature meant that this building must be watched by people who were allies of the addict inside.

Nature is right, I can't stay here. He walked on pretending like he'd only stopped for a moment to marvel at the building. He kept checking it out as he passed it by, trying to appear bored as he did.

Next to the gate, he caught sight of an ornate plate of metal with lettering engraved over the symbol of a sleeping cat next to a bag of coins. The letters read,

The Offices of the Noren Trading Company.
No Entry Without Invitation.

"Interesting," Em said, as he rounded the end of the street. He looped the block until he came back to the road that would lead him back to the fountain walkway. "Ghen-*sa* picked up a tail then?"

Ghen had said that this 'Nedain' held a grievance against him, and her employer was a man named Noren. The addict could have been hired by either the employer or this guard to find Em.

"But why?"

If it was the merchant, then he should know Ghen would go home soon, and how he would get there. If Noren wanted to reach him, Ghen could not avoid him, so there was no reason to spy on him. If it was the guard Nedain, then why was the spy in the office? The sentry at the gate hadn't argued, so he was either expecting that addict or someone like him. Was this Nedain so important as to have that authority?

Neither felt right. Em pored over possible answers as he retraced his steps down the main street of Henaden. He knew generally what direction he needed to go and about how far. Master D'gui's home didn't seem to be built the usual way, so he thought he could find it without much trouble.

"Em?"

Em stopped and was jostled as someone pushed past him to keep going down the road. When Em turned, he found Master D'gui looking at him curiously.

"What are you doing here?" she asked.

Bumped again by another traveler, this one calling him a 'Little fool!' as he went by, Em stepped out of the flow to stand next to the mystic.

Em couldn't think of any reason to hide what he'd been doing. "Your forgiveness, master, but I found someone listening at a window of your home."

"What?" Her eyes widened before her features became stern. "Tell me everything."

Quickly, he explained who had been listening and to where he'd followed them. Master D'gui softened slightly once she heard that the spy had reported his findings to the Noren Trading Company.

"... but there is much that does not make sense to me. Something of this spy leads me to think there is more I do not understand," Em finished.

Master D'gui said nothing and took her time in thought.

Minutes passed before she proffered an answer. "I'm afraid my new recipe will need to wait. I've finished selling Ghen's root and that's enough for now. Let's go back home, but Em," her gaze hardened, "keep an eye out for more spies or this same one again if he is foolhardy enough to return. If you see anything, I want you to tell me immediately. Do you understand?"

"Yes, master," Em said with a bow.

She climbed on her horse and looked down from Lena's back. "Oh, and don't tell Ceahan. Not yet at least, he can be... excitable when it comes to prowlers."

"Yes, master."

With that, they waded into the crowds of Henaden.

Master D'gui was far more familiar with the streets of Henaden and she ignored all of the vendors' various calls for her attention as she rode straight for home, Em walking at her side.

The moment they got back, she stopped outside her front door and got down from the saddle. Without a glance at Lena, she walked straight to her door but did not open it. Instead, she observed it as if looking for some sign that Em could not see.

He heard her sigh of relief before she turned and walked back down her front steps.

"We will go in the back," she said before taking back Lena's reins and leading her toward the back gate.

"What were you surveying, master?" Em asked.

"Nothing important. Just a little something I have to let me know if anyone has opened my door without using the proper key."

"The man never stepped up to your door, master," Em said.

"Yes, but can you be sure he worked alone?"

Em was surprised by how seriously she was taking this prowler. "He did not strike me as the kind who would want to share whatever reward was offered to him." They rounded the side of her home and walked to the gate. "I cannot guarantee that, but it is my opinion."

Master D'gui opened her gate and walked through. "I certainly hope you're right."

Putting Lena back in her pen, Master D'gui strode purposefully home and stepped inside.

Ghen and Ceahan looked up in surprise at the master's return, clearly expecting Em.

"That was fast," Ceahan said.

Then they saw Em come in behind her.

"There you are, kid," Ghen said, "We didn't have a clue where you wandered off to."

"Yes," Master D'gui said before Em could answer. "I found Em pacing the street on my way back. I returned because the clouds were getting dark, and I didn't want to risk being rained on. I wasn't able to find all I wanted to buy, but I was able to sell all I needed to."

She drew out a small pouch and set it before Ghen, who scooped it up quickly, grinning at the full weight of the little pouch.

"Yes!" he said in excitement, then looked embarrassed at his outburst. "Uh, sorry miss. I just... this means a lot to me."

"Oh, I don't mind. I'm glad I could assist and thank you ahead of time for caring for my home."

"You're good folk, Master D'gui. I'll take good care of things here."

"Excellent. When I return from my trip, maybe I shall have to visit your home as well. You speak so highly of..."

"So," Ceahan whispered, stepping next to Em, "where did you go? I looked out in the street, and I didn't see any sign of you."

Em couldn't decide if Ceahan was suspicious of Em or generally curious. "I went to check on the man we saw earlier, he was strange. He appeared to be frightened, but he wandered off into the main street."

"The patch addict? Why?"

"Yes, the same man. As I said, he was strange."

"Yeah, he was jumpy, but I think that was because of Master D'gui. Did you see his face when she used magic?" Ceahan grinned. "He went paler than that poison he rubs on his skin."

"Just so," Em agreed simply, letting the conversation simply fall away.

Master D'gui continued rambling, and Em found she'd strayed from Ghen's ranch home to the agricultural habits of the colder north of Ifeldia.

Ceahan, hearing his master rambling, rolled his eyes and went back to the books he was reading before they'd come in.

Em watched the master and apprentice through new eyes that had nothing to do with a loss of memory. Something about the master's suspicion and Ceahan's own, they were very careful people. Too careful, perhaps?

So, what if they had secrets? Was it his business? Probably not.

"But I still wonder," Em said to himself.

Em did not feel he was in any danger. It wasn't like Master D'gui had come into his home and begun acting strange, if anything it was the other way around. He had no other option than to trust her.

However, there was no obvious reason for Master D'gui's request that he watch out for more spies unless she had a reason to suspect them.

"Should I worry about it?"

The presence of Instinct rose to give his opinion. *It may be tied to their problems, Little Em, but while you're here, aren't they yours too?*

Em had to nod his agreement at that.

Stealing a moment, Em walked to a bottle of ink with a quill and wrote a hasty note on the back page of his journal. He remembered Master D'gui's warning about Ceahan's agitation should he learn of a stalker, so he wrote the note in the language he'd spent the morning translating. That way, no one but him could read it.

Be vigilant. Something stalks the house of Master D'gui.

CHAPTER 32

"S'CUSE ME, MASTER D'GUI," Ghen finally interrupted.

Master D'gui had rambled long enough about history that she'd strayed further and further from her original point, and now it was a commentary on the historical significance of the plum in dwarfish folklore.

"Oh, yes?" she asked, snapping out of the trance of her own thoughts.

"After you left, we were talking with Em. He said you had some idea about what we should do tonight. Something other than messing with the faker."

Ceahan looked up at this change of topic, and Em turned from his peering into the street through the window.

Master D'gui tapped her lip. Had she such an idea? "That's right! Oh, I know what he means. I wouldn't call it an idea yet, more of a thought."

"What was it, master?" Ceahan asked.

"Well, I found no mention of the faker in the list of viruses in the studies of Mangorin and Sebliah's published work. So, I tried to learn more about the small network the faker damaged instead."

"You said the faker had attacked this place more than once, correct?" Em asked.

"That's my guess, considering we saw some healing had already occurred in places that weren't freshly damaged. I couldn't find that network in the research but that isn't surprising. It's only a mass of a few hundred pathways, that sounds like a lot, but when among billions it does not even earn a footnote in such research, if it's noticed at all. Still, I see no reason why the faker should have damaged this part of Em's mind. My thought was that maybe we should try to find out, using a more active method."

Ceahan nodded, catching on. "So, something like using magic to heal the damage. Then we can learn if it has something to do with the continued amnesia or is something else to do with the faker specifically."

Master D'gui smiled proudly. "Precisely. That being said, I'd like to do this while Em is awake. We don't know what it will do if an impulse runs through there, but if one does, then Em may have a reaction that will help us understand its purpose. Also, while Em is awake, the faker seems to be less active. Hopefully, we shouldn't need to fear interference from it."

There was a silence as everyone considered the idea.

"How safe is it?" Ghen asked. "You said healing was tricky."

"It is," Master D'gui confirmed, "but I do have some experience. We can go as slowly and carefully as we need. Ceahan will assist, but I will restrict him to monitoring the faker. No offense, Ceahan, but your control issues make anything you could do to help with the healing a thousand times more dangerous than it already is."

"Oh, I'm not offended, master," Ceahan said, honestly relieved.

Master D'gui smiled. "Thank you for understanding. Overall, while this could be tricky, I think the risk is lower than going back to the faker directly."

"I like this plan, but will it do any good?" Em said. "I expect the faker will return later to undo your work."

"So, what if it does?" Ceahan countered. "We can fix it again if the damage isn't too severe. Also, I bet tearing it all up takes energy. We suspect the faker is starving, so it may decide that breaking this crossroads again, isn't worth the effort."

"Even if it does decide to tear it up and use the energy," Master D'gui chimed in, "we may still learn why they were broken in the first place. That information will let us learn more about the faker."

Em nodded, satisfied.

There was a brief moment of silence before Master D'gui inquired, "Any other questions, comments, or complaints?"

All eyes drifted towards Ghen, who shook his head. "I'm not the expert, but it sounds like the safest choice we have."

"It most likely is," Master D'gui assured him.

After a moment, Ceahan leaned back in his chair to get a view out of the window. The sky was dark because of the clouds, but it wasn't late yet. All the same, it was getting towards the middle of the afternoon. "Master, if we are going to do this, we need to do it before nightfall. I'm guessing the more tired Em gets, the more awake the faker will be. The afternoon is already fading away."

She looked out the window too. "I'm glad I came back early then. It seems it may not rain after all, at least not today, but had I stayed out, we would be fighting the time. Perhaps we should go ahead and start our preparations."

"Should I get your magic dirt?" Ghen asked.

"Dirt?" Em muttered, confused, having forgotten the mapping sand.

No one heard him, and when he noticed, Em didn't feel like repeating the question.

"Maybe not, Ghen. If I'm wrong and it does rain, the sand will be useless. It falls apart in water and will have to be dried. That is an annoying and tedious process. Perhaps for this little venture, we can perform it inside. Em can use my chair." She pointed to the padded seat sitting near the southwest hallway. "Ceahan and I will be able to stand behind him. I'll do the healing, and he'll keep an eye on the faker."

With that, more instructions were doled out and before long they were ready to start.

Ceahan moved over to Em, who was already seated in the chair.

"Master, may I go ahead and search for the faker? It wasn't easy to find the first time, and so it may take a moment."

"Go ahead," Master D'gui said without looking up. "As long as it's alright with Em, of course."

"Is there anything I must do, Ceahan-*so*?" Em asked, looking over the back of the chair at the apprentice.

"Sit back and relax. You get the easy job."

Em rolled his eyes. "The pleasure of the fattened pig."

"More or less." Ceahan grinned.

The apprentice then closed his eyes and opened the floodgates of his power. As always, it came out in a rush that filled the room from floor to eaves. Ceahan had almost no control over the volume he used, but he had at least learned how to give it form. He began to pour the magic through Em's mind, and it rebounded back to him with images and feelings that expressed what it found within. Now, with his senses attuned, Ceahan began his search. Not randomly, as they had last night, but homing in on the feeling of the faker he'd encountered.

Ceahan's sense of magic came to him like a sense of smell. He breathed in the images that his magic brought to him of the mind, its impulses, and the sense he was looking for. The one thing so far that just did not fit with the rest of Em, was the faker. In the magic, it simply smelled different when compared to the rest of Em's mind. He hadn't detected it originally because he hadn't even known what to search for, but now that he did, was able to start tracking the faker quickly.

"By the way," the apprentice asked Em as he completed this simple task, "that *sa, so* thing you add to our names. I know it's an honor thing, so why don't you do it for Master D'gui?"

"I do," Em said. "She is master, that is her honor. Just like *sa* is Ghen-*sa*'s honor."

"Okay, so that counts instead of the little things."

"It does."

Ceahan thought he caught the scent of the faker for a moment and zeroed in on the feeling. However, it proved too general and fleeting. Still, it was close now, so he searched on.

"Because of my master, I know there are other cultures that use things like that, but aren't there exceptions? Like with family?" Ceahan asked.

Em nodded absently, but the movement messed with Ceahan's connection. Em felt Ceahan's hand shift to get a hold of him again and Em stiffened his neck to hold his head in place.

"Oh, forgive me, Ceahan-*so*."

"No problem." the apprentice said dismissively.

Em almost bowed his head again but held back. "To answer your question, yes. I would not use these with family or those who I can be less formal with."

"I understand. By the way, I know we aren't close, but you don't have to be formal with me. I know Ghen has accepted it, and it makes sense for the master, but you can just call me Ceahan. I do a kind of double take every time I hear the *so* since I'm not used to it."

"I will try to remember that, Ceahan."

Ceahan caught another sensation of the faker and drew in closer, but couldn't find it. "Hey, out of the two of us. Who do you think is older?"

"I assumed I was. I could be wrong, how old are you?"

"I'll have seen sixteen falls the next time the leaves turn."

Em thought about it.

You are older, Nature said. Em would have expected it to be Instinct who replied, but clearly it was Nature who knew the answer.

"Nature says I am older."

"Nature, huh? Well, even if you are, it can't be by much, can it?"

"No, not by much."

"Well... wait a moment," Ceahan said, cutting himself off. His magic was finally rebounding off of the faker and Ceahan was getting a clear picture of it.

It appeared to be in a dormant state. It didn't move, only wrapped around a single pathway. It didn't have the strong scent like an impulse, instead the faker's odor was vague as if it was hiding itself.

"Did you find something?" Master D'gui said. She happened to be listening to their little conversation and noticed when Ceahan cut off.

"I found the faker. I think it's sleeping or something like that," Ceahan said.

"Let me see." Master D'gui walked over and, attuning to Ceahan, observed it herself. Her magic had a smell to it, too. It was close and intelligent, like the smell of a library, but there was always a sweet earthy scent hidden in it. As if that library had a vase of wildflowers at the end of every shelf, which bloomed in bright colors and kept the air fresh with their peaceful aroma.

"There it is," she said, catching the feeling of the faker for herself. "Is it just me or does it have less presence than yesterday?"

"It could be part of its resting. Hiding basically while it sleeps."

"Or perhaps it serves two purposes. Consider, what if it is both camouflage and an efficient way to save energy? A way to burn less of its food while it cannot hunt. I wonder if it's always like this while Em is awake."

Ceahan tilted his head. "Master, is it where I think it is?"

"What do you mean?" she asked.

"Can you feel the slight damage around here? I think this is where the faker attacked after we pushed it last night."

Master D'gui felt around with her magic. Ceahan was right, she realized. Her eyes narrowed. "This could be a coincidence or just its normal resting place, but it almost feels like it's taunting us."

"What? Like, 'I can get to him, and you can't stop me.'"

"Something like that. However, my guess is this is just its resting place. Good for threatening and not far from where it can go to get food."

"Should we be worried?" Ceahan asked.

The master shook her head. "If it's hibernating, then no damage is being done at the moment. Besides, we don't plan to disturb the faker, anyway. It can rot for all I care."

Ceahan grinned again. "I'll keep an eye on it as you heal."

"Excellent, I'm nearly ready." Master D'gui wandered off and quickly reread a passage in the book on the human mind, and then on a scroll Ceahan recognized as a resource from her days as an apprentice. She must be reviewing her old instructions from when she studied medicine.

Master D'gui was confident in her abilities to heal Em's mental paths and was only using the scroll for cursory review. It wasn't long before she announced, "Alright, I have everything I need. So, if there aren't any final recommendations, we can begin."

When no one spoke up, she let her magic sing.

Ghen kept his nose in a book, attempting to distract himself, but couldn't help looking up anxiously as Master D'gui began her work. He was trying hard to read and be helpful, but every time he finished reading a section, he realized he hadn't absorbed a word. He was too nervous about what was going on with Em, especially since he couldn't follow along like before.

Laying her hand atop Em's head, Master D'gui's magic rolled out of her. Unlike Ceahan, it was in a far more controlled stream, and she used it like her student to explore the depths of Em's mind once more. Instead of images being breathed in like a smell, she heard the song of her magic and listened for the tune of the damaged pathways from the night before. Because she remembered where to look, she found them quickly and easily. A survey of the network told her nothing obvious had changed throughout the day.

She took a deep breath, and with a whisper said, "Let's go."

Warmth ran down her arms and, instead of a jolt of power, the magic reached out slowly. The melody of Master D'gui's magic wrapped around the torn edges of the mental byways and coaxed new growth out of them. A performer playing her favorite instrument, she worked slowly and played carefully. A song of healing depicting what was broken made anew, each note plucked in tune.

The weave of the magic worked rhythmically along the edges of the paths, and Master D'gui settled into the rhythm with them as she'd been trained to do long ago. The waves of power thrummed like the strings of a harp and the magic slowly swayed, bringing the broken ends a little closer together with each movement. To Master D'gui's imagination, her magic was like many little dancers who gently pranced in a subtle dance of healing. As long as everything moved in tune, all would be well again.

Hearing her own mystical music and seeing the dance, Master D'gui's blood stirred. The satyr in her felt that music, that dance, as their tribe often did. An old satyr song came back to her from long ago, and before she knew it, that became the rhythm her magic moved to. Where she'd learned the song, she couldn't recall, but every word and note came back clearly to her now. To that subtle sound of healing's rhyme, she couldn't help but quietly hum along.

The fields are bare, and nests are empty.
Yet pray, hear my voice.
Winter is gone, change has come, and
now spring draws near.
I beseech you hurting hollows I hold so
dear.
Long I've wished to hear your song, to see
your flowers grow.
This is how I'll know that Life anew is
here.

Pray, sing blooming blossoms. Fly high
budding birds.
I slowly dance to Life's song and wait for
you to dance along.

Sleepers wake to the clopping of my
joyful prance.
Twirl with me little lilies in the step of
your water dance.
I know what troubles came, and that
I'm in part to blame.
Hear the song of wounded hearts that
mend.
I sing to you that Life has come again.

Pray, sing blooming blossoms. Fly high
budding birds.
I slowly dance to Life's song and wait for
you to dance along.

Deer of spring, large and small. Can't
you hear my call?

New days and new seasons have come at
last. The burdens we bore are in the past.
Life's quiet song said death has met its
end. I beg of you, show your life again!
I slowly dance to this song and wait for
you...

"... to dance along," Em finished for the master.

"Oh," Master D'gui said slowly, "you know the song?"

"I suppose," Em replied.

Despite her usual excitability, Master D'gui merely smiled calmly, keeping up the healing rhythm of her work. "I'd all but forgotten that song until the tune suddenly came back to me a moment ago. I'm glad it did, I like it."

Out of sight, the voice of Instinct smiled. *It's one of my favorites personally.*

Since Em said nothing of the voice he alone heard, Master D'gui kept on humming quietly to herself. With each beat to the mystical rhythm, she drew out the burned ends of the pathways, continuing to do so for some time. Yet minute by minute, verse by verse, the little roads slowly met at their ends, the dancing magic finishing its work.

When Ceahan could sense that his master's work was nearing completion, he said, "No movement from the faker, master. It may not be able to tell that anything is happening."

"That would be nice. Then tonight we will... Is something the matter, Em?" Master D'gui became more serious as her patient began to twitch.

"My arms, they burned for a moment."

"Please take off your coat," Master D'gui requested, pausing her work.

Em jostled under her hands as he worked his coat off his shoulders. It was an awkward process since he couldn't move much with both Master D'gui and Ceahan having at least one hand laid on his head. Once he succeeded, the master and apprentice peered at Em's bare arms. There were no twitching muscles or signs of distress.

"Is it still happening?" Master D'gui asked.

"No, it was only for a moment."

"I don't think this has to do with my work, but there is still a chance. Em, would you like me to continue with the healing?"

"Yes." Em said confidently.

"Alright then."

She was about to return to her work when Ceahan said, "Master, wait a moment."

"Is something the matter Ceahan?"

"The faker, it's doing something."

"Is it moving?"

"No, it's still, but it's no longer in that dormant state."

"Hmm... Mr. Em, does this change your mind?"

This time there was a delay in Em's response, but only a slight one. "No, please continue."

Master D'gui considered the situation. A moment ago, the aches Em felt seemed like a coincidence, but the faker's response gave her pause. She spoke slowly, still considering. "We will continue. For now, at least. Ceahan, tell me if the faker does anything, anything at all."

On the opposite side of the room, Ghen's reading sat totally ignored as he looked over at all of them. The rancher tapped his foot anxiously. Master D'gui pitied him because, without the mapping sand, Ghen was only able to listen and go off their reactions.

Master D'gui went back to her healing. She did not hum this time and paused whenever Ceahan so much as twitched. She focused on the practicum of her work, but remained careful in her execution since healing was dangerous and she was so close to completion.

Luckily, it wasn't long before Master D'gui breathed a long sigh of relief. "I'm done."

Ghen and the boys also relaxed, blowing out their own held breaths.

"I'm not skilled enough to bring the passages back fully, but they are in working order," Master D'gui said. "What of the faker?"

Ceahan shut his eyes and focused.

"Nothing, in fact, I think it may be starting to slip back into hibernation."

"Why'd it come out at all, then?" Ghen asked from across the room.

"My best guess... It must have been something to do with my work," Master D'gui hypothesized. "Coincidence is real, but if I were to guess, I think Em's mind sent something of a probe to check out what was happening. It might have sent an impulse or two through some of the newly repaired pathways, and I didn't see it. The faker may have realized that, which is why it was partially roused."

"You assume then that the faker awoke because it became aware of something moving through these paths?" Em said.

Master D'gui nodded and let Em go. "Something like that."

Ghen and Em nodded and looked pleased, both assuming anything that made the faker worry was to their benefit. Ceahan, on the other hand, looked pensive.

"Master, if an impulse ran through the repaired paths, and if that is what caused Em to ache," Ceahan began tentatively, "should we consider the possibility that the faker could be trying to help him?"

"What?" Em and Ghen asked in unanimous surprise.

Master D'gui waved them off. "Absolutely, we should."

"Why?" Ghen asked, sounding almost annoyed.

"Just because we have one good theory Mr. Ghen, does not mean we should ignore others. Yes, the faker has a strangely alien feel about it, but that is not conclusive and Ceahan and I can make mistakes. This faker could be a part of the mind the researchers didn't see, or perhaps we simply lack a crucial understanding of it. I believe I said something of the sort when we first discovered it."

"How is the faker's attack on my memory helpful?" Em asked in genuine confusion.

Master D'gui thought of possible explanations. "That could be more of a side effect. Imagine if these roads we fixed do pose a kind of danger. I'm not sure they do," she clarified, "but we should consider the possibility. The faker could be a destroyer your mind created to keep them in check. That would simply make it an overzealous worker of sorts."

"How do we figure out which it is?" Ceahan asked.

"Well, to start with, you said it felt alien as if it wasn't a part of Em, and I agree with you. That seems to support the idea that it is *not* part of Em. Personally, I think we were on the right track before. Also, Em can't feel our magic, yet the faker used magic that we felt. More reason to think it's not part of Em."

Ceahan nodded. "I've been looking all day for something other than a tribesman that could use magic, and I couldn't find any record of such a thing."

"Yes, and foreign or not, it won't change our plans much. Even if it is a worker the mind created, that doesn't make it a good thing. If anything, it's become a cancerous one and is doing more harm than good in its overzealous action. If that's the case, it needs to be neutralized anyway.

"If we discover these paths are dangerous, we can then cut these mental passages ourselves, and make sure they never heal. On the other hand, if they are fine and the only problem is that the faker is an invader, we remove the invader as we planned originally."

Everyone considered this for a moment before Em asked, "If this creature is from outside me, how do you explain the pain I felt?"

Master D'gui shrugged. "First off, they could be unrelated. We don't know for sure that the pathways were the source of your discomfort. That is only a possibility we are considering. If they were the cause, then there are explanations. The easiest one is that it could be atrophy."

Ghen raised his hand like a schoolboy. "Sorry Master D'gui, I know more than most farm and ranch folk, but what's atrophy?"

Ceahan smirked. "Atrophy is when something has been asleep too long and becomes worn down from not being used. My master is suggesting that, if the mind used an impulse on those paths, it might have been painful because it hasn't been used in a while."

"So, it's like Em's head is trying to use a rusted tool?" Ghen suggested.

"That isn't an exact analogy, but you seem to have the basics of it."

Master D'gui touched Ceahan's shoulder to get his attention. "That's good enough for now, Ceahan. However, this situation does present a new risk."

"What risk is that?" Despite the risk clearly being to him, Em didn't sound worried.

"When we started, I was hoping the faker would either react while I was healing you, or not at all. That would mean we could know for certain when the faker would move and be ready for it. But, if the faker may wake up whenever these pathways are used, and since we can't know when they will be used, it means the faker could spring into action at any time."

"Could you or Ceahan use magic to put something in my head to tell you if it starts to wake up again?" Em said.

"I know mystics who probably could, but I don't know how," the master admitted. "Since my apprentice has never studied except with me, Ceahan won't know either. This isn't the time for us to experiment, so we are stuck watching."

"Watching?" Ghen asked. "So, one of you has to keep one eye pointed in his head day and night?"

"Nothing so aggressive," Master D'gui assured him. "All the same, one of us should be at Em's side at all times. If anything is out of the ordinary, Ceahan and I can come running. We can't be sure anything will happen but... I have a feeling we may still be in for a few more surprises."

CHAPTER 33

MASTER D'GUI LOOKED UP from her reading materials as orange light streaked across the page. The sun had finally lowered itself enough that its rays crept beneath the hem of the clouds that had hidden them throughout the afternoon.

"My word, is it that late already? Well, I suppose it is." After Em's healing, the master had returned to her studies on how she might contain the faker and had fully lost herself in the pursuit. Now that she was looking up, she was beginning to hear her stomach begging for attention. "Is anyone else hungry?"

"Just a bit ma'am," was Ghen's reply. "Would you like me to try and put something together for us all?"

Master D'gui nodded. "If you are willing to cook, that would be nice, but please allow me to assist since I know my way around my own kitchen."

"Much obliged, master," Ghen said as he stood from his seat.

"Ceahan," Master D'gui instructed, "stay by Em and get me if—"

"Yes, master, I'll call you if anything happens," Ceahan assured her.

"Good." With that, she set her materials aside, before going with Ghen into the other room.

Ceahan expected he had the easy job since, so far, Em had been just sitting quietly and translating. Once the master and the rancher left though, Em put his things aside as well and picked up his long and short sword.

"Where are you going?"

Em stretched. "Nature says I've been sitting too long and that now is the time to train."

"Yes, well," Ceahan felt uneasy discussing these voices Em heard, "you've probably been journeying for months on end. Shouldn't uh... Nature give you a break today?"

Em's eyes went distant as he discussed the matter with the invisible teacher. "He is insisting, and I admit I am restless."

The apprentice sighed. "I'm guessing you can't do it in here, so I don't have to move to stay near you."

"Not unless you think the master wouldn't mind a few of her books knocked over."

Ceahan rolled up the scroll he'd been reading. "You do that and I'm going to get blamed for it. We're going outside."

Em smiled slightly and led the way out into the backyard. As they passed the kitchen, Master D'gui poked her head out to make sure Ceahan was going with him, but when the apprentice gave her a nod, she went back to aiding the rancher.

As Ceahan descended the two steps into the yard, Em was already starting. His long sword flew from its scabbard and Em moved in three quick cuts before stepping back.

"So did 'Nature' teach you how to fight then?"

"I do not remember." Em said with the utmost simplicity and Ceahan suddenly felt stupid for asking.

"Okay well... Is Nature going to make you practice with only that sword, or are you going to use both?"

"I do not know. If I have time, I think I would like to train with more than just my long and short swords." Em paused a moment before adding. "Nature says, he trains me in many ways, even how to fight unarmed."

"Fighting hand to hand?"

"Yes, not that my hands will be met with others unless you want to join."

Ceahan took a step back. "I've never learned anything like that. I'd rather not be beaten up."

Em grinned, then tilted his head. "Nature said to tell you, 'Fighting with your hands is the easiest to learn, but the hardest to master.'"

"You think?" Ceahan said a little creeped out that 'Nature' was talking to him now through Em.

Em thought about it before giving his answer. "We can all fight with hands, it comes naturally." As Em spoke, the inspiration for his words flowed from his hidden teacher. "Even so, there are many bad habits that are also natural and get in the way of mastery."

"Okay, I get that. Learning magic is similar in that way. It's a part of you, not like a tool. That doesn't mean it's easy to control."

Em suddenly remembered the master's comments about Ceahan struggling with control. "It is the same, then. Yet maybe one can help with the other."

"What do you mean?" Ceahan asked.

Em grinned again. "Show me how you strike."

"What?"

"Throw a punch," Em said in a fairly bad attempt to talk in an Ifeldian accent.

Ceahan made a face, threw out his arm lazily, and then crossed his arms.

"How terrifying," Em said, with a roll of his eyes, "why would you practice magic when a strike like that would flatten armies?"

"Very funny," Ceahan said with a humorless smile. "Fine."

Ceahan uncrossed his arm and punched the air, his shoulders shuddering, as he gave it real effort.

Em had to make an effort not to shake his head. He took a step closer to the apprentice. "I think you can improve. Try that against me."

"You want me to punch you?"

Em took his stance. "I want you to *try*. Do not fear, I will not hit you."

Ceahan watched Em carefully and punched lazily again.

Em slapped the lazy hand away with a *SMACK!*

"Ow!"

"I mean it, try to hit me," Em repeated.

Ceahan obliged, irritated now. This time, he threw a punch with all his strength.

Ceahan wasn't practiced like Em was, so it wasn't all that strong, but Em treated the attack with respect. He caught the blow with the length of his arm and turned with the momentum, deflecting the force.

Em grinned.

Ceahan grinned back. "Again?"

Em nodded.

This time Ceahan punched twice in quick succession, a right and a left.

Em turned both away and stepped in quickly to deliver a counter. He stopped the blow inches from Ceahan. The counter was so quick that the fist was stopped by the time Ceahan reacted.

"Hey!" Ceahan complained as he stumbled back. "You said you wouldn't hit back."

Em shrugged. "Did I hit you? No, I only acted like it. In its own way, pretending to attack is an excellent defense."

"You sound like the philosophers Master D'gui makes me read."

Em chuckled. "Perhaps they and I hail from the same lands."

Ceahan smiled again. "No, they're all tightwads from Roldea, I think."

"Too bad. Now, what did you think?" Em asked.

"Of what?"

"Your attacks, were they good?"

Ceahan didn't seem to know how to answer the question. "I guess not. I didn't hit you, and you didn't act like I was much of a threat."

Em nodded and circled Ceahan. "You punch like you are standing on a chair."

"What does that mean?"

Em put his feet together. "You stand like this. When I stepped forward, all you could do was fall back. You had no balance. If you had hit me, you would have stumbled too. Standing like that while you fight will also tire you out faster, your arms do all the work. Bring a foot back slightly." Em took his stance to show what he meant. He leaned one way and another to show the balance, throwing quick punches, and quickly stepping forward and back. "I can move and turn my body. My back turns with me and my feet push off the ground. Even if you can punch hard with just your arms, it does not mean you can punch well."

Ceahan looked on, curious, as he began to take some interest in the conversation. "Isn't punching hard and, well, the same thing?"

Em asked knowingly, "Is using magic well the same thing as using all of it? If so, why did Master D'gui tell us the flaw in your magic was that you use too much?"

"Okay, that's a fair point. Except, using magic isn't about how you stand."

"Neither is fighting with your hands." Em said. "Still, it is a good place to start."

Ceahan rolled his eyes. "Maybe you are from the same place as those philosophers."

Em decided to show off a bit, and his slower turns and strikes became fast and precise. A quick kick, a dodge, another quick flurry of blows. He sidestepped quickly, aiming a heavier blow at an imaginary opponent's exposed midsection... and collapsed to the ground.

Em gasped, falling to his knees before his voice boiled up into a scream of agony.

It's happening, Instinct said nervously.

Nature's words rolled like thunder. *The Akai.*

Em's left hand flew to his right side, gripping his arm tightly as if to stem the flow of pain. The pain started in his arm but was growing like a smoldering fire that had found new fuel. The arm was only its starting point, the fire already now covered his right hand and was crawling up his shoulder.

"Master! Master, come outside!" Ceahan yelled as he leapt to Em's side.

The rear door of the house was flung open and Master D'gui flew across the yard as her half satyr legs carried her swiftly to where Em struggled.

There she froze. Master D'gui and Ceahan were petrified by utter shock.

"Th.... That's impossible," Master D'gui breathed.

Em's riot of pain brought with it an unreal clarity. A fog he hadn't noticed cleared in a moment. He looked down. His arm still burned as if it was set alight... and it was. Inside his arm, a visible red glow was beginning to grow larger and far brighter.

The forgotten fire, beginning to burn once more.

Up on the walkway above the home of Master D'gui, eyes watched a red glow flicker against the walls of her garden. They were the eyes of a silhouette in the dark, strong and masculine. The only thing visible from the street was the symbol of an upturned crown sown in gold on their shirt. Watching from the shadows, Eznem, the Inverted King smiled.

"Now that's unexpected."

"And does it change what you will do?" asked a voice behind him.

The moment the voice spoke the Inverted King felt pain in his chest and knew his rival had returned.

"Do?"

Eznem turned, and while his grin never left his face, seething hatred surged as he saw who stood behind him. In the light of the fading sun was a man leaning on a simple staff, he was plain and unremarkable by sight, but the Inverted King knew better. Though he looked like a normal common worker in a city, this 'workman' was much more.

"I don't plan to 'do' anything *yet*," Eznem said. "I admit I'm surprised, but I'm actually glad to see the return of the red blades. You may remember, they didn't all serve you."

The workman said nothing and looked unphased by the comment.

"This explains, why you put those two phantoms on that boy. I'm glad I wasn't able to break him after all. Is that why you've come? Are you here to keep me from harming him?"

"I've come to tell you, I'm watching you, spirit. Neither your schemes here nor in the far lands have not escaped my sight." The workman warned.

The Inverted King gestured to the home below where raised voices could be heard and the red light still glowed. "And you think your schemes have escaped me? Oh, primordial builder, do you really think you're the only one with servants? I may not be able to strike you now, but I know what you are up to."

The workman smiled. "Is that so?"

Then, without a flash or a flicker, he disappeared.

Eznem's gaze lingered where the workman had been a moment before, and his smile became a snarl.

What did that mean? In fact, why did he come to me at all? Was it simply to provoke me?

The Inverted King turned toward the red light of the Akia once again. Had he missed something? Or was this another of his rival's games, a play to make him doubt himself?

No, he's building up to something. That must be what the red blade is for.

Eznem drummed his fingers on his side. Despite his own words he had planned to unleash a surprise on the servants of the workman, but perhaps he needed to change his timing.

"I won't move now... but soon. I'll gather those I need and then wait. I'll let *him* make the first move. Until he shows his face again, I'll wait, I'll watch, and I'll be ready. Everything will be prepared for whatever he decides to do."

CHAPTER 34

"I... I CAN'T SENSE it," Ceahan stuttered.

Master D'gui snapped out of her shock first. "Yes, yes, I know!"

The light was going further and further up Em's arm. Master D'gui reached out to touch Em but hesitated. Was it safe to touch the glowing limb?

Em groaned as the pain overwhelmed him, reminding Master D'gui that there was no choice but to risk it. She quickly clasped his arm, letting go just as quickly, expecting some heat or shock.

There was none.

More slowly, she reached out again and took his arm. Despite the glow seeping out from underneath her hand, she couldn't feel anything. Nothing abnormal at all, not even the magic she was sure she should be able to sense.

Em groaned as another wave of pain washed over him. The red glow flared slightly. It had already spread all over his right arm from fingertips to his shoulder blade and was still growing.

"Whatever it is, we can take hold," Master D'gui announced.

Ceahan remained where he was, staring in awe.

"Ceahan! Later! This has to do with these pathways, I'm sure of it."

Ceahan finally began to rouse himself. "Uh, yes, master."

"Find the faker, now." Master D'gui ordered. She clasped Em's head and forced her way in, trying to find the mental passages she'd repaired earlier. Em's mind was a symphony of impulses of all kinds, but the brightest point was the very point she was looking for. The repaired paths bustled with as much life as Henaden's main street. Impulses raced and light shone brightly, not only within the mental roads, but the very essence around the paths flickered with red light similar to Em's arm.

Ceahan placed a hand on Em's head and began his search for the faker. "I found it," he said almost instantly.

"So fast?" Master D'gui asked in surprise.

Ceahan struggled for words. "See for yourself, it's... it stands out now."

Master D'gui paused. Should she look at the faker or watch these mental lanes? Which was more important? These paths were obviously the source of Em's pain, but if there was something to do with the faker, could she miss the opportunity to see it?

Em grunted again, but less fiercely. Perhaps the pain was lessening, or he was adjusting to it. Either way, he'd be fine for another moment.

"I'll take a look."

Already the light had reached Em's mind, and when she looked for the faker, she found it easily. The faker was a dark purplish silhouette against the fiery sky Em's mind had become. It was the only thing that light didn't seem to come from. Watching the faker, Master D'gui's breath caught.

"What is it?" Ghen asked nervously. He came outside and looked on in confused dismay.

"Master," Ceahan said, ignoring Ghen. "The light, do you see it? Its..."

"I see it," she interrupted. "Em? Em, can you hear me?"

The light spread quickly. Already under Ceahan's hand on top of Em's head, black hairs glinted with flecks of crimson. His arm, where the glow had started, seemed to have reached its maximum with a steady shimmering illumination. The red glow flowed out in waves from wherever it covered and beneath his skin looked like the sun glimpsed from underwater.

Despite reaching what might be its highest on his arm, its spread was unfinished. Already, faint glimmers reached towards Em's legs. Em's fist was clenched as he fought the pain. His eyes were pinched tight, and he was in deep pain, yet... he smiled.

"I can hear you," he said carefully through gritted teeth, still split with a grin.

"What's happening? Can you tell us anything about this!?" Master D'gui shouted, trying to get some clue as to what the right course of action was.

Em's chest fluttered, but not in pain. If anything, it looked like he was about to laugh.

"Em, Em! What's happening?!" she repeated, fearing this was some symptom of mania.

"The faker is reacting!" Ceahan yelled moments before Em renewed his painful convulsions.

His smile fell and Em yelled, pressing on the sides of his head as new waves of pain exploded.

"Hold him down!" Master D'gui yelled.

Ghen jumped in and pinned Em's small body down to keep him from struggling in the arms of the two mystics.

"The faker is attacking Em," Ceahan said.

"Not again." Master D'gui growled. "I'll destroy the lanes and stop this at the source."

"It's going berserk!" Ceahan called anxiously.

Master D'gui pressed into Em's mind once more, and...

"STOP!"

Em's voice rang out just as Master D'gui began to feel the pathways that created the strange glow, ready to cut them apart. But the moment Em called out, the pathways obeyed and fell silent.

The glow faded, and Em's convulsions slowed.

"What... what did you do?" Ghen asked, still holding Em down.

"Ceahan, the faker?" Master D'gui asked, unable to find it herself. Without the light, the faker was hard to find once again.

"It's going back to sleep," Ceahan said with a sigh.

Master D'gui leaned back and wiped her brow. "By all of the seven layers of the world, what was that?"

The whole group seemed to take this moment to catch their breath. By the time Master D'gui recovered, Em was still lying on the ground with an arm over his eyes.

"Are you still in pain, Em?" Master D'gui asked, equal parts curious and concerned.

"Only my head," Em muttered. He pulled his arm away and flexed it. "I think I am a little sore, but with my head like this, it is hard to tell."

"What is going on!?" Ghen repeated louder and slightly annoyed.

"Calm Ghen, calm," Master D'gui soothed. "The moment of panic has passed. As for what just happened, that seems to be complicated."

"Was that magic?" Ghen asked.

"No, that was *not* magic," Ceahan said.

"Now, now," Master D'gui was still slightly out of breath, "that is not definitive. However, I admit that was... unexpected."

"It was not magic?" Em looked at his arm in confusion. "Did I imagine the light?"

"No, that was very real," Ceahan affirmed.

"Then how was it not magic?"

"I'll explain," Master D'gui said before Ceahan could state his own feelings. "As you may or may not know anyone, with magic, even a small amount, can see or feel what we normally call magic. Think of it like an extra sense we have as magicians. How we experience the sense differs from person to person, but we should be able to still sense magic when it's used. Usually, we can also sense details like what the magic is being used for, even if it's foul black magic. What stunned me and my apprentice is that you shined bright as my fireplace, but I felt as much of your power as I expect Ghen did."

Ceahan nodded his agreement.

Ghen voiced the question in all their minds. "If it wasn't magic, then what was it?"

Master D'gui laughed. "I haven't a clue! This has got to be the most fun I've had researching in ages."

No one laughed with her.

"Do we need to sever the mental paths that caused this?" Ceahan asked.

Surprisingly, Em pulled away from Ceahan at the suggestion.

Master D'gui would have said no, but instead of answering she focused on her patient. "Em, is there some reason we shouldn't?"

Em hesitated, looking down at himself. "I... I was better, for a moment."

"What do you mean?" Ceahan asked.

"Before," Em recounted, "I think my thoughts were clouded. It was hard to tell because I do not remember being any other way, but a moment after the pain started, I felt... I still feel... better? Even now, it is hard to explain how." He flexed his hand. "It's like I move more easily or think more easily."

Master D'gui suddenly recalled a detail of their research they'd overlooked until now.

"Ceahan."

"Yes, master."

"Last night as the faker passed over pathways. The sand showed us nothing, but you mentioned the mental lanes were being 'warped' somehow, I believe."

Ceahan brightened, having totally forgotten the fact until now. "Yes, that's right. They softened, or something like that. Are you suggesting that by going red, or whatnot, Em undid that?"

She shrugged. "I have no idea, but going forward when the faker moves, I want to monitor that warping more closely. Next time Em 'goes red,' I want to monitor it more closely too."

"Next time? You're going to leave those roads put together?" Ghen asked.

"Oh absolutely," Master D'gui said with a smile. "You didn't see all that we did. Also, as of right now, I think we have more evidence that the faker is an outside virus and something to be removed or destroyed."

Ceahan nodded, but Ghen and Em looked at her in confusion.

"That light," she explained, "it covered everything. Maybe I couldn't feel it the same way I feel magic, but when we looked into Em, it was a dazzling show. Every fiber and drop of blood glowed with the light. The faker, however, was like a dark shadow. It couldn't hide in that light, because I guess, unlike the rest of you, it couldn't produce it."

"I think we also learned why the faker destroys those pathways and why it freaked out a moment ago," Ceahan added, then turning to the guests of the house, he added context. "It wasn't just that it was easy to see, but it was so clear it was obvious. And it looked like that light almost burned the faker."

Em nodded slowly as he followed along. "So then, the red is something from inside me. So, the faker destroys those paths for its own protection?"

"Hang on Em," Ghen said. "If it's part of you, then why did it hurt?"

Em considered for a moment then looked at Master D'gui. "Could the pain be... what was your word... ato, no atre..."

"Atrophy?" she suggested. "Possibly, but we passed out of my frame of reference long ago. Anything I say at this point is almost guesswork. I do agree with Ceahan, however, that the light was hurting the faker, and that self-preservation explains the faker's actions."

"Then what—" Ghen started, but Ceahan interrupted him after sniffing at the air.

"Hold on, rancher. I'm all for this conversation, but unless Em is that burning smell, I think one of you left our food over the fire."

Master D'gui took a whiff of the air. "Oh heavens!" she said. "Em, stay here, and you stay with him." She looked pointedly at Ceahan before running back into the house.

Ghen hesitated, looking at Em, but said nothing and finally ran after her.

Left in the awkward silence, Ceahan and Em looked at each other. Then, even though neither could have explained why, they laughed.

Ceahan was still chuckling slightly. "Looks like I'm not the only one who can't control their strange powers."

Em's head bobbed in agreement. "It was what I deserve for trying to show off."

When his laughter cooled, Ceahan asked, "Can you think of anything in your journal that could have warned us about that?"

Em took a moment but shook his head. "No, I made no notes of anything like this."

"Well, usually I would ask if this has ever happened before. Except, from your perspective, I've known you longer than you've known yourself."

"True," Em grinned. "Should I ask you then if this has happened before?"

The apprentice rolled his eyes. "Oh, be quiet."

It wasn't long after that Master D'gui returned, bringing with her bowls of the hash Ghen had thrown together with a slice of bread protruding from the edge of each bowl.

"It's not much, but it will do." Master D'gui looked at the sky. "Yes, the rain seems to be holding off for now. We'll eat out here and discuss our plans for the evening."

"Thank you, master," Em said with a bow as she handed him and Ceahan their portions. Before long, she and Ghen were back with their own meals.

As twilight faded overhead, the group used a small fire pit kept in the master's back yard to build up a small fire. The flames were weak but broke the small chill of the oncoming night.

"I suppose I ought to bring up the bad news," Master D'gui said regretfully when they were reaching the end of the meal.

Em paused, food halfway to his mouth. "What is it, master?"

"In short, we need to make an attempt at the faker this evening." She saw the hesitation in Ghen's eye and explained before any questions were raised. "I think it's clear that 'the faker', as we've named it, is a specimen we know little about. What we do know is that it has destructive tendencies and that, over the past day, we have pushed it around a lot. I knew we would, but with that red light, I'm guessing we pushed further than I ever meant to. Prodding it yesterday was one thing, but if the faker suffered real wounds as Ceahan suspects, it could need food badly for its own health."

"Not to mention," Ceahan added, "the faker will probably go on a rampage the moment Em drops out. If it really got hurt, I bet it won't rest until those pathways we fixed are broken to pieces."

Master D'gui agreed. "Simply put, we have no idea exactly how the faker will act but can be fairly sure that it will act and do so aggressively."

Ghen sighed. "I'm no fan of leaving Em to this little bugger, but shouldn't we consider letting it alone at least tonight? You know, let it rest so that it'll be all calmed down when you're ready to work on it?"

Master D'gui shook her head. "It might make the faker more comfortable, but do we even know if the faker can survive its current injuries? If it's dying, what will it do? We just don't know, and that is very dangerous. As I said before, this is something I think we *must* do."

"What do you have planned?" Em asked.

"That's right," Ghen chimed in. "Didn't you say yesterday you weren't sure what you could do with it?"

Master D'gui raised an eyebrow. "What did you think I was looking into all day? Ceahan was looking for a comparable virus, but I was looking at other things. I already said that in my search last night, I found nothing on the pathways we fixed this afternoon. After I found nothing then, I instead shifted my focus onto old medical research. I've come up with some... *theories* on how I can try to trap it."

Even Ceahan looked skeptical. "Theories, master?"

She shrugged. "It's what I have to work with. Still, it's not as if I'm making wild guesses. The methods are based on tested spell craft, which I've modified slightly. I can guarantee they will have some effect, I'm just not certain how great the effect will be. While it's been a while, I tried to find solutions I at least have some experience with from my time as an apprentice. I think I've found some reasonable ideas that fit the criteria."

Hearing that it was based on true techniques she had experience with, Em and Ceahan relaxed.

Ghen still looked tenuous. "Em, when you think of going through all this, how do you feel about it?"

All eyes turned to Em.

How did he feel? Excited, yes; afraid, assuredly; desperate, definitely. None of those would settle Ghen's mind, though. There was something else though, another feeling, harder to define.

He tried to put it into words, it was a feeling from almost outside himself. Not Instinct, but Em could feel this direction was... something. Even so undefined, that 'something' was comforting. Yet, how could he explain that?

Setting aside his bowl, Em didn't say a word but did what felt right. Taking his right hand, he pointed to his heart with an outstretched thumb and looked at Ghen expectantly.

Ghen stared dumbstruck, while Master D'gui and Ceahan traded looks of confusion. Neither had any clue what the gesture meant.

Ghen was silent and closed his eyes, tilting his head this way and that, as if trying to listen. After some time, his eyes opened again, and he got up and started pacing in a circle, mumbling to himself.

Master D'gui and Ceahan watched the rancher with a mix of curiosity and amusement.

Mid-stride, Ghen froze. He'd found his answer. The rancher turned back to them, his eyes were sad, but he was calmer.

"Fair enough," Ghen said, although Em wasn't sure if the rancher was talking to him or someone else. Ghen pointed to his heart the same way Em had. He lowered his hand a moment later and shook his head, disappointed. "You know I've been really down and out all day about how little help I've been."

"Actually, Mr. Ghen—"

"No, Master D'gui, thank you for whatever you were about to say, but no," Ghen said firmly. "I've not been very helpful, in fact, I've been less than. Thinking about it, I've been a downright burden. Instead of trusting you to do your work, I've questioned you at every step. That ain't what good folk ought to do, and I know better. The kid's right," he added, looking at Em. "I think peace and the Boss are going your way and I'm set to follow. That being the case, I'll try and be more supportive. What can I do to help?"

Master D'gui looked at her guests curiously. "I won't pretend I understood all that you've said. However, if you are willing to help, I will let you know how you can later."

"What do we need to do to prepare?" Em asked, now that it seemed the decision was made.

"Most of what we need is already in place from yesterday," Ceahan said.

"Except your sand," Ghen pointed out "Unless we're going to be inside again."

"No, we'll be outside," Master D'gui decided. "I'm still worried about the rain, but I would prefer the mapping sand for this."

Em looked from one face to another, still trying to figure out what Ghen meant by 'sand.' When he couldn't work it out, he decided it was better to wait rather than ask. Clearly, he would find out soon enough.

"Anything else?" Master D'gui asked.

"Nothing big," Ceahan muttered through a mouthful of hash.

"Great." Ghen nodded, looking around the yard trying to think if there was anything they were neglecting. He couldn't think of anything, but something slightly different did come to mind. "If we're all good on that, do you mind if I change the topic slightly?"

Master D'gui shrugged. "I guess not. Was there something else you wished to discuss?"

Ghen nodded. "Sure, miss. It's just when we get this little bugger out. What's next?"

"We don't know if we will get it out yet," Ceahan said. "This is theoretical. Remember?"

"And I'm being supportive now. Remember?" Ghen said, with a grin. "Let's make a plan of what to do once the little twit is dealt with."

Master D'gui smiled back. "Ah, I see. Well... hmm... admittedly we will need to keep Em another day or two if we get the faker tonight. Even if all is well at first appearance, there is more we need to determine." She used her spoon to count off the items on her fingers. "First, this red light. Then, if there are any lingering effects of the faker. Lastly, of course, making positive confirmation that the faker is the root of the amnesia Em suffers. Incidentally—"

Ceahan looked at Em, cutting off the lecture Master D'gui was on the edge of falling into. "Em, I'm curious. Once you're cleared by the master, what do you want to do then? Where will you go once this is over?"

Master D'gui pursed her lips, pouting at being interrupted, but was too interested in Em's answer to fuss about it.

Em considered. "Master, is there any chance I can regain everything I've forgotten when the faker is gone?"

She winced slightly. "Well... I can't speak with certainty, but I doubt it. Our current theory is that the faker's warping the pathways, along with the loss of impulses, is what causes your forgetfulness. That would imply the loss is most likely permanent. While we hypothesized a moment ago that your red light might have reversed the damage somewhat, that doesn't mean it would put everything back to the way it was originally. If you do recall anything, it could be different from how things actually happened, or too muddled and confusing to understand."

"I see... I... I guess, I do not know what I want to do then."

"We'll find something for you, kid," Ghen said. "I'll help you."

Master D'gui nodded her agreement. "Don't fret about it. You are too young to give up hope yet. With my research, I live in a world of lost history. So, you can take it from me that you may discover your past eventually even if you can't remember it. Even if you don't, you have plenty of time left to make a good ending for your story. I've personally thought for a long time that the most important marker of our lives is our..." she hesitated "... well, our legacy."

These last words came out slowly, and much more somber. Em saw the same sadness he'd seen in her earlier when discussing her tribe. This time, she didn't need Ceahan to cheer her up. Instead, she brightened up by herself. Glancing at her apprentice, pride sparkled in her eyes.

"Thank you Ghen-*sa*, Master D'gui," Em said bowing to each in turn.

"My pleasure, kid," Ghen said grinning.

Master D'gui nodded.

For a moment, an awkward silence started to build, and Em felt responsible for it. To break things up, he quickly asked, "Ceahan, what will you do once this is over?"

"I'll go back to my studies."

"What I mean," Em clarified "is that the master mentioned you are going on a journey soon. What are you traveling to do?"

Ceahan became nervous as the topic shifted to his future plans. "I'll get better control of my power and learn to get even stronger from there. Learning from Master D'gui and others."

"Even stronger?" Ghen laughed jovially. "How strong do you need to be, kid? Planning to take on an army?"

"No," Ceahan said. "I just... you know, want to be safe."

Em nodded, believing he understood. "Hmm, will you go to Korodai then? To study with other masters, or is that already part of the trip you have planned?"

Ceahan squirmed under the question but was relieved when Master D'gui saved him. "Ceahan and I are planning to make a stop at Korodai. That, however, is a very private affair. I tell you this since you asked, but please keep it to yourselves."

"I can do that, miss," Ghen assured her without hesitation.

"You have no reason to fear my spreading it." Em shrugged. "I have no one to tell, even if I remember it tomorrow."

They talked on for a while longer, about Ghen's hopes for his ranch, and then Master D'gui's told them of all the cities she planned to visit on their upcoming journey. Then she strayed to tales of even further places, some in distance, some in time long past.

Master D'gui was an enchanting storyteller. She used her words to bring dead cities back to life and showed as much as told them the stories of the secret histories of places that still existed. She told them of the destruction of Juseana a hundred falls before King Roleius was ever born, described the depths of the underground city of Kenthuru, sang the praise of the hanging cities of the fae which were still suspended in the Borgiden Mountain range, and of many more places.

As the moon climbed up to peer down at the meeting at Master D'gui's, it found the group happy and content. Everyone knew that hard times were on the horizon. But, for now, they were willing to wait on those and enjoy this simple moment.

CHAPTER 35

As NEDAIN ENTERED NOREN's office, she found the merchant pouring wine into one of his goblets. "Noren, we may have word on the sylwerd's location."

Noren showed as much reaction as if she'd said the sky was blue. "And?"

"And this is how you start your plan to work with your 'friend', isn't it?" Nedain asked, confused.

"So, it is. I have a question though, when you say 'we may have word', can you be more specific?" Noren gestured to his desk where a stack of pages sat separate from the rest. "I received five such reports today. Among them, three have my interest."

"Is one of them about the mystic?"

"Ah, you mean the report from the addict. Yes, that one is of the three of interest," Noren said. "I thought you'd already heard of these reports. Still, I appreciate you bringing this to me straight away after hearing to make me aware."

Nedain dropped herself into a chair. She sat with arms crossed and was frankly disappointed. She'd arrived with what she thought was big news, but Noren had probably already worked it all out.

"Have you told your elf friend then?" Nedain asked.

Noren looked up from his cup, amused. "About what, a bunch of rumors? Even if I wanted to, how do you expect me to reach him? He never exactly gave me a way to do that."

'A bunch of rumors.' Nedain cocked her head, maybe he didn't know. "You're taking this one with the mystic rather lightly, aren't you? I would have thought that you'd take a closer look at it."

Noren raised a skeptical eyebrow. "Did you see the man who brought the report? I caught a glance of him on his way out. He was starving for his poultice. He probably sees dragons in the cobblestone shadows. However, he was too excited to have seen nothing, which's why it made my interesting pile."

Nedain tilted her head. "So, you didn't talk to him yourself?"

"No, should I have?" Noren asked, his amusement becoming curiosity.

"He said some interesting things." Nedain grinned. "I heard a word or two from him as he was pushed out the door. I thought he might be out of it too, until he added a detail that caught my attention. So, I did some checking."

Noren walked over to sit across from her. "Do tell."

"He said that there were two other people in the house. A man he called a farmer, and a young, short guy with a strange accent."

Noren thought for a moment before his eyebrows rose slowly. "Do you mean Ghen and his strange little friend? Oh, what was his name...?"

"Em."

"Yes, that was it, Em." Noren nodded. "So, they were the others at this 'witch's' house?"

"He didn't remember their names exactly. When I pressed him, he did remember the shorter one had strange clothes, and the farmer was trying to take care of a mule."

"Sounds like our boys, but what would they be doing there, of all places?" Noren pondered aloud.

Nedain shrugged. "No clue, but I was curious. I've never heard of a mystic in Henaden, but I thought the registry office would have noted it if there was one. I decided to stop by before they closed doors."

"It's not as if mystics have to register themselves and, if there was a mystic on the registry, I would think I would already know."

"You're probably right." Noren's spies in the city watched for anything of interest and someone able to use magic would be one thing they were sure to make note of, so Nedain had to admit that was true. "There's more in that office than official records though."

"Like what?" Noren asked, intrigued. He almost felt like Nedain was holding back some detail.

"Like gossip. When I went by, there was a talkative kyate-siv at the desk. I asked if there was anyone who could use magic in the city. She said there wasn't that she knew of but that two men came in just the other day looking for a person they said was supposed to be a sorcerer."

"No," Noren said dramatically, a smile tugging at his lips.

Nedain nodded. "She remembered when the two of them talked that the more rural one called the other 'Em' by name."

Noren leaned back. "That is an interesting turn of events."

"I thought so too." Nedain looked pointedly at Noren's wine jug.

He noticed the look. "Help yourself," he said distractedly, focusing more on his internal thoughts.

Nedain didn't need a better invitation.

As she poured her own drink, Noren asked, "Did this kyate-siv girl say anything else?"

Nedain shrugged. "Nothing I can make much out of. It sounded like Ghen was kind of a guide, and it was Em looking for this Master D'gui."

"Who? Oh, is that the woman who owns the home?"

"Yeah, that's the mystic's name. Apparently, she's a researcher on paper."

"This does make a kind of sense. I can't see Ghen getting wrapped up with sorcerers. However, a mysterious foreigner who is skilled enough to kill one of my guards. That contract's worth a halak."

"If you ask me, that adds weight to our little addict's story as well," Nedain added.

"I think you are right," Noren agreed. "This moves his report to the top of my pile. I'll read it again in a moment to see if there are any other details I overlooked. Excellent work, Nedain."

Nedain didn't work for praise, but she was glad that Noren wasn't mocking her anymore. She had his respect again, and the fact that Em might be involved with this sylwerd business had her excited. It was a chance to settle the score. "So, what do we do?"

"Do?" Noren said, sitting up. "We do nothing and do it intentionally."

"Seriously?" Nedain said, between sips of her cup. "Shouldn't we make a plan to take the sylwerd?"

"And botch it royally? No, this is too important to be impulsive. Don't forget, Em surprised you alone before. Now he's with at least one person who can probably use magic, and I don't have a clue what the sylwerd can or can't do. We also don't understand their full relationship. I won't jeopardize our relations with my patron simply to make it quick."

Nedain raised her hands in surrender. "Fine, I see your point. We can't just sit on our backsides and hope, though."

"Yes, I guess I misspoke earlier when I said we'll do nothing. We are going to do something, just nothing overt. Consider this your first task as our 'Dark Arm of Henaden', as I put it before.

"That home is on the steps, isn't it? Organize lookouts at both ends of the step who won't be conspicuous. Have them tell you anything they see and make note of everyone who goes in and out. I will keep an eye on the other sylwerd leads in case this mystic turns out to be a hallucination. While we do that, I will also ask around to find out what I can about this Master D'gui discreetly. Be sure to keep any of our people who know about the sylwerd off of the mystic's step. We can't risk tipping our hand."

"I'll get one man to make rounds on the step above them every so often. Not to peer down at them, but to give us a glance and maybe see something important. I'll get someone who knows their business there and on the side streets, but Noren, if we want people good enough to be quiet about this, it will cost."

The merchant didn't even blink. "I'll cover it." Then Noren grinned. "Sounds like you are going to take to your new role well."

Nedain didn't smile back. "Thanks, but what do we do if they try to leave the city?"

Noren's grin fell. He rubbed his chin for a while, taking the occasional sip of his wine.

When he was ready to speak, the merchant was serious. "I don't care about Ghen as much anymore. If he's only a guide, he can burn for all I care, but that only applies if he's leaving by himself. Em should be followed if it can be managed. The mystic and sylwerd, however... No, no matter what, they *do not* leave the city. Is that understood?"

"Perfectly."

Noren opened his mouth to add something, but Nedain already knew the question and the answer.

"If it comes to it, the sylwerd will be captured alive and unharmed."

"For now, we wait and watch, but soon..." Noren smiled hungrily and raised his goblet. "To our coming success."

Nedain smiled back with a raised cup and dagger edged smile. "To settled debts."

CHAPTER 36

"THIS IS GOING TO be a *night to remember*!" Master D'gui announced loudly, giggling at her own joke.

Ceahan merely turned away, slightly embarrassed. Ghen looked confused, and Em pretended he hadn't heard.

"Get it?" she asked. "A 'night to remember' is a common phrase, but in this case, we want Em to—"

"Oh!" Ghen said. "I get it now." He chuckled "That's clever."

Ceahan rolled his eyes. "Was it?"

"Oh, you're no fun," Master D'gui said.

Again, Em pretended not to hear.

Master D'gui saw her patient looking pointedly away and decided he wasn't any fun either. These boys just didn't have the same highly developed sense of humor she did.

"Fine," she said, "let's get on with this. Let's count everything off. Ghen, do you have the ink and parchment?"

"Yes, ma'am."

Master D'gui lamented having neglected the faker's lane warping effect for so long. So this time, Ghen was aside with a lamp and a small table to write down anything she or Ceahan told him so it wouldn't be overlooked later.

"The mapping sand?"

"Right here, master," Ceahan said pointing to the tall jar.

"Go ahead and spread it out," she commanded.

Em watched with interest as the grains of fine powder were poured out but said nothing.

"Perfect." Master D'gui clapped when the jar was emptied. "I have the tea and the mix. Yesterday, we never used the mixture to wake Em up, but we will be doing that tonight. If things go as I hope, we may even do it repeatedly." With everything in place, she asked, "Are you ready, Em?"

His voice came out little more than a whisper. "Yes."

Em laid back in the seat and Ceahan took his place behind him. Soon the mapping sand thrummed to life and once again everyone stared at the shining wonder in motion. To Em the idea of having someone in your head was odd, and the magic tingled as if a feather duster was being used on the inside of his skull.

"Last call," Master D'gui said. "If you need to visit the necessary, I suggest you do it now."

No reply.

"Once we begin, I fear things will start to happen quickly," she continued. "As we agreed, it is too large a risk to let the faker remain unchecked. We've already seen the faker will fight if it feels threatened, so the plan is simple.

"First, get it away from its current location. While I am not an expert on the mind, our quarry chose this nest intentionally, probably because of how it can hurt Em. However, this location will give it none of the food we currently suspect it desperately needs. Like it or not, the faker has no choice but to leave.

"When it's out of the nest, we will test various ways of slowing the faker, if not stopping it outright. This will include both using magic and also waking Em up. It, so far, has not been active when Em is awake. If that trend continues, we will try to use that to our advantage. Are there any questions, or anything else before we begin?"

Ceahan paused for Ghen or Em to reply before he did.

"No master."

She nodded. "It's time then. Ceahan, the first thing is to analyze. Have you located the faker?"

"The faker is dormant," he said quickly, having already located it. "It's right where we left it."

"Show us."

The sand spread into the now familiar web of Em's mind. Em and Ghen gawked in renewed wonder at the spectacle. Neither, whether they remembered seeing it before or not, were used to such sights. Soon, the view of the sand focused on a set of passages. Among the golden roads was a small and dark purple mass, the faker.

"I thought it would be bigger," Em commented.

"Yes well, it looks smaller than I remember as well," Master D'gui said.

"It looks right to me," Ceahan said. "Maybe it gets a little bigger when it wakes, but if it does it can't be by much."

"Please note that Ghen," Master D'gui said. A moment later, she added, "Now that I think about it, you're right. If it was much larger it couldn't impersonate being in the pathway like an impulse. I guess my imagination inflated it."

Ghen paused in the middle of a stroke. "Should I keep writing then?"

"Yes, just note that it could be a mistake. The details are inconclusive."

"Yes miss." Ghen scratched his head, trying to figure out how to spell 'inconclusive,' and decided to just write that it was 'muddy' instead.

The cross-tribe mystic pushed her glasses further up and stared intently at the grains of dark sand. "Be warned, little mite," Master D'gui whispered, "I'm a fan of history, and the fact you seem to erase it makes you no friend of mine. Subject of study or not, I won't play fair."

"I don't think anything has changed since our little red event," Ceahan said, referring to Em's colorful display of strange power.

"That's fine. I can't think of anything else we need to confirm. Em, I think it's time you took a nap."

Em nodded sadly.

After Master D'gui poured him a cup of her soothing concoction, she gave him a pat on the shoulder. "Don't worry, this is a light dose. You won't be asleep long. Unless I miss my guess, when you wake up, your memory will be as sharp as one of your swords."

Em smiled softly. "Thank you, master." He took a deep draft of the mixture and laid back, doing his best to relax.

Master D'gui turned from Em as he began to slip away, her eyes focusing on the sand.

"Ceahan, tell me the instant Em is asleep. Also, the moment you feel a change in the faker."

"Yes, master."

Master D'gui knew what she was about, and her potion worked well. It wasn't long before Em was overcome by the deep breaths of rest.

"He's out," Ceahan confirmed.

Master D'gui didn't reply, only nodding her head. The moment she heard his words, she began to tap her foot rhythmically.

"One... two... three..." she counted under her breath.

When her count reached forty-three, the apprentice gave his second report. "The faker is beginning to change. It's not awake yet, but its presence is building."

Back to one then. "One... two... three..."

This count took much longer, and more than once Master D'gui doubted if she'd double counted or skipped a number.

The specs of sand began to glow a slightly brighter purple, looking less like a shadow on the path and more like an impulse inside it.

Ceahan looked up at his teacher. "It's awake."

"Ghen," Master D'gui dictated, "note that from first rest to the faker's awakening was around forty-three seconds. The faker's full awakening process was somewhere between two minutes and twenty to two and forty seconds."

Ghen didn't reply, but she heard the scribbling of his quill.

The faker slowly began to move along the pathways, now fully taking to its role of hiding among the mind, pretending to be an impulse. Master D'gui walked back to Em and quickly did her own reaching into his mind.

She didn't seek the faker, instead, she checked in on the newly repaired mental lanes. One of her largest worries was that the red glow from before would return while Em was asleep. If another event like that occurred, anything could happen. The unknown was always interesting, but in her experience, it could be very dangerous too.

Luckily, for now, all was silent.

"Has the faker gone far?" she asked, looking back at the sand.

"Not yet. I think its course is towards the repaired paths, but if it is, it's taking a detour to get there."

"Looking for a meal?"

"Possibly master," Ceahan said.

"Keep track of it, and—"

"Wait! The faker is shifting directions," Ceahan announced, cutting Master D'gui off.

The master was in no way offended by the interruption. "Can you tell where?"

Ceahan took a moment to answer. "I think it's located a meal. The faker is speeding up and fast."

The sand began to blur as Ceahan kept pace with the tiny creature.

The faker charged along paths, but occasionally reached across, only barely holding onto the pretense of being an impulse in favor of speed.

Master D'gui grinned. "That seems risky, and lines up with the starvation theory."

Ceahan shifted uneasily. "Should we wait until it enters where the memories are?"

"No, let's wake Em now," Master D'gui decided. She picked up her prepared mixture and pulled the cork out of the bottle. Waving it in front of Em's face, the hard scent of the encapsulated powder brought Em out in moments, shaking his head in a daze.

"Wh... What is happening?" he asked lazily.

"The faker moved to attack, but shifted towards your memories after a moment," Master D'gui explained.

The visualization on the mapping sand showed that the faker was slowing in its movement.

Ghen smiled off to the side. "It's the moment of truth, folks."

"Indeed it is, Ghen." Master D'gui could see the faker was slowing in the sand, but it was impossible to tell if it was starting to hibernate. "Ceahan, is it going dormant?"

"No. I don't think it is, master."

They had yet to confirm exactly what the faker would do if Em awoke suddenly and many of their plans depended on it. It could return to the nest it started from, ignore Em being awake to continue its hunt or try to wait for Em to go back to sleep by hibernating where it was.

The faker slowed until it stopped in the middle of the pathway, but its color did not fade.

"Ceahan, are you sure it isn't hibernating?"

"Yes, master."

It just sat there.

"What is it doing?" Master D'gui wondered aloud. She hadn't expected it to stop and not hibernate. The response did not sit well with her. "Hmm…" She needed more information. "Do any of you have any insight as to what it's doing?"

"No master."

The rancher shrugged. "Sorry miss, not this time."

"Perhaps it suspects a trap." Despite having only just woken up, Em's mind was already sharp.

Master D'gui was willing to follow this line of thought. "Please explain, Em."

"You wanted to force it into sleep, away from its hiding place, yes?"

"That was my hope. Without the opportunity to kill you, we could lock it up while it was immobile."

Em nodded. "What if the faker suspects this?"

She considered this. "Interesting hypothesis. However, that indicates a higher intelligence than the base instinct we would assume such a small organism follows. What you suggest implies it has guessed it's being watched by an outer presence and trying to outsmart it. That's very advanced thinking."

Ceahan chewed his lip. "Will you make a move against it, master?"

"No, but I think it's time Em had more tea."

"Master, if Em goes back to sleep, my guess is that the faker will go back to what it was doing before." Ceahan sounded worried. "That means Em either loses memories or the faker attacks those paths again."

"My thinking aligns with yours, then." Master D'gui's eyes were locked on the mapping sand.

Ceahan still wanted more of an explanation. "Then why put him to sleep? Right now, it's got to be burning energy, and it's not eating anything. If we wait, the faker will be forced to make a choice."

Master D'gui shook her head. "Tonight, the most frightening thing is the unknown. Whether the faker is intelligent or not, Em returning to sleep should put it back on the same course as before. That means we can at least predict its actions. Knowing what it will do within reason will make catching it that much easier. If the faker is suspicious somehow and we force it into a decision, it may do absolutely anything, and we won't have any way to predict what it will do. That is the worst-case scenario for us right now."

The apprentice nodded his understanding.

Master D'gui didn't need to give Em more relaxant. His eyes were already beginning to look drowsy again, the effect of the mixture fading.

"Lay back, Em. We will take good care of you."

Dreamily, the boy said, "Thank you master, I have chosen to trust you. After all, you make me think of Ins..." Em's drowsy words faded to gibberish. He fought the sleep, and his eyes opened and closed multiple times, but the tea took hold of him quickly.

"He's out again," Ceahan announced, but Master D'gui had seen that already.

Even now, she was tapping her foot again. "One... two... three..."

Minutes passed, and eventually, she lost count.

"Bah!" she cried. "I was somewhere around seven minutes. Has there been any change that we can't see on the sand?"

"Em's sleep is getting deeper, but I can't feel any change in the faker."

"This is what we get for trying to make an attempt to capture the faker today. Not that we had a choice," Master D'gui said angrily. "We don't know enough to make effective predictions. This behavior isn't what I expected at all. Ghen, note that the faker did *not* go back to sleep when we woke Em and that it hasn't moved for a long time after he was out again."

The sound of the scratching pen flew out from Ghen's desk.

"I don't understand it either," Ceahan admitted. "It's still burning a lot of energy and getting nothing for it."

Master D'gui began to pace in front of the mapping sand. "It could be waiting to see if Em will wake up again. I'm still not sure why, but it appears to be highly averse to acting while Em is awake."

Ceahan shrugged without breaking his focus on Em's mind. "Can't we go back to your first plan, then? If the faker's going to just sit there, we can trap it now."

"Yes, but we are working with tools I've only just put together. We also aren't sure how the faker will react to my magic. Add to that, I'm not sure where the faker even is."

Ceahan's face became confused. "Master, I can show you where it is."

"Not like that. I mean we don't know how important these passages are. If we try to trap the faker here, there's a chance it could kill Em the moment we tried to act."

"Should we give up then?" Ceahan asked. "Simply watch and try again later."

"What?" Ghen asked in surprise. "I know I wasn't the biggest plan of poking the thing to start with, but didn't you say it was risky to leave it alone with that red stuff happening?"

"Yet again," Master D'gui said thoughtfully, "we face a choice where neither option looks like the right one."

Ghen, looked uneasy at the thought. "So, what do we do?"

"Make our own way." Master D'gui grinned, as an idea began to form. "Okay, here is what we'll do. A bit of 'wait' and a bit of 'go.' Poor Em will probably lose more memories than I'd like, but compromises must be made."

Ceahan looked skeptically at his mentor. "Compromises? Exactly how big a compromise are we making, master?"

"Nothing drastic," she reassured. "As I said before, I have prepared a combination of ways to try to trap it. Instead of going straight to trying to put them to full use, we will test them.

"Our evidence suggests the faker is starving, and so far, all it's done is burn energy. If we are correct, hunger will make it do something soon. While it chases a meal, I'll put a kind of wall in its way. Far enough ahead that the faker shouldn't deviate. We can monitor it to see if our faker avoids it. If it doesn't, we'll be able to see if my ideas will stop or slow the faker. The compromise is that the faker will get the chance to feast while I work out the flaws in my method."

"Well, he's gone this long without memories. It can't hurt too bad to lose a last few."

Ghen didn't look like he agreed with Ceahan, but was smart enough to see that this was the best solution at the moment.

No complaints were raised, so they waited.

It was another few minutes before the faker moved again. Master D'gui guessed slightly over fifteen.

"Master," Ceahan whispered excitedly. "I think I know why it waited."

"Speak quickly. We can't lose it."

"Yes, Em's in a deeper sleep. His mind shifted again as his sleep deepened. It was right after that change that the faker started to move."

Master D'gui nodded her understanding. "It was waiting for it then. Hiding until it was more likely Em would stay asleep. Ghen?"

"Already writing," he said.

"Perfect."

The faker ran slower than before this time and did not jump paths.

"Back to the imitation game, I see. You're no longer willing to take the risk of running fast," Master D'gui said to the sand.

"It could be Em was right, and it suspects something is happening. Maybe not so specific as Em suggested, but a sense of danger at least."

Master D'gui was glad to see Ceahan was putting real thought into the case.

"That's possible, Ghen please note that down. Also, note that it could be that instead, the faker feared that it had made too much noise running earlier and that it thought it woke Em up."

Ceahan grimaced.

"What is it?" his master asked urgently.

"Nothing," he said quickly. "I just... well, your theory's way better than mine."

"Don't worry about that. Your idea was good, I'm glad you are willing to admit that you might be wrong, but I might be too. That's why we noted both." Master D'gui winked.

Laying a hand on both Em and Ceahan, Master D'gui tied her senses in with her apprentice's so that she could feel the faker as he did. There was depth to the little creature. Its song was an ominous one to be sure, and she could imagine it as ravenous. Yet there was something else about it. Layers beyond the innate, some which resounded with the quiet music, called magic. It was a song no creature like this shouldn't be able to sing, yet it could. A fact the master hoped to use to her advantage.

"Ceahan, confirm for me, where is it heading?"

"To eat I believe."

"Directly, or is it still circling towards the healed pathways?"

Ceahan hesitated and sounded confused when he found his answer. "Directly."

That was what she had hoped and feared. Those pathways were bringing out Em's power, and that power had burned this little intruder. Naturally, it should counterattack. Starting out, it had gone to do just that, but now its priority had changed.

"Ghen, note the following. I suspect that since it used some of its energy to stay awake, the faker shifted its goal. Food is now more pressing than the risk those pathways present."

"More evidence to the starving theory," Ceahan said to himself.

That and more, Master D'gui knew. Whatever that red light was, it was a threat to the faker's survival. To ignore such a big risk could only mean there was an even bigger one. If that threat was starvation, it might mean the faker didn't have enough energy to destroy the mental lanes and still hunt enough to survive.

Master D'gui feared how the others would react, but to be present of mind, she needed to say it. "I fear our target is reaching the end of its life. If it has the inclination to take Em with it, that could happen tonight. I don't know if anything for sure, but I think at this point there is no stopping."

The silence after her announcement was palpable.

To fill the empty air and stay focused, Master D'gui explained what she was doing as she crafted her spell. "I'm going to test my trap by putting a barricade ahead of it. Let me know if the faker becomes aggressive. My first barrier is a medical technique designed to let the body's functions flow while stopping alternative living components. I'm not sure how it will affect the impulses, so I'm going to layer it around the mental lanes."

"Do I need to write that?" Ghen asked nervously. He hadn't caught half the words and understood even less from what he had.

"No, I'm testing a wall. Write down, if 'wall one' fails or succeeds."

"Yes ma'am," Ghen said more confidently.

Using directions from Ceahan, she placed the first barrier in the faker's course.

"Now let's see how it likes this." Despite the seriousness of the situation, Master D'gui could feel herself beginning to grin from ear to ear. The discovery, the intrigue, the excitement!

On the mapping sand, grains shifted to give a quickly approaching pathway a halo of glittering silver as Ceahan's senses picked out his master's power.

The faker never altered course, and it collided directly with the barrier.

"Yes!" Master D'gui shouted. She leapt with excitement as the barrier held, and the faker was suddenly stopped in its tracks.

The purple mass on the sand seemed to push against it but soon gave up with little effort. It stretched to a new mental lane and continued its journey.

Ghen smiled brightly and quickly wrote,

First one worked great!

"It held master. You should be able to catch it with that." Ceahan's voice was infected with excitement.

Master D'gui took three deep breaths, calming herself. "No, that was good, but we don't know for sure that this will let us capture the faker. The barrier was effective, which was the point, but I'm not sure how much effort the faker put into breaking it. Also, don't forget the magic it unleashed against Em yesterday. That barrier won't so much as dampen such magic. For safety, we must keep testing."

"So, this next one will be a different wall?" Ghen asked.

"Yes, 'wall one' was a success. This will be 'wall two.' I'll admit, this one I'm more hesitant about after Em's red light."

"What is this one?" Ceahan asked.

"Well, it's not actually medical. It's something a sorcerer came up with to try to catch other people with magic. A way to slow only those who have the art. I thought, since the faker has some magic and Em had none, it would work as a selective net. However, this red glow changes things."

"Sorry to interrupt, master, but the faker is going to catch an impulse."

"Let it," Master D'gui said without hesitation. She followed up with a quote from an old dwarven general: "'Life is a resource, and this is a part we can spare.'"

She went back to Em and attuned again to Ceahan. Instead of focusing on the faker and putting a barrier in its way, Master D'gui set up a very small part of her second barrier elsewhere in Em's mind to observe its effects.

Nothing, or nothing noticeable, happened. She watched as other inhabitants of the mind, the defenders and workers that kept the mental roads intact naturally, mill through the net as if it were decorative.

"Okay, we'll try this one on the faker too." Finding the faker with Ceahan's help, she set up a second test in the faker's way. This time making the 'wall' smaller, still fearing side effects.

The sand moved as the magic took shape. The barrier looked like a net, with threads of white coiled around the road and reaching out in a starburst. The faker came to the second barrier and passed right through it. The faker didn't even seem to realize it was there. The only effect it had was that the purple form shivered as it went through.

"I think it slowed, master, but not much, if at all," Ceahan reported, disappointed.

"Ghen note that down," Master D'gui said sadly, taking a moment to remove the second wall from Em's mind.

"So, it didn't work?" Ghen tried to confirm.

"That's not exactly correct. It could have been that there was too little netting, or that the faker's power was too weak. We'll consider it inconclusive."

"Got it," Ghen said, scribbling down the note in his own words once again.

"Do you have any other barriers, master?" Ceahan asked nervously as he watched the faker catch up to yet another impulse, leaving a trail of warped passages in its wake.

"Not that I need to test. There is one more, but it's a common medical spell made for amputation. That's our most drastic option. We'll save it until we absolutely need it."

Ghen looked up from his paper, clearly not following the conversation between the two mystics.

"Nothing about that needs to be noted," Master D'gui informed him. "I'll explain if it comes to using that method, but I'm hoping it won't."

There was a pause as Master D'gui watched, biting the tip of her nail in thought, as the faker closed on another target. It was now in its hunting grounds and would eat until content or until it figured it was well enough to turn back to its original goal of destruction.

"Master?" Ceahan asked when she didn't say anything. "What's next?"

She sighed. "I guess now we go for the big one."

"The big one?"

"Yes, Ceahan. First, give us a wider view of where the faker is now."

The glittering sand scattered and reformed into a view further out, where the purple light of the faker was only one of many colorful travelers journeying down Em's private roads.

"Good, now draw me an outline around the faker. Round up, in size, I'm going to trace this and begin to build a large cage to contain the faker. Once in our large cage, I'll progressively make smaller and smaller ones, cornering the invader."

Along with what he felt in Em's mind, Ceahan imagined a sphere of glittering red marking a wide birth around the purple dot. The sand acted accordingly. Grains flew from all over the projection to form the glittering orb.

Master D'gui nodded gratefully. "That will do nicely. Be sure to set it slightly ahead, I don't want to shift things around a lot. To start with, I'll use our first wall. Once it's smaller, I'll add a thicker layer of the second inside the first. Ready?"

"Yes."

"Should we wake Em?" Ghen asked off to the side.

Master D'gui considered the notion heavily. "I want to catch the faker unaware. If it has any sense of danger, it might be better if it feels it can hunt freely. In the case that it finds a way to break out, we may try again with Em conscious."

With her hands already pressed to Em's head, Master D'gui began her work. Her gaze flicked between Em and the red sphere Ceahan projected in the sand as she went along, tracing the orb's outline. The silver halo glistened as it spread over the map.

As she traced it out, Ceahan shifted the sand, the red flecks free to turn silver to show the growing change in Em's mind.

While turning between Em and the sand, Master D'gui spotted something that made her slightly nervous. "Ceahan, is the faker chasing an impulse in the sphere?"

"Not anymore," Ceahan said. At his imaginings, an impulse flared a little brighter as it left the sphere, the purple light of the faker on its tail.

Master D'gui quickly covered that space with the barrier and worked from that point to spread out the veil of silver.

"Then let's hope this works," she said nervously.

The faker reached the edge of the barrier quickly enough and was once more stopped, colliding with the wall in a soundless impact. It pushed, but quickly gave up, opting to stretch to a new road and continue the chase. Yet this one was blocked too. The faker pushed again, and again gave up, changing paths only to find itself still unable to continue.

It pushed again, but when it failed this time, it didn't switch paths. Instead, it pushed again. The sand couldn't show it, but Master D'gui could feel through her art the little form pushing with great might to break through. For all its efforts though, it wasn't enough. The faker failed, and the silver wall towered before it.

Master D'gui smiled, and, just as it gave in, she completed the sphere. "It's trapped."

Yet her smile didn't last long.

"The faker is storing up its power. I feel it." Ceahan's voice was soaked in apprehension.

"It's trying to break the barrier." Even as Master D'gui spoke, the faker fired a pulse of magic. A flash like the one that had sent Em into a seizure, only smaller, tore down the passage, leaving it scarred and burned.

Signals of pain fled from the wounds, and Em's face twitched slightly.

The wall, however, was unaffected. The faker's power had no structure that the wall could even attempt to halt. Thus, the attack and defense merely passed one another by, like strangers in the markets.

"Master, use your second wall if it attacks again," Ceahan suggested. "I felt something in that. That flash or pulse or whatever is based on our same power."

"It's worth a try. Let me know when it's going to try another burn."

The faker, its attack done, rammed the silver wall once again and was disappointed to find that its efforts did not affect its cage. Not that even the point of getting through remained any longer. Its quarry was too far, and the faker sensed closer game that could satiate its cravings. The faker gave up and reversed course further into the sphere, chasing a new impulse. This one, they all saw, was inside the cage.

Ceahan, as was his duty, announced what they'd already noticed. "It's changed its target."

"I don't think it can feel the barrier until it hits it," Master D'gui said. "Otherwise, why change paths twice to try to press through, unless it didn't know it couldn't go around? Ghen?"

The quill scribbled.

She continued, "I'm going to build another barrier. One which will be much smaller. I don't need to be as cautious if it can't see the walls."

The mapping sand glittered as a new silvery orb was crafted within the first, possibly half the size of the original. Master D'gui was able to create it much faster by using part of the original sphere to make the second. This saved much needed time and made it so the new orb kept the faker nearer to its center, where the creature couldn't easily escape before the ball was fully formed.

The moment it was finished, Master D'gui dispelled her larger creation. Grains of sand scattered to make new impressions as the larger silver halo vanished from sight.

Ceahan adjusted his view, and the sand shifted again making the sphere larger so that they could watch what was happening inside in more detail.

The sand consolidated into this new form just as another impulse vanished beneath the small purple mass. A memory lost, but one gone, so that others might yet remain. A tragic, but Master D'gui knew, unavoidable sacrifice.

"It's found another," Ceahan muttered.

The faker took off, roaring towards the nearest wall of the barrier. On the other side, its prey ran, unaware of its pursuer.

It was attempting to stretch from one lane to another when it met the wall, its body of purple and black ooze feeling the obstruction. It had no force to push, so the faker tried to go around and found it couldn't. There the faker paused.

The strange being did not try to force its way but seemed to almost observe pressing against the barrier to figure out why it couldn't go forward. Slowly it pushed harder and harder. Its form again became amorphous as it looked for a crack or flaw, yet the invader couldn't even begin to understand the silver halo's texture.

"It's pooling power again!" Ceahan warned.

Master D'gui wasted no time to reply. She weaved a subtle net all around the faker of her second barrier. If the second wall type couldn't stop the faker, maybe Ceahan was right, and it could stop its attack.

"Here it goes!"

The sand flashed just after Ceahan shouted. The light flickered and fizzled, burning away Master D'gui's web, but the attack did not escape the web itself. It was trapped in the heart of the blaze, and Ceahan wondered if there was any chance that the faker would be seared with its own malcontented fire.

The moment the light faded, flickers of impulses streamed from the path the faker rested on as it cried out in pain, and the mind's defenders ran to investigate. Like a thief caught in the lamplight, the faker didn't wait a moment after the flare faded but darted off its speed beyond what an impulse should be capable of.

"Wall two succeeded in stopping the faker's attack." Master D'gui announced triumphantly.

Parchments scrambled as Ghen set his current page aside and got a new one to keep taking notes on.

"Where's it going?" Ceahan asked, watching the faker flee quickly away.

"I don't know," Master D'gui said slowly observing the sand.

It was moving in a direction similar to the way it had come. Both the master and apprentice wondered if it was going back to where it nested, but maybe not. They saw its heading would be off if that were the case. That direction was closer to the pathways they'd repaired in the afternoon, but that direction wasn't quite right either. Yet it was moving oddly. It followed many paths as if trying to fake being an impulse, but wasn't afraid to swing to a different road either. It seemed to sway one way and then the other as it moved through the open space within their unseen cage.

"Is it trying to decide where to go?" Ceahan asked.

"Unsure whether to retreat and take Em hostage or destroy the pathways? Possibly, but I don't know. Indecision requires intelligence beyond the instinctual."

"I guess it doesn't matter what it chooses," Ceahan said, "both places it wants to go are outside its cage."

"As the faker will soon learn," Master D'gui agreed as they followed the purple speck while it closed in on yet another wall of the barrier.

"Hang on," Ceahan said, "it's slowing."

"Really? No... wait."

The representation wasn't so sharp to show everything, but now the faker was slowing enough that it was becoming obvious even on the mapping sand. It wasn't just slowing, it settled into the rhythm and speed of an impulse, sliding more and more in line with the direction for finding the repaired pathways.

"I think it's made its choice," Ceahan said.

"Ceahan, you'll see it first," Master D'gui said intently "tell me the moment it touches the wall. I'm going to make a sphere around it the moment it does."

Master D'gui looked from the sand to Em again, feeling her halo of silver. She might feel the hit of the faker herself, but she needed to be sure. The moment it found the edge of their ball she'd trap it in an even smaller cage.

As Ceahan focused more on the faker, so did the sand, unintentionally. The view zoomed close until it was a mass of purple light with only the fringe's golden line of the path at its edges.

Soundless in the sand, the faker thudded against the wall.

"Now!"

At Ceahan's cry, Master D'gui moved with a cold calm, unwilling to allow the loss of focus that could be detrimental to her craft.

The silver halo exploded with new walls from the point of impact as she closed the faker in once more with a shell only a fourth of the size of the sphere before. The smaller sphere made quick work but was still almost too slow.

Hitting the wall, the faker reversed its direction immediately and sprinted away in the opposite direction.

Had Master D'gui made the sphere any bigger it might not have closed before the faker escaped its far end. Alas, she was successful, and the faker found itself again barred from going any further.

She took her hands away with a long breath of relief, dispelling the bigger sphere. "Wow... Well, that was close."

Master D'gui wiped sweat from her brow and realized this was beginning to take a toll on her too. She didn't have the endless reserves of power that Ceahan did, but the strain was more mental than physical in this case. Such precise work, and needed so quickly, was difficult at any level of skill and it had been a long time since she'd had to practice this.

She took a quick breath and went back to Em. She wanted to rest, but if the faker did another attack, then...

It was as if Ceahan, or the faker, were reading her mind.

"It's going to attack!" the apprentice yelled.

Master D'gui leaped forward to string up another defense, but it was going to be too late!

The sand flashed, in a way, but it was as if the attack dribbled out from around the faker instead of its strong burst like before. The light crackled pitifully, only burning the near edges of the pathway.

Master D'gui froze. "What's it doing Ceahan?" She wondered if this was something new.

The mapping sand was still almost all a view of the faker, so there was little to tell from the purple blob alone. A single impulse of pain came out from the mental lane, announcing that some annoyance had appeared.

Ceahan didn't reply.

His master made a small clap of her hand to snap him out of it. "Ceahan, what's happening?"

The apprentice looked up at her slowly. "Master, I think... it's going to sleep."

CHAPTER 37

"I BEG YOUR PARDON," Master D'gui said tersely. "It's what? Show me... show us, on the sand!"

The glittering grains raced to their new places as Ceahan's mind took a wider view.

There it sat, the purple mass, motionless once more. Slowly its color was fading deeper and darker. Reducing what energy pulled its life together.

Ceahan grinned. "It's going to sleep. That attack, if it failed, what if it's out of strength? A well without water."

Master D'gui watched the sand carefully but said nothing.

"Then... you did it?" Ghen asked hopefully. "You starved it out?"

"Yeah... yeah, I think we did!" Ceahan pumped his arm, and the mapping sand began to fall apart as he looked away.

"Enough!" Master D'gui clapped with enough magical force that the sand shivered, and the sound echoed around the walled garden.

She brought all the excitement to a shuddering halt and left the two in silence.

"Something is not right," she said darkly.

Focusing on Em, she created yet another internal barrier, closing the faker in an even smaller prison. This one was small enough that she felt comfortable layering it with her second type of wall on the inside, in case of some new attack. She left the larger outer barrier in place this time in case the faker broke out in some surprising display.

"What's wrong, master?" Ceahan worked up the courage to ask.

"I don't know... not yet."

She attuned her senses to the sharper ones of her apprentice's and searched around the faker for minutes, trying to find what it was that bothered her.

The faker faded to its darker hibernation. However, she noticed that bursts of light occasionally flickered on its surface. The amorphous invader was a black thunderhead, the lights its bolts of destruction meandering behind its cloudy veil.

"What is wrong with this picture?" she asked herself. She pulled away from Em and began to pace. "It met the barrier, ran to escape, failed, attempted to attack, failed, and then went dormant."

Where was the flaw? Something nagged at her, ate at her, screamed at her from the back of her mind, but she could not make out the words. The more she strained to hear it, the louder it yelled, still unheard.

"Something... something about what it did? Maybe what it didn't do? Let's see, its goal was... Ha! That's it!" she yelled in excitement, loud enough that Em shifted under Ceahan's hands despite the drug.

Ceahan watched her tentatively. "Master?"

She turned on him excitedly the moment he spoke. "Ceahan! Your theory, not the most recent," she clarified, "the one before. Do you remember it?"

"Which one... uh, wait... Master, I'll admit I'm lost."

She wanted to scream! "The faker, it went back and forth, before it hit the wall and we trapped it. You said it was deciding where to go, yes?"

"I thought so."

"Do you stand by that?"

Ceahan shrank under her urgent gaze. "Should I?"

"I should hope so. However, more than the theory itself, where was it trying to go before we caught it?"

"To the repaired paths..." he said, confused and unsure, "... to destroy them?"

"Exactly!" she said triumphantly. "Follow that logic. The faker goes through all this work to get food so that it can destroy the mental lanes we repaired. Then it decides it has enough energy to undo all our work, but it gets caught. Here is what's been bugging me, the faker didn't do anything to burn much energy before we caught it, but what happens then? It runs out of strength anyways?"

"That doesn't make sense," Ceahan said thoughtfully. "If it thought it had the strength to destroy the repaired paths, it should have at least had enough for a single attack."

"Full marks," Master D'gui said, turning her eyes back to the sand to turn her mind towards the next problem.

"So, it's not over?" Ghen asked, fear creeping into his voice.

Ceahan shook his head disappointedly. "Not yet, rancher. But master, if it's not dying from starvation, what is it doing?"

"A good question. Waiting for more impulses to come to it? No, it's possible, but that seems unlikely. Another question is why stop its attack? It didn't sputter out because it was tired, which means the magic was intentionally aborted instead."

"Maybe it knew it didn't have the gumption to fight out and break the roads," Ghen suggested hopefully.

Master's head bobbed left and right, weighing the idea. "Then why go to them in the first place?"

"Maybe, master, it had eaten just enough to go, break the roads it needed to, and come back to hunt or go back to sleep at its hostage spot," Ceahan suggested.

"Just enough?" Master D'gui peered at the faker and noticed a splotch on her glasses. She took them off to clean the lenses. "That suggests it stopped its own attack because it reached or passed its usable limit to meet all its needs and survive."

There was little Master D'gui hated more than not knowing, and they knew next to nothing. While this experiment was fascinating it was also becoming infuriatingly confusing.

"That takes a complex understanding of its own natural limits. Can you tell me how much you can do before you run out of strength to such an exact measure, or even give a guess you would call reasonably precise?"

Ceahan thought for a second but had to shake his head.

Master D'gui finished polishing off the spot on her glasses. "Either knowledge or a guess would take an intelligence even greater than the idea of planning ahead. This organism is incredibly small, it can't possibly think in so many layers. The closest option that could explain something like this would be like when those cruel life-shapers use magic to set conditions on living creatures they've made into wea..."

A chill wind blew through the garden and Master D'gui was stricken silent. It was like she was turned to stone with her glasses still frozen in her hands. The only part of the master that moved were her ever searching eyes. They darted back and forth as her mind raced and an ominous chill crawled up her spine.

Ghen and Ceahan stared at her. Her mutterings were too quiet for either of them to follow what she'd said, and they waited expectantly for her to come to some conclusion.

When Master D'gui found her answer, she was horrified. "Please... no," she gasped. Like the small crackle of pebbles before a landslide, her words were the precursor to a flurry of motion. Her hands shook wildly as she fought to get her glasses back on her face. "Ceahan, Ceahan! The faker, what's it doing!"

"Um, nothing. It looks the same."

"No... No! Don't look, listen! Is there a sound, a signal, a vibration, debris being released, I don't care if it's singing *The Lay of Juniper* in the ember tongue, is it sending out anything?!" She jumped from where she was to Em's side in one inhuman leap.

"Uh..." Ceahan gaped for a moment but gave up on replying. Instead, the powerful apprentice poured his efforts into 'listening' to the faker.

The mapping sand shimmered at its edges as Ceahan's focus blurred from the visible. Yet as the image blurred, it did not do so uniformly. The faker was stable, a dark mass that flowed loosely in an orbit of sand.

Master D'gui waited by his side without saying a word, fearing to disturb him. However, she unknowingly started to urgently tap her foot.

"Stop... knocking," Ceahan said, focus not being his best trait.

Master D'gui pressed down on her foot, squatting slightly, to make it stop. For a moment, there was silence.

"Th-There is something," Ceahan muttered.

"Something?"

Ceahan opened his eyes and pointed to the sand.

From the faker, the sand shaped into transparent waves that poured out from the strange body at its source.

"I don't know what it is," Ceahan admitted. "It's like small... things I guess, coming from the faker. I don't think it's an attack, but maybe... a signal?"

Master D'gui almost fainted. She stumbled, and Ceahan reached out to catch her, but she caught herself.

"Keep an eye on Em!" she snapped, refocusing.

Ceahan went rigid at the reprimand and turned his attention back to their patient.

Master D'gui began to pace again, even faster in a small circle. Her frenzied mutters poured out like water. "This is impossible, but there it is. How, though? It's too small. I thought a mouse was the limit. No one has the experience and skill to do this, why even Dread R..."

Without warning, Master D'gui spun on her heel and stared at Em, or more accurately, his clothes, in fear. A *Yongarad* Marauder uniform. Pieces of the puzzle were beginning to finally fit together but into an awful image.

A million thoughts raced through the master's mind as it all came together. Her nails dug painfully into the palms of her hands as she clenched her fists and tears stung in her eyes. There was someone in Yongarad who could have done this, and the thought was sickening.

Too quietly for Ceahan to hear, Master D'gui growled the name.

"Rose."

Ghen stood from the desk and walked around it toward Master D'gui. "Ma'am, are you alright?"

"Designed?" Master D'gui hissed, in reply. Her face burned with wrath. "Using perverted black magic to do this to someone intentionally... that... that... that hag!" she screamed.

Ghen and Ceahan both took a step back.

The sand collapsed as Ceahan lost focus, but he jumped back to his place and the sand pulled itself back together quickly. However, the falling sand was enough to pull the master from her tantrum.

"Okay." She took a deep breath. "Okay." Another deep breath. "I'm okay," she said, with one more breath for good measure, and lifted her glasses to wipe her eyes.

Her demeanor was calm, but Ghen didn't dare step any closer. That anger and rage were still there, only contained. The fury burned behind her eyes hot enough to boil oceans. Those same eyes, while holding back that pain, turned toward Em with urgent purpose.

She strode to him and set straight to work.

Ghen looked on via the sand to see her tear away all her barriers around the faker until it was bare and completely free.

Ceahan stared wide eyed. "Master what are you—"

"They don't matter anymore," she said, cutting him off, "and it won't be free for long."

A new wall, azure blue in the sand, was laid like a tile near the faker. Then another, and another. Like pieces of a mosaic, Master D'gui put azure tiles in place one by one, working them into a shell around the small creature.

When a mental path was in the way of the tile, Master D'gui didn't hesitate, a bolt flashed, and she blew apart the road with her magic. Then she slipped a new tile in the newly freed space.

"What's she doing?" Ghen asked Ceahan, too scared to ask Master D'gui herself.

"She's isolating it, I think. I don't know what's going on, but she must be using that amputation spell to cut the faker off from Em completely."

"Burn it all!" the master cursed all of a sudden. "Ceahan, I told you to watch the faker!"

"What?" Ceahan snapped up, surprised at her sudden anger. She never yelled like this. He hadn't even lost control of the sand. It was still seeing everything. The shell, the paths, the faker they were all as clear as... "Oh."

He felt it now. The faker was clear, too clear.

Ghen peered at the sand. "Is it getting bigger?"

It was. Ceahan watched in dismay as the faker inflated. Growing steadily bigger. The bigger it grew, the faster it grew. He should've noticed it sooner.

"I'm sorry master I—"

"Not now!" she said urgently, working to finish the shell before the faker expanded enough to reach the edge.

Too late. She pressed a magical tile down, but the bulge of the faker got there first. It bulged out of the gap and whitened, threatening to burst like a stretched wineskin.

The strong spherical shape she'd attempted to create couldn't accommodate the bulge of the faker's new size. Master D'gui couldn't risk pushing against it. If it burst, who knew what it could release? Instead, she added more tiles, smaller and faster. They were weaker, but she had to fill the gap.

Two, three, four...

"Done!" she said with relief and waited to see if it would hold.

The sphere of azure tiles had a bulging deformation on its far side. Master D'gui knew how weakened the structure was by the oblong shape, but still, it might be enough. For tense moments, she waited.

Inside the sphere, the pathways that'd been caught along with the faker were lost to view beneath the black and purple mass of flesh. Yet, despite the push of the faker's attempts to keep growing, the seal held.

She turned and walked to the chair Ghen had been sitting in and dropped down hard.

"That's it," she said, out of breath. "We'll do the cleanup, but we're done for the night."

"Should we wake Em?" Ghen asked.

"No!" the master called urgently and tried to stand, but only plopped back into the chair, realizing just how exhausted she was. "At least, not yet. Try not to move him, either. I just created a huge obstruction in his head. I don't want it moving around, I'll secure it so that it will be safe enough... or I will in a minute anyways."

"I'll get you some water," Ceahan suggested, but Ghen stopped him.

"You stay here kid. I'll get the water." The rancher ran to the house.

He returned quickly with a small jug of water, which Master D'gui drained quickly.

Blinking in surprise, Ghen went back to the house and filled it up again. He also filled cups for himself and Ceahan.

When Master D'gui finished the second cup, she sighed with relief. "Thank you very much, Ghen. That was more excitement than I've had in a very long time, and I hope the most I have for an even longer time."

Ghen looked from master to apprentice and back. "So, what in blazes happened there?" he sounded desperate. "Ceahan said it was dead, you said it wasn't, you asked if it was talking or something, and turns out it was and then you shut it up? I'm so lost it ain't even funny, miss."

Master D'gui smiled with pity. "I'm sorry Ghen, quite a lot happened very quickly. I'd like to explain, but I'm too tired. I still need to finish up my work in Em, I can't let the shell interrupt the workings of his mind. Then I'm going to bed. In the morning, I will give a full account to you and Em. For now, let him rest."

Ghen nodded. "So... is it over now?"

She sighed. "That I guess I should answer. Despite how dire things might have seemed for a moment, that was excellent progress. I think we've learned some things, things that give me a much better guess at what the faker is and how this all came about. However, Em's troubles aren't over yet."

"Can you answer what's left, master?" Ceahan asked, still keeping an eye on the sphere, adamant not to let details slip past him again like the faker's growth.

"Well, as you might guess, the faker is sealed. If that truly was the root cause of Em's repeated amnesia, then this should be the end of it. I only hope the faker stays sealed. My work was shoddy at the end and the faker has surprised us too many times to assume it's out of tricks. We need to monitor Em for days, maybe even weeks, to make sure."

"Should we take turns watching him like we did last night?" Ghen asked.

"I'm sorry Ghen," Master D'gui said tiredly. "I'm not sure you can this time. Last night we had reason to believe things would go as they normally do for Em. We had reason to believe he'd be alright, and that if anything did happen, we could manage it easily enough. Tonight is too different, that seal alone is what must be monitored." She pointed to the azure shell in the mapping sand. "Sadly, you cannot watch the faker as we can. Don't blame yourself there's nothing for it. As for me, I'm sorry, but I'm too tired to take a shift. I'm very drained."

"I can stay up."

"Thank you Ceahan," she said slowly, "but even you will tire by morning. I would appreciate it if you would try, though. Do your best, but be sure to rest now and again for short spurts. Oh, and I'm sorry for shouting earlier."

"It's alright master, I made a mistake."

She shook her head slowly and lazily. "We all make mistakes, but that doesn't mean I should have been so snippy. Granted, it was urgent, and I was genuinely angry, but I shouldn't have been." She wiped her face, utterly exhausted.

"Yes, master. Thank you," Ceahan said, finding no better words for the situation.

Master D'gui took a deep breath and, with an effort, stood. "Alright, I need to finish my work. Then you two can take Em to an actual bed. He deserves a good rest."

She took a step toward Em, but paused, her eyes laden with pity. She went back to Ghen's little desk and borrowed the quill and a new slip of parchment. She bent over to write, for if she sat, she wasn't sure she could get up again without help.

"Miss? What are you writing?" Ghen asked, peeking around her shoulder.

Master D'gui finished and folded the page. "It's a note for Em. Tomorrow he's going to wake up and he's probably going to remember. He's going to be... so happy..." she sounded as if on the edge of tears. "I just don't have the heart to tell him face to face that, while his amnesia may be at an end, his trials aren't over yet."

CHAPTER 38

SLOWLY, EM OPENED HIS eyes. It was dark and he couldn't see much except for a dim light. His head felt strange, but he looked around the room. Sleep fogged his mind, but he recognized that he must be in Master D'gui's house. Every shelf and flat surface upheld unmistakable piles of cluttered research materials.

Em couldn't remember going to sleep in this room, but he did remember... He *did* remember! Em's addled mind snapped awake, and he sat up excitedly. As he shifted in bed, he heard the crackle of parchment.

The dim light came from a low burning candle on a bedside table. From its feeble light he saw that, in his haste, he'd rolled onto a sheet of folded parchment which was lying on his bed. He hoped it was not part of the master's research, after all, he did not want to upset her if she'd managed to...

I'm sorry, Em.

The first line jutted out of the fold after Em rolled onto it. Reading it, his thoughts came to a swift halt and so did his excitement.

Even before unfolding the page, Em suspected that things were amiss. As he'd realized only a moment before, he didn't remember entering this room. Maybe there was more he still couldn't remember.

I'm sorry, Em.
If by chance you do not know your name, then please know
you are Em. Nearby we should have set a journal of yours that

will explain more. I recommend reading it before continuing this letter.

If you do know this name and that the journal belongs to you, I have news. Some of it good, and some not.

You may be pleased to hear that the faker, what I believe to be the root cause of your memory loss, was contained. I truly believe that soon, if you can't already, you will be able to remember again.

The bad news is that the faker, while being contained, had a final surprise for us. None of us fully understand what happened yet.

However, it is already clear that between the faker's final surprise and this red glow you displayed, our work isn't finished yet. I'm sorry, but you need to persevere a little longer.

I will explain more in person when I have the chance, but first I wanted to give you time to rest.

Sleep well.

Signed, Master Ida D'gui.

As he finished the letter, Em's spirit fell. "Still more? All I have done, all I have suffered, and there is still more?"

A soft, unseen hand laid itself on Em's shoulder and Instinct's old kind voice came from the shadows sitting on the side of his bed.

Oh, Little Em. Any song may have a somber verse, but remember that doesn't make the tune a dirge. Ida's taking good care of you, and all she said was that it wasn't over, nothing more. Who's to say that the worst isn't behind you? Take this moment, Little Em, and remember that you can remember.

Em turned to look at Instinct, but while he could feel the presence of the voice, he still couldn't see a thing.

"I... Thank you," Em said awkwardly.

He felt foolish talking to nothing, but then Instinct seemed to smile back at him, and he felt a little less foolish even if he couldn't describe why.

Before Em knew it, he was feeling a little better. The voice was right, if nothing else he could remember again. Though Master D'gui's letter implied that there was still a chance that he might have forgotten a few things.

Em looked around and quickly found his journal atop the nearby chest of drawers. He wished to read it, but the candle was burning lower and lower. Opening his journal, he saw the light had already faded so much that it was harder to read than when he'd read the letter.

As the light continued to dim, he perceived another light from beneath the door of the master's guest room. Quietly, Em stood, and taking the journal, left the room and padded silently down the hallway. One glance out of the window told him that the sun hadn't yet broken the horizon but soon would. As he turned toward the living room, he found the source of the light.

A second lamp burned on a side table in the parlor next to a large chair. In that chair sat Master D'gui wrapped tight in a blanket with a book open on her lap.

Em was too quiet for her to notice him at first, and at the entrance of the sitting room, Em stopped to study the mystic for a moment.

She wore one of the same style of robes as the day before, but this was the first time he recalled seeing the scholar with her hair not tied tightly and neatly on top of her head. With the silver streaked hairs let down, the small pale horns she often hid poked through.

Something about having her hair down like that made Master D'gui appear younger, relaxed, and more at peace. More of the classic carefree satyr showed in her in that little moment than Em had yet seen in her. Slowly, she turned the page of her book and smiled as she continued to read.

It wasn't in the book, in her hair, or in anything she did but, despite remembering her from yesterday, Em had a strange feeling as if recognizing her from somewhere else. Something about her was familiar in a way she hadn't been before.

Behind his shadow, Instinct smiled, and while Em could not see Instinct, he was sure there were tears in his eyes. *It looks like you're Ida D'gui after all,* said the voice with a hopeful emphasis on her last name.

Yes, of course that's who she was. Who else would she be?

Finally, she became aware of Em. When she saw him, Master D'gui smiled and nodded his way. Em bowed in return and, taking a few steps forward, sat down before her and laid his journal on his lap. He was quite comfortable sitting on the floor, only grabbing a cushion to place under himself.

Master D'gui gave him a curious look but did not comment. The master seemed to understand that he wanted to read, and nodded her approval before returning to her own book.

Looking down at the small leather notebook, Em wondered where it came from and where he was from too. Then, as he had many times before, Em opened it and read...

> You go by the name Em Dér.
> I know you are confused, and I know why. You have forgotten again. I am writing this message to warn you. If you sleep, you will forget. I know this because I am you, a you that has been forgotten. That is what our life has become, living for a day to die in our sleep. Then, a new Em rises tomorrow with no memory of who we were.
>
> Em, even as I write this to you, I wonder how long we have been this way. I do not know who we once were or who we are supposed to be now. All I know is what I have been told, which I will pass on to you. We forget everything each day, but there is a chance to be whole again. This curse or sickness we have can be cured, Em.
> In the city of Henaden is a master of magic known as Master D'gui. Our guides told me Master D'gui will help us. I do not know why, but this may be our only chance. Trust Instinct and Nature, they will see us to our goal.

Also, you should know that whatever has been done to our mind has not affected everything about us. You will find that our body remembers much of what our mind cannot.

Seek Henaden, find Master D'gui, and find who we are supposed to be.

That is all we have to remember.

From the Em of yesterday.

Except that as he finished, he realized that it wasn't. Finally, this message and this journal were not all he had to remember, not anymore. The master's letter made it clear that there was more to come, but for the moment, Em paused to remember.

Leaning back from the journal, he turned his head towards the front of the house and the front window. The window faced east and with Henaden's staircase architecture, no building obstructed his view of the red light of dawn as it began to color the night sky.

Distant clouds rumbled a threat of foul weather, but despite the darkness, the morning light broke from beneath the shadow. The morning's sunrise brimmed on the horizon of every dawn for both the rich and the poor of this trade city. The light rose for each of them equally, and even with the storms still on the horizon, Em took a moment to appreciate the dawn beneath the storm. This would be a day he could finally remember.

"The Em of yesterday, of tomorrow, and myself here and now. We each can see this and keep it as one mind again." Em smiled. "That is all we have to remember."

EPILOGUE

TO THE NORTH AND west of Henaden, two figures sat upon a hilltop, watching the same sunrise break through the veil of night and shadow as Em. Both were in matching uniforms, each one very similar to the one that Em himself wore. However, compared to Em's, theirs were cleaner, newer, and did not have the same wear from long travel. Also, pinned clearly to their breasts, were metal signets. The sign of true marauders.

The signets on both were metal circles with an inlay shaped like the skull of an ox. Yet their signets weren't identical. Around its edge, Landrin's signet bore a single star stamped in it, speaking to his rank. Quell's signet bore no stars but needed none. His was made of black steel, instead of the normal silver. Despite its light-devouring black metal, it never lost the clarity of the symbol emblazoned upon it. The black badge named him not just as an officer, but as *the* officer. Only two other marauders wore black badges and only they equaled his rank.

Each of them headed a cohort of the Yongarad Marauders, each serving the needs of one of the Dread of Yongarad. That Quell had traveled so far into Ifeldia would have been unthinkable had it not been ordered by his Lord Dread in particular.

Their strange camp lay hidden near the cabin of a smuggler, or it would be his cabin if he were still alive. A loud smacking of lips and gulping sound meant that the Wodjok were having their morning meal.

Landrin groaned at the sound. "Do they have to do that every morning?"

"You'd swallow every meal whole too if you only had eight teeth," Quell pointed out to his junior officer.

"Then can't they do that somewhere else?"

"They could," Quell said. "If you want to tell them to move, be my guest."

Landrin didn't stir.

"I thought so," Quell said with a nod.

Of all the tribes of man, the wodjok tribe was one of the most set apart. Not only did the wodjok know that fact, but the scaled men reveled in it. They'd rather eat their overgrown pet bugs than take an order from someone like Landrin, who they saw as a weak outsider. They only took orders from their own or from someone they'd learned to fear.

"Wretched swamp filth. Why did we even have to bring them along?" Landrin complained, running a hand through his long kyate-siv hair.

"Because they're better trackers than you are, and they aren't all swamp filth. Don't forget, those two big shiny ones are desert filth."

Landrin huffed. "I still don't like them."

Quell sighed. "You need to learn not to swallow curd, if you don't have to. Wodjok aren't pleasant company, but it could be worse. Imagine if they were usarumai. They'd be even better trackers."

Landrin rolled his eyes. "Like hunting with a rabid dog. I admit sir, it would certainly be interesting, but I'd rather leave the beastmen to those under the dagger or maw." He was talking about the marauder factions whose signets bore a dagger or a depiction of open jaws as their mark instead of the ox skull.

Quell nodded. "They're interesting troops, but we've got the better of them. Dread Muden is a better backer than Dread Grevarion or old Dread Rose."

Landrin took a moment before he looked over both shoulders to make sure no one was around. Even though they were on the edge of camp, he still whispered.

"Does he actually think we'll find his sylwerd out here? He's been searching for the boy for ages now."

Quell grinned, shaking his head. "You're more skilled than smart, Lanny. If Dread Muden says he's here, he is. That power of his is no joke."

Landrin looked doubtful, but still whispered when he asked, "He really sees the future?"

Quell shrugged. "How would I know? I can't use magic. Ask Nero, maybe he can tell you. I don't honestly care. All I know is that Dread Muden seems to know things I don't."

"The wodjok haven't found a sign of him for weeks and, as you pointed out earlier, the only reason we brought them was that they're supposed to be our trackers. How long are we going to hunt around here?"

Quell stood up and dusted himself off. "Until the Lord Dread says we go somewhere else."

"But..."

"Shut it!" Quell said firmly and loud enough that the camp went quiet. Even the wodjok ceased their incessant gulping. "I don't give two drops that you've got complaints. I allow you to ask questions, but I've already given you an answer. We stay. Clear?"

Landrin was smart enough to only nod.

"Good lad," Quell said as he turned away.

When the lead marauder began to drift further away, the sound of the hissing laughter of the wodjok followed as they mocked Landrin amongst their little group.

The one-star marauder stood and glared at them, but made no challenge. Instead, Landrin went to take out his frustration on any lazy subordinate who'd been unfortunate enough to sleep late.

As Quell crossed the campground, the tent flap on the largest of the camp parted. From it stepped an elf. His hair was black as night and his face pale as the moon. Despite the early hour, the elf was clothed in all black buttoned up to the neck, covering every part of free flesh below his face. Quell preferred it that way, it even gave him the creeps, to see what was beneath those clothes.

"Quell." The elf beckoned.

The lead marauder changed direction, instantly walking straight to the tent where he dropped to a knee. "Dread Muden, sir, how may I serve?"

The figurehead of power gazed at Landrin in the distance. "What was the disturbance?"

In Yongarad, 'Dread' was a title like an Ifeldian royal 'High Lord' so Quell was a little surprised Muden cared about such a display. Usually, such a thing was beneath his notice.

"Nothing I thought important sir, I was correcting a young man's behavior. Landrin only earned his first star, right before we left home. He's too young and hotheaded, he wouldn't know sense if it stuck its finger in his eye."

"What was his sin?"

Poor boy should have known to keep his mouth shut. There'd be no saving him now. "He was complaining that our efforts haven't had results."

"Sentiments I share," Muden said with mild anger. "Yet there is something else, he talked of some descent? Did he not?"

Quell huffed. "Discontent, yes, but I'd not say descent, sir. But of course, you know best."

"That I do."

"Yes..." Quell agreed slowly. "All he said aloud was a wish to go home and be away from the trackers."

"Is that all?" Dread Muden asked with interest.

"Yes sir." Maybe there was hope for Landrin yet.

Dread Muden took a few steps and then stopped. His gaze drifted over the air curiously. "This was one of your marauders?"

"Yes sir."

"His name?"

Or maybe there wasn't hope after all. "Landrin sir," Quell reminded him.

Dread Muden turned to cast his eyes over the camp, searching the various tribespeople and the air around each of them. "Landrin!" he called out in a loud voice.

Lanny stood up at attention, already aware of who called his name.

"Is he an archer?" Dread Muden asked quietly.

"Not usually, but he's serviceable as one." Quell breathed an internal sigh of relief. That question meant it might only be a maiming then.

A moment later, for no reason Quell could see, Landrin's left eye exploded in its socket and the kyate-siv dropped to the ground, screaming and rolling in pain. Quell didn't bother to watch Lanny but kept his head bowed to Dread Muden.

The sickly pale elf looked at the sky above, amused. He'd already forgotten Landrin existed. "Such a little thing, and yet the threads of fate shift so greatly. It has been a long time since they have been so volatile. Something is coming or has already come."

Whenever the dread talked of fate so openly, Quell knew to take it seriously. "What does it mean, my Lord Dread?"

Muden pondered this question. "It means that greater things are at work. I have no doubt the sylwerd is a part of this, if not at the center of it." He paused, peering intently at what Quell couldn't see. "Why do you sway so in this direction?"

Quell knew who or what Muden was talking to wasn't him. People claimed Dread Muden could see all futures. All that might happen or all that would not, or some slush like that. Quell wasn't sure what to believe, but he knew it was the 'threads of fate' the dread was talking to now.

"Quell, you are from this land by birth," the dread said suddenly. "What lies to our south?"

Quell didn't point out that he'd only been born in Ifeldia and had left as a child. Even when he had been Ifeldian, he wasn't even from this region. Of course, he was prepared enough to know the answer, anyway.

"Only a few towns and the city of Henaden. Some random farmlands I think as well."

"Henaden," Muden repeated. "Fate once more brings me to you, Noren." Then to Quell, he said. "I will visit Henaden and my agent there. Dispatch with me some who can track and be ready to follow with haste."

"Should I prepare to come with you as well?"

The dread shook his head. "Fate is too wild at this time. Something stirs in that city, but I will not have the sylwerd overlooked for what could be idle distractions. Command everyone else yourself."

"Two wodjok and two of my men then?"

Muden looked to the sky again for a long time before nodding. His eyes were focused above where he watched fate toss in the wind.

Knowing better than to disturb him when he was like this, Quell drifted away just like many of the other shadows in the light of early dawn.

Dread Muden kept his eyes above for some time, seeing, hearing, and feeling the threaded spirits beyond this layer of the world. Each string whispered to him secrets of fate, of the possibilities that spun about the tapestry of the world. Caught up in the visions of fate, a deathly whisper dribbled from Dread Muden's pale lips.

"Ancient powers move. I see an upturned crown opposed by a worker's hammer. There is a strange sword wrapped in shades of scarlet... And... a storm? Yes, a storm is coming."

The red blades began with a promise.

The woodcutter and his wife kept to their word and found Azaz was true to his.

For, while they were still poor, they found they had more than ever before.

Soon the wife delivered a son, strong and handsome. Later, the couple rejoiced over a daughter, who from birth, was beautiful beyond compare. After these, they were excited for their third child, who was promised a gift unlike any other.

Yet when the child came, they were dismayed. The child, a girl, was disfigured on her left side. Her arm was missing, and her body and face twisted on that side like marred clay.

Only seeing these faults and nothing else, the woodcutter and his wife despaired. "Did not Azaz promise that all our children would be beautiful, what is this that has been born? Where did we fail that the promise was broken?"

Then the wife said. "Perhaps this is not meant to be our child. Let us disown this one and try for another. Then the promised child may still be born. This child will serve in our home, and we will treat her well, in honor of the promise to Azaz."

The husband agreed, and without seeing what they'd done, this daughter became family to none.

Yet the couple's plan to force their will on Azaz's design came to not when the wife soon fell ill and died.

The woodcutter tried to go on, telling the children of their promise, but when fortunes fell, he soon forgot it. To make this girl useful in all of his labor, the father tied a small axe to the servant daughter.

Yet even as she was seen as a tool, the third child called servant, remembered the promise.

It came that one day, when all went wrong, that the woodcutter flew into a rage.

In fear of his wrath, the small child still tied to the axe, was forced to run away.

She ran and ran till she ran out of breath. Only then did the small one, look to see she was lost.

Unsure where to go or what to do, this little one curled against a tree and cried herself to sleep.

It was deep in night when she awoke and cried once again as she felt all alone.

It was then, as she sat against the tree, that light began to shine from where she could not see.

When she sought to find from where the light came, she found a man she'd never seen, but at once knew his name.

The beginning and the end.

Azaz had come once again.

www.ingramcontent.com/pod-product-compliance
Lightning Source LLC
Chambersburg PA
CBHW011915130726
47903CB00016B/2845